The Stone Circle

Also by Elly Griffiths

THE DR RUTH GALLOWAY SERIES

The Crossing Places
The Janus Stone
The House at Sea's End
A Room Full of Bones
Dying Fall
The Outcast Dead
The Ghost Fields
The Woman in Blue
The Chalk Pit
The Dark Angel

THE STEPHENS AND MEPHISTO SERIES

The Zig Zag Girl
Smoke and Mirrors
The Blood Card
The Vanishing Box

OTHER WORKS

The Stranger Diaries

As Domenica de Rosa

One Summer in Tuscany
(previously published as *Summer School*)
The Eternal City
Return to the Italian Quarter
(previously published as *The Italian Quarter*)
The Secret of Villa Serena
(previously published as *Villa Serena*)

ELLY Griffiths

The Stone Circle

A Dr RUTH GALLOWAY MYSTERY

Quercus

First published in Great Britain in 2019 by

Quercus Editions Ltd
Carmelite House
50 Victoria Embankment
London EC4Y 0DZ

An Hachette UK company

A CIP catalogue record for this book is available
from the British Library

HB ISBN 978 1 78648 729 2
TPB ISBN 978 1 78648 730 8

10 9 8 7 6 5 4 3 2 1

Typeset by CC Book Production

Printed and bound in Great Britain by Clays Ltd, Elcograf S.p.A.

For Jane Wood

CHAPTER 1

12 February 2016

DCI Nelson,

Well, here we are again. Truly our end is our beginning. That corpse you buried in your garden, has it begun to sprout? Will it bloom this year? You must have wondered whether I, too, was buried deep in the earth. Oh ye of little faith. You must have known that I would rise again.

You have grown older, Harry. There is grey in your hair and you have known sadness. Joy too but that also can bring anguish. The dark nights of the soul. You could not save Scarlet but you could save the innocent who lies within the stone circle. Believe me, Harry, I want to help.

The year is turning. The shoots rise from the grass. Imbolc is here and we dance under the stars.

Go to the stone circle.

In peace.

DCI Harry Nelson pushes the letter away from him and lets out something that sounds like a groan. The other people in the briefing room – Superintendent Jo Archer, DS Dave Clough, DS Judy Johnson and DS Tanya Fuller – look at him with expressions ranging from concern to ill-concealed excitement.

'He's back,' says Clough.

'Bollocks,' says Nelson. 'He's dead.'

'Excuse me,' says Jo Archer, Super Jo to her admirers. 'Would someone mind putting me in the picture?' Jo Archer has only been at King's Lynn for a year, taking over from smooth, perma-tanned Gerald Whitcliffe. At first she seemed the embodiment of all Nelson's worst nightmares – holding meetings where everyone is supposed to talk about their feelings, instigating something unspeakable called a 'group huddle' – but recently he has come to view her with a grudging respect. But he doesn't relish the prospect of explaining the significance of the letter to his boss. She'll be far too interested, for one thing.

But no one else seems prepared to speak so Nelson says, in his flattest and most unemotional voice, 'It must have been twenty years ago now. A child went missing. Lucy Downey. And I started to get letters like this. Full of stuff about Gods and the seasons and mystical crap. Then, ten years on, we found a child's bones on the Saltmarsh. I wasn't sure how old they were so I asked Ruth – Dr Ruth Galloway – to examine them. Those bones were nothing to do with the case, they were Iron Age or something, but I got Ruth to look at the letters. She thought they might be from someone with archaeological knowledge. Anyway, as you know, we found Lucy but another child died. The killer was drowned on the marshes. The letter writer was a Norwegian professor called Erik Anderssen. He died that night too. And this,' he points at the letter on the table, 'reads like one of his.'

'It sounds like someone who knows you,' says Judy.

'Because it goes on about me being grey and sad?' says Nelson. 'Thanks a lot.'

No one says anything. The joys and sorrows of the last few years are imprinted on all of them, even Jo.

After a few seconds, Jo says, 'What's this about a stone circle?'

'God knows,' says Nelson. 'I've never heard of anything like that. There was that henge thing they found years ago but that was made of wood.'

'Wasn't the henge thing where you found the murdered child last time?' says Jo, revealing slightly more knowledge than she has hitherto admitted to.

'Yes,' says Nelson. 'It was on the beach near the Saltmarsh. Nothing's left of it now. All the timbers and suchlike are in the museum.'

'Cathbad says they should have been left where they were,' says Judy.

Judy's partner, Cathbad, is a druid who first came to the attention of the police when he protested about the removal of the henge timbers. Everyone in the room knows Cathbad so no one thinks this is worth commenting on, although Clough mutters 'of course he does'.

'This is probably nothing,' says Jo, gesturing at the letter which still lies, becalmed, in the centre of the table. 'But we should check up the stone circle thing. Nelson, can you ask Ruth if she knows anything about it?'

Once again everyone avoids Nelson's eye as he takes the letter and puts in his pocket.

'I'll give her a ring later,' he says.

'How did you know about the stone circle?' says Ruth.

Nelson is taken aback. He has retreated into his office and shut the door for this phone call and now he stands up and starts to pace the room.

'What do you mean?'

'A team from UCL were digging at the original henge site just before Christmas. They think they've found a second circle.'

'Is this one made of stone?'

'No,' says Ruth and he hears her switching into a cautious, academic tone. 'This is wood too. Bog oak like the other one. But they're calling it the stone circle because a stone cist was found in the centre.'

'What's a cist when it's at home?'

'A grave, a coffin.'

Nelson stops pacing. 'A coffin? What was inside?'

'Human skeletal matter,' says Ruth. 'Bones. We're waiting for carbon-14 results.'

Nelson knows that carbon-14 results, which tests the level of carbon left in human remains, are useful for dating but are only accurate within a range of about a hundred years.

He doesn't want to give Ruth the chance to explain this again.

'Why this sudden interest in the Bronze Age?' says Ruth.

'I've had a letter,' says Nelson.

There's a silence. Then Ruth says, her voice changing again, 'What sort of letter?'

'A bit like the ones I had before. About Lucy and Scarlet. It had some of the same stuff in it.'

'What do you mean "the same stuff"?'

'About corpses sprouting, shoots rising from the earth. Imbolc. The sort of stuff that was in Erik's letters.'

'But . . .' Nelson can hear the same reactions he witnessed in his colleagues earlier: disbelief, anger, fear. 'Erik's dead.'

'He certainly looked dead to me when we hauled him out of the water.'

'I went to his funeral. They burned his body on a Viking boat.'

'So it can't be him,' says Nelson. 'It's some nutter. What worries me is that it's a nutter who knows a bit about me. The letter mentions a stone circle. That's why I rang.'

'It can't be this circle. I mean, no one knows about it.'

'Except your archaeologist pals.'

'Actually, they've got funding for a new dig,' says Ruth. 'It's starting on Monday. I was planning to drop in for a few hours in the morning.'

It's Friday now. Nelson should be getting ready to go home for the weekend. He says, 'I might drop by myself if I'm not too busy. And I'd like to show you the letter because, well, you saw the others.'

There's another tiny sliver of silence and Ruth says, 'Isn't the baby due any day now?'

'Yes,' says Nelson. 'That might change my plans.'

'Give Michelle my best,' says Ruth.

'I will,' says Nelson. He wants to say more but Ruth has gone.

CHAPTER 2

Ruth reruns this conversation on a loop as she drives to collect her daughter from Sandra, her childminder. She has deliberately been keeping her interactions with Nelson to the minimum. She sees him every other Saturday when he takes Kate out for the morning but she manages to keep their conversation general and upbeat; they sound like two breakfast TV presenters handing over to the weather forecast. 'How are you?' 'Fine. Getting sick of this weather.' 'Yes, when's the sun going to come out?' But this latest development takes her back to a time that still feels dangerous and disturbing: her first meeting with Nelson, the discovery of the bones on the marsh, the hunt for the missing children, her last encounter with Erik. Over the last ten years she has, by and large, dealt with these memories by ignoring them but the discovery of the new henge in December, and now Nelson's mention of the letter, has brought everything back. She can still feel the wind on her face as she ran across the uncertain ground, half-land half-sea, knowing that a murderer was on her trail. She can hear Lucy's voice calling from deep underground. She can see the police helicopter, like a great misshapen bird, stirring the waters of the tidal pool that had taken a man's life.

Corpses sprouting, shoots rising from the earth. That's what Nelson had said, the words sounding strange in his careful policeman's voice, the vowels still recognisably Lancastrian even after more than twenty years down south. It had to be a coincidence and yet Ruth does not trust coincidences. One of the few opinions that she shares with Nelson.

Kate, her seven-year-old daughter, is drawing at Sandra's kitchen table and acknowledges Ruth with a friendly, yet dismissive, wave.

'I'm doing a Valentine's card,' she says.

Ruth's heart sinks. She has managed to forget that it is Valentine's Day on Sunday (VD she calls it in her head). In her opinion, the whole thing is an abomination: the explosion of bleeding hearts in the shops, the sentimental songs on the radio, the suggestion that, if you are not in possession of a single red rose by midnight, you will die alone and be eaten by your pet cat. Ruth has had her share of Valentines in the past but this doesn't lessen her distaste for the whole business. She's never had a card from Nelson; their relationship is too complicated and clandestine. *Roses are red, violets are blue. You've had my baby but I can't be with you.* She tries not to think about Nelson presenting his heavily pregnant wife with a vast bouquet (he will go for something obvious from a florist, red roses tied in ribbon and encased in cellophane). She wonders who is the intended recipient of Kate's artwork.

Ruth doesn't ask though and Kate doesn't tell her. She puts the card, which seems to show a large cat on a wall, in her school bag and goes to put her coat on. Ruth thanks Sandra and has the obligatory chat about 'thank goodness it's Friday, let's hope the rain holds off'. Then she is driving off with her daughter, away from the suburbs towards the coast.

It's dark by the time that they get home. When they get out of the car they can hear the sea breaking against the sandbar and the air smells brackish which means that the tide is coming in. Ruth's cottage is one of three at the very edge of the marshes. Her only neighbours are an itinerant Indigenous Australian poet and a London family who only visit for the occasional weekend. The road is often flooded in winter and, when it snows, you can be cut off for days. The Saltmarsh is a bird sanctuary and, in the autumn, you can see great flocks of geese coming in to hibernate, their wings pink in the sunlight as they wheel and turn. Now, in February, it's a grey place even in daylight, grey-green marshes merging with grey sky and greyer sea. But there are signs that spring is coming, snowdrops growing along the footpaths and the occasional glimpse of bright yellow marsh marigolds. Ruth has lived here for twenty years and still loves it, despite the house's increasing inconvenience for a single parent with a child whose social life now requires a separate diary.

It was on the beach at the edge of the marshes that the henge was first discovered. Ruth remembers Erik's cry of joy as he knelt on the sand before the first sunken post, the sign that they had found the sacred circle itself. She remembers the frenzied days of excavation, working desperately to remove the timbers before the sea reclaimed them. She remembers the druids protesting, the bonfires, the burning brands. It was during one of the protests that she first met Cathbad, now one of her dearest friends. And now they have found a second circle. Ruth worked on the dig in December and performed the first examination on the bones found in the stone cist. Now, during this second excavation, a lithics expert will look more closely at the stones and archaeologists will try to date the wooden posts. Ruth is looking forward to visiting the site again. It will never be the same as that first discovery though, that day, almost twenty years ago now, when the henge seemed to rise from the sea.

'Hurry up, Mum,' says Kate, becoming bored by her mother staring out to sea. 'Flint will be waiting for us.'

And, when Ruth opens the door, her large ginger cat is indeed waiting for them, managing to convey the impression that he has been doing this all day.

'He's hungry,' says Kate, picking the cat up. There was a time when he seemed almost bigger than her; even now on his hind legs he reaches up to her waist.

'There's food in his bowl,' says Ruth. But, nevertheless, she removes the perfectly edible cat food and replaces it with a fresh offering. Flint sniffs at it once and then walks away. He isn't really hungry – he has just consumed a tasty vole – but he does like to keep his human minders on their toes.

Kate switches on the television, a habit that never ceases

to annoy Ruth but she doesn't say anything. She starts to cook macaroni cheese for supper, one of her stock of boring but acceptable dishes. She tries to read the *Guardian* at the same time, propped up behind the pots which should contain tea and coffee but are actually full of mysterious objects like old raffle tickets and tiny toolkits from Christmas crackers.

She has left her phone in her bag by the front door but Kate calls to tell her it is ringing. She manages to catch the call in time. Frank.

'Hi,' he says. 'How was your day?'

'OK. Phil is more megalomaniacal than ever. I'm expecting him to make his horse a senator at any minute.' Phil is Ruth's boss at the University of North Norfolk. He adores publicity and is very jealous of the fact that Ruth occasionally appears on television.

'Same here.' Frank is teaching at Cambridge. 'Geoff now continually refers to himself in the third person. "Geoff is disappointed with student outcomes", "Geoff has some important news about funding".'

Ruth laughs and takes the phone into the kitchen.

'Frank was wondering if you wanted to go out for dinner tomorrow.'

'Ruth doesn't know if she can get a babysitter. Shall we stop this now?'

'I think we should. I could come over and cook?' Frank, a single father for many years, has his own small store of recipes but at least they are different from Ruth's.

'That would be nice.' Please don't let him mention VD.

'I'll come to you for seven-ish. Is that OK?'

'Great. Kate would like to see you before she goes to bed.' Which, on a Saturday, is becoming later and later. Ruth will have to bribe her with an audio book.

'See you then.' Frank rings off but seconds later she receives a text:

Are you pleased I didn't mention Valentine's?

Ruth doesn't know whether to be pleased or slightly irritated.

Ruth is glad that she has the evening to look forward to because the shadow of VD looms over Saturday. It's not one of Nelson's Saturdays so Ruth takes Kate swimming in King's Lynn and even at the pool there are red balloons and exhortations to 'Treat yourself to a Valentine's Day Spa'. At least she has arranged to meet Cathbad and his son, Michael, and, after their swim, the children play in the circle of hell known as the Soft Play Area and the adults drink something frothy which may or may not contain coffee.

'Are you taking Judy out for Valentine's Day?' asks Ruth, dispiritedly eating the chocolate from the top of her 'cappuccino'.

'No, but I'll cook us something special,' says Cathbad. In jeans and jumper with his long wet hair tied back in a ponytail, Cathbad looks like any ageing hipster dad. He still wears his cloak sometimes but Ruth has noticed that more and more, when he's with his children, especially Michael whose embarrassment threshold is low, Cathbad mimes a slightly offbeat version of conventionality. Apart from running a few evening classes in meditation and past life regression, he's the full-time carer for Michael, six, and Miranda, three, and seems to enjoy the role. Ruth often ponders on the fact that this apparently makes Judy a 'working mother' and Cathbad a 'stay-at-home father' as if mothers never have jobs outside the home and caring for children isn't work. Nelson is, presumably, a 'working father' though no one would ever label him in this way. Ruth's mother often used to describe her, rather apologetically, as a 'career woman' but Nelson, who is consumed by his job, will never be described as a 'career man'. Will Michelle go back to work as a hairdresser after this new baby is born?

Time to stop thinking about that.

'Valentine's is crap though, isn't it?' she says.

'I don't mind it,' says Cathbad, waving to Michael who is about to descend the tubular slide. 'I like ritual and saints' days. And it's another way of marking the coming of spring. Like Ash Wednesday and Imbolc.'

Nelson had mentioned Imbolc, Ruth remembers. But she doesn't want to tell Cathbad about the new letter.

'When is Imbolc?' she asks. 'Beginning of February?'

'It's flexible,' says Cathbad, 'but usually the first or second of February. It used to be a feast dedicated to Bridgid, the goddess of fertility, but then it got taken over by Christianity and Bridgid became St Bridget. In Ireland children still make rush crosses for St Bridget's Day.'

Cathbad grew up in Ireland and was raised as a Catholic but, like the feast day, he is flexible, incorporating both pagan and Christian traditions into his belief system. Ruth sometimes thinks that what he really likes is any excuse for a party.

'Are you seeing Frank this weekend?' asks Cathbad.

'He's coming over tonight to cook me a meal.'

'That's nice,' says Cathbad. His expression is bland but Ruth thinks she knows what he's thinking.

She takes pity on him. 'It's going well with Frank. We've got a lot in common.'

'He's a good person,' says Cathbad. 'He has a very serene energy.'

There's a brief silence during which Ruth knows that they are thinking of someone who could never be described as serene. She says, 'Michelle's baby is due any day now.'

'I know. Judy says Nelson is worse tempered than ever at work. It must be the worry.'

'Or maybe it's just bad temper.'

'No, he has a good heart really.'

'Let's hope the baby isn't born on Sunday,' says Ruth, 'or he'll have to call it Valentine.'

'I like the name Valentine,' says Cathbad. 'It's got a certain power.' His children, though, all have names beginning with M, for reasons that are not entirely clear to anyone, even him. He also has a twenty-four-year-old daughter called Madeleine from a previous relationship.

'Valentine Nelson,' says Ruth. 'I can't see it.'

'Of course 2016 is a leap year,' says Cathbad. 'There's a certain power in being born on 29th February. Funnily enough, in Ireland leap years are associated with St Bridget. She's said to have struck a deal with St Patrick to allow women to propose to men on one day of the year.'

'Bully for her,' says Ruth. 'I'm sure Michelle doesn't want to wait until the 29th to have her baby.'

She thinks about this conversation intermittently over the rest of the day. She doesn't envy Cathbad and Judy their relationship, or even Nelson and Michelle. By and large, she is happy with her life in her little cottage on the edge of the marshes with her daughter and her cat. If she has ever dreamed of a life with Nelson, the dream ended after the rapturous love-making and hasn't encompassed life in a confined space with a man who takes up too much room, literally and metaphorically. It's just that, on days like this, she does wonder if she'll ever have a romantic relationship again. But, at seven o'clock, there is Frank, bearing chocolates, wine and two steaks in a rather bloody bag. Kate has already had her supper but she insists on showing Frank her collection of Sylvanian animals and all her spelling/maths/reading certificates (this takes some time as Kate seems to win a new award every week). Eventually, though, Kate is tucked up in bed listening to Stephen Fry reading Harry Potter and Ruth and Frank have their meal.

It's a nice evening. They talk about work and the idiocies of their relative bosses. They talk about Kate and about Frank's children in America. Even Flint sits next to Frank and purrs at him loudly with his eyes closed. But, at eleven o'clock, Frank picks up his car keys and sets off home. They kiss on the doorstep, both cheeks like acquaintances at a smart party. Ruth locks the door, turns off the lights and goes upstairs, followed by Flint. What is happening with Frank? They had once had a proper relationship, complete with extremely good sex. Is Frank now just a friend who cooks her meals and takes her out sometimes? Is he seeing someone else, a stunning classicist from Christ's or an economist from Girton with a PhD and a thigh gap?

But, as Ruth is about to turn out the light, she sees that she is not in bed alone. On her pillow is a card showing a fat ginger cat on a wall.

'Happy Vallentines Day Mum,' it says.

Nelson is woken by a knock on the door. Three knocks actually. Staccato and self-important. Bruno, the German shepherd, barks in response. Is it the postman? But it's Sunday and – Nelson looks at the clock radio – 6.30 a.m. Michelle is asleep, lying on her back, her stomach a mound under the bedclothes. She is finding it increasingly difficult to sleep in these last days of her pregnancy and Nelson doesn't want to wake her. His daughter Laura, living at home while she studies to become a teacher, was out late last night and will be dead to the world. Nelson gets up as quietly as he can and pads downstairs in pyjama bottoms and a 'No. 1 Dad' T-shirt, a bit embarrassing but all he could find to wear last night.

'Coming,' he mutters irritably. Bruno is standing in the hallway staring at the door. He's actually not much of a barker; he prefers to assess situations and then act accordingly. Nelson thinks this could be because he came from a litter destined to be police dogs. 'Good boy,' says Nelson. He opens the door. There's no one there. Nelson looks up and down the street but the cul-de-sac is still asleep, no movement except for a ginger cat walking very slowly along a wall. The cat reminds Nelson of Ruth. He turns to go back into the house and it's only then that he notices the brown paper bag on the step.

In the kitchen, watched intently by Bruno, Nelson tips the bag upside down on the table. Inside is a stone with a hole through the middle and a note, black writing on red paper.

'Greetings,' it says, 'from Jack Valentine.'

CHAPTER 3

'It's an old Norfolk tradition,' says Tom Henty, the desk sergeant who has been at the station for as long as anyone can remember. 'Three knocks on the door and, when you go to answer it, there's nobody there but Jack Valentine has left a present, usually in a brown paper bag.'

'I've never heard of that tradition,' says Clough, halfway through his second breakfast of the day, 'and I was born and brought up in Norfolk.'

'It's an east Norfolk thing,' says Tom. 'I was born in Yarmouth.'

By now Nelson is used to the local belief that Norfolk is a vast place where the north, south, east and west regions are separated by massive, immovable barriers. As for Suffolk, it might as well be on a different planet.

'Whoever left me this is from east Norfolk then,' he says, pointing to the stone and the note on the briefing room table. Judy picks up the stone and looks through the hole.

'Cathbad would say that this is a witch stone. Stones with holes in are meant to be magical.'

Clough laughs and chokes on his Egg McMuffin but Nelson has learnt to listen to Cathbad's pronouncements.

'In what way?' he says.

'I'll ask him,' says Judy. 'I think they're meant to ward against evil.'

'I'll ask Ruth,' says Nelson, not meeting anyone's eyes. 'I'm going to drop in on the dig in Holme later. Just to follow up on that stone circle thing.'

Tom's thoughts are as slow and deliberate as his speech. 'Then there's Snatch Valentine,' he says now.

Clough chokes again.

'Present on the doorstep with a string attached,' says Tom. 'Child goes to grab the parcel but the string moves it just out of reach. Child chases the present until it's out of sight. Child is never seen again.'

There's a brief silence.

'Bloody hell,' says Clough, dusting himself for crumbs. 'That's a cheerful little story.'

'Where there's light there's dark,' says Judy. 'Some cultures believe that Father Christmas is accompanied by an evil imp who punishes bad children.'

'It's probably nothing,' says Nelson, 'but it worries me that it was delivered to the house. I haven't said anything to Michelle. I don't want to upset her. The baby's due any day now.'

No one says anything. They all know that, in the summer, someone else found Nelson's house, a man with a gun and a grudge against Nelson. Michelle and her daughter were both held at gunpoint and Tim, a police officer who had once been with King's Lynn CID, was killed. They all understand why Nelson has not told his wife about this new development.

'Do you think it's got anything to do with the other letter?' says Clough. 'The one about the corpse sprouting?'

'Don't know,' says Nelson. 'The first letter was typed, of course, so we can't get a handwriting match. But what are the odds of two nutters writing to me at the same time?'

'Pretty high, I would think,' says Clough.

Ruth drops Kate at school and drives back to the Saltmarsh, following the signs to the birdwatching trail. The car park, with its boarded-up ice-cream kiosk and notices about rare birds, reminds her irresistibly of the time when she first met Nelson. He had wanted her opinion about bones found on the marshes and they had driven here from the university – her first experience of Nelson's driving – parked by the kiosk and walked to the shallow grave where she had seen the dull gleam of an Iron Age torque and had known that this corpse, at least, would not be bothering the tall, rather intimidating, man at her side. She remembers Clough following them, carrying a bag containing litter found on the path. How alien they had seemed to her then, these grim-faced policemen, concerned only with what they referred to as 'the crime scene'. She knows more now, has attended many such scenes, but she knows that, in some ways, she'll always be an outsider.

There are several other cars in the car park, mud-spattered vehicles that look as if they might belong to archaeologists.

Ruth gets her oldest anorak out of the boot and puts on her wellingtons. As she does so, she feels a faint stirring of excitement. This is a dig; a place where, unlike a crime scene, she will always feel at home. It's a cold day, the air damp and grey, but it's not actually raining and this, in England in February, is also a cause for celebration. As she sets off along the gravel path between the reeds, Ruth wonders if Michelle's baby was born over the weekend. Would Nelson have let her know? The child will be Kate's half-brother, after all. Or will it? Whilst Nelson knows that the baby is a boy he doesn't – as far as Ruth can make out – know whether it's his or Tim's. If the latter, then the paternity will be obvious. Tim, as he was fond of pointing out, was one of the few black police officers in Norfolk.

The walk seems longer than it did nine years ago or maybe Ruth is even less fit. She glances at her wrist where a Fitbit, a Christmas present from her brother Simon and sister-in-law Cathy, sits smugly. She presses the button and it tells her that she has walked 2,007 steps since getting up (it tracks her sleep too). Surely it's more than that? She sometimes suspects Cathy, at least, of less-than-charitable motives in giving this particular present, a sort of mini-Cathy that nags her all day about doing more exercise. Ruth fears that her relationship with the Fitbit is already an unhealthy one. She worries about its good opinion of her (otherwise why not take it off?) but she also resents its chirpy bullying. *Almost there! You've nailed your step target for the day!* Never trust anyone, or anything, that uses that many exclamation marks.

She must have been going uphill (why doesn't the Fitbit give you more credit for this?) because suddenly she can see the sea, shallow waves breaking on the sand, seagulls flying low above the spray. The sun has come out and it sheds a hazy, Old-Testament beam of light on a small group of people standing just above the tide line. They are wearing hi-vis jackets and are grouped in a circle. Ruth walks towards them, stumbling over the sandy, grassy ground. She's about to call out but something stops her. The people seem very still and one of them, a man with a long blond ponytail, raises his arms to the sky. As Ruth approaches, he turns and Ruth sees a weather-beaten face, strong nose and bright blue eyes, eyes that seem to see into her very soul. Seagulls call, high above, and a sudden wind whips sand into Ruth's face.

'Erik?' she stammers.

CHAPTER 4

The man laughs and puts out a hand as if to steady her.

'My name's Leif Anderssen,' he says. 'I'm Erik's son. You must be Ruth Galloway.'

Erik's son. Ruth remembers that he had grown-up children, two girls and a boy. She'd kept in touch with Erik's wife Magda for a little while but their relationship hadn't been able to survive Erik's death and the events leading up to it. She hasn't heard from Magda in nearly five years and, besides, Magda wasn't one for talking about her adult children. She hadn't known that the son was an archaeologist but Leif Anderssen is very clearly in charge of this dig. He's a professor at Oslo University, he tells her, but has been seconded by UCL because of his expertise with stone artefacts. When Ruth had first approached Leif had been greeting the nature spirits, as he always does at the start of an excavation. Oh, he's Erik's son, all right.

'My father talked about you a lot,' says Leif as they walk towards the first trench. 'He always said you were his favourite pupil.'

Even after everything that has happened, Ruth can't suppress a small glow of pleasure.

The site is about a hundred metres west of the place where the henge was discovered almost twenty years ago. In December a team from UCL had discovered what seemed to be a second circle of wooden posts. Further excavation had uncovered the cist, a shallow rectangular pit lined with stones and containing a single urn and what looked like a fully articulated human skeleton.

'Cists are usually Bronze Age, aren't they?' says Ruth, panting slightly in order to keep up with Leif who, like his father, is tall and rangy.

'Yes,' says Leif. 'Later graves typically hold cremated remains. The fact that this one contained bones might mean that it's early Bronze Age.'

'Like the henge,' says Ruth.

'Yes, like my father's henge.'

This is, in fact, how Ruth thinks of the henge but she knows that, to others, the description would sound like sacrilege. Cathbad, for one, is of the opinion that the wooden circle belonged only to the sea and sky.

'It's possible,' says Leif, 'that the first henge was built to mark the death of an individual, like a cenotaph. It could be that we have found the grave of this person.' His English is near perfect; only the faint sing-song accent and the precision of his syntax mark him out as a non-native speaker.

'Have you had the dendrochronology results?' asks Ruth. Dendrochronology, the science of dating tree rings, was what gave them the date for the original henge.

'We're still waiting,' says Leif, 'but the wood looked similar: bog oak, intertwined with branches. Did you examine the bones?'

'Yes,' says Ruth. 'They looked old but we won't know for sure until we get the carbon-14 sample back.' She notices how, despite all the science at their fingertips, both she and Leif have fallen back on intuition; the wood and the bones had both 'looked' right.

'I heard that you thought that they might be female.'

'I'm pretty sure they are. The pelvic bones were intact and the skull definitely looked female; the brow ridges weren't developed, nor was the nuchal crest. From the size of the bones I'd say that it was a young woman, probably in her late teens.' She doesn't add that the skull has a particularly rounded and delicate chin which made her think that the owner had probably been rather beautiful.

They are at the trench now. Ruth can see the cist, solid slabs of stone interspersed with smaller pebbles, a dark void in the centre. A young archaeologist is kneeling down scraping away lichen but it looks almost as if he is in prayer.

'The roof stone was a metre wide,' says Leif. 'Quite a substantial tomb. Particularly for a young woman.'

Does Leif mean that a woman couldn't deserve an impressive memorial? Erik would never have implied such a thing. He knew that there are many prehistorical graves where women were buried with great care and ritual. And, even if some of these women had been killed as sacrifices to some cruel and faceless god, they were still important.

Ruth looks around her. The sand stretches away on either

side, grey and blue, giving way to windswept grass and marshland. The henge must have been visible for miles, silhouetted against the sky. She thinks of Erik's words: *The landscape itself is important. This is a liminal zone, between land and water, sea and sky . . .*

'Cists are sometimes called flat cemeteries,' says Leif, reading her mind in a way that she finds rather disturbing. 'They often occur in environments like this, flat land on the edge of water. It could be that the water represented rebirth or renewal in some way.'

Ruth feels that, with the reincarnation of Erik standing in front of her, she should steer clear of the subjects of rebirth and renewal. 'Have you looked at the grave goods?' she says briskly. 'There was an urn, wasn't there?'

'Yes,' says Leif. 'It contained seeds from wild fruit – blackberry, sloe and hazelnuts. Sustenance for the afterlife. There was something else though that I thought was significant.'

'Oh,' says Ruth, 'what?'

'A stone with a hole through the middle, found beside the urn. Such stones have powerful magical qualities.'

He smiles as he says this, reminding Ruth not of Erik, but of Cathbad.

'Stones like that have been found in Neolithic sites,' says Ruth. 'I was reading about a causewayed enclosure in Whitehawk, near Brighton. There were bodies buried there alongside fossils called shepherds' crowns, stones with holes through them too.'

'Hag stones,' says Leif. 'Odin stones. Holy stones. They have lots of names. They are meant to guard against witches and all kinds of evil. Some stories say that if you look through the hole you will see the fairy folk.'

Once again, Ruth feels that they are wandering along a slightly dangerous path. She does not want to discuss the fairy folk – or Odin – with Erik's son.

'Was it just one stone?' she asks.

'Yes,' says Leif. 'That makes it more significant, no?'

'Perhaps,' says Ruth. 'Could I look in the trench now? I'd like to see the layers.'

Ruth enjoys the chance – rare these days – of doing some actual excavation, the combination of heavy labour and precision, the feeling of working in the open air, the February sun surprisingly warm on her back even though her fingers and toes are soon frozen. She is just starting to work on an interesting section when a shadow falls over the neat line of soil and subsoil.

'Found anything interesting?'

Ruth straightens up. 'Hi, Nelson.'

He looms above her, blocking out the sun in his dark police jacket. Ruth tries to climb nimbly out of the trench but ends up having to take Nelson's proffered hand. His grip is very strong. Ruth lets go as soon as she is on solid ground.

'Is this the stone whatsit?' he says.

'The cist? Yes.'

'It's just a hole with some stones in it.'

It's lucky that Nelson says annoying things like this sometimes. It stops Ruth fantasising about him.

'It's probably early Bronze Age,' she says. 'A very significant find.'

'It's near the other one, isn't it?'

'Yes.' Ruth knows that they are both thinking not of the
wooden henge, but of the child's body she found inside it.
She remembers the moment with all her senses; the mist
rising from the sea, the waterlogged ground under her feet,
the seagulls calling high above, the little arm emerging
from its shallow grave . . .

'Who's in charge?' Nelson is saying. He is pawing the
ground like a horse, a characteristically impatient gesture.

'Well,' says Ruth, 'this might come as a bit of a shock . . .'

But it's too late. Leif is walking towards them, smiling a
welcome, teeth very white against his tanned skin.

'Leif,' says Ruth, 'this is DCI Nelson from the King's Lynn
police. Nelson, this is Leif Anderssen, the archaeologist in
charge of the dig. He's Erik's son.'

Leif continues to hold out his hand and, after a second's
hesitation, Nelson grasps it.

'DCI Nelson,' says Leif. 'I've heard a lot about you.'

'None of it good, I'm sure.'

'Not at all, my father had a great respect for you.' Ruth
wonders how Leif can possibly know this, unless he was in
closer contact with his father than she thought. Erik always
used to say that he saw his children as 'free, independent
spirits', which also seemed to be an excuse for rarely seeing
them.

'It's all water under the bridge now,' says Nelson,
employing a rather unfortunate cliché, given Erik's death

from drowning. Erik's body had been found in a marshy pool only a few hundred metres from where they stand now.

'Indeed,' says Leif. 'The world turns and life continues. To what do we owe the honour, DCI Nelson?'

Ruth can see Nelson thinking as clearly as if there was a bubble over his head. She knows that he won't want to tell Leif about the letter but how else to explain his presence?

'I came to see Dr Galloway,' he says at last. 'I need her help on a police matter.'

'I should be going anyway,' says Ruth. 'I've got a seminar at twelve. Do let me know when you get the test results.'

'Of course,' says Leif. 'I hope to see you again.'

Ruth holds out her hand but Leif leans forward and kisses her on both cheeks. Even though he is standing behind her Ruth can tell that Nelson is glowering.

They sit in Nelson's car, which is parked next to Ruth's. Nelson drums his fingers on the steering wheel as Ruth reads the letter.

'It's very like the others,' she says at last. 'Even the quote from T. S. Eliot.'

'Where's that?'

'"That corpse you buried in your garden, has it begun to sprout?" I think it's from *The Wasteland*. Also the bit about our end being our beginning. That sounds like T. S. Eliot.'

'Your friend Shona. She helped with the literary stuff last time, didn't she?'

Ruth is silent for a moment. Shona Maclean, an English

Literature lecturer at the university, did help Erik with the letters last time but, over the years, she has allowed herself to forget this. At the time she had felt betrayed but friends are too valuable to lose. Shona has a child now too and that has formed another bond. After a holiday in Italy last summer, Ruth and Shona are closer than ever.

'Anyone can find quotes like this,' she says.

'Anyone who knew what the previous letters were like.'

'Who would have known?'

'We never made them public,' says Nelson. 'Didn't want any copycats sending us their lunatic scribblings. But word always gets out. Everyone in the station must have known.'

And Shona knew, Ruth thinks. And Cathbad.

'There are certainly similarities,' she says. 'The way he addresses you personally, the Biblical references. "Oh ye of little faith."'

'That's Doubting Thomas, isn't it?' says Nelson. 'The one who doesn't believe that Jesus has come back from the dead.'

'Full marks for religious knowledge.'

'He's one of my favourite characters. Always ask for evidence. Thomas would have made a good policeman.'

Ruth wonders whether Nelson is contemplating calling his son Thomas. Kate says the new baby will be called George but Ruth doesn't know where she got this information. Ruth looks at the typed letter, in its plastic sleeve, on her lap. *The year is turning. The shoots rise from the grass.* What did Leif say just now? *The world turns and life continues.* It's a fairly standard new-agey sort of phrase but there is an uncomfortable echo. Is it just a coincidence that Leif appeared at the same time as the letter?

'Actually the phrase occurs a few times in the Old and New Testaments,' she says. Her parents were evangelical Christians, fond of quoting the Bible. 'But it's nice to know that you've got a favourite saint.'

Nelson doesn't rise to the bait. 'There's another thing,' he says. 'You know it was Valentine's Day yesterday?'

'No,' says Ruth. 'Was it?' This is partly ironical (who could escape it?) but also she doesn't want Nelson to think that she spent the whole day waiting in vain for a card that never came.

Nelson misses the sarcasm anyway. 'Someone left a paper bag on my doorstep,' he says. 'There was a note with it. "Greetings from Jack Valentine." Apparently it's some sort of Norfolk tradition.'

'What was in the bag?'

'Just a stone.'

'With a hole through it?'

Nelson stares at her. 'How the hell did you know that?'

'There was a stone with a hole in found inside the cist,' says Ruth. 'We think it dates back to the Bronze Age.'

'So whoever sent me the letter might have known about the dig?'

'Maybe,' says Ruth, 'but those stones are fairly common. There are lots of legends attached to them.'

'I know,' says Nelson. 'Judy was telling me some of them. She gets it all from Cathbad. But it's a coincidence and I don't like coincidences.'

Ruth is about to answer when she sees a figure running across the car park towards them. It's the young archaeologist from the dig. Nelson winds down the window.

'We need Dr Galloway,' pants the archaeologist.

'Why?' says Ruth. But she already knows.

'We've found some bones.'

Ruth and Nelson follow the man, whose name is Vikram, back along the gravel path towards the sand dunes. The brief burst of sunshine has gone and the day is grey and cold again. When they reach the site they find Leif in the trench with two other archaeologists, a man and a woman. They stand aside for Ruth.

The bones are about half a metre down, white against the sandy soil. Ruth can see an arm, possibly a radius or an ulna. Silently Leif hands her a trowel and a brush and, for a few minutes, Ruth works to expose the bones. She doesn't want to excavate them yet because the context will be important. She can see already that there is a grave cut in the soil above. Someone has put this body in the ground deliberately. It takes about twenty minutes for Ruth to be sure of two things. One, there is a complete skeleton here. Two, it's relatively recent.

'How can you tell?' says Nelson, leaning over her shoulder.

Ruth points her torch to where part of the skull is visible. A piece of metal glints back at them.

'A filling,' says Nelson.

'Yes,' says Ruth. 'That will be useful for ageing. And there should be dental records too.'

There's a third thing too. The rounded ends of long bones, the epiphyses, are still growing in children as new cartilage gets added. In late adolescence these fuse with the main part of the bone. The bones are slender too, fragile-looking. Ruth is pretty sure that she is looking at the bones of a child.

CHAPTER 5

'We need to look at missing children from the last ten or twenty years,' says Nelson. 'Maybe even thirty. Ruth couldn't be sure of the exact age of the bones without doing more tests but there was a filling, the old silver sort.'

'They haven't been used since the eighties, have they?' says Judy. 'It's all white fillings now.'

'I haven't got any fillings,' says Clough, grinning to show annoyingly perfect teeth.

'That's amazing,' says Tanya seriously, 'given the amount of sugar you eat.'

'How old did Ruth think this child was?' asks Judy, who is taking notes on her iPad.

'She thought early teens, about twelve or thirteen. Apparently bones have end bits on them that disappear when children finish growing. Different bones fuse at different rates – I didn't follow it all – but the humerus hadn't fused and that usually happens at about fourteen. So we're almost certainly looking at a prepubescent.'

'Do we know if it's a boy or a girl?' asks Clough.

'Ruth says that she might be able to tell from the pelvic bones when she does the full excavation but apparently it's difficult with a prepubescent skeleton.'

'Can she get DNA from the bones?' asks Judy.

'Possibly. But again that depends on all sorts of things. You know what these archaeologists are like. They never give you a straight answer.'

The team are used to Nelson's impatience with all experts, including Ruth, but there is a palpable sense of anticipation in the briefing room. They have a body and there's a chance that they will be able to close one of the cases that all police forces dread, when a child apparently vanishes into thin air.

'If they've been missing for more than ten years we'll have done a review,' says Tanya, opening her laptop.

'That's true,' says Nelson, 'so we need to look at the neighbouring forces too. There can't be that many cases that are still open. I'll speak to my old sergeant Freddie Burnett. Who else was working here thirty years ago?'

'Tom Henty,' says Clough. 'He's been here for ever.'

'And Marj Maccallum,' says Judy. 'She came in to see me last year. When I was acting DI,' she can't help adding. 'Marj was a WPC here in the seventies and eighties, when such things existed.'

'I remember Marj,' says Nelson. 'She was still here when I was first made DCI. She was a good cop, very sharp.'

'I'll ring her,' says Judy.

'Good idea,' says Nelson, 'but there's something else I want you to do first. Clough and Fuller, you keep looking in the files.'

Both Clough and Tanya look briefly mutinous as Nelson ushers Judy into his office. Then Tanya turns back to her laptop and Clough finds a half-eaten Mars bar in his pocket and eats it thoughtfully.

Ruth is forced to cancel her seminar and so is met by Phil muttering about 'client expectations'. 'Now that people are paying nine grand a year they expect a better service.'

'They're not clients,' says Ruth, unlocking her office. 'They're students. I'll reschedule the seminar but I couldn't really leave the site. They'd just found a dead body.'

She can see that Phil is torn between wanting to know about the dead body and wanting to lecture her about time-keeping. In the end curiosity wins.

'Is the body modern?' he says, sliding into her office as soon as the door is open.

Ruth's office is so small that two people standing up make it feel crowded. Ruth sits behind her desk and, after some hesitation, Phil takes the visitors' chair. Her poster of Indiana Jones looks down at him disapprovingly.

'The bones don't look that old,' she says. 'I'll excavate tomorrow and send samples for carbon-14 and isotope analysis.'

'Is it a murder case then?' says Phil. Ruth knows that he is deeply envious of her links with the Serious Crimes Unit. Phil is also Shona's partner, which means that he is up to date with the gossip.

'Possibly,' says Ruth. 'DCI Nelson was actually at the

site when the bones were uncovered.' She hopes she isn't blushing.

'*Was* he? Why was that?'

'Just checking up on the dig, I expect. Do you know who's running it?'

'Someone from UCL?'

'Leif Anderssen. Erik's son.'

Phil's lips purse in a silent whistle. 'Erik the Viking's son? What's he doing in England?'

'He's an expert on stone artefacts, apparently. You know they found a stone cist in the centre of the circle?'

'I read the reports. They wanted my opinion but I didn't have time to visit the site. There's so much extra work now I'm Dean.'

Phil mentions his recent appointment as Temporary Dean of Natural Sciences roughly once every fifteen minutes.

'Lucky I've got so much free time, then,' says Ruth. 'The timbers and the cist look early Bronze Age. We're still waiting for carbon-14 on the bones in the cist.'

'Just like old times,' says Phil. 'You and Nelson hunting for a killer on the Saltmarsh.'

Ruth stares at him. Can he really be saying those words so lightly? Can anyone, even Phil, not be aware of how much the last case cost her, how many lives were lost or changed for ever?

'Let's hope it doesn't come to that,' she says. 'If you'll excuse me, I need to prepare for my next seminar.'

But after Phil has oozed out Ruth stays staring into space for the next ten minutes. Does the discovery of the bones mean that she is about to be involved in another murder investigation? What will it be like to be working closely with Nelson again, especially with Michelle's baby about to be born any day? The whole thing – the dig on the Saltmarsh, Erik's son materialising – feels uncomfortably like one of those dreams where the past replays itself but with certain details subtly altered. When she first dug on these marshes she was in her twenties, single, just about to embark on her academic career. Now she's still single but she has a seven-year-old daughter and an extremely complicated romantic past. Her career, too, seems to have stalled. She's a senior lecturer at UNN but it's a fairly lowly institution in the middle of nowhere. She should really be looking for a new job at a better university. She has written two books which were well received in academic circles even if they didn't trouble the best-seller lists. She gazes up at her poster. What would Indy do?

She is roused by a buzz from her wrist.

'Only 1,000 steps to go!' exhorts her Fitbit chummily. 'You're in it to win it!!!'

'You want me to interview Shona Maclean?' says Judy.

'Not interview exactly,' says Nelson. 'Just ask her a few questions. After all, she was involved the last time.'

'She wasn't charged though.'

'No, but I'm pretty sure that she helped Erik Anderssen with the letters. All that stuff from Shakespeare and T. S. Eliot. After all, Shona teaches English literature. Ruth says there's an Eliot quote in this one too.'

'Do you really think Shona could have something to do with the new letter? Why would she want to upset you? She's Ruth's friend. They went on holiday together last year.'

'Don't remind me,' says Nelson. 'I don't think Shona is necessarily involved but she might have some idea who's behind it. Erik Anderssen's son is running the dig on the Saltmarsh.'

'Is he?' Judy wonders why Nelson hadn't mentioned this earlier. She has only the vaguest memory of Erik although she was there when they pulled his body out of the water.

'He's called Leif,' says Nelson, with distaste.

'It's a Norwegian name,' says Judy. 'Is he an archaeologist?'

'Apparently so. Pretty pleased with himself too.'

'Do you think he could have written this new letter?'

'It's a bit of a coincidence that they both turn up at the same time. And there are things in the letter that were never in the public domain.'

'There are always leaks though. Maddie says that the local press know everything that goes on here.'

Madeleine, Cathbad's eldest daughter, is currently working on the local newspaper, the *Chronicle*. Maddie's mother was Cathbad's ex-girlfriend Delilah, who later married Alan and had three children, the youngest of them being Scarlet Henderson, the little girl whose body was found on the marshes ten years ago. Maddie has always felt that the King's Lynn police wasted too much time suspecting Scarlet's family of her abduction and murder and so she has strong opinions about police malpractice. But then Maddie has strong opinions about everything. It's one reason why Judy is glad that she's living in digs and not with her and Cathbad.

'Maybe,' says Nelson, 'but there are a few too many links for my liking. They found one of those witch stones on the site. It was buried next to the bones.'

'Do you think it's connected to your Jack Valentine parcel?'

'I don't know. It seems a pretty big coincidence, although Ruth says these stones are fairly common.'

'They are. Cathbad's got a collection. We keep them by the door because that's supposed to mean good luck.'

'You don't surprise me. But why would this Leif write to me or send me a stone in a paper bag? Just to make trouble? It doesn't make sense. That's why I want you to talk to Shona. Find out if she knows anything. But subtly, mind. We don't want her claiming police harassment.'

'You know her better than me. You should talk to her.'

'You'll do it better,' says Nelson. 'I'd just put her back up. And Cloughie and Tanya would be even worse.'

'She'd probably love to be interrogated by Cloughie.'

'I don't want to give her the chance to flirt or get on the defensive,' says Nelson. 'Just a nice woman-to-woman chat.' He says this like it's a new language.

'That's sexist,' says Judy, but she picks up her bag all the same.

'Is it?' says Nelson. 'But I said woman not girl.'

'You're learning,' says Judy. Very slowly, she adds to herself.

*

Nelson follows Judy downstairs and stops for a word with Tom Henty. To his surprise, Tom comes up with a name at once.

'Margaret Lacey,' he says. 'Aged twelve. Went missing in 1981. The year Charles and Diana got married.'

'How do you remember that?'

'You always remember the ones that weren't found, don't you?' Tom looks at him and Nelson finds himself nodding. He will never forget Lucy Downey or Scarlet Henderson. The lost girls.

'What do you remember about Margaret?'

'It was a street party for the Royal Wedding. That's why I remember the year. Margaret and her friend had been at the party in Lynn. They wandered off and no one thought much of it. Later, Margaret's mother – Kathy, Kelly, one of those names – went looking for her and turns out she hadn't been seen for hours, since she parted company with her friend by the quay. There was a massive police hunt but Margaret was never found.'

'Anyone charged?'

'No, there was a lot of suspicion of the parents, particularly the father, but no charges. There was the usual local weirdo but he had an alibi, as I remember. The case was reviewed in 1991, just before you arrived, but there were no new leads.'

'Tell me about the weirdo,' says Nelson. 'Did he have form?'

'Not really. A few cautions for prowling. This was before all this porn on computers malarkey. No, he was just a nutter who liked collecting stuff from the beach. The Stone Man, they called him.'

CHAPTER 6

Shona is surprised, but not displeased, to see Judy.

'No one ever comes to see me now that I'm part-time,' she says, clearing some books off a chair so Judy can sit down. 'Or were you looking for Ruth?'

'No,' says Judy. 'I wanted a quick word with you.'

Shona's office is similar in size to Ruth's but it's far less functional. There are throws over the chairs and a jar of spring flowers on the table. There are pictures too, a poster of woman drowning in flowers (Ophelia?) and several playbills in tasteful colours, which make the room seem more like a student bedsit than a lecturer's office. Even Shona's books are cosier than Ruth's, the orange spines of the Penguin classics and several shelves of leather-bound volumes. Judy fixes her eyes on the playbill over Shona's head. *Women Beware Women.*

Shona offers coffee – she even has a cafetière and proper cups – but Judy refuses politely. They exchange a few remarks about their children. Shona's son, Louis, is almost the same age as Judy's Michael. Then Judy says, 'I wanted to see you because DCI Nelson has received a letter.'

Shona is still smiling but Judy thinks that she has suddenly become very still.

'A letter?' she says.

'Yes. An anonymous letter. But the thing is it seems very similar to the ones Nelson received ten years ago, when Scarlet Henderson went missing.'

Shona says nothing. It was Judy who had questioned her about the letters and about the disappearance of Erik. Judy knows that they are both thinking about this now. Nelson was wrong; she is the very worst person to have this conversation.

'The first letters were written by Erik Anderssen, weren't they?' she says, after a pause.

Shona looks like she's going to deny this but then she shrugs and says, 'Yes.'

'With your help?'

'I supplied a few literary references.'

'And you were in a relationship with Anderssen?'

'Years ago,' says Shona. 'When we were working on the henge dig. I was a volunteer. That's when I first met Cathbad.' She looks at Judy. There's a definite challenge in her gaze. Is Shona implying that Cathbad had fancied her too? It's probably true; Shona is very beautiful, even if she is several years older than Judy. Cathbad's age, in fact.

'I was just wondering,' says Judy, trying to sound like this is a cosy 'woman-to-woman' chat, 'whether you had any idea who could have written this new letter. Some old friend or colleague of Erik's perhaps?'

'His son's working on the new dig,' says Shona. 'Ruth told me.'

'Do you know him, the son?' Judy doesn't want to let on that she knows his name.

'No,' says Shona. 'I never met any of Erik's family. Apart from his wife, of course.' Her voice is flat.

'Well if you do think of anything,' says Judy, 'can you let me know?'

'Of course,' says Shona. 'Anything to help the police.'

Judy does not like her tone.

Ruth is packing her bag. She supposes she should stay late as she missed most of the morning but she's damned if she's going to. Besides, she needs to pick Kate up from Sandra's. She hasn't got any lectures or seminars tomorrow which is why she will be free to excavate the body found on the Saltmarsh. Even so, she bets that Phil will make a thing of it. Or, worse, turn up.

She glances out of her window. It's only five o'clock but already nearly dark. Hard to believe that the clocks will go forward next month. The artificial lake, grubby and often litter-strewn in the daylight, looks attractive in this light, lit by the mushroom-shaped lights around its circumference. As Ruth watches, a man strides along the lakeside path, holding a child by the hand, another child walking behind him, occasionally patting a mushroom. It's rare to see children on campus and Ruth looks more closely before realising that she knows this family. It's Cathbad with Michael and Miranda. What's he doing here? Meeting his old colleagues in the chemistry department? As Ruth watches, another man approaches. He, like Cathbad, has long hair in a ponytail. The two men embrace warmly and the newcomer bends down to talk to Miranda. Michael, as ever, remains slightly aloof.

Ruth stands back from her window but she continues to watch. She wonders why Cathbad didn't tell her that he and Leif Anderssen are obviously close friends.

By the time Nelson gets back to his office, Tanya has put the Margaret Lacey file on his desk. Nelson reads through it quickly, noting dates and names. On 29 July 1981, Margaret Lacey, aged twelve, attended a street party near her home in King's Lynn. At some point during the afternoon she slipped away with her friend, Kim Jennings. Margaret's mother, Karen Lacey, reported her missing at eight o'clock that evening. Margaret had last been seen with Kim in front of the Custom House by the quay. According to one witness the two girls had been arguing but Kim insisted that they had parted amicably. Margaret had wanted to see the Punch and Judy man in the Tuesday Market Place and walked off in that direction. Kim went back to the street party. A massive police search started that night, combing the streets that were, presumably, still full of monarchist revellers. Frogmen searched the river and sniffer dogs tracked as far as South Wootton. The investigation, as far as Nelson could see, focused on the parents, Karen and Bob. There were two older children, Annie who had been fourteen at the time of Margaret's disappearance and Luke, who had been fifteen. Bob, who was a plasterer, was known to have a temper but he swore he'd never laid a hand on any of his children. He had been drinking in the pub most of the day, until alerted by Karen at about seven. There were several witnesses who claimed to have been with Bob but Nelson knows that drinking companions do not make good alibis. It would probably have been possible for Bob to have slipped out for an hour without anyone being much the wiser.

John Mostyn, the so-called Stone Man, emerged as a suspect quite early on, because of his previous convictions. He had also been seen talking to Margaret and Kim earlier in the day, 'showing them some pebbles he'd found on the beach'. But John had spent most of the day looking after his wheelchair-bound mother, Heidi, and she gave him a firm alibi. Some schoolfriends said that Margaret had talked about a boyfriend in London but this proved to be a false trail. Despite numerous appeals, Margaret was never seen again.

Nelson stares down at the file, now furry at the edges with age. Nelson was fourteen in 1981. They'd had street parties in Blackpool too but his mother had disapproved of them for some long-forgotten sectarian reason. Nelson remembers his mother and his sisters watching the wedding on television but he and his father had escaped to the park. They'd played football, he remembers, one against one, until some local lads had joined them. Come to think of it, that might have been the last time he'd had a kick-around with his dad. Archie Nelson had been an enthusiastic supporter of his son's schoolboy footballing career but he wasn't much of a player himself, childhood polio having left him with one leg shorter than the other. And, a year after the Royal Wedding, Archie was dead from a heart attack. It's an odd feeling. Nelson would have been only two years older than Margaret. He could have played football with her older brother, hung around on street corners with her big sister. Where are the family now? He emails Tanya and the answer comes back immediately. Bob Lacey died of cancer two years ago but Karen is still alive. She divorced Bob soon after Margaret's disappearance, married again and has two sons with her new husband. Margaret's sister Annie is married with children and lives in Lynn. Luke lives in London. John Mostyn is seventy and still lives in the house where he once cared for his mother.

Are they Margaret's bones that have been discovered buried on the Saltmarsh? Dental records should make identification possible even if they don't have DNA. At least this will give the family some closure, some remains to bury.

Nelson has left a message for his old sergeant Freddie Burnett. He suspects that Freddie is out on the golf course but, when he gets a call back, it transpires that Freddie is on holiday in Tenerife. 'Bit of winter sun,' says his old colleague, his voice mellow with vitamin D. 'You should try it.'

'Maybe I will one day,' says Nelson though he can't think of anything worse than a week of golf, cocktails and after-dinner entertainment. He tells Freddie why he is calling.

'Margaret Lacey,' says Freddie. 'Well, well, well.'

'Do you remember the case?'

'Very well. I was pretty sure who killed the poor girl too.'

'The father?'

'No, the prowler. John Mostyn.'

'He had an alibi.'

'His mother. She would have sworn black was white for him. No, Mostyn was the type. He was always hanging round the little girls. Pervert. Him and his pebble collection. If I had my way, I'd castrate the lot of them.'

Nelson tries to stop Freddie before he gets going on one of his crime and punishment diatribes.

'Well, if it is Margaret,' he says, 'we can reopen the case. There have been lots of advances in forensics since the eighties. We might still get the perpetrator.'

'I bloody hope so,' says Freddie. As Nelson is saying goodbye and wishing Freddie and his wife a pleasant holiday, his phone buzzes. It's Laura.

'Dad, you'd better come home. Mum says her contractions have started.'

CHAPTER 7

Laura meets Nelson at the door. She has her jacket on and car keys in her hand.

'Thank God you're here, Dad. Mum keeps saying that there's plenty of time but I don't think there is.'

Michelle is in the sitting room. She looks quite calm but she is staring intensely at the coffee table in front of her. Bruno is watching anxiously and there's an overnight bag by the door.

'Come on, love,' says Nelson. 'Time to get going.'

'It's fine,' says Michelle, not shifting her gaze. 'Contractions are still fifteen minutes apart.'

Nelson has such a strong attack of déjà vu that he almost feels dizzy. He and Michelle leaving their house in Blackpool in the middle of the night, Michelle in the early stages of labour with Laura, neither of them knowing what to do, Nelson breaking all the speed limits on the way. Laura had been born in a cubicle in A&E, there being no time to get to the maternity ward. Rebecca had taken her time, almost ten hours of Nelson pacing and questioning and absent-mindedly eating the ham sandwiches he had made for Michelle. Now Laura is a grown woman who is, even now, texting her sister in Brighton.

'Rebecca says hurry up. She wants to meet George.'

'We all do,' says Nelson. 'Come on, love.' He helps Michelle to her feet and they walk slowly out of the room, Michelle already doing her breathing, shallow pants that make Bruno cock his head with interest.

'Shall I come with you?' says Laura.

'No,' says Nelson. 'You stay and look after Bruno. I'll ring you as soon as there's any news. Don't worry.'

'I won't,' says Laura, worriedly.

He puts the blue light on the car and they are at the hospital in ten minutes. They go up to the labour ward where the midwife seems to spend an inordinate amount of time asking Michelle useless questions. The contractions are obviously closer now and lasting longer. Still the midwife writes slowly on her pad, stopping to answer an orderly's question about the birthing pool.

'We need to hurry up,' he says. 'The baby will be here any minute.'

'Don't worry, Mr Nelson,' says the midwife, 'we've got plenty of time yet.'

'It's DCI,' growls Nelson. Preoccupied as she is, Michelle finds time to give him a look.

'Michelle's in labour,' says Judy, reading Nelson's text.

'We should pray to Hecate,' says Cathbad. They are in the café at the University of North Norfolk. Leif is buying the coffee and, from what Judy can see, vast amounts of chocolate for the children.

'I thought Hecate was the goddess of witchcraft,' says Judy.

'Childbirth too.'

'That figures.' Sometimes Judy thinks that she would quite like another child (if she could stand another M name) but can't bring herself to go through pregnancy again. Besides, she wants to take her Inspector exam soon. She watches Miranda skipping along beside Leif as he manoeuvres his tray towards them. Miranda seems to have taken to Leif, which is unusual because the only adults she really likes are her parents. Actually, sometimes just her father.

'Why didn't you tell me that you knew Leif?' says Judy.

'You didn't ask,' says Cathbad.

Judy is used to answers like this – seemingly frank but actually frustratingly enigmatic – by now. 'I told you about the letter,' she says. She feels rather guilty about this. 'You could have told me that you were in touch with Erik's son.'

'I wasn't in touch with him then,' says Cathbad. 'He only emailed me today. I've met him once before, years ago, when he was still a student. And I wanted you to meet him. That's why I suggested meeting here, at the university.'

'What's he doing here?'

'Visiting a friend in the history department apparently.'

They have to stop talking because Leif and his tray have arrived. Michael sits reading on his Kindle. Judy feels conflicted (reading: good; technology: bad) but doesn't say anything. Besides, Miranda is making up for it by watching delightedly as Leif turns his paper napkin into a swan.

'Again!' she says.

'Do you want one, Michael?' asks Leif.

'No thank you,' says Michael politely.

'How long are you in England for?' Judy asks Leif as she sips her cappuccino. Ruth told her recently that, in Italy, it's considered shocking, almost rude, to drink cappuccino after midday. Judy is rather pleased to think that she's being a rebel for once.

'For as long as the dig lasts,' says Leif. 'Probably about two weeks.'

'What about the modern bones that you've discovered? Won't that delay things?'

'Ruth thinks that the excavation will only take a day. She seemed pretty confident.'

'She's very good at her job,' says Judy. 'She'll be very thorough.'

'She seems an altogether admirable person,' says Leif. Something in the way he says this makes Judy look at him sharply but Leif is smiling pleasantly while his hands are busy with another piece of origami. This time it's a frog for Michael. Despite his earlier refusal, Judy can tell that Michael is pleased with the gift.

'It's sacred land,' says Cathbad. 'That's what your dad would say. That's why you've found a second circle.'

'The second circle might have been a burial mound,' says Leif, 'with the cist at the centre. Or a sky burial.'

'What's a sky burial?' asks Judy.

'Bodies left in the open to be consumed by animals and carrion birds,' says Leif, taking a bite of chocolate brownie. 'They could be offerings to the sky gods or simply part of the natural cycle. Animals and plants feed on the remains, death and rebirth. We'll know more when we have the results back on the bones.'

'What about the modern bones?' says Judy.

'A policewoman's question,' says Leif, smiling.

'I prefer police officer,' says Judy. 'When do you think the modern bones were buried there?'

'Ruth thought they might have been interred fairly recently,' says Leif. 'She mentioned the grave cut. I suppose you are looking into your . . . what do you call them? Cold cases?'

'Yes, we are,' says Judy.

'I'd love to see the site,' says Cathbad. 'I have very happy memories of the first excavation. Despite what happened later.'

Leif seems quite moved. He puts his hand on Cathbad's. 'Come to the site,' he says. 'Come early one morning and we will salute the dawn together.'

'I'll have to do the school run first,' says Cathbad.

Nelson stares at the beauty spot on his wife's cheek. They are in the zone now. Michelle seems oblivious of him; she concentrates on breathing, occasionally waving her hands as if trying to conjure something out of mid-air. Just once, she stares at him, really stares, as if she's seeing him for the first time.

'If anything happens to me,' she says, 'look after the baby.'

'I will.'

'Promise!'

'I promise.'

But then, suddenly, she's pushing and it's all screaming, grunting and panting and horrible silences and then, just like in the films, a slithery rush and the first angry cries.

'A beautiful boy,' says the midwife.

She puts the baby on Michelle's chest, still with the umbilical cord attached. The room smells of blood.

'Does Dad want to cut the cord?'

But Nelson can't tear his eyes away from the baby. This miracle child. His son.

'Hallo, George,' he says.

CHAPTER 8

Ruth doesn't hear until halfway through the next morning when Clough turns up at the excavation. She has exposed the margins of the visible bones and has taken pictures next to a scaling rod for measurements. Now she is in the process of lifting out a femur. She's not sure if there's a complete skeleton; the bones aren't articulated, and don't seem to have been buried with any particular care. By contrast, the remains in the cist had clearly been arranged with reverence, almost in foetal position, with the grave goods, the urn and seeds, at their side. Ruth is more certain than ever that the modern bones were buried in a rush and fairly recently.

Ted, from the field archaeology team, stands by to number and label each bone. It's a sunny day, though bitterly cold, and Ruth plans to let the bones dry out in the sun for a while, which should harden them. She is concentrating on the job so doesn't see Clough until he appears at the edge of the trench. She sees his feet first, tough-looking boots that also manage to look as if they're at the cutting edge of fashion. That's how she knows it's not Nelson.

'Have you heard the news?'

'What news?' says Ruth, pushing the hair out of her eyes. She is simultaneously hot and cold and her back aches. She is desperate for coffee but Leif tells her that the site is a caffeine-free zone: 'No poisons, only good energy here.'

'Michelle's had the baby.'

'That's great.' Ruth wonders how she can voice the question that crowds all others out of her mind. Is there some subtle way she can ask, without offending or shocking Clough?

'Oh, and it's not black,' says Clough, climbing into the trench. 'So we know it's the boss's. I brought you some coffee.'

So even Clough knows! Does everyone at the station know? Were they having bets on whether Michelle's baby was Nelson's or Tim's? Clough's face gives nothing away. He hands over a Starbucks cup, which probably completely violates the karma of the dig, and looks around the trench with apparent interest. Ruth drinks the coffee gratefully. The baby is Nelson's. This means it will cement Nelson and Michelle's marriage for ever. She can't see Nelson walking out on a baby and, anyhow, does she still want him to walk in her direction? She doesn't know. At that precise moment she is conscious only of the caffeine making its way into her system and of the relief of standing upright, easing her back. The other emotions will come later.

'Born last night,' Clough is saying. 'Seven pounds, six ounces. Not as big as Spencer was.' Since becoming a father, Clough has directed some of his relentless competitiveness into boasting about his offspring. He hands Ruth his phone to show the photograph sent by Nelson last night. Ruth looks at the baby wrapped in a blue shawl, eyes closed, fists clenched. Nelson's son. Kate's brother.

'Mother and baby both doing well,' says Clough. 'They should be home later today.'

'That's great,' says Ruth again. 'I'll send some flowers.' She takes another swig of coffee.

'How are your bones?' says Clough, peering at the half-exposed femur, which Ted is clearing with a pointing trowel.

'Don't touch anything,' says Ted. 'I know what the police are like. And why didn't I get coffee?'

'I've never seen you drink anything that isn't beer,' says Clough. 'How old do you think the bones are?'

'We won't know until we have the carbon-14 results,' says Ruth, rather wearily, 'and even then we won't have an exact date. The burial looks fairly new but the bones are older. We'll do isotope tests on the teeth. That will tell us where this person grew up.'

'The boss said you thought it was a child.'

'Yes, from the look of the bones I'd say it's an early adolescent. The bones still have epiphyses on them and we've got teeth, which is a great help with ageing. The eruption of permanent teeth happens within fairly set timescales. I'll know more when we excavate the skull.'

'Girl or boy?'

'We can't be sure unless we get some DNA. Girls have shallower pelvises and less pronounced brow-ridges but this isn't always easy to discern in adolescents. These changes occur gradually during the pubescent years.'

'You know we've got a possible name? Margaret Lacey, a twelve-year-old who went missing in 1981. That's strictly confidential, by the way.'

Ruth is pretty sure that Clough shouldn't have told them at all but he's always been a terrible gossip. Having a name makes all the difference though. She looks at the skull, which is still embedded in the earth and thinks: Margaret.

'I remember Margaret Lacey,' says Ted. 'Disappeared during a street party, didn't she?'

'Were you living in Lynn then?' asks Clough. 'You'd be about the right age.'

'No, I was still in Bolton in 1981,' says Ted. 'That was before I had to leave.'

Ted always makes it sound as though he was chased out of his home town by a pitchfork-waving mob but, as far as Ruth can make out, he simply left to attend Liverpool University.

'Are Margaret's family still living in the area?' asks Ruth.

'The mother and sister are,' says Clough. 'Father's dead, brother's in London. From what you've said, I think we'd better warn Margaret's mum that this might be her.'

'Who's in charge now the boss is on paternity leave?' asks Ted, with a wink at Ruth.

Clough puffs out his chest. 'Who do you think?'

'Judy,' says Ruth.

Michelle and George are home by lunchtime. Nelson drives them back as if he's advertising a safer roads initiative. Rebecca has come up from Brighton and she and Laura have attached blue balloons to the front door. Both sets of neighbours come out to welcome them.

'I feel like royalty,' says Michelle, getting carefully out of the car. She's still wearing maternity clothes but she has dry shampooed her hair and it glows in the sunshine. Both girls come out to hug her but they turn immediately to the occupant of the baby seat that is being proudly displayed by Nelson.

'He's gorgeous,' says Rebecca. 'He looks just like me.' And it's true that George, like Rebecca (and Kate) has inherited Nelson's dark hair.

'He's a bonny baby,' says Brenda next door, who likes to emphasise her Scottish ancestry.

'Can I hold him?' says Laura, who is trying to stop Bruno jumping up at his master.

'When we get inside,' says Nelson. 'It's a bit cold out here.'

After a few more pleasantries, the family go indoors; Nelson holding the baby seat with Bruno at his heels, Rebecca and Laura either side of their mother. Brenda turns to Alan, the other next-door neighbour. The cul-de-sac is not normally a very chatty place but the events of the last few months have brought them all a bit closer together.

'It's nice to see some happiness after everything that happened in the summer,' says Brenda.

'Yes,' says Alan. 'Michelle looked radiant, didn't she?' He has always had a soft spot for Mrs Nelson.

'I still think about that day,' says Brenda. 'That poor young man being shot like that. Tim Heathfield, his name was. Derek and I went to his funeral. The church was packed out.'

'Well that's all in the past now,' says Alan, trying to edge back inside.

'Poor Tim,' says Brenda, looking at the Nelsons' house, the balloons dancing in the breeze. 'I'll never forget him.'

It's late afternoon by the time that Ruth has finished her excavation. The scene-of-crime officers have left. Ted has numbered each bone and Ruth has filled in her bone chart. It seems as if they have a complete skeleton and, from the look of the skull and the pelvic bones, Ruth thinks it is that of a young female. The bones lie in paper bags, ready to go into the pathology crates. They are well-preserved, a factor that makes Ruth think that they were originally buried else-where, in a more anaerobic environment, with little oxygen to cause decay. There's nothing obvious to point to the cause of death. A healed fracture is evident on one humerus but this injury probably occurred in early childhood. The other bones show no abnormal signs of stress. The most precious clue is the presence of some blue household rope, strands that may have once bound Margaret's arms and legs. Traces of material were also found near the jawbone, possible evidence of a gag or even a means of asphyxiation. These fragments have been carefully bagged and documented. If DNA is found on them then the police might have a suspect at last. Ruth is just about to ring Clough when Ted says, 'What's this?'

Ted is taking soil samples and is kneeling looking into the crater left by the skull. Ruth comes to join him and, as she does so, she is aware that Leif is now standing behind them. Ted points at something white, half-embedded in the soil. At first Ruth thinks it's another bone but then she sees the pitted surface and realises that she is looking at a round piece of chalk. Ted picks it up carefully with gloved hands. The stone is the size of a small apple and there are two holes going through it. The positioning of the holes makes them look disconcertingly like eyes.

'A witch stone,' says Leif. 'Was it buried with the body?'

'I think so,' says Ruth, looking closer. 'This is a sandy beach, there's not much chalk around.'

'It looks like a skull,' says Ted. 'Maybe that's why it was buried there.'

'Maybe,' says Ruth. 'Let's bag it up and send it for tests. There could be DNA on it. Or fingerprints.'

'You think like a policeman, Ruth,' says Leif. 'It's clear that this is an offering of some kind.'

'Nothing's clear at the moment,' says Ruth, rather annoyed at this comment. 'Now, if you'll excuse me, I need to box up the bones.'

It rains later that evening. Michelle feeds George and goes to bed early. Nelson stays downstairs watching a Swedish crime drama with his daughters. He keeps falling asleep but he knows that the presence of the baby's cot in his room will mean that he wakes every hour in the night to check that George is still breathing. The trouble is, every time Nelson's eyes close he thinks of Ruth. Will she have heard about George by now? He sent texts and pictures to Judy and Clough. A massive bunch of flowers has already been delivered, 'From everyone at King's Lynn CID'. What did Judy say about news leaking from the police station? Presumably the whole town will know by now. He needs to tell Ruth. For one thing he wants Katie to meet her half-brother, though that will be tricky with Laura and Rebecca here. His head nods.

'Why don't you go to bed, Dad?' says Laura. 'We'll take Bruno out.'

His girls have been wonderful all evening, so excited about the baby, so kind to their parents. There's not a trace or resentment or jealousy in either of them. Maybe they would welcome Katie in the same wholehearted way.

'No, you're all right,' he says. 'I want to see if that Sven bloke killed the man dressed up as a moose.'

Ruth sits at her computer as the rain lashes against the windows. Kate is in bed, still oblivious to the fact that she is no longer an only child. Ruth has been expecting Nelson to ring all day but now it's nearly midnight and she knows that she won't hear from him. She should go to sleep – she has a nine o'clock lecture tomorrow – but she googled Margaret Lacey a few hours ago and now can't stop reading about the case.

'Family's anguish as Street Party Girl still missing.'

Margaret became 'Street Party Girl' very quickly in the days after her disappearance. Ruth was thirteen in 1981, almost the same age as Margaret is, was, would have been.

As Douglas Adams said, the problem of the past is largely one of grammar. A confirmed republican, Ruth is rather embarrassed to remember that she too had attended a street party, just off Eltham High Street. She remembers the bunting and a ribald song about 'Lady Di' but little else. Now Lady, later Princess, Diana is dead too and the whole thing seems like it happened in a different life.

To some papers Margaret was also 'Maggie' although there was no evidence that her family ever called her by this diminutive.

'Did Maggie have a London boyfriend?'

The answer was almost certainly no but some of Margaret's schoolfriends mentioned 'a boy in London', a 'penfriend' according to some. Ruth had almost forgotten penfriends. She'd exchanged letters with Beatrix in Germany for almost a year before the correspondence petered and died. Where was Beatrix now? she wondered. All Ruth could remember was that she'd been keen on 'prog rock' and *Starsky and Hutch*. At any rate, Margaret's penfriend never materialised. There was only one London train from King's Lynn that afternoon and none of the passengers remembered seeing a twelve-year-old girl wearing jeans and a Fruit of the Loom T-shirt. No CCTV in those days, of course.

There was TV though and Ruth manages to track down a documentary from 1988 called *The Missing* about unsolved cases. Margaret pops up on screen, first in her school uniform – purple blazer, fat tie, blonde hair in plaits – then in a bridesmaid's dress, her hair loose and curly. She was a pretty girl with a heart-shaped face and big blue eyes. In 1981, the days when Jimmy Savile was considered a lovably eccentric entertainer, many of the papers commented on Margaret's looks or speculated that she might have had 'admirers', despite being only twelve. 'She looked older,' said one report, lascivious even in print.

Margaret's mother, Karen, features strongly in the documentary. The father, Bob, doesn't speak much apart from, once, saying he'd like to kill the person who took his little girl. Ruth can see why Karen was chosen as spokesperson. She was attractive, like her daughter, with short blonde hair and an impressively straight gaze.

'Margaret wouldn't have run away,' she said, more than once. 'She was happy at home. Her brother and sister doted on her. She was the apple of our eye. We all adored her.'

Margaret certainly looked like the adored youngest child, the golden girl. Ruth is a youngest child too although it's hardly the same with two and, besides, she always felt that both parents preferred her brother, Simon, who got married, produced children and kept his atheism decently hidden behind dutiful churchgoing. Annie and Luke Lacey both appear on the documentary. Annie would have been twenty-one at the time but looked older, a solid-looking girl with an impassive stare. 'Someone knows what happened to my little sister,' she said, 'and we won't rest until we find them.' Luke, a year older, was more nervous, ducking his head so that his eighties fringe covered his eyes. 'It's not knowing that's quite hard,' he said, with rather touching understatement. 'It would be better really if we knew she was dead. Then we could grieve.'

Well now they might have a body and the grieving and the questions could start all over again. When Ruth had finished her excavation and gave it as her considered opinion that the body was that of an adolescent, probably female, who had died about thirty years ago, Clough said that he and Judy would visit Margaret's mother 'to prepare her'. How can you ever be prepared for news like that, even after thirty-five years? Ruth looks at the time at the bottom right-hand corner of her laptop: 00.28. She should go to bed. She knows, without looking round, that Flint is staring at her, wanting his late-night snack. But, when she shuts her laptop, she continues to gaze at the window, at the rain and the darkness.

CHAPTER 9

The sun rises over the marshes, turning the inland pools red and gold. The sand stretches out in front of them, rippled like a frozen sea. A flock of birds flies from the reed beds, zigzagging into the light. Leif raises his arms: 'Goddess of the earth. Bless our endeavours today.' Cathbad makes a suitable answer but he finds himself thinking, not of Brother Sun and Sister Moon, but of whether Judy will get to work in time after dropping the children at school and nursery. It was kind of her to offer to do the school run, especially when she has a possible murder case on her hands and Nelson is still away on paternity leave. He hopes that she remembers Michael's special vegetarian lunch box.

'The energies are good,' announces Leif. He selects a stone that is glimmering on the edge of the water. He weighs it in his hand for a moment and then sends it spinning into the sea. It skips over the shallow waves, once, twice, three times.

'A votive offering.' Leif turns to grin at Cathbad who has a sudden desire to pick up his own stone and send it spinning into the air, describing a perfect parabola as it flies. Stone skimming is a speciality of his, much admired by his children. He's surprised at the pettiness of his thoughts. He supposes that Leif, with his height and golden looks, arouses feelings of inferiority and competitiveness in other men. It's just a disappointment that he's not immune to such things.

'The new circle is very near the sea,' he says, as they turn and walk inland.

'Yes,' says Leif. 'Of course the sea has come much closer over the years but I think the setting is important.'

'Ruth said that the bones might be female,' says Cathbad.

Leif stops. 'The modern bones?'

'No,' says Cathbad. Judy has, in fact, told him the possible identity of the modern bones but he knows that this isn't in the public domain yet. He wonders why Leif jumped to this conclusion. 'She said that the bones in the cist were early Bronze Age and probably female, post-pubescent but still fairly young.'

'Yes,' says Leif, seeming to recover his poise. 'It's interesting that a young girl was buried here with such ceremony. There were grave goods too. An urn containing berries and seeds and a stone with a hole through the middle.'

'A witch stone?'

'Yes, or hag stone. Funnily enough, one was found with the modern bones too.'

They have reached the site and Leif takes the tarpaulin off the trenches. Cathbad looks at the clean lines, the layers of soil, the scaling rods laid on the grass. It reminds him of digging with Erik in the early days. Erik, despite his eccentricities, was very strict about methodology. You weren't even allowed to sit on the edge of your trench, Cathbad remembers, in case you spoilt the edges.

Leif shows Cathbad the cist, a rectangular space lined with stones.

'The bones were roughly in foetal position,' he says. 'The urn at her head, the stone by her feet.' The female pronoun makes all the difference, thinks Cathbad. He finds himself praying for the Bronze Age girl as well as for Margaret, if that is the identity of the later body.

'Were there wooden posts around the cist?' he asks.

'We think so,' says Leif. 'We've excavated six of them. This is a sketch of the possible shape.' He shows this, not on a notebook, but on his iPad, which seems rather sad to Cathbad. But the reconstruction is impressive, a palisade of posts in a roughly oval shape.

'It's not really a circle, is it?' says Cathbad.

'No,' says Leif. 'It reminds me of stone ships. Have you seen these? You get them in Scandinavia, around a thousand years BCE. The Jelling stone ship in Denmark is famous. It's a grave surrounded by stones in a leaf pattern that resembles a ship. It's thought to link to the Viking belief that the dead sailed to Valhalla over the sea. But some say that the burial also meant good luck and fertility for the surrounding lands. Ships in fields, they're sometimes called.'

Cathbad looks out across the flat marshland. He remembers guiding Nelson across the quicksand in the dark, using the ancient posts as a guide. He likes the thought that the Bronze Age grave might have meant good luck for the surrounding land. But he finds the notion of stone ships rather disquieting. He once had a very vivid dream – or hallucination – about Erik sailing a ship made of stone.

'I remember your dad so well,' he says now. 'He was a great influence on me. I switched from chemistry to archaeology because of him. He was my lecturer at Manchester.'

'He talked about you often,' says Leif. 'I think you were very dear to him.'

'Maybe,' says Cathbad. 'I was useful to him, at any rate. I've sometimes felt that things didn't end well between us. Maybe that's why I think of him so often.'

'Perhaps there is some way that we can achieve closure,' says Leif. He's looking intently at Cathbad. His eyes – so like Erik's – disconcertingly bright.

'Perhaps that's why you came here,' says Cathbad.

'I was summoned here,' says Leif. 'By the dead girl.'

'The girl in the cist?'

'No,' says Leif, 'the poor spirit whose bones we found the other day. I feel sure she is a girl and that she is calling to us.'

He smiles at Cathbad, a radiant beam that recalls Erik at his most messianic. But, at that moment, Cathbad does not find the memory reassuring.

Judy drops the children at their educational establishments without incident. She forgets Michael's lunch box but stops off at the Co-op to buy him a cheese sandwich and some grapes. She puts these in a police evidence bag which, for Michael, makes his whole day worthwhile. At the station, she finds Clough eating a bacon sandwich which makes her mouth water. Doing without bacon is the single worst thing about living with Cathbad.

'Want some?' says Clough.

'No. Yes. Just a bit.' Clough tears off a piece of bread and bacon, dripping with tomato sauce. It tastes like heaven.

They have arranged to call on Karen Benson, Margaret's mother, at nine o'clock. On the phone Judy only said that they'd made a discovery which might be linked to Margaret's disappearance. She also suggests that Karen has someone with her to receive the news. When they get to the neat terraced house they are met at the door by a large woman in a nurse's uniform who says that she's Karen's daughter, Annie Simmonds.

'Margaret's sister,' she adds, fixing them with a rather belligerent stare. It's obvious that Annie, at least, regards the police with suspicion. Karen is a gentler, more nervous, presence. She's a small woman and that makes her look oddly childlike, despite ash-grey hair and a face that bears the lines of a lifelong smoker.

Annie offers them tea which Judy accepts because she feels that it'll put the visit on a friendlier footing. If the bones do turn out to be Margaret's, they will be seeing a lot of her family in the next few weeks. Annie puts mugs in front of them, together with a plate of biscuits. Clough takes two. Karen gets out a cigarette and looks at it longingly.

'You know Pete doesn't like you smoking in the house,' says Annie. Karen puts the cigarette back in its packet. *Smoking Kills*, is the bald message on the gold box.

Pete Benson is Karen's second husband, a mild-looking man with white hair who looks older than his wife. He barely speaks as the women hand out plates and mugs. And he doesn't comment on the cigarette.

'Thank you for seeing us,' says Judy. 'As I said on the phone, we've made a discovery which we think might be connected to Margaret's disappearance. It's early days but we just wanted you to know so that you can prepare yourselves and so that we can support you.'

'Have you found her?' interrupts Annie. The question sounds as if she really expects them to have found Margaret alive. As if a blonde-haired woman in her late forties is about to come into the room with her arms outstretched.

Judy says, 'We've found some human remains which we think might be those of Margaret. I'm sorry. This must be a terrible shock.'

Karen makes a noise that is halfway between a gasp and a sob. Pete reaches over and holds her hand. Annie takes a sip of tea, eyes hard.

'We've found some bones on the coast near Titchwell,' Judy continues. 'The forensic archaeologist thinks that they might be the remains of a child Margaret's age.'

'An archaeologist?' says Annie. 'What's an archaeologist got to do with it?'

'The bones were found on an archaeological site,' says Judy. 'And the police often consult archaeologists in cases like this.'

'And you think it really might be ... that it might be Margaret?' Karen's voice is trembling.

'We'll see if we can get some DNA from the bones,' says

Clough. 'And, if not, we can check dental records. One way or another, we should have a definite answer for you.'

It's almost the first time Clough has spoken – he prefers to leave the family liaison stuff to Judy – and Judy is annoyed to see both women turning to him with respect and attention. Superintendent Archer hasn't put anyone in charge in Nelson's absence. 'Let's try a collegiate approach,' she said, when asked directly (by Tanya). But there's nothing that admirable about the way colleges and universities operate, as far as Judy can see.

'How long will it take?' asks Annie.

'About two weeks,' says Clough, plucking a timescale from the air. Karen and Annie take it as gospel.

'So in two weeks we'll know,' says Karen. 'We'll know . . . we'll know what happened to her.'

'Easy, love.' Pete looks at his wife rather anxiously.

'These things take time,' says Judy. 'I know it's very hard, the waiting.'

'We've waited thirty-five years,' says Karen, with a harsh laugh that turns into a smoker's cough. 'Our Annie's just become a grandmother. I'm a great-grandmother. But it's as if Margaret disappeared yesterday.'

Judy looks at the wall behind Karen's head, where a giant flat-screen TV is surrounded by framed photographs: children, grandchildren and pets. Her eyes are immediately drawn to a studio portrait of a blonde girl in a pink bridesmaid's dress. Margaret. Forever young, forever missing.

'It's tough on the mother,' says Pete, with the air of one passing on a state secret.

'Tough on everyone, Pete,' says Annie. 'Our Luke still has nightmares about it.'

'Well, hopefully we'll have some news for you soon,' says Clough, standing up. 'Thank you for letting us come round today.'

'Thank you, Detective Inspector,' says Karen, addressing Clough.

'We'll be in touch,' says Judy.

'You didn't correct them about the rank,' says Judy as they drive back to the station.

'I didn't like to upset them,' says Clough, 'not at this emotional time.'

'Bloody sexist. Assuming the man is in charge.'

'I know,' says Clough, driving carefully through the maze of streets. 'It's shocking. I'd write to the *Guardian* about it if I were you.'

'You're going the wrong way,' says Judy. 'It's left here.' Karen and Pete still live in the house where Margaret was brought up. Once council, it's now privately owned, as are many on the estate. But, while the pebbledash houses display signs of individuality – a conservatory here, a loft extension there – the overriding impression is still that of uniformity, row upon row of identical houses, each with their small stretch of garden, roads named after First World War Generals: Haig, Allenby, Marshall, Byng. Clough takes a right down Allenby Avenue.

'Where are you going?'

'I think this is the one.' Clough slows down as they pass

a corner house, the same as the others in the street except shabbier, a decaying sofa in the garden, dirty blinds at the upper windows.

'What . . . ?' begins Judy.

'This is the house where John Mostyn lives,' says Clough. 'The prime suspect.'

Judy wants to tell Clough that John Mostyn's not an official suspect so they can't stalk him like this but she's secretly impressed that Clough has both read the file and remembered the address. 'It's very close, isn't it?' she says.

'Yes,' says Clough. 'The families knew each other.'

'Incredible that Karen hasn't moved away,' says Judy.

'Maybe she didn't want to leave with Margaret still missing.'

Judy thinks of Karen saying 'it's as if Margaret disappeared yesterday'. Has she, all this time, been half expecting her youngest daughter to walk through the door, golden-haired and unchanged? Does she feel, on the nights when the wind and rain rush in from the sea, that Margaret is out there somewhere in the dark?

Clough pulls in at the kerb and they both stare at the end house. Judy knows from the file that John Mostyn has lived on his own since his mother died almost twenty years ago. The Stone Man, they called him, and she has a sudden vision of the house's occupant sitting calcified in his chair, flesh becoming stone.

'Let's go,' she says. 'Time enough to interview Mostyn when we have a DNA match.'

*

When they get back to King's Lynn police station, the duty officer – a newish woman constable – tells Judy that her daughter is waiting for her.

'What?' says Judy. She imagines three-year-old Miranda sitting in the waiting area, clutching her teddy bear.

'I thought you were too young to have a grown-up daughter,' says the PC, blushing.

'I am,' says Judy. But by now she has spotted the blonde hair and the parka and knows who is waiting for her.

'Hallo, Maddie.'

'Hallo, Mum,' says Maddie, grinning. Judy and Cathbad aren't married so, technically, Madeleine isn't her step-daughter but it would be churlish to point this out. Besides, Maddie has a perfectly good mother of her own so Judy isn't required to fulfil that role. What they have instead is a rather uneasy semi-friendship. Maddie's not that close to Cathbad either although she adores Michael and Miranda.

'Have you got a minute?' says Maddie.

'Of course. Come on up.'

'Hallo, Maddie,' says Clough. 'You still working for that crap paper?'

Maddie laughs but Clough has succeeded in putting Judy on her guard. She knows now why Maddie is paying her this visit.

The open-plan office is empty apart from Tanya, sulkily writing up some notes. Judy offers to make coffee and Maddie proffers her own herbal teabags. She follows Judy into the kitchen and says, 'I hear you've found Margaret Lacey.'

'Is that why you're here?' says Judy, splashing boiling water into a mug.

'Come on, Judy,' says Maddie. 'Just say yes or no. It would be such a scoop for me.'

'I can't say yes or no,' says Judy, 'because I don't know.'

'But you have found some bones. Cathbad told me.' Maddie always refers to her father by his name (or, rather, his druidical name). Her stepfather, who brought her up, is Dad.

'Look, Maddie.' Judy tries for a calming tone. Maddie's startling green eyes are fixed on her face. She has an intensity that sometimes seems to edge towards something darker. 'You can't mention the name Margaret Lacey in connection with these bones. Not until we're sure. Her family have suffered enough. But, if this is her, you'll be the first to know. After the next of kin, of course. Is that a deal?'

'What about John Mostyn?' says Maddie. 'He still lives locally, doesn't he? Will you bring him in for questioning? Get a DNA sample?'

'I can't say,' says Judy.

'John Mostyn could have killed Scarlet too,' says Maddie. 'He used to work for the paper as a photographer. He knew all about the henge dig.'

'He didn't kill her,' says Judy.

'Scarlet was found buried in the centre of a Bronze Age circle,' says Maddie. 'That's where you found Margaret too.'

'Maddie,' Judy lowers her voice, 'we know who killed Scarlet and he's dead too. Don't do this to yourself.'

'You'll never understand about Scarlet.' Maddie sweeps out of the room leaving Judy standing there, a mug of boiling water in her hand.

CHAPTER 10

Clough was right; it takes two weeks for the DNA results to come back. And it's a match. The bones found buried by the Bronze Age grave are the remains of Margaret Lacey, aged twelve. Judy and Clough break the news to Karen and, before the police put out an official statement, they drive out to the Saltmarsh so that the family can put flowers at the site. The archaeologists have been warned to stay away.

It's a misty morning, the sky streaked pale blue and pink, the sea limpid and calm. They walk in file along the gravel path. Judy leading, followed by Karen and Pete, Karen holding a bunch of flowers hastily purchased from a garage, Clough and Annie bringing up the rear. Judy visited the dig yesterday but is struck by how different the Saltmarsh looks in different times and moods. Today the sand seems completely featureless and, if she hadn't seen the measuring rods, she might not have been able to identify the site. They climb the sand dune, picking their way through beach-grass and plants that look like huge cabbages. Then the ground levels out and the trench – the grave – is there, just at the edge of the tide. Someone (Judy suspects Leif) has marked the place with a rough cross made from driftwood and tied together with grass. Karen lets out a small cry and then puts her hand to her mouth.

'Why was she buried here?' says Annie, out of breath from the walk but angry again. 'It's miles from anywhere.'

'Ruth, the archaeologist,' says Judy, 'thinks that Margaret was originally buried somewhere else and her bones transferred here fairly recently. She can tell by the preservation of the bones.'

'Then why are we here?' says Annie, sitting heavily on the grassy bank.

But Karen has walked up to the trench and has placed her flowers by the cross. Then she falls to her knees. Pete hesitates then goes to stand beside her. Clough and Judy keep a respectful distance away. After a moment, Annie gets to her feet and joins her mother. The three of them are silhouetted against the skyline, like a religious tableau, the woman kneeling, the man and the younger woman standing one on each side. Judy can hear them speaking but it's a few seconds before she recognises the words. The Hail Mary. The family are Catholic, she knows, but Karen told her that she hadn't been to mass since Margaret disappeared. But they are praying now, the rhythmic mutter counterpointed by the cries of seagulls and the sound of the incoming tide. Judy, who was brought up a Catholic, thinks that they will say the prayer ten times, a decade of the rosary. She feels her lips forming the words but stops when she sees Clough looking at her.

'Pray for us now and at the hour of our death.'

Karen gets to her feet. Then she crosses herself and heads back towards the sand dunes, without looking back. Pete, Annie and Clough follow but Judy takes one last look at the site. The beach is still deserted apart from someone walking by the sea's edge. Something about the figure reminds Judy of Cathbad and she realises it's because they are either wearing a hooded coat or a cloak. But Cathbad will be dropping Michael off at school now. Judy stays watching as the figure comes closer, walking slowly but with great purpose, footprints disappearing into the wet strand. When the cloak-wearer is almost level with the site, it turns towards the sea, raising its hands to the sky. The hood falls back and Judy sees bright hair gleaming in the hazy sunlight.

CHAPTER 11

Superintendent Jo Archer speaks to the press at midday. Nelson is due back at work the next day but she's not about to wait for him. She speaks fluently and well, asking the assembled journalists to respect the Lacey family's privacy 'at this difficult time'. Judy, watching from the back of the room, spots Maddie sitting near the front. Judy kept her word and telephoned Maddie two hours ago with the news about Margaret. When Jo invites questions Judy half expects Maddie to ask about possible links to the Scarlet Henderson case, but her stepdaughter keeps silent.

Someone asks about DNA.

'The technology has come on in leaps and bounds since the eighties,' says Jo, managing to convey the impression that this decade is only a distant memory to her. 'We're hopeful that there will be some DNA on the remains, or on objects found with them, that will allow us to reopen the case and catch Margaret's killer.'

This is a real teaser for the press pack. Several people ask about these mysterious objects but Jo says that she is not divulging this information 'at this point in time'.

'Will you be reinterviewing past suspects?' says a man from one of the nationals.

'Again, I can't comment on that,' says Jo.

But Judy knows that the answer is yes. They already have a DNA sample from Karen, that is how they were able to identify Margaret. Now they need DNA swabs and finger-prints from everyone involved in the case, 'to eliminate them'. Judy and Clough are going to call on John Mostyn. 'He doesn't have to cooperate,' Jo reminded the team, 'but it will be interesting to see his demeanour. He'll have heard on the news about us finding Margaret's remains.'

Judy notes that Jo expects everyone in the world to have seen her press conference but, when they reach the shabby corner house late that afternoon, John Mostyn says that he never watches or listens to the news. 'It's always bad,' he says. 'I prefer to think of nice things.'

John Mostyn is a slight figure who looks older than sev-enty. Judy's mother is a seventy-five-year-old spring chicken who does yoga and wears skinny jeans. Mostyn is shrivelled and frail-looking, wearing a baggy jumper and corduroys. His house, too, seems to teeter on the edge of squalor; the sitting room knee-deep in cardboard boxes, the kitchen a nightmare of sticky brown units and overcrowded surfaces. Judy and Clough sit at the kitchen table after Mostyn has moved several books, a bubbling vat of what looks like beer and a hamster in a cage.

'So you haven't heard that the police have found Margaret

Lacey's remains,' says Judy, trying not to look at the mountain of newspaper in the corner which seems to be moving.

Mostyn sits opposite them. His faded blue eyes look open and guileless. 'No. I hadn't heard that. Poor girl. But it's good for the family. After all this time.'

'We're contacting everyone connected with the case and asking if we can take fingerprints and a DNA sample,' says Clough. 'Just so that we can rule people out.'

'It's very simple,' says Judy as Mostyn is looking rather alarmed. 'Just a swab from inside your cheek.'

'Will I have to go to the police station?'

'It's very quick,' says Judy. 'You'll be in and out in ten minutes.' Nelson has told them to bring Mostyn to the station if possible.

'People will see,' says Mostyn, 'and they'll think I did it. They'll throw things.'

Mostyn and his mother had suffered abuse at the time of Margaret's disappearance. It's in the files and Judy has seen the headlines. 'Loner was last person to see Maggie alive.' 'Police question so-called Stone Man.' Such coverage probably wouldn't be allowed now for fear of jeopardising the case.

'We can send someone here if that's easier,' says Judy.

'The neighbours will see,' says Mostyn. 'People round here know everything that goes on.'

The same comment had been made in 1981 but, all the same, a girl had managed to disappear in broad daylight. Judy wonders whether Mostyn has become more paranoid with age and isolation. The house certainly doesn't look like it belongs to an entirely well man. She is sure that something is moving under that newspaper.

'I'll come into the station,' says Mostyn at last. 'Don't call for me. I'll make my own way.'

'That's very helpful,' says Clough, 'thank you. Shall we say nine thirty tomorrow morning?'

'All right,' says Mostyn. 'I'm up early most mornings. Beachcombing.'

Judy has already noticed the stones. They are everywhere, amongst the flotsam and jetsam in the room, stones of every shape and colour, from glittering hunks of quartz to tiny piles of pebbles, like the droppings of a petrified rabbit.

'Have you always lived near the sea?' she asks.

Mostyn smiles for the first time. His teeth are discoloured and rotten but the expression is surprisingly benign.

'Yes,' he says. 'I was born at Caister-on-Sea. It used to be a Roman port once. I found a Roman coin in the sand when I was a boy. I sent it to the British Museum and they wrote a nice letter back. I've got it somewhere.'

He looks around as if he might, amid the detritus of years, find the letter written some sixty years ago.

'You must have found some interesting things over the years,' says Judy.

'I certainly have.' Mostyn is still smiling but now he turns away and starts searching along a shelf packed with books and yellowing magazines. 'I've found shepherd's crowns, sea lilies, brittle stars, all sorts of things. I've got something here somewhere . . . Yes. Here it is.' He scrabbles under some ancient copies of *Punch*. 'Have this, my dear. For luck.' It's a witch stone, a perfect oval with a single hole running straight through the middle.

Outside, in the car, Clough says, 'My money's still on Mostyn. He's as creepy as hell.'

'He was scared,' says Judy. She is still holding the stone. It fits perfectly in her hand.

'Yes, but why was he scared?' says Clough. 'And, did you notice, he didn't ask where Margaret was found? Surely that should have been his first question. We've found Margaret. Where?'

'I did notice that,' says Judy. 'Well, if his DNA's on the rope, we've got him.'

'And he could have written that letter,' says Clough. 'He's interested in history. Remember what he said about the coin?'

Once again, Clough surprises Judy. She had thought that he was too revolted by the house to be listening closely to Mostyn's ramblings down memory lane. But he's right. Mostyn did show an interest both in history and archaeology. Not to mention the sea.

'And he's from east Norfolk,' she says. 'Caister is right near Yarmouth and Tom said that's where the legend of Jack Valentine is from. He could have left that witch stone on the boss's doorstep. He found this one for me. I bet there are hundreds of them in the house.'

'That house,' says Clough and shudders. Clough and Cassandra are extremely tidy, despite having a baby and a puppy. Judy often fears that her own household will one day descend into chaos. Cathbad keeps things fairly clean but he doesn't like to dust because he admires spiders. But, at the end of their interview with Mostyn, when the newspaper mound finally erupted and a furry shape emerged, Judy hadn't been able to stop herself screaming. 'Tuppence!' exclaimed Mostyn. 'That's where you've been.' He cradled the little creature in his hands and Judy saw that it was another hamster. Mostyn held out his hands and Judy stroked the quivering fur. Now she puts the stone in her bag and fumbles for hand sanitiser.

'He needs help,' she says. 'He's a hoarder.' She passes the plastic bottle to Clough.

'We should do a proper search of the house,' says Clough, rubbing the gel on his hands.

'They got a search warrant at the time,' says Judy. 'They didn't find anything. And thirty-five years have passed.'

'There's more than thirty-five years of rubbish in there,' says Clough, starting the engine.

On the other side of King's Lynn, Ruth and Kate are also waiting in a car. Ruth has collected Kate from school and they are on their way to see the new baby. The day after George was born, Nelson drove round with some photographs and explained to Kate that George was her half-brother, 'because you both have the same daddy'.

'But not the same mum,' said Kate, who likes to get things straight.

'No,' said Nelson. 'Michelle is George's mum.' He hadn't looked at Ruth when he said this. She wished she had left

Nelson to have this conversation in private but had thought that she should be there in case Kate needed some questions answered. But, if Kate had queries, she kept them to herself and favoured her parents with a rendition of 'Food, Glorious Food' from her acting class, complete with gestures.

Now they are sitting outside the Nelsons' house and Ruth is gathering her courage. Kate, clasping a wrapped present, is watching her intently.

'Let's go in, Mum,' she says.

'In a minute,' says Ruth. She has never been in this house before, although Kate has. It's a modern detached, square and somehow reassuring, like a child's drawing of a house. Hard to imagine the horrors that occurred behind this front door – white with patterned glass – last summer. The front garden is a neat square of grass, the driveway wide enough for two cars, Nelson's Mercedes and Michelle's Micra parked side by side. Does Nelson mow the lawn? Ruth is ready to bet that he does.

'Come on, Mum.'

'I'm coming.'

Nelson is obviously on edge too because he opens the door before they have time to knock.

'Come in,' he says, over-heartily. 'Michelle and George are in the front room.'

The front room. Ruth thinks this must go back to Nelson's childhood home. She's sure that Michelle calls it the sitting room or the lounge.

Michelle is sitting on the sofa, buttoning her blouse. The

baby, obviously satiated from his feed, lies in the crook of her arm, his mouth half open. Ruth can see dark hair and long eyelashes, both inherited from Nelson.

'Hallo,' she says.

'Hallo, Ruth,' says Michelle, rather tightly. But she gives Kate a lovely smile. 'Come and say hallo to Baby George.'

Kate approaches, holding the present out in front of her. 'He's asleep,' she says.

'He sleeps all the time,' says Nelson. 'Except at night.'

Michelle smiles. Ruth thinks that she looks tired but lovelier than ever; no make-up, the brown roots showing in her hair, eyes ringed with violet shadows.

Kate touches George's cheek. 'Hallo, baby.'

'Do you want to hold him?' says Michelle.

'Are you sure?' says Nelson but Michelle ignores him. Kate sits next to her on the sofa and Michelle puts George in her lap. The three adults stare at them, Kate sitting very upright, the baby still sleeping, the winter sun illuminating both their faces.

'I should take a picture,' says Nelson, breaking the spell. He goes to get his camera, obviously not trusting the moment to his phone.

'How are you?' says Ruth to Michelle.

'Oh, OK,' says Michelle. 'Tired. You know.'

'Yes,' says Ruth. 'I don't think Kate slept through the night for the first year.'

Kate is interested. 'Why didn't I?'

'I don't know. Sometimes babies don't.'

'George is quite good,' says Michelle. 'He slept from

midnight until five last night. It's just that Harry keeps waking up to check on him.'

Ruth had forgotten that Michelle calls Nelson Harry. The thought of them sharing a bed, the baby next to them, causes a wave of jealousy so intense that Ruth feels almost sick. Nelson comes back into the room and takes several pictures. Michelle reclaims her baby and puts him in a Moses basket on the floor. Kate unwraps the present, a cuddly giraffe, and plays with it herself. Nelson offers to make tea and this is declined, although Michelle asks for a pint of squash.

'You get so thirsty breastfeeding,' she says.

'I remember,' says Ruth, although she doesn't really. Nature seems to grant you amnesia about childbirth, which is probably the only reason why women go on to have more children. But Ruth is clearly only going to get one chance at motherhood so she wishes that she remembered the early days better.

Nelson brings squash and biscuits for all of them. Ruth sips the orange liquid. She hasn't drunk diluted squash since childhood. It reminds her of church youth clubs. Kate drinks hers quickly and puts the glass down on a coaster. Ruth is proud of her.

'Where's Laura?' she says.

Kate met Laura last year, although she doesn't seem to have worked out that she too is a half-sibling.

'She's at college,' says Nelson. 'She's training to be a teacher.'

'Rebecca was here last week,' says Michelle. 'She's working in Brighton.'

'I like Brighton,' says Ruth. There's a rather awkward silence. George saves the day by waking up and starting to cry. Nelson picks him up and pats his back with an experienced hand. Ruth averts her eyes.

'Give him to me, Harry,' says Michelle.

'We should go,' says Ruth.

Kate blows a kiss to George, who is still crying, though in an angry, raspy way.

'Bye, Michelle,' says Ruth. 'Thank you for letting us see George. He's beautiful.'

'See you soon,' says Michelle. She sounds distracted and probably lets this phrase slip accidentally from her social lexicon. Ruth is pretty sure that Michelle would be happy never to see her again. Michelle is fond of Kate though; Ruth will always be grateful to her for that.

Nelson walks to the car with them.

'Did you hear?' he says. 'They've confirmed the identity of the remains found on the beach. It is Margaret Lacey.'

'I heard the press conference on the radio,' says Ruth.

'I'm back at work tomorrow,' says Nelson. 'No rest for the wicked.'

Ruth doesn't believe a word of it. She thinks that Nelson can't wait to return to the fray. He looks as if he's already thinking about the case, about marshalling the team and finding Margaret's killer. He won't rest, Ruth knows, even though so many years have passed. Nelson sees her looking at him and smiles. Because he so often looks serious, the smile transforms his face completely.

'George is gorgeous,' says Ruth.

'He's not bad,' says Nelson.

'I'm happy for you,' says Ruth. 'For you both. Really.'

'I know you are,' says Nelson.

There's a charged silence broken eventually by Kate's peremptory tap on the car window. Ruth says goodbye and gets into the driving seat. Nelson is watching as they drive away.

CHAPTER 12

Nelson is at the station by seven thirty the next morning. By the time that Tanya gets in at eight thirty, Judy at eight forty-five and Clough at nine, he has created an incident room display with Margaret Lacey's picture at the centre. Arrows point out to her parents, Karen and Bob, the latter with RIP scribbled across his forehead. Sister Annie and brother Luke are also there, alongside Kim Jennings and John Mostyn.

'We need to interview Kim Jennings,' says Nelson, after acknowledging the team's greetings and congratulations. 'I've been reading through the transcripts and I think there was something she wasn't telling the police at the time. I've checked and she still lives in Norfolk. She's got a shop near the beach in Wells. That's your neck of the woods, Judy.'

'Yes,' says Judy. 'I'll go and see her.'

'And talk to Marj Maccallum,' says Nelson. 'She was a good officer. I'd like to have her take on the case.'

'What did DS Burnett say?' asks Clough, who, as usual, is chomping his way through a McDonald's breakfast. 'I remember him. Hard as nails.'

'Freddie thinks it's all down to Mostyn. Well, he may be right.'

'Mostyn's coming in at nine thirty to give a DNA sample,' says Clough.

'Good,' says Nelson. 'Let me know when he's here. I'd like to take a look at him.'

'He's an unsavoury specimen,' says Clough. 'Lives in a house full of cardboard boxes and rats.'

'They were hamsters,' says Judy.

'He took a liking to Johnson,' says Clough. 'Gave her one of those stones with holes in.'

'Did he?' says Nelson. He notes that the team who, according to Jo, have been working together in perfect harmony during his absence, are back to vying for position. 'Well, Mostyn was the original prime suspect but there was nothing at the time to tie him to the crime. He was seen talking to Margaret during the street party but he had an alibi for the whole afternoon and evening. Admittedly it was from his mother and, as Freddie reminded me, she might well have been prepared to lie for him.'

'I think that it was Mostyn who wrote you that letter and left the stone outside your house,' says Clough. 'He's interested in history and literature and all that. There were all sorts of books around the house. And he talked about finding Roman coins on the beach.'

'And he's from east Norfolk,' says Judy. 'So he'd know the Jack Valentine legend. And there was a witch stone found with the remains.'

'Yes,' says Clough. 'Ruth thought that it had been placed there deliberately because you don't find chalk on that beach. She also thought that the bones hadn't been there long. She reckoned they'd been buried somewhere else first, in anaer-whatsit conditions. It's in her report.'

'I've been reading it,' says Nelson. 'She thought the bones had previously been buried in peaty soil that was rich in nitrogen.'

'What does that mean?' says Clough.

'Horse manure,' says Nelson, 'or some sort of silage.'

'So we're looking for horse shit,' says Clough.

'Again,' says Judy.

'The stone and the rope are both promising leads,' says Nelson. 'Also the material found near the mouth. The killer's DNA could be on them. You've taken samples from the mother and sister?'

'Yes,' says Judy. 'They were the first people we went to.'

'We need to get the brother too,' says Nelson. 'He's a bit of a shadowy figure in all this. He was fifteen when Margaret disappeared. That's old enough.'

'Do you think he could have killed his own sister?' says Clough, always one for saying the unsayable.

'I'm just saying we ought to talk to him,' says Nelson, 'and get a DNA sample. Fuller, can you get on to it?'

'Yes, boss,' says Tanya. 'Is the case officially open again?'

'Yes,' says Nelson. 'It may be thirty-five years too late but we're going to get justice for Margaret. Let me know when Mostyn comes in, Cloughie.'

*

Ruth is also looking at a report. She is reading the results of the isotope analysis on Margaret's teeth. There is nothing too surprising as it confirms that the teeth belonged to someone who was brought up in Norfolk, specifically the coastal north-east region. This would fit Margaret, who was born and bred in King's Lynn. The carbon-14 report confirms that the bones are fairly recent but has nothing much to add to the investigation. The best hope of a lead lies with the bones themselves. If Ruth could find out where they had originally been buried, then it might point the police in the right direction. Ruth has a lecture in half an hour but she opens her desk drawer and gets out a map entitled 'Geology of Norfolk'. Ruth loves old maps, the pinks and greens, the lines showing contours, the crosses for churches and the picks and shovels for mines. Reading maps is an essential skill for an archaeologist. But now she is looking at soil. The area around King's Lynn is marked as 'tidal flat deposits' and she knows that this will be clay and silt, built up during the millennia north Norfolk was covered by the sea (Lynn is the Celtic word for lake), so the soil is shallow and lime-rich over chalk or limestone. But Margaret's bones were buried in richer earth and there were definite traces of nitrogen which could come from manure. This might mean farmland. Ruth searches further inland, where you would expect to find loamy clay soil with a peat surface. This would fit with the preservation of the bones, typical of waterlogged anaerobic conditions. Taking a pencil Ruth traces a circle around King's Lynn, taking in agricultural land near the River Great Ouse.

She is so deeply engrossed that she doesn't hear the knock on the door. Debbie, the department secretary, has to put her head round the door. 'Ruth?'

Ruth jumps. 'Sorry. I was miles away.'

'A letter's been delivered for you.'

'A letter?' In these days of email, actual post is rare. Her publishers send royalty statements where the earnings are so tiny, both in monetary and typeface terms, that they are almost impossible to find. But they write to her home address. If the post has come to the university, it must be a sales catalogue of some kind. But Debbie's face seems to indicate that this delivery is rather more intriguing.

Debbie hands over a white envelope. 'Hand delivered,' she says impressively.

Ruth waits until Debbie has gone and then slits open the envelope with her special Victorian paperknife – a present from Frank. Inside is a brief typed note:

You found Margaret. She called from the depths and you answered. Her soul is now at peace. May the Gods of earth, sky and sea bless you, Ruth.

Ruth stares at the words for a long time. She doesn't move until her Fitbit buzzes and exhorts her, bossily, to 'get up and stretch for ten'.

Kim Jennings' shop, called Little Rocks, is on the quayside at Wells, only a few hundred metres from Judy's cottage. She texts Cathbad and suggests meeting for fish and chips after her interview. It's a lovely spring day, the sea sparkling and the boats clinking in the harbour. Although it's only March there are a few tourists wandering around and taking photos of the beach huts. Little Rocks, with its window display of crystals and fridge magnets in the shape of crabs, is empty though. There are trays outside displaying stones and pebbles, some rough-edged, some polished to shine like jewels. Judy recognises a couple of the shepherd's crowns mentioned by John Mostyn. These are really fossilised sea urchins, grey stones with a darker pattern of rays protruding from the centre, like a star or the spikes of a crown. She looked up sea lilies and brittle stars too, though she can't see any of them in the shop. These fossils are usually found in sandstone and can look rather sinister preserved in the stone, like scaly claws or alien faces. The most attractive stones outside Little Rocks are chunks of amber, clear yellow or red-gold, some flecked with what might be the remains of tiny prehistoric insects. But still no one is buying anything.

Kim Jennings, a short woman with Cleopatra hair, says that business is bad. 'People browse but they don't buy. I think that's rude.' Judy sympathises but she can't see anything in the shop that anyone would actually want to buy, unless you fancy bracelets made from pebbles and books entitled *Crystal Healing: How to Attract Wealth and Reduce Stress*.

On second thoughts, maybe that would be worth a read.

Kim switches the driftwood sign on the door to 'Gone fishing' and leads Judy into a back room. They sit amongst cardboard boxes which reminds Judy of John Mostyn's house but Kim offers to make coffee, which certainly wasn't on offer at the Mostyn residence, and the parts of the floor which can be seen are, thankfully, free of rodents.

'You've heard that we've found Margaret's remains,' says Judy, accepting a cup of instant coffee in a mug proclaiming, probably erroneously, that 'Mermaids Exist'.

'Yes,' says Kim. 'I heard it on the news. Poor Margaret. You know, for a long time I really thought that she was still alive. I kept expecting her to turn up at my house as if nothing had happened. "Hi, Kimbo," she'd say, "what's the gossip?" No one calls me Kimbo now.'

'It must have been very hard for you,' says Judy.

'It was awful,' says Kim, winding a large onyx ring round her finger. 'For years I was just "Margaret's Friend", "The Last Person To See her Alive". Newspapers hassled me, people stopped me in the street.'

'But you didn't move away?'

Kim shrugs. 'Norfolk's my home. My family have lived here for ever. Why should I move away? And things died down after a while. But now you've found her, I suppose it'll all start up again.'

'I'm sorry,' says Judy. 'But it does give us a chance to bring Margaret's killer to justice. There have been so many advances in forensic science since 1981. We're really hopeful that new evidence will come to light.'

'I hope so too. For Karen's sake mostly. It's been hell for her.'

'Did you know Margaret's family well?'

'Yes, we were in and out of each other's houses all the time. Karen was lovely. The sort of mum who didn't care if you came in with muddy shoes. She was so pretty, really slim with feathery blonde hair, like someone from Pan's People. I used to wish my mum looked like that.' She laughs. 'My mum looked like a mum, that was all.'

'Did you know Margaret's brother and sister too?'

'Annie was a bit of a cow. She was always jealous of Margaret. I had a bit of a crush on Luke. All the girls did. He was blond too, and an ace footballer. He had loads of girlfriends though. He never noticed me. I was a dumpy little thing in those days.'

'What about Margaret's dad, Bob?'

'Bob was all right. He had a short temper though so we kept out of his way. Bob was a mate of my dad's and Dad said that he was devastated when Margaret went missing. He searched for her for years. I think that's what killed him in the end, not the cancer.'

'I know it's a long time ago,' said Judy, 'but could you bear to tell me again what happened that day, the Royal Wedding day, the last day you saw Margaret?'

Kim laughs hollowly but answers readily enough. 'I could recite this in my sleep. I even did a reconstruction for the TV with Annie being Margaret, even though she didn't look anything like her.'

'Just tell me in your own words,' says Judy. 'Try to cast your mind back.'

Kim looks up and to the right. A good sign, according to a neural linguistic programming course that Judy once attended, because it means that Kim is remembering past experiences.

'We were at the street party,' she says. 'It was a really sunny day, I remember that. The party was lots of fun at first, food and games and everyone having a good time. Then the grown-ups starting singing these old songs and it got a bit embarrassing. Margaret and I slipped away. It was after lunch, about three-ish. We went for a walk to the quay because we liked seeing the swans. There was a Punch and Judy show in the Tuesday Market Place and Margaret wanted to go but I hate that sort of thing. I went back to the street party and I sat with my mum and sisters. They were all singing Beatles songs. "All You Need Is Love". I still can't hear that song without wanting to cry. The last time I saw Margaret she was walking up by the Custom House, across the little bridge, her head up and her hair blowing in the breeze. She looked so beautiful, she really did.'

There's no envy here from Kim, the woman who remembers her twelve-year-old self as 'a dumpy little thing', just sadness. Judy sympathises with her over the Punch and Judy show, she hates that form of entertainment herself and not just because of the name; it glorifies wife beating, in her opinion.

'Did you argue with Margaret?' she asks. 'Some onlookers thought you looked as if you were quarrelling.'

'The police asked me this at the time,' says Kim, with a trace of impatience. 'We often used to argue, about silly things really. Margaret said I was posh because I had a pony, even though he was just a shaggy little thing left behind by some gypsies. I used to say that Margaret was big-headed, she thought she was so pretty, just because she had blonde hair and had her ears pierced.'

Some of the papers had even mentioned Margaret's earrings, Judy remembers, as if they were a sign of sexual precocity that would surely end in abduction and death.

'Was Margaret angry when you wouldn't go to the Punch and Judy show?' she asks.

'She was a bit annoyed,' says Kim, 'but nothing serious. She waved goodbye and blew me a kiss. I'll always remember that.'

She is silent for a moment, twisting her ring.

'Did you see John Mostyn on your walk?' asks Judy.

'That was earlier,' says Kim. 'He came up to me and Margaret and some other girls and asked if we wanted to see some pebbles that he'd found on the beach. He was always doing that but the stones were lovely sometimes. I think that's where I got my interest in crystals from.'

'I know you've told this story lots of times before,' says Judy, 'but is there anything that you've remembered over the years, something that came into your head, maybe something that doesn't seem to fit with the rest?'

'There is something,' says Kim, unexpectedly. 'Seahorse.'

'Seahorse?'

'It came to me about five years ago that Margaret had said something about a seahorse or seahorses. That's when I started collecting them in the shop. It was a sort of tribute to her.'

Judy dimly remembers the seahorses; keyrings and charms, a few cuddly versions with iridescent tails. It strikes her as oddly fitting that these tiny, beautiful, almost other-worldly, creatures remind Kim of her dead friend.

'But you can't remember the context of the seahorse comment?' she says.

'No,' says Kim. 'Memory's a funny thing, isn't it?'

'It is,' says Judy. As an expert in the art of forensic interviewing, memory is her job but she often feels as if she doesn't understand it at all. She thanks Kim for her time and asks if her parents still live in the area.

'Mum and Dad are still in Norfolk,' says Kim. 'They still live in the house I grew up in. It's not far from here. And, of course, Uncle Pete lives in Lynn.'

'Uncle Pete?'

'Mum's brother. He married Karen. Didn't you know?'

CHAPTER 13

Clough informs Nelson when John Mostyn is in the building. He gives it about twenty minutes and then goes down to the interview room where a young PC called Jane Campion is guiding Mostyn through the DNA procedure.

Nelson watches through the two-way mirror for a few minutes. Mostyn looks nervous, but that could be just because he's in a police station. He also looks so much like a stereotypical sex offender – scruffy clothes, unwashed look, shifty gaze – that Nelson is almost predisposed to think that he is innocent. It's no wonder that the police focused on him at the time, weird loner living with his mother, wandering round showing young girls his pebble collection. It's only a surprise that Roy Brown, who'd been the superintendent in 1981, hadn't locked him up as soon as look at him. Nelson remembers Superintendent Brown, known to the station as 'Chubby', and he wasn't a man to let lack of evidence stand in the way of an arrest. Freddie Burnett has already been on the phone demanding to know if Mostyn is going to 'get away with it again'. Strictly speaking, of course, it wasn't a murder investigation the first time round but now it is and Nelson is determined to do things by the book.

Nelson pushes open the door. Campion jumps and looks flustered, although she is a highly competent constable and is handling the procedure perfectly.

'Good morning.' Nelson addresses Mostyn directly. 'I'm DCI Nelson. I'm in charge of the inquiry into the abduction and murder of Margaret Lacey.'

He means to intimidate Mostyn with his rank and with the reminder that this is now, officially, a murder case but the man just blinks at him mildly.

'I know who you are,' he says.

'Thank you for voluntarily providing a DNA sample,' says Nelson. 'We're hopeful that we've been able to retrieve DNA from the scene. It means we'll be able to bring the killer to justice.'

'That would be good,' agrees Mostyn.

'And we'd like a handwriting sample from you too,' he says.

For a second a flicker of alarm seems to cross Mostyn's face.

'Handwriting?'

'Yes. Just a few words will do. PC Campion will show you what to do.' The words 'Greetings from Jack Valentine' were in capitals and there's probably not enough writing to get a match but Nelson wants Mostyn, if he is the sender, to know that they're on to him.

'Happy to help,' says Mostyn, recovering his poise.

'Thank you,' says Nelson. 'We'll be in touch,' he adds,

managing to make this sound more like a threat than a promise. He goes to leave the room and is surprised when Mostyn calls him back, 'DCI Nelson?'

'Yes?'

'Is DS Burnett still on the force?'

'No,' says Nelson. 'He retired some years ago.' And is currently sunning himself in Tenerife.

'Well, give him my regards,' says Mostyn. 'If you see him, that is.'

Cathbad and Judy are eating fish and chips in a tiny café overlooking the quay. It's lunchtime so the place is full and they're sharing the table with two pensioners and a greyhound in a tartan coat. For this reason, Judy doesn't mention the morning's interview. They talk about the children, how Miranda is enjoying nursery and how well Michael is doing with his reading.

'I think we should get him piano lessons,' says Judy. 'I'm sure he's musical.'

'Lessons are so prescriptive,' says Cathbad. 'Let him find out about music for himself. Maybe we should buy him a ukulele.'

'He can find out about music all he likes,' says Judy, 'but he won't be able to play an instrument properly unless he has lessons.' She has already earmarked a second-hand piano on Gumtree.

'I used to play the guitar,' says Cathbad, offering a chip to the greyhound. 'Erik taught me. And I played the accordion at school. '

Judy doesn't remark that, in this case, even Cathbad had lessons of a sort. She says, 'Are you going back to the archaeological site? Leif's site?'

'I don't know,' says Cathbad. 'It's a beautiful place and it's interesting archaeologically too. But, I don't know, it felt odd being there with Leif. Too many memories of his father, perhaps.'

Judy thinks of her trip to the site with Karen, Pete and Annie, the Hail Marys rising into the mist, the sad flowers in their cellophane wrapping. She remembers the figure that she saw on the beach, the hooded man looking out towards the sea. Had that been Leif, saluting the dawn?

'What was Erik like?' she asks. They have never really talked about him before.

'He was a visionary,' says Cathbad. 'He could make you feel as if you were seeing the landscape through ancient eyes. He was an amazing teacher too. He made you think, really think, throwing out all your old assumptions and preconceptions. I was quite dazzled by him, at first. But now I think that he exploited me, used me to do his dirty work. Shona too. She was in love with him, you know.'

'She still seems quite bitter,' says Judy. 'But she didn't have to help him write those letters. They wasted a lot of police time.'

'Love does odd things to you,' says Cathbad. Judy turns to smile at him but he's looking at the greyhound, offering it a chip.

*

Nelson's phone buzzes as he goes up the stairs. He sees 'Ruth' on the screen and so waits until he's in his office to call back.

'Ruth? What is it? Is it Katie?'

A deep sigh. 'No, it's not Kate. It's me. I've had a letter.'

'A letter? What sort of letter?'

'One that reads like it was from the same person who wrote to you. Listen.'

As Ruth reads, Nelson can almost feel his blood pressure rising. He remembers the letters arriving when Lucy went missing and then later with Scarlet. The same mocking, erudite, menacing tone. *She called from the depths and you answered.* It's the same person, he's sure of it.

'Is it typed?' he asks.

'Yes.'

'Did you touch it?'

'Yes, of course I touched it. How else would I have opened the envelope?'

'Well, don't touch it any more. Put it in a freezer bag or something.'

'I've put it in an evidence bag.'

'Good. Hand delivered, you say? I don't suppose anyone saw who delivered it?'

'No. The department secretary just brought it in. It was delivered to the main reception.'

'To you personally?'

'Yes. To Dr Ruth Galloway.'

Nelson can't stop himself smiling. Ruth does like people to use her full title.

'It does sound like the same person. "Out of the depths" – that sounds religious.'

'"Out of the depths I cried unto thee, O Lord",' quotes Ruth. 'Psalm 130. Also that bit about earth, sky and sea. That's from a hymn. "Holy, Holy, Holy".'

'I'm going to talk to that Leif,' says Nelson.

'Do you really think it's him?'

'Judy and Clough have got the idea that it's someone involved in the original case. A loner who collects stones. But I still think Leif Eriksson's our most likely suspect. Like father like son.'

'I don't think writing anonymous letters is the sort of thing that runs in families, Nelson.'

'You never know,' says Nelson. 'Take extra care at home. Lock all the doors.'

'The letter writer sounds pleased with me, if anything,' says Ruth. 'Maybe I'll find some flowers on my doorstep.'

'Remember the last time someone left something on your doorstep,' says Nelson. 'Lock the doors and make sure the security light's on. I'll come round to see you tonight.'

Marj Maccallum seems delighted to see Judy.

'I like to keep in touch with the force,' she says. 'And I'm always glad to see a woman officer doing so well.'

Judy can't help feeling pleased. Sometimes she feels that her career has stalled; with three detective sergeants at King's Lynn, there's not really anywhere for them to go. Her only options are to take her Inspector's exam or move.

Marj makes them tea and they sit in her sunny conservatory watching Mabel, Marj's stunningly white Westie, running round the garden.

'Lovely weather for early March,' says Marj. 'Almost warm enough to swim in the sea.'

Judy had inadvertently stepped into the sea at the weekend, when on the beach with the children. It had been like standing in melted ice. But Marj has the fit, weather-beaten look of someone who swims all year round.

'It is a lovely day,' she agrees. 'Thank you for seeing me. As I said on the phone, we're keen to talk to anyone who remembers the Margaret Lacey case.'

'I remember it all right,' said Marj soberly, offering Judy a biscuit. 'That poor girl. That poor family. Well, I hope that they find some peace now.'

'What do you remember about the investigation?' asks Judy.

'Superintendent Brown and DS Burnett were sure it was the prowler. John something.'

'John Mostyn.'

'That's right. But, I don't know. I thought we should have looked more closely at the family.'

'At the father, Robert Lacey?'

'No, not Bob. He was the type who might kill a man in a pub fight, but not his daughter. He worshipped Margaret. No, I always thought the brother and sister were a bit odd.'

'In what way?' Judy remembers Kim saying that Annie had been a 'cow' and jealous of Margaret.

'Annie was very highly strung. Well, that's a kind word for it. She was the sort who was always shouting or in tears. I remember her yelling at her mum that nobody cared about her, only about Margaret. She argued with her dad too but I heard that she didn't get on any better with her stepfather. The boy, Luke, just didn't seem that interested. Normally youngsters – especially boys – are excited about a police investigation, despite themselves, even if it involves a family member. They want to know about fingerprints, clues, all that stuff. But Luke kept himself to himself. I thought at the time that he might be hiding something.'

'That's what DCI Nelson said.'

'Well, he's a shrewd man, Nelson. Not a dinosaur like Chubby Brown. He'll dig down and get to the truth.'

It's odd that people use dinosaur as an insult, thinks Judy, as she drives back along the coast road. Marj used it to mean someone stuck in old ways but dinosaurs were experts at evolution, that's why they lasted nearly two hundred million years. Humankind is never going to match that. She looks at the sea sparkling in the distance and thinks again of the mysterious figure on the shore. Marj had said that Nelson would dig down to get the truth. But archaeologists seemed to dig for days and find more questions than answers. She wonders how much Leif Anderssen knows about his father's past.

Nelson is also thinking about Erik Anderssen. It's hard not to, seeing as how he's standing with Erik's son very near the place where the Norwegian archaeologist breathed his last. And very painful breaths they must have been. Drowning must be the worst of deaths and, even now, Nelson doesn't like to think about that night: the storm, the chase across the treacherous ground, the desperate search for the missing girl. Today, though, the marsh looks very different, the grass flecked with little yellow flowers and the sun shining on the distant sea.

'It does your soul good, doesn't it?' says Leif, breathing in and expanding his chest like an advertisement for body-building.

'I wouldn't go that far,' says Nelson.

He'd rung Leif as soon as he'd spoken to Ruth. 'I'm on the site,' said Leif, 'but you could meet me here if you like.' Nelson knew that he should delegate the interview to Judy and Clough. He has reports to write and teams to lead. He should, as Jo is always telling him, 'be the hub of the wheel and not one of the spokes.' But, on the other hand, he's the one with the history here. He's the only one who can really ask these questions about Erik. And, besides, the archaeo-logical site is also now a crime scene. Really it's his *duty* to be there.

The site looks busy today, full of people digging and sifting and brushing soil away from what look like very ordi-nary bits of stone. The trench where Margaret was found is directly in front of them. Ruth says that the grave was fairly new – something about cuts and infill – but it still seems odd to Nelson that someone made this potentially perilous journey across the Saltmarsh to bury the bones with these other prehistoric remains. Almost against his will he remembers something Erik once told him. *It's the landscape itself that's important. Don't you see?* And Nelson does see that there is something special about this place even though, in his mind, it's special in the way that accident hot-spots are special.

'Would you like a tour?' says Leif, waving a hand towards the diggers and the trenches.

'No, you're all right,' says Nelson. 'I wanted to talk to you because some letters have been received.'

'Letters?' Leif tilts his head. He's taller than Nelson, which is annoying.

'Letters that recall other letters,' says Nelson. 'The ones your father wrote.'

'My father wrote you letters?' Leif sounds interested, even slightly amused, but Nelson doesn't entirely buy the act. He thinks that Leif is also wary; his arms are crossed which Judy would say is a sign of defensiveness.

'Your father once wrote me a series of letters,' says Nelson, 'which significantly impeded a major crime investigation. He would have been charged with wasting police time if he hadn't . . . died.'

Leif glances over his shoulder at the marshland, bright with spring flowers. So he does know where his father died.

'I didn't know,' he says. 'We weren't always that close, my father and me. He was a free spirit.'

A phrase that, in Nelson's opinion, hides a multitude of sins. He says, 'Were you at the University of North Norfolk this morning?'

Now Leif really does look uncomfortable. He looks away, uncrosses his arms and crosses them again. Nelson waits.

'I did call in at UNN,' he says. 'I've got a friend there. In the history department.'

Nelson is not a betting man but he's willing to wager that the friend is female.

'While you were there,' he says, 'did you drop anything off at the archaeology department?'

'At the archaeology department? No. Why? Is this about Ruth?'

Nelson lets this hang in the air.

'Are you a fan of T. S. Eliot?' he asks.

'Who?'

'British-American poet,' says Nelson. 'Died in 1965.' That's what Wikipedia says, anyhow.

'Oh,' says Leif. 'The man who wrote *Cats*.'

Nelson is not sure if he is joking or not. 'If you say so. You've heard of him, then?'

'Vaguely. I don't know much about English Literature.'

'Speaking of which, are you acquainted with a lecturer in English Literature called Shona Maclean?'

'I've heard the name,' says Leif. 'I think she was a friend of my father's.'

'She's not your friend at UNN?'

'No. My friend's in the history department. Her name's Chloe Jackson.' Leif smiles, seeming to recover his poise. The sun gleams on his yellow hair. Nelson eyes him coldly.

'Can I trouble you for a sample of your handwriting?' he says. The letters were typed but he has the Jack Valentine note. Besides, he thinks the request might wipe the smug smile off Leif's handsome face.

On a scrap of paper which he finds in his pocket, Leif writes: *To DCI Nelson. Tireless seeker after truth.*

It's meant to be funny, Nelson realises, but it's interesting nonetheless.

Michelle is also enjoying the sunshine as she walks to the village hall. For one thing, it will lighten her hair. Not having time to get her roots done is the single worst thing about having a new baby. But the sun also helps with the depression that she felt settling on her that morning as soon as Harry had gone to work and Laura to college. It's a cloud that has been hovering over her ever since George was born. George is wonderful. He's beautiful and really very good. Sometimes Michelle feels her heart almost exploding with love when she looks at him. But there's also a feeling of isolation, almost of loneliness, that seems to be lying in wait for her, ready to pounce even when she's with her family. Michelle tries to give herself pep talks: What have you got to complain about? You've got a loving husband and two gorgeous grown-up children. You've got a job waiting for you, appreciative employers (Tony and Juan sent a baby hamper from Harrods with a note saying, *We miss you but enjoy this precious time with Baby*) and lots of friends. Your baby is healthy and your mother is coming down next week to help look after him. You should be counting your blessings. In answer to this Pollyanna-ish monologue, Michelle can only answer: but I don't have Tim.

Did she love Tim? Sometimes, now, when she thinks about his face and his smile, the way his eyes softened when they looked at her, she thinks that she did. He had certainly loved her. He gave his life for her. It's such a dramatic, Sunday School sort of phrase, but in this case it is literally true. He gave his life so that she and Laura could live. And she loves him for this. But she also knows that she would never have left Harry for Tim. Her love for Harry has been the most powerful emotion in her life for over twenty-five years, a quarter of a century. It's a strong plant, this love, even if it has become slightly thorny over the last few years. It would take more than Tim's grace and beauty to uproot it.

But what if the baby had been Tim's? This had been a very real possibility, something Michelle had hardly dared to admit, even to herself. If George had been Tim's it would have been awful. Everyone would have turned against her, Harry would have divorced her – and, no doubt, married Ruth – and even her daughters would probably have disowned her. But at least she wouldn't have this feeling that Tim has disappeared altogether and soon there will be nothing of him left. In her last months of pregnancy it was as if some essence of Tim was still wafting about, wanting to find out if he was the father. But now he's gone and that is almost the hardest thing to bear.

Maybe the mother and baby group will help. She remembers these gatherings from the first time round. Her NCT class and the local toddler group had proved invaluable sources of female friends and playmates for Laura and Rebecca. It had been hard to replace these friends when they'd moved down to Norfolk but she'd managed it, assiduously following up playground chats and meetings in the park or at the swings. But now, of course, those friends all have grown-up children, some are even grandmothers. She'd been horrified to see her friend Liz referring to herself on Facebook as 'Nanny Beth'. Who the hell was Nanny Beth? Not Liz who liked to drink cocktails and once confided to Michelle that she'd had to resign her gym membership after she'd had sex with her personal trainer in an empty squash court.

As soon as Michelle pushes open the door of the Nissen hut that calls itself the Village Hall and manoeuvres the buggy inside, she realises her mistake. These aren't mothers, they are *children*. Some of the women look younger than Laura, younger than Rebecca. They sit casually on the floor in their skinny jeans and crop tops, texting and chatting whilst their babies lie on their backs on a slightly grubby 'activity rug'. A child wearing a hijab looks up. 'Oh, are you Michelle? I'm Saira, the community midwife. Come and join us.'

Saira is friendly enough, offering tea and coffee, cooing over George, but she's so *young*. How can she be a qualified midwife? Michelle would have trouble trusting her to babysit.

Michelle accepts a cup of burnt-tasting coffee and sits on a beanbag. George is mercifully still asleep. She feels overweight and overdressed in her Boden jeans and loose jumper. She is sure that the lounging girls think that she is George's grandmother. Nanny Miche.

'How old is your little boy?' asks an infant with pink hair.

'Just over two weeks,' says Michelle.

'Ooh.' The girl peers into the buggy. 'He's a good size, isn't he? Lots of hair. Is he your first?'

'No,' says Michelle, slightly cheered. 'I've got two older girls.'

'How old are they?' says Saira.

'Twenty-two and twenty-four,' she says. There is a silence, broken only by George waking up and starting to cry. As Michelle picks him up, one of the youngest-looking mums, a waif with (natural) silvery blonde hair says, 'Shall I hold him so that you can drink your coffee?'

It sounds like the kindest thing anyone has said to her for weeks.

'Thank you,' says Michelle, passing George to the girl.

'I'm Star,' she says, juggling George skilfully. 'My baby's Ava. She's over there, asleep under the baby gym.'

Star. She even seems to be glowing slightly.

CHAPTER 14

Ruth doesn't tell Kate that Nelson might be coming round that evening because, that way, Kate won't be disappointed if he doesn't turn up. But, at seven o'clock, she hears the familiar squeal of Nelson's brakes and, despite herself, feels the familiar surge of excitement that comes with seeing Nelson on her territory. It has been at her cottage that all their most memorable encounters have occurred and, although she knows all that is in the past, Ruth stops at the mirror by the door to let down her hair, which has been scrunched up on top of her head, and check her teeth for spinach (she has been trying to add more greens to their diet).

'What are you doing, Mum?' says Kate, who is lying on the floor putting her Sylvanians to bed – unlike Kate they have a very strict bedtime regime.

'It's Dad,' says Ruth, opening the door.

'Daddy!' Kate throws herself into Nelson's arms.

'Hallo, love.' Nelson comes into the room with Kate wrapped round him. Ruth feels a pang. She realised a year or so ago that she would probably never be able to pick Kate up again. Not in the easy, casual way that Nelson does, anyway. Her back is feeling the effects of three decades of digging and Kate now comes up to her chest.

'Hi, Nelson,' says Ruth. 'Do you want a cup of tea?'

'That would be grand,' says Nelson, depositing Kate on the sofa. 'I can't stay long.'

'Are you going back to see Baby George?' says Kate.

'That's right.'

Ruth says nothing. She leaves Nelson and Kate to enjoy some time together while she makes the tea, trying not to feel resentful that Kate gets ten minutes of her father's company while 'Baby George' gets him all evening, all day, for the rest of his life.

In the end, though, Nelson stays until Kate goes to bed.

'Is Dad coming to say goodnight?' asks Kate, as Ruth tucks her in.

'I'm here,' says Nelson from the doorway.

'You can both read me a story if you like,' says Kate.

'Another time,' says Ruth. 'You can listen to an audio book tonight.'

She kisses Kate and leaves the room. Downstairs, she gets the anonymous letter, still in its plastic wrapping, from her backpack. That is what Nelson is here for, after all. To look at a possible piece of evidence. Ruth sits on the sofa, listening to Nelson's deep voice and Kate's laughter. Flint comes to sit next to her but goes off in a fluffy huff when he sees Nelson coming back down the stairs.

'That cat hates me,' says Nelson.

'Maybe he can smell Bruno,' says Ruth.

'The whole world can smell Bruno,' says Nelson. 'Is that the letter?'

'Yes.'

Ruth notices that Nelson holds the note at arm's length to read it. Does he need glasses? She can't imagine it somehow.

Nelson says, 'It certainly sounds like the same person. As you say, it's not threatening. Rather the opposite. But, all the same, someone knew that Margaret was buried in the stone circle and that person may well be the murderer.'

'I'm pretty sure that the bones weren't on the coastal site for very long,' says Ruth. 'From their preservation and general condition I would say that they were initially buried on cultivated land.'

'I read your report,' says Nelson. 'So someone, presumably the killer, buried Margaret and then dug up the bones thirty years later. Why?'

'So they would be found?' suggests Ruth. 'After all, that first letter tells you where to look.'

'Do you think the bones were buried at the site after excavations began in December?' says Nelson. 'There must have been a lot of digging going on. Surely they would have been found earlier if they were there?'

'Not necessarily,' says Ruth. 'You can only dig something up if you know exactly where to look. But I do think the burial was fairly recent. It's hard to tell because the soil was already disturbed but the grave was shallow and the infill looked new.'

'So someone could have found out about the dig and decided to bury the bones where they would be found?'

'I suppose so but who would have known? The dig wasn't even on the local news.'

'Leif Anderssen knew.'

'But how could he know about Margaret's murder? That was more than thirty years ago. He would have been a child, living in a different country.'

'I know,' says Nelson. 'But the letters do seem so much like the earlier ones. The ones his father wrote. And I'm not sure I trust Leif. I went to see him today.'

'You did?' Even for Nelson, this sounds like quick work. 'What did he say?'

'He denied all knowledge of the letters, of course. But he looked a bit rattled when I asked for a handwriting sample.'

'What good is that? The letter was typed.'

'Remember the note that was delivered to my house on Valentine's Day? "Greetings from Jack Valentine"? That was handwritten.'

'And was it a match?'

'I don't think so. The so-called expert says there's not enough of it to be sure.'

'So it's quite probable that Leif wasn't involved.'

'I suppose so.' Nelson glowers into the fire. 'It's just that these letters do sound a hell of a lot like the other ones. The ones Erik wrote.'

'I'm not so sure,' says Ruth. 'Some of the allusions are the same but I think the tone is different. The others were nastier, more threatening.'

She stops because she has heard something. Nelson hears it too and stands up. A car is approaching. This is rare enough to be slightly alarming. Hers is the only occupied house. Bob, the Indigenous Australian poet, is off on his travels and, as far as she knows, the weekenders aren't due until Easter. Headlights shine in at the window, disconcertingly bright, then the engine is switched off and footsteps approach.

'I'll go to the door,' says Nelson.

Ruth wants to protest but she feels unaccountably scared. Maybe it's because she was talking about those other, darker letters, maybe it's the thought that someone is out there, watching her. So she lets Nelson answer the door.

He opens it about an inch and Ruth hears a familiar American voice say, 'Oh . . . hi . . . I was looking for Ruth.'

She gets up and joins Nelson at the door. 'Hallo, Frank. Come in.'

'I was just passing,' says Frank. 'I've got takeaway.' He holds up a bag from a Chinese restaurant on the Hunstanton road.

'Just passing?' says Nelson. 'No one passes this godforsaken place.'

'I had a meeting at UEA,' says Frank, although Ruth would have told him that he doesn't have to explain himself to Nelson. 'I'm on my way back to Cambridge.'

'Your satnav's wrong then,' says Nelson. And it's true that Ruth's cottage is definitely not on the route from Norwich to Cambridge.

'Sit down, Frank,' says Ruth. 'I'll get some plates. Are you staying, Nelson?'

'No, I've got to get back,' says Nelson. He is still standing in the doorway though and makes no move to leave. Flint comes sauntering in and, with what looks like deliberate provocation, tries to sit on Frank's lap.

'Hallo, buddy,' says Frank.

Ruth turns to say something to Nelson – something easy and light to ease the tension in the room – but he has gone.

Nelson drives back across the dark marshes in a fury. What is that American doing, hanging round Ruth and Katie? Driving all the way from Norwich on the pretext of having a Chinese meal. He must be sleeping with Ruth. No doubt he wants to sweep her and Katie off for a new life in the States. Before Nelson knows it, Katie will be riding around in a yellow school bus, wearing a jumper with a letter on it and calling him Pops. Well, he won't allow it.

By the time he reaches home, he has calmed down slightly. After all, he is driving home to his wife and baby. He can't really control who Ruth eats Chinese takeaways with. Even so, there was something about Frank's familiarity with the house (and that bloody cat sucking up to him too) that makes him wish he could arrest him for something. There are lights on upstairs. Michelle must be trying to get George to sleep. Nelson presses the remote-control button to open the garage – something that never fails to give him childish pleasure – and drives in. He can hear Bruno barking from inside the house and hopes that the dog isn't driving Michelle mad. The trouble is that Michelle doesn't have time to take Bruno for walks during the day and, although they employ a dog walker – something that seems, to Nelson, to be the epitome of soft southern laziness – Bruno still has a lot of unused energy. Also, he has heard the car.

'Down, boy.' Nelson tries to restrain – or at least quieten – Bruno's ecstatic welcome. He'll have to take him out for a walk but it's nine o'clock now and he's starving.

'Hallo, Harry.' Michelle is coming down the stairs. She looks different but he can't work out why.

'Hallo, love,' says Nelson. 'Sorry I'm late. There was a lot to catch up. First day back and all that.'

'Shh.' He doesn't know if she's addressing him or the still capering dog. 'George is asleep.'

'Does that mean he'll wake up later?' says Nelson, in what he hopes is a muffled tone. He's never been good at whispering. It's a northern thing, he tells his daughters.

'I don't know,' says Michelle. 'But the point is he's asleep now. Do you want a beer?'

Nelson suddenly feels that he would like a beer very much. Michelle certainly seems in a good mood. It's been a long time since she's suggested anything as frivolous as alcohol and she hasn't complained about him being late. Also he realises what's changed about her appearance: her hair is loose and she's wearing a T-shirt instead of a baggy jumper. Michelle complains that pregnancy has left her with extra weight but Nelson actually prefers her figure like this. He goes in for a kiss as she passes. She laughs and moves away but it doesn't really seem as if she minded.

'Where's Laura?' he asks, following Michelle into the kitchen.

'Out with some friends. I've made a shepherd's pie. Yours is in the oven.'

'Champion,' says Nelson, getting a beer from the fridge. 'George must have been good if you had time to cook.'

'He's always good,' says Michelle, getting out a plate and a glass. 'But I do feel a bit better. Maybe it was just that the sun was out today. Oh, and I met a nice woman at the mother and baby group. She's called Star.'

'I don't think DCI Nelson is my biggest fan,' says Frank, arranging foil cartons on the table.

Ruth is in the kitchen looking for a bottle of wine. 'Nelson's not much of a one for small talk,' she says.

'No,' says Frank. 'I imagine his talk is pretty big.'

Ruth has located a bottle and is now looking for a corkscrew. Since when did she buy wine with a proper cork? Phil must have brought it on one of the rare occasions when he and Shona came to dinner. She thinks that she detects an edge to Frank's words. She has never told Frank that Nelson is Kate's father but she knows he knows. She has also never revealed the identity of the mysterious 'someone else' in her life, the reason she has never been able to commit herself to Frank. But, again, she is pretty sure that Frank has cracked the code.

She comes into the sitting room with bottle and glasses and puts them on the table. They share out the food in a companionable manner, chatting about takeaways in England and the US and about the respective merits of egg-fried versus plain rice. Then Frank says, spearing a sweet-and-sour something or other, 'Why was Nelson here tonight?'

'It was about the bones we found on the Saltmarsh,' says Ruth. 'I told you about them.'

'Pretty late to make a business call.'

'It's his first day back,' says Ruth. 'I think it was a long day.' She wonders if she is revealing too much knowledge about Nelson's schedule.

'Is there . . .' Frank stops and takes a gulp of wine. 'No. Forget it. Forget I said anything.'

'Well, you didn't really,' says Ruth.

'Ruth. Are you . . . Are you still involved with Nelson? I know I haven't got any right to ask.'

Ruth sighs. She knows that Frank doesn't have any right to ask. She knows that she doesn't have to answer. But part of her wants to explain, to see if the words make any sense when said aloud.

'We are still involved,' she says. 'Nelson's Kate's father.' Frank makes a slight movement but says nothing. 'So that means we'll always be involved in a way. But it's difficult. He's married. He doesn't want to break up the family. And I'm used to my own company. I wasn't even sure if I wanted us to be together. Then, last year, I did think that I wanted it. Nelson felt the same. At least, I'm pretty sure he did. But then Michelle, his wife, announced that she was pregnant and now they've got a newborn baby. I couldn't ask Nelson to leave his baby. I wouldn't want him to.'

She stops and reaches for the wine. The bottle is nearly empty and, though she knows it's not the best etiquette, she pours the remainder into her glass. Frank is driving anyway.

'It's a tough situation,' says Frank and Ruth has the impression that he's choosing his words carefully. 'I guessed some of it and, for what it's worth, I think you're doing a great job. Kate's a great kid and you're a great mom.'

'Thanks,' says Ruth. And she is touched, although there are too many 'greats' in that sentence and she's never been called a 'mom' before. It sounds like a character in an American sitcom.

'And I know you don't want a man in your life,' says Frank. 'But, if you did, I'd be keen to apply for the position.'

Ruth has to laugh. 'That's an academic speaking,' she says.

'I've got an impressive research record,' says Frank. 'Five books and numerous articles in scholarly journals.'

'You can send in your CV,' says Ruth.

Nothing more is said on the subject. Ruth clears the table, putting the cartons in the bin. Frank stacks the dishwasher and Ruth makes coffee. They drink it in front of the fire, the embers now glowing like tiny dragons.

'I should be going,' says Frank. Ruth looks at the clock on the mantelpiece. It's nearly midnight. She has work tomorrow and Kate has school. Frank is right, he *should* be on his way.

'Drive carefully,' she says.

Frank turns to her. His face is suddenly very serious.

'Ruth,' he says. And kisses her.

*

Nelson is dreaming. He's on the beach at Blackpool. It's just as he remembers it from childhood except that the sand stretches into infinity. He knows that, if he can only find the sea, he will be able to swim and escape from whatever is following him. He walks and walks but the water is always just out of his sight. Then, suddenly, he's on the beach by the Saltmarsh and a Viking longship is approaching. Leif Anderssen is at the front, his hair blowing back in the wind. As Nelson watches from the shore, Leif turns into Michelle and then Ruth. The longship becomes a boat on the Norfolk Broads and Ruth is beside him saying, 'Don't die, Nelson.' A bell is ringing, becoming more and more insistent. *Never send to know for whom the bell tolls; it tolls for thee.* He wakes up with a start. His phone is buzzing. Blearily he picks it up. 'Control', says the screen.

'DCI Nelson? A body's been found at the Canada Estate. Looks like murder.'

CHAPTER 15

It's five a.m. and, miraculously, George is still asleep. Nelson gets out of bed without waking Michelle. He grabs his phone and texts Clough and Judy, then heads into the bathroom for a shower.

The Canada Estate is a business park built on a brownfield site that was once a gasworks. There were initially grandiose plans that included apartment blocks, a park, even a school, but these projects were stalled by local objections and by the unarguable fact that there wasn't any money left to develop them. The few businesses that moved to the Canada Estate now exist in splendid isolation looking down on an empty plaza and an unfinished fountain. Nelson drives right into the circular space where two uniformed police officers and a man in a hi-vis vest are standing beside the fountain. The sun is rising over some abandoned cranes and the whole scene is bathed in a pinkish light.

'DCI Nelson.' He shows his card but he knows one of the officers, PC Bradley Linwood, by name and the other by sight. The third man introduces himself as 'Pat Eastwood, the night watchman'. They keep their distance and stand aside to let Nelson see the body that is slumped in the shallow stone basin, the head by the base of a half-finished sculpture that was meant to represent King's Lynn and the Hanseatic League. Nelson recognises the dead man immediately. It's John Mostyn and he's been shot.

Clough and Judy arrive within a few minutes of each other, Clough wearing a woollen beanie hat and looking like an off-duty boxer, Judy in her Barbour with the hood up. It's very cold in the empty plaza even though Pat Eastwood has made them all mugs of coffee from a kettle in his Portakabin. Nelson has made everyone move away from the body and is waiting for the scene-of-crime team to arrive but he gestures to his sergeants to come and look.

'That's him all right,' says Clough. 'Poor bastard.'

'Shot through the heart,' says Judy, leaning closer.

'One shot,' says Nelson. 'Looks professional.'

'Who found him?' asks Clough.

'Night watchman from the security company doing his rounds. Found the body here in the empty fountain. No sign of the assailant.'

'Was he shot here, do you think?' asks Judy.

'No. I think he was shot somewhere else and brought here. There are some bloodstains on the step that looks as if the body was dragged along. There's CCTV everywhere so if we're lucky we might get something. Pat, the security guy, says half the cameras don't work though.'

'Why bring the body here?' says Clough, looking round at the empty offices, half of them boarded up, most of them sporting 'To Let' signs. 'This place is a bloody wasteland.'

But Nelson is looking round too. The sheer wall of buildings forming a ring around the central space with the dry fountain in the middle.

The Stone Circle.

Ruth wakes up to Radio 4 telling her that Hillary Clinton is ahead in the race for the US presidential election. That's good, she thinks sleepily, when the final votes are counted in November she will look forward to waking Kate with the news that the most powerful leader in the world is a woman. There are still too many men in top posts, including in universities. Then she sits up. There are currently too many men in her bed. One, to be exact. Dr Frank Barker, visiting lecturer in nineteenth-century history at the University of Cambridge, is asleep next to her, as silent as a cat, his naked chest rising and falling gently. Oh God.

Ruth realises that she too is naked and grabs her dressing gown. It's seven a.m.; soon Kate will come bounding in babbling about school and asking Ruth to do her hair in a French plait. She must head her off. Kate knows and likes Frank but the sight of him in Ruth's bed would raise questions that Ruth is not yet prepared to answer. What happened last night? She doesn't remember much beyond Frank saying 'Ruth' and leaning in to kiss her. She remembers that she had been dimly worried about smelling of chow mein but soon that had been buried with all the other everyday concerns, drowned out by her overwhelming need for someone to hold, someone to make her forget Nelson going back to his newborn baby, someone to make her forget that she is nearly fifty and, in the Bronze Age, would probably have already been dead for twenty-odd years.

And it had been great, Ruth remembers, as she pads out onto the landing to forestall Kate. The sex had been fun and tender and unembarrassing; the best she could hope for from someone who isn't Nelson. Flint is waiting outside the door, looking at her accusingly. 'Don't you start,' says Ruth.

She opens the door of Kate's room. Her daughter is still asleep, her face stern in repose, her cuddly toys arranged in a neat line by the wall.

'Time to get up, Kate,' says Ruth. 'Your uniform's on the radiator.'

Kate is awake immediately, one of the perks of being seven and not forty-seven.

'I've got PE today,' she says. 'We're going to play dodge-ball.'

Ruth has no idea what that is but she quails at the thought of retrieving Kate's PE kit from the laundry basket. 'I'll put your kit in a bag,' she says.

'The pink bag with Hello Kitty on it.'

'I'll see what I can find.'

Ruth has a lightning shower and then goes back to her room. Frank is awake, rubbing his eyes. 'Hi, baby,' he says to Ruth. *Baby?* What's happened to them?

'I must get dressed,' says Ruth. 'Kate and I need to leave at eight.'

'Do you want me to lie low up here?' says Frank, understanding at once.

'Please,' says Ruth, searching vainly for a clean top. She has a lecture at ten and doesn't want to look more than usually untidy.

By the time that Kate is up and dressed, the hastily ironed kit in the Hello Kitty bag, untidy French plait completed and breakfast made, Ruth feels slightly calmer. If they can get out of the house without Kate seeing Frank then all will be well. Ruth packs her lecture notes in her backpack and notices the letter, still in its evidence bag. Nelson must have forgotten to take it last night. She puts it in her desk drawer. *Thought for the Day* is on the radio, which means it's nearly time to leave.

'Have a last-minute wee,' she tells Kate. 'Use the downstairs one.'

Ruth puts on her coat and gets Kate's anorak, hat and scarf ready. It's still very cold outside in the mornings, the frost glittering on the window panes.

'I want to say goodbye to Flint,' says Kate, putting on her gloves.

'I think he's outside,' says Ruth. 'We'll probably see him in the garden.'

They make it to the car without incident. Frank's car is parked in front of the weekenders' cottage so Ruth hopes that Kate won't notice it. Ruth scrapes her windscreen with her gym membership card. It's the most use it ever gets.

Then she climbs in and starts the engine, the hot air dispersing the last flakes of ice.

'Let's go disco,' says Ruth, revealing her age.

'There's a man at your bedroom window,' says Kate informatively.

CHAPTER 16

John Mostyn has no known next-of-kin so Nelson applies for a warrant to search his house. When it arrives Judy and Clough drive to the estate in King's Lynn. As soon as they park in front of the pebbledash house they know that something is wrong. The front door is open, swinging gently on its hinges.

'Keep behind me,' says Clough, as they approach.

Judy ignores him. She hates it when Clough gets into one of his Jack Reacher moods. She pushes past him, although she is careful to put on gloves before touching the door.

There are bloodstains in the hall and, in the crowded front room, a bullet hole in the back of the sofa, where Mostyn must have been sitting when he was shot.

'This is the crime scene,' says Clough, getting out his phone to call the station.

'No sign of a struggle,' says Judy, looking round the room.

'How could you tell?' says Clough.

But, in fact, it is easy to see that the fragile towers of cardboard boxes haven't been disturbed. There's a narrow channel from door to sofa and both victim and murderer must have travelled the same way. Clough peers at the faded green chenille of the sofa.

'Bullet's not in there. Murderer must have pocketed it.'

'The boss said it looked like a professional job,' says Judy. 'Looks like Mostyn was just sitting on the sofa when someone burst in and shot him dead.'

'The door was kicked in,' says Clough. 'But the wood was rotten. It wouldn't have taken much force.'

Judy looks at the sofa. There's a dull red stain and a scorch mark where the bullet entered the fabric. Not much blood though. The killer had known exactly where to shoot. 'Come on,' she says, 'we'd better leave this room before we contaminate it any further.'

They retreat to the kitchen where the hamsters are on their hind legs in their cage as if they know something is wrong.

'Poor things,' says Judy. 'We'll have to find a home for them. Would Cassie like them? Make nice pets for Spencer.'

'You must be joking,' says Clough. 'Cassie hates mice. And Dexter would eat them.' Dexter is Clough's dog, a bulldog puppy. Cassie is his wife and Spencer his one-year-old son.

Judy looks round the kitchen. There are some signs of order in here, some vestiges of a daily routine. John Mostyn seemed to have lived on tinned soups; they are lined up on the worktop: mulligatawny, oxtail, pea and ham – flavours Judy did not know still existed. His bowl, spoon and cup are washed up on the draining board. He grew herbs in pots on the window sill and has a 1992 'Beaches of Norfolk' calendar on the wall showing February, Hunstanton. He obviously sat at the kitchen table to read and to watch a small colour television balanced on a pile of children's encyclopaedias. Judy examines some of the paperbacks ranged around the chair.

'Clough!'

'What?' Clough is looking out of the window for the SOC team.

Judy points to the books. *The Wasteland* by T. S. Eliot. *The Four Quartets. The Complete Works of Shakespeare.* The *Good News Bible. The Sunday Hymnal. The Enthusiast's Guide to Pagan Festivals. The Oxford Dictionary of Quotations.*

Clough shifts some of the papers on the table.

'Look at this.'

It's a typed letter.

DCI Nelson,

You have found Margaret but this is only the beginning. It is the best of times and the worst of times. You must finish what you have started. Courage, my friend. Remember we know not the day nor the hour . . .

'It's not finished,' says Judy.

'Why print out an unfinished letter?' says Clough. 'Mind you, there's no printer. No computer either.'

But, under a pile of BBC cookery magazines, they find a laptop, only a few years old by the looks of it. There's a printer too.

'We should seize the laptop,' says Judy. She takes a plastic bag from one of the many bags that are full of them and carefully slides the slim computer inside. The forensics team arrive and start to erect an awning over the front door. 'One way in, one way out,' that's the rule. The house is suddenly full of people in white coveralls.

'We'd better get back to the station,' says Clough.

'I'm taking the hamsters with me,' says Judy.

'So John Mostyn was killed by someone who broke into his house, shot him at close range and then drove the body some three miles to leave it in an industrial estate.' In the briefing room, Nelson is rattling through the facts with his usual deadpan delivery. Judy, Tanya and Clough watch him. In the background, the hamsters run wildly on their wheel.

'We might get some CCTV from the Canada Estate,' says Nelson. 'It's quite a way from the car park to the fountain.'

'And someone may have seen or heard the killer breaking into Mostyn's house,' says Clough. 'It was probably pretty late at night though.'

'Maybe not,' says Judy. 'After all, he was sitting on the sofa and not in bed.'

'He probably slept in there,' says Clough. 'I think I saw a sleeping bag.'

'He was sitting upright,' says Judy.

'Watching TV?' suggests Tanya. '*DIY SOS* was on last night.'

'The TV was in the kitchen,' says Judy. 'And I don't think that he was much of a DIY fan.'

'We'll have to see what the SOC team finds at the house,'

says Nelson. 'And we need to ask why the killer took the body to the Canada Estate. Surely it would have been easier just to leave it in the house?'

'Maybe they just wanted to distract us,' says Clough. 'Misdirection, like in magic tricks.' Clough rather fancies himself as a magician and, after a few beers, is prone to trying to do a trick with empty glasses and a pound coin.

'I think the location itself might be important,' says Nelson. 'The plaza was a circle surrounded by buildings. It's a kind of stone circle.'

He looks slightly embarrassed to be voicing such a Cathbad-esque thought but Judy is impressed. The boss is right, there was something rather symbolic about the placing of the body, the shuttered buildings, the empty fountain.

'But if Mostyn wrote the letters,' says Tanya, 'he was the one who was obsessed with stone circles.'

'Maybe someone else knew about the letters,' says Nelson. 'Remind us what the letter said, Judy, the half-finished one you found in the house.'

Judy has given the letter to Forensics but she has a photo on her phone. She reads the words aloud. '"DCI Nelson, You have found Margaret but this is only the beginning. It is the best of times and the worst of times. You must finish what you have started. Courage, my friend. Remember we know not the day nor the hour . . ."'

'It certainly sounds like the other ones,' says Nelson. '"Best of times" is a quote, isn't it?'

'Yes, it's the beginning of *A Tale of Two Cities*,' says Judy. 'By Charles Dickens. I looked it up.'

'What about "we know not the day nor the hour"?'

'It's from Matthew's gospel. "Therefore keep watch, because you do not know the day or the hour." I think it's about being ready for the Second Coming.'

'Mostyn certainly wasn't ready,' says Clough. 'He can't have expected someone to burst into his house and shoot him dead.'

'Maybe that's exactly what he did expect,' says Nelson. 'Maybe he knew that someone was coming after him. Finding Margaret's bones must have stirred up lots of memories and he was the key suspect at the time. We should have offered him police protection.'

'We offered to take him into the station yesterday,' says Clough, bristling slightly. 'But he said he wanted to make his own way.'

'Because he was scared,' says Judy. 'He said that he and his mother had suffered abuse when Margaret first went missing.'

'So who would have wanted him dead?' says Nelson. 'Someone who thinks – or knows – that he killed Margaret?'

Judy thinks that, despite his low-key manner, the boss is actually relishing being involved in a murder case again. Tanya and Clough too seem galvanised at the thought of a dead body. For her part, thinking of the tins of soup and the 'Beaches of Norfolk' calendar, she just feels rather sad. She must be losing her edge.

'If Mostyn wrote the letters,' she says, 'he wanted us to find Margaret. Why would he do that if he was the one who had killed her in the first place?'

'Maybe his conscience was bothering him,' says Clough.

'And how did he know where she was buried if he wasn't the one that killed her?'

'Remember Ruth thinks that the body was moved,' says Judy. 'So Mostyn might not have been the one who originally buried her. He might have known who it was though.'

'He knew too damn much for my liking,' says Nelson. 'About Lucy, about the original letters, where Margaret was buried. Maybe he knew too much for someone else's liking. Well, we'll know more when we hear from the geeks.' He means the Computer Forensics team, currently examining Mostyn's laptop. Judy wonders if she should make a point by pretending that she doesn't understand the term but decides that it's not worth the hassle.

'What about Margaret's family?' says Tanya. 'I'm seeing Luke, the brother, later today. I'm going up to London,' she adds, rather importantly.

'The streets aren't paved with gold, you know,' says Judy.

Tanya ignores her.

'Margaret's father, Bob, was a suspect too,' says Clough. 'Maybe Mostyn knew that Bob had done it and someone killed him to keep him quiet.'

'Yes, but why now?' says Nelson. 'Mostyn had thirty years to inform on Bob Lacey. If he was intimidated, surely he could have spoken up after Bob died? But we can't ignore the possibility that the same person killed Mostyn and Margaret. We should keep looking at the original case, at least until we get the DNA results back from the remains. Judy, where are we with Margaret's friends and family?'

'I spoke to Kim Jennings,' says Judy. 'I thought I'd speak

to her parents too. The two families were close and Karen's second husband is Kim's uncle. I've tracked down Margaret's English teacher, Carol Dunne. She's a headteacher now. I though she might have some useful insights.'

'Good idea,' says Nelson. 'Talk to the sister, Annie, too. Cloughie, you liaise with the Forensics team and find out about CCTV. Judy, we need to tell Karen today about Mostyn, prepare her for the media making the link with Margaret. We've got about a day before this hits the press.'

'I'm not sure about that,' says Clough. 'I saw Judy's stepdaughter outside just now. She must know something's going on.'

'That girl's as much trouble as her father,' says Nelson. 'Judy, can you talk to her?'

'I haven't got any influence over Maddie,' says Judy. 'Or Cathbad, for that matter. I suppose we could offer her an exclusive if she keeps quiet for twenty-four hours.'

'Good idea,' says Nelson. 'Though I can't imagine any relative of Cathbad's keeping quiet for that long.'

He's forgotten that my children are Cathbad's too, thinks Judy. But she too often finds it hard to remember that they are related to Maddie.

CHAPTER 17

'What do you mean, he's dead?' asks Karen Benson. 'Did he have a heart attack or something?'

Judy and Clough look at each other. They don't want to release too many details about Mostyn's death but Karen deserves to know some of the truth. Besides, it will be in the papers tomorrow.

'We are treating his death as suspicious,' says Judy, falling back on police-speak. 'I must ask you to keep this to yourself for the time being. We'll make a statement tomorrow.'

'Suspicious?' Pete Benson who, as usual, is sitting quietly by his wife's side, speaks up for the first time. 'Does this mean that he was murdered?'

'It's an ongoing investigation,' says Clough and, to Judy's irritation, once again husband and wife both turn to him as if the oracle has spoken. 'We just wanted to prepare you because, when this hits the press, people will remember that Mostyn was originally questioned about Margaret's disappearance.'

Karen looks up at Margaret's picture on the wall,

something that she does, almost unconsciously, every few minutes.

'I never thought he did it, you know,' she says. 'People were quick to point the finger at John because he was a bit odd but I always thought he was harmless. I couldn't have gone on living near if I thought he'd killed her.'

'I saw him a few weeks ago,' says Pete. 'We talked about gardening.'

'Was he interested in gardening?' asks Judy, thinking of the overgrown wilderness at Allenby Avenue.

'I don't think so,' says Pete. 'Stones were his thing. He liked collecting stones.'

Judy thinks of the hag stone that was her gift from Mostyn. It's still in her bag, warding off evil. She too hadn't thought that Mostyn seemed like a killer. But, as the boss had said, he certainly knew too much.

'Why did people suspect John of being involved with Margaret's disappearance?' asks Judy.

'I think just because he was odd,' says Pete. 'And he was seen talking to the girls that day.'

'He was talking to everyone,' says Karen. 'He'd found a fossilised sea urchin or some such thing.'

'Sea urchin?' says Judy. 'A shepherd's crown?'

'I don't know,' says Karen, looking confused. 'A sea urchin's the name I remember. I can picture it now. A grey stone with a sort of star-shape in it.'

'You don't remember a seahorse at all?' says Judy. Clough looks at her quizzically.

'No,' says Karen. 'I just remember John going round

with this sea urchin thing. He showed it to the girls and he showed it to me too. Then, later on, I remember him sitting with his mother, Heidi, at one of the long tables. John was devoted to Heidi. He looked after her so well, took her everywhere. She was in a wheelchair, you see. A nice lady. She could be sharp-tongued but she had a good heart.'

And Heidi had been John's most stalwart advocate, thinks Judy, giving him an alibi that even the dinosaur Superintendent Roy Brown hadn't been able to shake. She wonders what it was like for Mostyn after his mother died. Did he feel any sense of freedom or was he scared, all alone without his champion? At any rate, he'd stayed in the same house, letting the clutter silt up around him.

'Was John Mostyn with his mother all afternoon?' asks Clough.

'I think so,' says Karen. 'But I've been asked this so many times. What happened that afternoon, when I last saw Margaret, what time I told Bob, where Annie and Luke were. And I've tried to remember everything, I've written down times, drawn maps, but there are parts that are still a blur. I think John was with his mother all afternoon but I can't be certain.'

Karen's voice has become almost hysterical. She reaches for her cigarette packet. Pete puts his arm round his wife.

'It's hard,' he says, addressing Judy and Clough. 'It's hard being asked to remember all the time.'

'I hate to ask,' says Judy, 'but do you have any idea who could have killed John Mostyn?'

'No,' says Karen. 'I'm sorry he's dead. I'm sorry about everything.' She's crying now.

'Could it have been a burglar?' says Pete. 'There have been a lot of burglaries on the estate recently.'

But, as far as they could see, nothing had been taken from the house on Allenby Avenue. And no burglar, disturbed mid-crime, would have killed with a single shot and then taken the body to an industrial estate on the other side of town. Much as Judy disapproves of the word, this was an execution.

Michelle is sitting on a comfortable sofa, George on her lap. She is watching Star carefully adding what looks like a large thistle to a collection of leaves steaming in a teapot.

'What's that?' she says.

'Blessed thistle,' says Star. 'It's very good for increasing your milk supply. You are breastfeeding, aren't you?'

'Yes,' says Michelle.

'Fenugreek too,' says Star. 'And fennel and goat's rue. I've got so much milk that I could be a wet nurse, Mum says. I'm expressing too. What about you?'

'I hate expressing.' Michelle is not that keen on breast-feeding, to be honest, but she did it with the girls so she is determined to give George the same start. She'll stop after ten weeks though. She doesn't say this to Star because she's so obviously revelling in the whole experience of mother-hood.

They'd exchanged mobile numbers yesterday but Michelle had been surprised to receive a text from Star suggesting that they meet for a 'cup of tea and a chat' at her house. 'It'll be much nicer than that baby group.' Michelle had been even more surprised when she turned up at the address to discover that it was a large modern house on the Ferry Road.

'It's my mum and dad's place,' said Star, opening the door with her baby, Ava, on her shoulder.

Michelle approves of the sitting room. It's rather like hers, neat and comfortable with a fitted carpet, three-piece suite and an array of cushions balanced on their tips. Children's toys are spread out on a patchwork quilt and sunlight streams in from large picture windows. Star says that she prefers wooden floors and 'things that are jumbled up a bit.' But she says that she knows she is lucky to be living with her parents. She's twenty-one – younger than Michelle's daughters – and a single mother. 'But Ava wasn't a mistake,' she says, passing Michelle a mug of aromatic tea. 'I wanted a baby but Ryan, her father, wasn't quite mature enough to be a dad.'

Michelle had married young; she was only twenty-one when she met Harry, twenty-four when they married. But she can't imagine going it alone and conceiving a baby with a manchild who isn't mature enough to be a father. Harry has always seemed grown-up, he was already in the police when they met and seemed able to cope with anything. She'd thought of herself as sensible too but she doesn't think she ever had Star's poise, her sweet seriousness that makes her almost seem the older one in the friendship. And they are already friends, Michelle realises with a slight shock, after two meetings.

Michelle puts George down on the quilt and sips her tea. It's almost tasteless and smells of grass cuttings. It's comfortingly hot though and there are home-made biscuits on the tray. Star tells her about her meditation classes and they watch the babies lying on their backs making underwater starfish movements as they gaze up at the little glass stars hanging from the ceiling.

'I put those there,' says Star. 'I think it's good to look up at the stars.'

'Are your parents at work?' asks Michelle.

'Dad is. He's a teacher. Mum's gone over to Grandma's. She lives nearby. Mum's taken some time off work to help me look after Ava.'

'That must be nice,' says Michelle. She is looking forward to her mother coming down next week. Even at her age, there's something about having your mother around that makes you feel safe.

'It is nice,' says Star. 'Grandma's been lovely too. She and Granddad even say they'll look after Ava when I go back to work.'

'What do you do?' asks Michelle. It's not that Star doesn't seem capable, it's just that Michelle can't imagine her doing an ordinary, prosaic job. She's too ethereal and otherworldly.

'I'm a qualified aromatherapist,' says Star. 'I want to set up my own business. I'd like to teach meditation too. I've been going to these fantastic evening classes. They're really inspiring.'

'I went back to work when my girls started secondary

school,' says Michelle. 'I'm a hairdresser. If I'd stayed near my mum I might have gone back sooner. I didn't really want to leave the girls with anyone who wasn't family.'

'I know what you mean,' says Star. 'I read somewhere that it takes a whole family to raise a child. Mind you, Mum can be a bit . . .' She pauses, looking up at the twinkling stars as if trying to think of the right word. 'A bit domineering,' she says at last. 'Of course she's had a difficult time in the past. Losing her sister like that, I mean. I think she had a complete breakdown when she was still in her teens. It's made her very protective of me. I know that. I make allowances.'

She sounds like a mother talking about a teenage child. Would Michelle's daughters be as understanding about her? she wonders. If they knew about Tim, for example.

'Of course,' Star is saying, 'Mum's a paediatric nurse. She knows all about babies and childcare but Ava's *my* baby.'

Ava is a fairy child with a tiny heart-shaped face and Star's silver-blonde hair. Next to her George looks big and almost rudely healthy, although Ava is actually a day older.

'That's so nice,' says Star. 'Like twins. Friends for life.'

'They can grow up and get married,' says Michelle.

'We don't know what their paths will be,' says Star, sounding like Cathbad. 'Marriage isn't for everyone.'

A sound in the hallway makes Star look up. She picks up Ava, although the child is still happily gazing at the ceiling. A large woman in a red coat comes into the room, bringing a chill of outdoor air.

'Have you heard?' she is saying. 'Mostyn's been killed . . .'

She stops when she sees Michelle.

'This is my friend Michelle, Mum,' says Star. 'And this is George.'

'Michelle?' says the woman, clearly expecting something more.

'Michelle Nelson,' says Michelle.

'DCI Nelson's wife?'

'That's right.'

'Mum . . .' says Star, on a warning note.

'My name's Annie,' says the woman. 'I'm Margaret Lacey's sister.'

It is some moments before Michelle realises the significance of the name.

Ruth is glad to dive into the comforting world of the university. She had dropped Kate off at school with some relief. Kate had asked if the man in the window was Frank. Ruth said yes, he had called in last night after Kate was in bed. This much was true at least and, for the present, lost in thoughts of dodgeball, Kate had seemed content to let the matter rest. Ruth arrived at UNN in good time for her lecture on The Archaeology of Disease which was greeted with the usual mix of enthusiasm and bafflement by her audience. Now she is in her office preparing for her seminar on Osteology. She has pinned a diagram of a skeleton on her cork board because, in her experience, students often get the radius and the ulna confused.

She almost ignores her phone when it buzzes but there's always the thought that it could be Kate's school (a fall, a sudden temperature, a freak playground accident) or

Nelson. But the display says 'Roz', Ruth's forensics contact. She presses 'answer'.

'Hi, Ruth. Thought you'd like to know, we've got some interesting stuff back on your bones.'

She means Margaret Lacey.

'Oh yes,' says Ruth.

'We've found some pollen and vegetable matter.'

'That's great news,' says Ruth.

'Yes, and some of it looks very specific. If you carry out a botanical morphological survey it could go some way to establishing the original burial site.'

'That's a big help,' says Ruth. 'Can you send me a list of the flora and fauna?'

'I'm emailing it now.'

She wonders whether to ring Nelson but she's still rather embarrassed about last night, as if Nelson will be able to tell, even over the phone, how the evening ended. In the end she calls Judy.

'That's great,' says Judy, sounding slightly distracted all the same. 'Will this pollen and stuff help us find the exact place where Margaret was first buried?'

'Roz did say it was specific,' says Ruth. 'So I hope we should be able to narrow it down a lot.'

There's a short silence. Ruth wonders if Judy's driving. Then Judy says, 'Have you heard the latest development?'

'No,' says Ruth. 'What?'

'John Mostyn, our prime suspect, has been found dead. Shot. This is confidential for now, by the way.'

'Understood.' There's no one Ruth could tell anyway. Kate? Flint? Her thoughts veer towards Frank and away again.

'I'd better go,' says Judy. 'I'm on my way to do some interviews. Can you come in tomorrow to talk about the pollen and the other results? About ten?'

'Yes, I think so.' Ruth looks at her timetable. She'll have to miss a department meeting but it will be worth it. 'See you then.' She can hear her students scuffling outside the door. She sighs and gets up to let them in.

'Good old Ruth,' says Clough. They have been listening on hands-free because Judy is driving.

'Yes,' says Judy. 'If we can find out where Margaret was originally buried, that'll be a great help.'

'I still think Mostyn was the most likely person to have killed her,' says Clough. 'That's why he was killed. It was a revenge killing.'

'This isn't *The Godfather*,' says Judy. Clough is obsessed with the Godfather films and can quote them at length. In order to stop him doing so she says, 'Shall we see Annie next? Then I can go on to interview Kim Jennings' parents, if you've got other things to do.'

'OK,' says Clough, who is looking at something on his phone, probably a message from Cassie full of heart emojis and kisses. He's silent for a minute, scrolling, then he says, 'Why did you say that thing about seahorses, when we were talking to Karen and Pete?'

'It was something Kim said,' says Judy, taking the turning where the Campbell's Soup Tower used to stand. 'I asked her if there was anything random that she remembered from the day Margaret vanished. She said "seahorses".'

'Is that one of your cognitive interview things?'

'Don't knock it,' says Judy. 'I've got results that way before.' But Clough is looking at photos of his beloved dog Dexter and doesn't respond.

CHAPTER 18

At Annie's house, Judy is surprised to find Michelle loading a baby seat into her car. She is watched by a blonde girl holding a baby and by Annie herself, who has her arms folded and is looking rather critical of Michelle's baby-wrangling skills.

'Oh, hi, Judy.' Michelle has succeeded in installing George in the back seat and looks up, pushing her hair back with one hand. 'What are you doing here?'

'I was going to ask you the same thing,' says Judy. Clough is making faces at George through the window.

'I'm friends with Star,' says Michelle, with a trace of something that sounds like defiance. 'We met at a mother and baby group.'

Judy had loathed mother and baby groups, the fake camaraderie, the subtle put-downs ('Oh, I remember Jordan doing that months ago'). It's another reason not to have another baby.

'Star?' she queries.

Michelle points to the blonde girl, which turns into a

wave. This must be Annie's daughter. Judy remembers Karen saying that Annie had just become a grandmother. But Star looks young enough to be Michelle's daughter, younger than her daughters, in fact. Judy is quite impressed by this inter-generational friendship.

'I won't keep you,' she says. 'Bye, Michelle. Bye, George. Stop that, Cloughie, you'll give him nightmares.'

'He likes it,' says Clough, straightening up. 'He's a little cracker, Michelle.'

Michelle gives him a genuinely warm smile and a modified version for Judy. She says goodbye and drives away. Annie greets them as they walk up the drive. 'I know why you've come. It's about John Mostyn. I've just come from Mum's.'

That was quick, thinks Judy. Mind you, they would have been there sooner if Clough hadn't insisted on stopping for chips.

'I'm going to put Ava down,' says Star. 'She's almost asleep.'

'Have you winded her?' says Annie.

'Yes,' says Star, with what sounds like elaborate patience. She smiles at Judy and Clough and retreats into the house. Annie ushers them into a modern kitchen, all gleaming surfaces and concealed gadgets. They sit at the breakfast bar, where the stools are just a little too high for Judy. She hates having swinging legs like a toddler. Clough grins at her but doesn't say anything.

Annie makes coffee with a certain amount of cup crashing but it's delicious and she gives them biscuits too.

'So Mostyn is dead,' she says. 'God rest his soul.'

This isn't said in a very religious tone, more in the way that Judy's Irish father tags the phrase onto reminiscences about unloved relatives, but it's interesting for all that. It seems that Annie, too, thinks that John Mostyn was innocent.

'Oh, he was just a simple creature,' she says. 'Going round showing us stuff that he'd found on the beach. I never thought that he'd taken Margaret. Even Dad didn't think that and he suspected everyone at some point.'

'Did he?'

'Yes.' Annie frowns into her coffee mug for a moment. 'The whole thing sent him a bit nutty for a while. Well, it did all of us.'

'John Mostyn's death is confidential for now,' says Judy, 'but it will come out in the press and, of course, people will make the connection with Margaret. We just wanted you to be prepared.'

'Oh, we're used to it,' says Annie. 'The things the papers used to make up about Dad, about all of us. Even Luke. Implying that he might have ... Margaret was his little sister, for heaven's sake.'

Judy has read the press cuttings and, whilst there are several veiled hints about Bob Lacey, she can't remember ever reading anything about Luke. But there must have been rumours, she's sure. She remembers Nelson's comment about him being 'old enough'.

'Can you think of anyone who *did* think that Mostyn killed Margaret?' asks Clough. 'Anyone who might have felt strongly enough to kill him?'

'A lot of people suspected him at the time,' says Annie. 'They used to shout things at him in the street, throw stuff at his house. I remember his mother, she was in a wheelchair, attacking these kids with an umbrella when they said something about John.'

Judy remembers Mostyn's frightened whisper. *People will see and they'll think I did it. They'll throw things.* She feels guilty all over again. Did they fail John Mostyn? Is this their fault?

'Can you think of anyone who felt particularly strongly?' says Clough. 'Maybe someone who could have got worked up by the recent publicity?'

Annie stares at them. She doesn't resemble her mother, or Margaret (although Star does), but suddenly there's an expression that reminds Judy of one of the pictures on Karen's wall. Margaret in flared jeans, sitting on a wall and looking straight at the camera.

'Everyone felt strongly at the time,' she says, 'but then people forgot because that's what they do. Everyone forgets.'

'Do you mind telling us your recollections of the day that Margaret went missing?' says Judy. 'We're reopening the case and we're doing everything we can to find her killer. We hope that her remains will give us some forensic evidence but anything that you can remember will help as well. Even if it didn't seem significant at the time.'

Annie gives them the stare again and, for a moment, Judy thinks she's about to refuse. But then she sighs and says, 'It was such a lovely sunny day. Everyone was happy. I helped Mum lay out the food for the party. Luke had disappeared off with his friends playing football. That's how it was in the eighties. Girls were still expected to help around the house and the boys got out of everything. I made sure that all my children learned to cook and clean, Matt as well as Sienna and Star.' She pauses, and Judy is afraid that she's going to go off on a tangent about modern parenting but, after an eloquent eye-roll, Annie drinks some coffee and continues. 'Margaret was there with her friend, Kim. They helped a bit but they were too busy being silly and messing around. When Luke came back, Kim got very giggly. She had a crush on him, I think. I can't remember when Margaret left the party. I was with some friends, we were singing, and someone had got hold of some beer. There was a boy I liked too, Jimmy Preston. I remember sitting on his knee for a bit. The first thing I knew was when Mum came over and asked if I'd seen Margaret. I said I hadn't. Kim wasn't there either – she'd gone home but I didn't know that – and I thought they might be at our house. I went home but there was nobody there. I started to worry then. Mum came back and rang Kim's parents but they hadn't seen her. Mum went to get Luke and Dad. I stayed home in case Margaret came back. It was strange, it was still broad daylight and kids went wandering off all the time then but even so I think I knew that something bad had happened. I remember sitting there in our kitchen and shivering, though it was a hot day. I think that, even then, I knew I wouldn't see her again.'

She stops and stares out of the window. Judy thinks that she's trying not to cry.

'We've heard that John Mostyn talked to Margaret that

day,' she says. 'Did you see anyone else with her? Anyone slightly unusual?'

'John Mostyn showed her his stones,' says Annie. 'He was showing everyone. Later on I saw him sitting with his mother. I told the police that at the time. No, I didn't see Margaret talking to anyone strange. There was no one strange there. It was just our friends and family.'

'This might sound odd,' says Judy, 'but did you hear anyone mention seahorses?' She doesn't look at Clough.

'Seahorses?' says Annie. 'No. Why?'

'It's something Kim Jennings said.'

'Oh her.' Annie turns away with a shrug. 'She's away with the fairies, that girl. Have you seen her shop in Wells? Full of old tat covered in glitter. No wonder no one goes in there.'

Tanya enjoys the trip to London. She likes the anonymity of travelling at midday, an enigma in her jeans and navy Barbour, too casual to be an office worker, too smart to be unemployed. She buys coffee and a bun at the Countryline café and reads *Private Eye* with an amused and worldly expression on her face. Sadly there are only two other people in the carriage to witness her sophistication: a teenage boy wearing headphones who occasionally twitches in response to some private rhythm and an elderly woman reading *Fifty Shades of Grey* with her eyebrows raised.

King's Cross is even more exciting because there's a chance that she, world traveller that she is, could be heading for St Pancras and the Eurostar. But instead she takes the Thameslink to Blackfriars, where Luke Lacey works as an accountant. They are meeting in his office, an anonymous building with a stunning view over the Thames. Tanya longs to live in London, to work within sight of St Paul's and Tower Bridge, to drink coffee in Covent Garden and shop at artisanal bread stalls in Borough Market. But Petra, her partner – shortly to be wife – would never leave Norfolk.

Luke was once a good-looking boy but there's little trace of that in the middle-aged man with greying blond hair who meets Tanya in reception. He was a football player too but Tanya, a fitness fanatic, looks with some disapproval at his spreading bulk, only partially concealed by an expensive suit. Luke Lacey is fifty this year and, in Tanya's opinion, he's just the right demographic for a heart attack.

'Thank you for seeing me,' she says. 'As you know we've reopened the case into your sister's death.'

'Yes,' says Luke. 'I'll be down to see my mother at the weekend. This is pretty hard for her.'

You haven't been conspicuous by your presence so far, thinks Tanya. It's Annie who has been supporting Karen.

'I know it's been a long time,' she says, 'but I'd really like your memories of the day that Margaret went missing.'

Luke looks at her, twisting his wedding ring. He has a wife, Rina, and two children, Betty and Felix. Tanya has been doing her homework.

'Is it true?' Luke says suddenly.

'Is what true?'

'Is Mostyn dead? That's what Annie said. She rang me this morning.'

THE STONE CIRCLE | 161

So Clough was right. The news is out. Tanya doesn't see that there's any point in denying it, especially if Maddie Henderson is going to run the story tomorrow.

'Yes, he was found dead last night.'

'Found dead? Killed?'

'It's an ongoing investigation. I'm not at liberty to say more.'

Luke sighs and leans back in his chair. Tanya tries to read his expression. Relief? Anger? Fear?

'So, twenty-ninth of July 1981?' she prompts.

Luke sighs again. 'There was a street party. I was there for a bit, had some food, listened to the songs, but then I went off with my friends to play football. At the Loke Road rec. It was all we thought about in those days. Football. I thought I'd play for Man U one day.'

Glory hunter, thinks Tanya. Why not Norwich City? 'When did you last see Margaret?' she asks.

'I think it was at the party. She was sitting with her friend Kim and her family. They were eating cake. Kim offered me some and some of my mates laughed.'

'Did she have a crush on you?'

'I don't think so. She was a funny little thing, Kim.'

'Did you see John Mostyn at the party?'

'Yes, he was hanging around showing people his stone collection. That's what he always did. We used to laugh at him.' Luke and his mates had done a lot of laughing that day, thinks Tanya. She wonders when the laughter stopped. She remembers something in Judy's report from the first interview with Karen Benson and Annie Simmonds. Annie had said that Luke still had nightmares about Margaret's abduction.

She asks Luke when he first heard that Margaret was missing.

'Mum came down to the rec to see if she was there. It was late, about seven thirty, but it was still light. Mum was really worried, I could see that. So I said I'd help search. I went to the park with some of my friends and up as far as the allotments. I went home when it was dark and the police were there. Mum had fetched Dad from the pub by then.'

'Was your dad . . . ?' Tanya tries to find a tactful way to put it.

'He wasn't drunk, if that's what you mean,' says Luke. 'Everyone tried to make out that he was but he wasn't. He was just in the pub with his mates. That's what everyone did back then.'

Except for the women, thinks Tanya, who were presumably left clearing up after the street party.

'What happened next?' she asks.

'Dad and his mates went out looking for Margaret,' he says. 'I went with them. It was dark but we had lanterns and torches. The police were out too, loads of them. They were searching the river. Frogmen and everything.'

'What about Annie? What was she doing?'

'She stayed behind with Mum. Mum was hysterical by then.'

'Do you remember who else was there? In the house or taking part in the search?'

'It felt like everyone was there. The house was full of

people. Lots of the neighbours were there, some of my friends and their parents. The police too. I remember a policewoman trying to comfort Mum. The men all went out looking for Margaret and Dad wouldn't come home. He stayed out all night, walking through the streets. He was crying, swearing, shouting out Margaret's name. I'd never seen him cry before.'

'Did you stay with your dad all night?'

'Yes.'

No wonder Luke still has nightmares, thinks Tanya.

'Is there anything else you remember about that day?' she asks, following Judy's lead. 'Anything that might not have seemed significant at the time but has stayed with you?'

'Not really,' says Luke. He looks at her but Tanya gets the impression that he's not seeing the faceless corporate meeting room but the dark streets, the torchlight, his father sobbing. 'It was horrible,' he says. 'You can't imagine it unless you've been through it. One day we were a family of five and then one of us just . . . disappeared. If she'd been ill or in an accident it would have been terrible but there would have been an explanation. A reason. But Margaret just vanished. Suddenly it was just Annie and me again.'

'Were you close, you and Annie? There was only a year between you.'

'I suppose so. When we were young. Mind you, she was always trying to boss me about. She used to make me do things.'

'What sort of things?'

'If she'd fallen out with someone at school, she'd want me

to beat them up.' He laughs suddenly. 'I didn't, of course. If I'd beaten up everyone Annie fell out with, I'd have been expelled.'

'Does she have a bit of a temper then, Annie?'

Another laugh, this time without humour. 'You could say that. Mind you, she had a lot to make her angry. Margaret going missing, Mum and Dad getting divorced, Mum re-marrying. It wasn't easy for us, growing up.'

'I'm sure it wasn't.'

'But we've both turned out all right. Annie's a nurse, full of good works in the community. I'm . . .' He gestures towards the window as if the Shard and the London Eye are tangible signs of his success. Which perhaps they are.

'Annie's got children now, hasn't she?'

'Yes, three. And now she's a grandmother. Her daughter Stella, or Star as she calls herself, has just had a baby.'

'And what about Margaret?' asks Tanya. 'Were you close to her?'

Luke smiles and, for the first time, Tanya sees a trace of the teenage heart-throb. 'Oh yes. We all loved Margaret.'

Judy drops Clough at the station and drives to the address given to her by Kim Jennings. Kim's parents, Steve and Alison, live on the outskirts of King's Lynn, in a house that was probably once surrounded by fields. Now there's just a small paddock, containing a skewbald cob. Judy stands for a moment by the gate watching the horse chew the grass, shaggy and mud-splattered in its winter coat. She had a pony when she was growing up though she, like Kim

Jennings, could hardly be described as posh. She thinks of Ranger now; his whiskery nose, his untidy mane, his divine horsey smell. Maybe she should get Michael riding lessons as well as piano lessons? She holds out some grass for the skewbald but the horse, correctly identifying her offering as worthless, carries on grazing.

Steve and Alison Jennings are a comfortable-looking couple, probably in their sixties, wearing matching Aran jumpers. Judy remembers Kim saying, 'My mum looked like a mum' and now Alison looks like a grandmother and a very competent one at that. The couple seem to be caring for two grandchildren, an elderly dog and an angry-looking cockatoo. Judy is tempted to ask them if they want some hamsters as well.

She asks about the horse instead. 'That's Patches,' says Alison. 'We got him from a riding school that was closing down. He's getting on a bit but the grandkids love to ride him.'

'Kim mentioned that she used to have a pony.'

Steve smiled. 'That was Cuddles. Kim named him. He was a little sod really. He'd been abandoned by some gypsies. We used to have quite a few rescue horses at one time.'

Judy, an enthusiastic patron of Redwings, a wonderful Norfolk horse sanctuary, warms to the couple. Alison brings in tea and home-made cake and Judy asks about Margaret.

'I remember her so well,' says Alison, expertly moving a crawling baby from the sleeping Labrador. The other child, aged about three, is watching *Peppa Pig* with the sound turned off. 'She was such a pretty young girl. I know everyone says that and, of course, looks aren't important, but that's how I remember her. So blonde and lovely, like an angel.'

'She was a nice girl too,' says Steve. 'Always very polite. Please and thank you and all that.'

Margaret hadn't always been polite to Kim, Judy thinks, teasing her about being posh and probably about having a crush on her brother. But maybe she was the sort who knew how to be nice to parents.

'Your brother-in-law married Margaret's mother, didn't he?' she says to Steve.

'Yes,' says Steve. 'We always thought Pete was a confirmed bachelor but when Karen and Bob got divorced he started courting Karen immediately. They make a good couple, I think.'

Judy doesn't think she's ever heard anyone using the word 'courting' in ordinary conversation or say 'confirmed bachelor' without meaning 'gay'. She thinks of the colourless man holding Karen's hand and saying 'It's tough on the mother.' Perhaps Pete was what Karen needed after the more volatile-sounding Bob.

She asks the couple what they remember about the day Margaret disappeared. Neither of them asks about John Mostyn and she hopes this means that the murder hasn't hit the press yet. Maddie has agreed to wait until tomorrow before breaking the news in the *Chronicle* but these days it's usually on Twitter or Facebook where a story first emerges.

'We were all at the street party,' says Alison. 'It was such a lovely day. Everyone was so happy about Charles and

Diana getting married. So sad when you think how that turned out. And Diana was only nineteen. That seems quite shocking now. Tammy, Kim's older sister, got married at twenty-one and I thought that was too young. Her kids are grown-up now.' She gestures at the baby, now on Steve's lap, and the TV-watching child. 'These are our great-grand-children.'

Kim is married, Judy knows, but she doesn't have children. There's a third Jennings daughter, Christina, but she has emigrated to Australia.

'Did you see Margaret at the street party?' she prompts.

'Yes, she sat with us for a bit. She always liked coming to our house. I think it was a bit more ordered than home, a bit quieter.' Kim had liked Karen Lacey, Judy remembers, because she was pretty and didn't mind mud on the carpets. She can imagine that the Jennings family, staid and conventional, had a similar appeal for Margaret.

'Margaret and Kim went off to look at the swans,' says Alison. 'We didn't think anything of it. We let our children wander then.'

'There were no mobile phones, you see,' says Steve, as if Judy can't possibly remember a time before such technology. 'You couldn't keep in touch.'

'Kim came back after about an hour,' says Alison. 'I think I asked about Margaret but I can't be sure. I felt terrible about that at the time. But you can't know what's going to happen, can you? We went home at about six. Chrissie was quite little and she was tired out. Kim had one of her headaches. Karen rang us at seven-ish asking if Margaret was with us. I said she wasn't. I rang back about an hour later and Karen was in a terrible state. So Steve got in the car and went to help look for Margaret.'

'We searched for hours,' says Steve, 'and, well, you know the rest.'

'Was Pete at the street party?' asks Judy. 'Did he help with the search?'

'No,' says Steve. 'He lived out Swaffham way then.'

'What about Bob Lacey? Did he help search?'

'Yes,' says Steve. 'I think he was in the pub most of the afternoon but Karen went and got him. Bob was a good man.' Steve fixes Judy with rather a stern look. 'People said all sorts of things about Bob but he was a good man, devoted to his family. He was frantic that night, literally tearing his hair out. Well, that's understandable. I would have been the same if it was one of mine. I think he stayed out all night, him and his lad, Luke. But we all helped. All the local men.'

It was the men with the search parties and the women at home with the children, thinks Judy, as she drives away with one last wistful look at the horse. She was only three years old in 1981. She doesn't think that she missed much.

CHAPTER 19

Judy's next stop is to see Carol Dunne, the woman who was once Margaret's English teacher but is now head of a primary school in Gaywood. St Paul's is a happy-seeming place, with a fence outside that looks like coloured pencils, a brightly coloured mural in reception and children's artwork on the walls. On the field a group of children are playing an energetic game of what looks like football but involves a beachball and several hoops. It reminds Judy of the school attended by Michael and Kate and shortly to be honoured with Miranda's presence. She senses that it's not league tables that dominate here but a genuine concern for pupils' well-being. This impression is reinforced when she meets Carol Dunne. She knows that Carol taught Margaret in 1981 so now must be at least in her mid-fifties but the woman looks like a teenager, with blonde hair tied back in a ponytail and the kind of energy that Judy can only achieve after three double espressos.

'I remember Margaret so well,' says Carol, moving a pile of poetry books so that Judy can sit down. 'She was very bright. She loved reading and used to come to my after-school drama classes. I was devastated when she went missing. It was my first teaching post and I suppose I got too attached to my pupils. I left at the end of the year and decided to transfer to primary. That was easier to do in those days.'

'And now you're a headteacher,' says Judy.

'That's not such an achievement,' says Carol with a smile. 'Stick around long enough these days and they make you a headteacher. It's a job no one wants with all the paperwork and the hassle from the government.'

Judy is not deceived. People say it's easy to progress in the police force but the top jobs are still dominated by men. For Carol to have become a headteacher at a relatively young age is still pretty impressive. She has been at St Paul's for eight years and the school is rated 'outstanding' by Ofsted. Judy has checked.

'You may have heard that we're opening a murder inquiry into Margaret's death,' says Judy. 'I'm try to build up a picture of Margaret and her family. I know it's difficult after so long but it really does help. Did you teach Annie and Luke too?'

'I taught Annie,' says Carol. 'She was in the fourth year, as we called it then, coming up to O Levels. She was bright too, very determined, not as sunny a character as Margaret. Funnily enough I taught Annie's children here. Matthew, Sienna and Stella. They were nice kids. Matt and Sienna both went on to university. Stella was always an original. I don't think she went on to university but I'm sure she's doing something interesting with her life. She calls herself Star now.'

'You said that Margaret had a sunny character?'

Carol smiles. 'She was one of those children who seem blessed. She was the baby of her family and everyone seemed to dote on her. She was clever, pretty, good at sport. Everyone wanted to be her friend.'

'What about Kim Jennings? She was Margaret's best friend, wasn't she?'

Carol pauses before replying and the late afternoon sun shines through the coloured glass in the window. Carol shields her eyes and her hand shines orange and purple and green. She gets up to pull down the blind.

'Kim was a nice girl,' she says, with her back to Judy. 'She was in Margaret's shadow, of course, but never seemed resentful about it. Poor Kim. It was awful for her when Margaret disappeared. Everyone looking at her, asking her questions. Her parents moved her to another school eventually.' She sits back down at her desk.

Judy thinks of Kim saying, 'She looked so beautiful, she really did.' The adult Kim also seemed remarkably lacking in bitterness. Is she happy, running her shop full of quartz and seahorses? Judy hopes so.

'What about Margaret's parents?' asks Judy. 'What were they like?'

Again, Carol seems to hesitate for a second. 'I didn't know them very well. It's not like a primary school, where you see people at the school gate. Her mother came to a parents' evening once. I thought she seemed a nice woman, she'd had little formal education herself but she was keen for her children to do well. And they have. I hear Luke's an accountant in the city.'

'Really?' says Judy, not adding that Tanya is probably interviewing Luke Lacey at this moment.

'Annie too,' says Carol. 'She's a paediatric nurse.' She laughs. 'I try to keep up with my ex-pupils.'

'What about Margaret's father, Bob?' asks Judy.

'I never met him,' says Carol, 'but I saw him on TV a few times after Margaret went missing. He seemed utterly devastated.'

'What do you think happened to Margaret? ' asks Judy.

'I don't know,' says Carol, with a certain headteacherly sharpness in her voice, 'I'm not a detective. The police and the press at the time seemed determined to pin it on Bob or on that poor simple man who collected stones.'

Is 'simple' a PC term? wonders Judy. It's the adjective Annie used too. She decides to take a risk. 'John Mostyn, the so-called Stone Man, has been found dead in suspicious circumstances,' she says. 'That's classified information for the present.'

Carol opens her eyes wide. 'Does this mean he did kill Margaret?'

'We don't know,' says Judy. 'We don't know anything at the moment but it certainly seems as if his death might be linked to Margaret's.'

'I never thought he did it,' says Carol. 'The Stone Man. It was just the strong ganging up on the weak. You see enough of that in the playground.'

Judy thinks of the press crowding round the police station

when they sense a story. That feels like bullying too sometimes. But, then again, the police have to be accountable.
As do schools.

'At the time,' she says, 'what did you think had happened
to Margaret?'

Carol thinks for a moment, adjusting a glass ornament on
her desk that is so horrible that it must have been a present
from a pupil.

'I think I thought it was an accident,' she says at last.
'That she fell into the river or something. I found it hard to
believe that someone could have deliberately taken her and
killed her. I still find it hard.'

Sadly, Judy finds it all too easy to believe.

It's getting dark by the time that Ruth leaves the university.
She's left it a bit late, catching up with marking, and now
she's anxious to get to the childminder's before the agreed
pick-up time of five thirty. Not that Sandra minds if she's
late, it's more that Ruth will feel that she has failed at one
of her many daily mother tests (test one: don't get caught
with a lover in your bed). As she fumbles for her new-
fangled Renault key a voice behind her says, 'Ruth?'

Ruth jumps and drops her keys.

A tall figure emerges from the shadow of the trees and
picks them up. It's Leif.

'Sorry to startle you,' he says. 'I wondered if I could have
a word. There's something I'd like to discuss with you.'

'I need to collect my daughter now,' says Ruth. 'Can we
do it another time?'

'Could I come with you?' says Leif. 'I came by bike.' Ruth sees that he's carrying a bulky bag presumably containing a fold-away bicycle.

'All right,' she says, slightly ungraciously. 'I can drop you off in Lynn.' She doesn't want to turn up at Sandra's with a long-haired Viking in tow.

Leif puts the bike in the boot and gets into the passenger seat. Ruth drives through the darkening campus, the mushroom lights coming on around the lake. There's a party in the students' union tonight. You can see posters for it all over the place. 'Spring has Sprung. Let's celebrate!' The student equivalent of Imbolc.

Ruth asks about the dig. Leif says that they are getting on well and are hoping to be able to commission a facial reconstruction of the woman whose skeleton was found in the cist. He knows a fantastic archaeologist sculptor in Sweden. 'He's called Oscar Nilsson,' he says, 'and he has a gift for conveying the actual character of the person. It's so important to have a face, then people can form a relationship.' Ruth shudders, thinking of faceless things, voices in the dark, hands reaching from the sea. There's something about Leif's presence that seems to disquiet her.

This feeling is reinforced when, a few minutes later, Leif says, 'I wanted to talk to you about my father.'

'Did you?' says Ruth, concentrating on one of the many roundabouts on the way to King's Lynn.

'When Dad died he left a letter for me,' says Leif. 'A lot of it was personal. We weren't that close. My parents were free spirits and that's not always easy for the children. But, in the letter Dad said that he was proud that I'd decided to become an archaeologist. He said that, if I could, I should come to north Norfolk to look at the henge circle. He also said that I should get to know you. He was very fond of you. My mother was too.'

'I was fond of them both,' says Ruth. Her mouth feels dry. She had once been very fond of Erik and Magda. She had stayed with them in Norway, sitting in the hot tub under the stars, taking the universe apart and putting it back in a different shape. They were her mentors, her idealised parents. She had thought that Erik and Magda had the perfect relationship, equals, friends and lovers, something to be aspired to and emulated. But it turned out that this too was not what it seemed. Both Magda and Erik had other lovers. Erik had a long-standing affair with Shona, something neither of them had shared with Ruth. And then there were the letters. When Ruth had first recognised Erik's handwriting on the pages, it was as if a monstrous shadow had fallen on their relationship. It meant that the Erik she knew – wise, compassionate, almost magical in his intuitive powers – was only ever an illusion.

'He said something though that I didn't understand,' Leif is saying. 'He said . . .' Leif takes a letter from an inside pocket and reads aloud, '"If you do make contact with Ruthie, tell her I'm sorry and that I loved her. Perhaps you will dance with the stone wedding party and pour a libation on the earth for me."'

For several minutes and several roundabouts Ruth can't speak. *Tell her I'm sorry and that I loved her.* This must have been written long before her last encounter with Erik but it's as if he knew everything: about Scarlet, about Lucy, even about his own terrible death on the marshes. It's as if Erik has given her his blessing from beyond the grave. He was the only person who ever called her Ruthie, although Cathbad sometimes does it to wind her up.

'What does he mean by the stone wedding party?' asks Leif. 'I think I have translated that correctly.'

'I don't know,' says Ruth. 'When he was my tutor at university, Erik was always saying things that I didn't understand. It meant that he wanted us to look them up, to find out for ourselves.'

'Will you look this one up?' says Leif. 'I'd like to make a libation to my father.'

'I will,' says Ruth. It sounds like an oath. Or a wedding vow.

Judy too finds someone waiting for her. Maddie is leaning against Judy's red Fiat, ostentatiously making notes.

'Have you been to see Carol Dunne?' she says. 'She used to teach Margaret, didn't she?'

'Why are you following me?' says Judy. She is tired and wants to go home.

'You can't think that Mostyn killed Margaret if you're still interviewing people.'

'I can't discuss the investigation with you,' says Judy. 'You've got your exclusive for tomorrow.'

'Who do you think killed John Mostyn?' Maddie gives her an enchanting smile, head on one side.

'I can't possibly answer questions like that,' says Judy, getting into the car. 'Do you want a lift home? Come for supper if you like. Cathbad's got one of his evening classes tonight but the kids would love to see you.'

'You're all right,' says Maddie vaguely. 'I've got some things to do. Tell them I'll see them soon.'

But, as Judy drives away, Maddie is still standing by the school gate, apparently deep in thought.

CHAPTER 20

It goes against the grain on the first day of a murder investigation, but Nelson leaves the station at five thirty. He's been at work for twelve solid hours but he still feels that he should be there all night, directing operations, moving arrows on a map like a plotter in a Second World War film. But, realistically, there's nothing more that he can do until he has the forensics results. The crime scene is sealed and he's had officers making house-to-house enquiries all day. Tomorrow Mostyn's identity will be in the papers and the link to Margaret will be public. The forensics on Margaret's remains, particularly on the rope, may well point to her killer. If that turns out to be John Mostyn, then the dead can bury the dead. It's a chilling phrase, thinks Nelson. Margaret's funeral is set for next week.

Bruno is still with the dog walker so the house is quiet when he gets in. Michelle is in the sitting room with George; he's sleeping in his Moses basket and she is watching one of those programmes where people buy a house in Tuscany and then seem surprised that everyone there speaks Italian.

'Hallo, love.' Nelson kisses her. 'Good day?'

'Yes, I saw Star. You know, the girl I met at the mother and baby group.'

'That's nice,' says Nelson, rifling through the post. 'Where's Laura?'

'Out at an evening class.'

'What's she studying? Isn't training to be a teacher enough for her?'

'She did tell me but I can't remember. My memory's terrible these days.'

Nelson bends over the basket to look at George. After all his fears, it's a ridiculous relief to be able to recognise himself in the little face. He can't stop himself picking up the sleeping baby and cuddling him, inhaling his sweetly pungent smell.

'Don't wake him up,' says Michelle. 'I met Star's mother today too.'

'Did you?' says Nelson, putting George down. He wonders if Laura has made anything for supper. He really should learn to cook. It's bad enough being dependent on your wife, somehow shameful to expect your daughter to look after you. He bets that smarmy Frank is a gourmet chef, the sort who talks about parmesan shavings and drizzling olive oil.

'She's Margaret's sister,' says Michelle.

'Who is?' says Nelson, who is lost in a pleasant fantasy involving deporting Frank.

'Star's mother. She's called Annie and she was Margaret's sister. The dead girl. Your dead girl.'

His dead girl. The trouble is, that's what it feels like.

'I've never met the sister,' he says. 'What's she like? It's odd to think of her being old enough to be a grandmother. This is tough on the family. You know the original chief suspect has been found dead? That's why I left so early this morning.'

'Yes,' says Michelle. 'I think Annie mentioned that. She seemed very upset when she came in. She knew who I was immediately.'

'You didn't say anything about the case?'

'I don't know anything about the case,' says Michelle. 'But Judy and Dave arrived just as I was leaving. I suppose they wanted to talk to Annie about this man's murder.'

'Yes, they were going to speak to all the immediate members of the family. Just to warn them, because it'll be in the papers tomorrow.'

'It's horrible for them,' says Michelle. 'Having the past raked up like that.' The press coverage of Tim's death had concentrated almost exclusively on the 'dead hero' angle but, even so, Nelson knows that it was almost unbearable for Michelle. For him too, come to that. He wants to say something, to reassure Michelle that the past horrors are behind them but, whilst he is still thinking of the words, she gets up and smiles at him. 'Are you hungry? There's some pasta sauce. Laura made a big batch and froze it. It's got Quorn in it but you can't taste that really.'

Laura is lying on the floor. There's a skylight in the ceiling and through it she can see stars and wisps of clouds.

'Lose yourself in the universe,' says a voice that seems to come, not from beside her, but from somewhere in the ether.

Laura closes her eyes and tries to hang on to her mantra but it's difficult in the dusty community centre with the traffic noise outside and the Italian Culture Class singing 'Funiculì Funiculà' in the next room. Last year, in the autumn before it got too cold, Cathbad took them into the woods at Sandringham and they had gazed up at the trees and it really was possible to feel part of the natural world and yet apart from it, both unthinking and yet deeply conscious. Cathbad says that you can meditate anywhere but she must be an undeveloped soul because, tonight, she can't stop thinking about that day's uni assignment, about George and Mum, worrying about whether Dad's collected Bruno from doggy day care. She tries again with her own personal mantra, listing amino acids in alphabetical order. Alanine, arginine, asparagine . . .

'Be aware of your breath,' says Cathbad. 'Be aware of the sensation of breathing. May everyone be happy. May everyone be free from misery. May no one ever be separated from their happiness.'

Usually his voice has a hypnotic effect on Laura but today she's not really feeling it. She opens her eyes and sees Star in lotus position, palms upwards, apparently at one with the universe. A feeling of entirely unspiritual irritation washes over Laura, like a dirty tide. She sits up. The two other members of the group, Malcolm and Felicity, are also fidgeting. Perhaps the Italian folk songs are too much for them too.

It's possible that even Cathbad feels it because he finishes the class a few minutes early, bowing in a slightly ironical 'namaste'.

'Are you all right, Laura?' he says as she rolls up her mat.

'Fine,' she says. 'No. I don't know.' There's never any point lying to Cathbad. 'I'm just a bit distracted.' Cathbad knows her parents, of course, but he'd never dream of asking if things were all right at home. Now, he says, 'Sometimes distractions are a way of pointing us in a certain direction. Maybe give some attention to those thoughts.'

'They're just trivial things,' says Laura. 'Like what I should have for dinner.' She thinks about food a lot, mainly about how to avoid eating it.

'Food is never trivial,' says Cathbad. Bloody Star is hanging about with a question about mindfulness so Laura shouts a general goodbye and heads for the door.

There's a man outside, standing in the little lobby with the fire extinguisher and the posters for long-forgotten fun runs. He's tall and muscular with golden-blond hair in a ponytail. He looks a bit like Thor in the Marvel films and is as out of place in this environment as if he were a real Norse god.

'Excuse me.' He has a faint foreign accent. 'Is this where Michael Malone, Cathbad, teaches?'

'Yes,' says Laura. 'He's in there.' She finds herself wishing that she wasn't wearing her oldest leggings, slightly frayed where Bruno tugged them out of the linen basket.

'Thank you,' says the man. 'My name is Leif.'

'Mine's Laura.'

'A beautiful name.'

Laura has never liked her name. It's too old-fashioned and has, to her mind, a slightly whiny sound, like the twang of a country and western guitar. In fact she was given the name because Michelle liked the song 'Tell Laura I Love Her'. But now she smiles and tosses her hair for all she's worth.

'Thank you. It's Laura Nelson actually.'

Now he can track her down if he wants to.

Ruth is at her computer, Kate is asleep upstairs and Flint is out on a night-time excursion. Outside her window the marshes are dark and silent and Ruth is looking up stories about the devil. Googling 'stone wedding party' brings up a variety of folklore and fairy tales, usually involving Saturday night revels that go on into the Sabbath. They remind Ruth of all-night parties at UCL. But the version that catches Ruth's eye involves the standing stones at Stanton Drew in Somerset. Stanton Drew is an impressive megalithic stone circle (actually three circles in total) and there is an appropriate legend linked to the site. There was said to have been a wedding at Stanton Drew, date unspecified but in that dusty era that Ruth sometimes ironically describes to her students as 'yore'. At the wedding party a mysterious fiddler, dressed in black, appeared and offered to play all night. The wedding guests danced, the music becoming more frenzied, until dawn broke on the Sunday morning and the fiddler, who was, of course, the devil, vanished in a puff of smoke leaving a circle of strangely shaped stones. The three largest are known locally as the bride, groom and preacher and there is a further group that is meant to represent the musicians. Frankly, it sounds just Erik's sort of place. Cathbad's too. The word Drew is apparently derived from the Celtic word for druid. Ruth is especially interested to learn that a geophysical survey in 1998 showed a series of concentric post-hole rings outside the main circle. So this site may once have been surrounded by a palisade of timber. Like Seahenge. Like Erik's henge.

Ruth stares at her laptop screen where the stones, misshapen and dark with lichen, do seem to be acquiring sinister proportions. Is this where Erik wanted her to go? Ruth remembers Erik once saying that the human journey is one from flesh to wood to stone. From the living body to the wood of the coffin to the stone of the grave. Maybe this is why there are so many myths and legends about petrification. Ruth thinks of *The Lion, the Witch and the Wardrobe*, one of Kate's favourite books. The White Witch turned her enemies to stone until Aslan breathed on them and brought them to life. There's too much overt Christian symbolism in the story for Ruth's liking but there's no doubt that this is a powerful scene; a room that was once full of statues suddenly teeming with life, lions roaring, giants wielding clubs, Mr Tumnus embracing Lucy. In Greek mythology, Medusa was famous for turning her enemies to stone, and then there's the basilisk, immortalised for a new generation by J. K. Rowling in the Harry Potter books, whose gaze is also meant to petrify, in both senses. Nearer to home there's the Lincoln imp, a mischievous creature that is said to have darted around the cathedral throwing things until an angel turned it to stone where it remains to this day, grinning from the wall. There is something primal about the thought that soft flesh becomes hard stone, dead but also everlasting.

She needs to talk to Cathbad. He'd understand all this stuff and he'd also understand why Ruth is considering trekking all the way across the country to look at some old stones. It's a pilgrimage of sorts and pilgrimages are not meant to be easy. She looks at the time in the right-hand corner of the screen. Nine o'clock. Not too late to ring. She's not surprised that Cathbad's mobile goes unanswered (he's very concerned about harmful vibrations and usually leaves it switched off, much to Judy's irritation) but when she tries the landline Judy tells her that he's still out at his meditation class. She sounds rather stressed and so Ruth doesn't stay on the line to chat. She looks at her Fitbit. Only two thousand steps today. She's felt rather twitchy ever since Shona asked her to become her 'Fitbit friend' which means she can see how many steps Ruth achieves each day. The app even gives you your rankings at the end of the week and Shona always wins. Ruth walks around the room a few times before giving up.

She goes upstairs to check on Kate (stairs give you extra points) and finds her fast asleep with her head on her cuddly chimpanzee. Flint, who is obviously back from his wanderings, is lying at the foot of the bed. He blinks at Ruth but doesn't get up. Ruth goes to her own room and stares out over the marshes. There are tiny lights glimmering at the point where the land meets the sea.

Phosphorescence. Will-o-the-wisps. Marsh lights. Cathbad would say that they are the ghosts of drowned children but there is also the legend of Jack O'Lantern, the miserable blacksmith forced to wander between heaven and earth, his path illuminated only by a spark of hellfire concealed in a turnip. The devil really does have all the best tricks as well as the best tunes. Ruth pulls the curtains and goes downstairs to bolt the door.

Nelson and Michelle sit in bed, watching an episode of *Breaking Bad* on Nelson's laptop. It's only half past nine, Laura is still out, but they both feel like it's the middle of the night. Michelle has been silent for about ten minutes. Perhaps she's asleep.

'Michelle,' says Nelson. She doesn't answer but he continues anyway. On screen a body floats in a swimming pool. 'I've been thinking,' says Nelson. 'We should tell the girls. About Katie. I should tell them, I mean.'

He looks at Michelle. She's not asleep, in fact she is staring at him intently. The dark roots make her blonde hair almost brown. She looks different, more serious somehow.

'Why tell them now?' she says.

'They'll know one day. You've been great to let me see Katie but, as she grows up, it's going to be harder to keep them apart. Also, I don't know, after last summer – all you and Laura went through – I don't think we should have secrets.'

Another silence and then Michelle says, 'Do you think I should tell them about Tim?'

When Michelle told him about the affair with Tim, Nelson hadn't felt in a position to take the moral high ground. And it had been such a strange time, they were all really just happy to be alive and the thought of the baby had sustained them. Even when Nelson had thought that George might be Tim's, he couldn't view his birth as anything other than a good thing, cosmically speaking, something bright to set against the darkness. Of course, there is jealousy and anger there too. Nelson hates the thought of Michelle sleeping with another man. He hates the thought of Ruth sleeping with another man, come to think of it. But Michelle has lived with jealousy over Katie for seven years.

'I don't think you should say anything about Tim,' he says at last. 'It's not as if he's . . .'

'Alive,' says Michelle.

'No,' says Nelson. 'What good would it do?'

'It might make me feel better,' says Michelle.

'Do you feel bad then?' says Nelson.

'Oh, Harry,' says Michelle, and he thinks she's near to tears. 'Of course I feel bad. I had an affair with Tim and now he's dead. He died because of me. I feel guilty all the time.'

'I feel guilty too,' says Nelson. But he doesn't say what for.

'But I'm happy as well,' says Michelle. 'Because of George. He's a miracle baby. Remember what that midwife called him? A menopausal miracle. I love him so much.'

Nelson wants to ask if she still loves him but George is a safer subject.

'He's a little cracker,' he says. 'I'll tell the girls at the weekend.'

'I'll help you,' says Michelle. 'I'll tell them that I'm happy for Katie to be in our lives.'

She is rewarded for this generosity by falling into a deep sleep but Nelson stays awake for a long time.

CHAPTER 21

Maddie's article appears in the *Chronicle* the next morning.

> The man found dead at the Canada Industrial Estate is confirmed to be John Mostyn, 70, of Allenby Avenue, King's Lynn. His death is being treated as suspicious. Mostyn was one of the main suspects in the disappearance of twelve-year-old Margaret Lacey in 1981. Margaret was last seen at a street party held to celebrate the wedding of Prince Charles to Lady Diana Spencer. Despite an extensive police investigation, opened again in 1991, no trace of Margaret was ever found. But, last month, archaeologists excavating a site near Holme in north Norfolk found human remains which were later confirmed to be those of the missing child.
>
> Margaret's parents Karen and Bob Lacey never gave up hope that their daughter would be found. Bob died of testicular cancer in 2014 but Karen still lives in the house that she once shared with Margaret and her siblings, Annie and Luke. She said that the discovery of Margaret's

remains would allow them to grieve at last. 'It's been hard,' she said, 'in some ways time has stood still since Margaret left us. I still think of her as that twelve-year-old girl who loved dancing and ponies and dressing up. Now we'll be able to bury Margaret and have a place to remember her. Maybe our family can finally find some peace.' Margaret's funeral is set to take place on Monday 7th March at St Bernadette's Church, King's Lynn.

The discovery of Margaret's bones has sparked a major police investigation led by DCI Harry Nelson, the detective who led the hunt for four-year-old Scarlet Henderson in 2008. Scarlet's body was found buried on marshy ground near Holme. No one was ever tried for her murder. Police wouldn't confirm a link between Margaret Lacey and John Mostyn but they admitted that they are still interviewing suspects in connection with Margaret's abduction and death.

'Did we?' says Nelson. 'Did we admit that?'

'I love the word "admit",' says Judy, who is looking slightly rattled. 'No, but Maddie saw me leaving the school after talking to Carol Dunne and she must have realised that the investigation is still ongoing.'

'The girl's a pro,' says Clough. 'She's even managed to get a quote from Karen Lacey.'

'She's got all the tricks,' says Nelson. 'Like saying "no one was ever tried" for Scarlet's murder. That's because the man was dead, for God's sake. She makes it sound like we never solved the case.'

'No mention of Lucy,' says Clough, 'who we did find.'

'That's because it's still all about Scarlet for Maddie,' says Judy.

'She's given a date for the funeral,' says Tanya. 'I didn't think that was set yet. Have Forensics finished with the remains?'

'They said they would release them to the undertaker today,' says Nelson. 'Maddie must have some inside knowledge.'

'St Bernadette's,' says Clough. 'That's the Catholic church, isn't it?'

'Yes,' says Judy. 'Remember, the family are Catholic. I don't think they go to church much though.'

'We should all go to the funeral,' says Nelson. 'It would be good if we could have some involvement, just to show that the relationship with the police is good. Judy, could you approach the parents? Maybe suggest that someone does a reading?'

'They like Clough best,' says Judy. 'They think he's in charge.'

'Christ, I don't want to do a reading,' says Clough.

Nelson looks back at the article which has upset him more than he cares to admit. 'She makes the link between Margaret and Scarlet,' he says, 'not overtly, but she says Holme for both of them when Scarlet was really found nearer Titchwell.'

'Is there a possibility that Scarlet's killer could have murdered Margaret?' says Judy. 'It was twenty years earlier but there was Lucy in between. And it *is* a similar location.'

'He wasn't living in Norfolk in 1981,' says Nelson. 'I checked. He was in the Shetlands or some such place.'

'The letters make the link too,' says Judy. 'If Mostyn did write the new letters he seems to be deliberately invoking the previous ones.'

'How did he know about them?' says Clough. 'We never made them public.'

'My guess is the *Chronicle*,' says Nelson. 'Mostyn used to do some photography for them. That place leaks like a sieve.'

'Bloody press,' says Clough. 'Who needs them?'

'We do,' says a voice from the doorway. It's Super Jo, newspaper in hand. 'Can I have a word, Harry?'

Ruth is on her way to the police station, suppressing the faint surge of excitement that always comes with being involved in a case. This is about finding a child's killer, she tells herself, not about seeing Nelson and being part of the team. Besides, her meeting is with Judy. Nelson might not even be there.

But, after she has signed in and been escorted to a meeting room, there's Nelson scowling behind the table and Clough eating a cheese and ham sandwich.

'Judy's just gone out to get some more sandwiches,' he says, rather thickly. 'In case the meeting goes on into lunchtime.'

Ruth glances at her watch. It's eleven thirty. She needs to be back at the university at one. 'What does Judy think about going on the sandwich run?' she asks.

'We take it in turns,' says Clough. 'This is a non-sexist workplace. We've got a certificate.'

'This is a non-working workplace at the moment,' says Nelson. 'Let's get on. What have you got for us, Ruth?'

Ruth gets out her file with Roz's forensics results and her own notes. Judy comes in and distributes sandwiches and bottles of water. Clough grumbles about the lack of chocolate. Ruth wonders where Tanya is. She usually never misses a strategy meeting.

'Forensic examination of Margaret's bones found traces of pollen, spores and wildlife—' she begins.

Clough interrupts her with a pained expression. 'Wildlife?'

'When the body was previously buried it would have been consumed by worms and maggots. Insects would have nested in the hair. Traces of their eggs remain. In addition, pollen was found in the nasal cavity. I have a report from an expert palynologist—'

'A what?' This is Nelson.

'A pollen expert. She traced the pollen found on the remains to this specific area.' Ruth gets out her map, the three police officers lean over to look.

'That's basically all of Norfolk,' says Clough.

'There's a place called Scarning Fen, near Dereham,' says Ruth. 'It's a very important wildflower reserve because there are some plants there that aren't found anywhere else in the country. There was moss on the bones that only grows in Scarning Fen.'

Nelson is frowning at the map. 'So Margaret was originally buried near Dereham?'

'It looks like it,' says Ruth. 'And there were damsel fly

eggs too. Scarning Fen is one of the few places in England where you find the red damsel fly.'

'If we go to this fen place,' says Nelson, 'do you think you can find where Margaret was buried?'

'I doubt it after all this time,' says Ruth. 'Vegetation will have grown so much and the fen is still such a large area. But having a location will help, won't it?'

'It will help a lot,' says Nelson. 'We've only really been concentrating on Lynn so far. Now we can find out who has links to this Scarning area. People always choose burial sites for a reason. It has to be somewhere they're familiar with, maybe a place where they walk their dog or where they camped as a child. Alongside the forensics from the rope, this might help us close in.'

'Have you got the forensics results?' asks Ruth.

'Tanya's at the lab. She should be back any minute.'

'That's her now,' says Judy. 'She always hums the *Rocky* theme when she climbs the stairs.'

Seconds later, Tanya bursts into the room looking important.

'What have you got?' says Nelson. 'Don't mind Ruth. She's one of us.' Ruth keeps her professional face on but she feels her cheeks glowing. One of us. One of the team.

'Mostyn's DNA is on the bones,' says Tanya. She pauses for effect. 'It's on the stone too, the piece of chalk that was found in the grave. But there's someone else's DNA too. The second DNA's not on the bones but it is on the rope and the gag.'

'So Mostyn's not the killer,' says Clough.

*

Nelson offers to walk Ruth downstairs. In the incident room she's surprised to see a cage with two hamsters in it.

'Is it bring your pet to work day?'

'They were Mostyn's,' says Nelson. 'We seem to have adopted them. Cloughie's named them Sonny and Fredo.'

'*The Godfather*?'

'What else?'

They walk down the stairs which are rather grand, with ornate banisters, a relic of the time when this was a gracious town house.

'Is this a breakthrough?' asks Ruth. 'The forensics?'

'I hope so,' says Nelson. 'I had Jo going on at me this morning. Apparently there's "concern amongst stake-holders" that we're not making enough progress. There's an article in the *Chronicle* today that makes us sound like the Keystone Cops.'

Nelson often uses these slightly archaic references. Perhaps he watched a lot of black-and-white films as a child. Another thing Ruth will never know about him. She can imagine that Jo would not be happy about the article, which Ruth read online that morning. Ruth has a sneaking admiration for Super Jo, although she would never admit this to Nelson.

'Is it still OK to take Katie out on Saturday?' asks Nelson, as they reach the bottom of the stairs.

'Yes, of course,' says Ruth. She has almost given up correcting him about the name. 'Have you got any plans?'

'I thought I'd take her to Redwings.'

'Good idea. She loves the horses.'

'Rebecca's coming down on Sunday to see George.'

They are at the main doors now but Nelson seems to have something else to say.

'I'm going to tell the girls,' he says, not looking at her. 'About Katie.'

'Oh.' Ruth doesn't know what to say. She always knew that he would tell them one day, of course, but there's no denying that she's dreading it. Nelson's 'girls' are grown women, women who will now hate Ruth.

'Good luck,' she says at last.

'Thanks,' says Nelson, rather grimly. 'What are you doing at the weekend?'

'I'm going to Cambridge on Sunday. To see Frank.'

'I hope it keeps fine for you,' says Nelson.

He looks like a thundercloud, though, which Ruth can't help finding slightly comforting.

CHAPTER 22

It's hard to find the right moment. Early on Saturday morning Nelson checks on the crime scene in Allenby Avenue. The house, surrounded by police tape, looks lonely and innocuous. A uniformed constable yawns on the door-step, straightening up when he sees Nelson approaching. Nelson rings Judy and asks her to visit Karen and Pete. 'Ask about the funeral and try to find out whether anyone's got any links to Scarning Fen.'

'I'm out all day,' says Judy. 'I'm not meant to be working this weekend.'

'Sunday then.'

'We're visiting my parents.' But she agrees to visit on Sunday morning. Then Nelson drives to the Saltmarsh to collect Katie. Ruth is friendly enough but seems rather dis-tracted. She has a pile of papers on her desk and is obviously planning to catch up on work. After a few brief pleasantries Nelson installs Katie in the back of his car and they drive to Redwings.

It's a bitterly cold day but he enjoys walking through the

fields with Katie, trying to engage the horses in conversation. He buys her hot chocolate in the café and she takes him to see the pony that she sponsors.

'I had to get a new one,' she says, pointing to a black and white blob in the distance.

'Did the old one go away for a holiday?' says Nelson, treading carefully.

'No, it died,' says Katie. 'I think I'd like a donkey next.'

Before they leave, Nelson fills out the adoption forms for a donkey named Wiggins.

When he gets home, his mother-in-law has arrived, which is the cue for lots of hugs and George-worshipping. Nelson gets on well with Louise, Michelle's mother, a smart ash-blonde who still works part-time and drives a pink Fiat 500. Seeing Louise, Michelle and Laura together is like watching a time-lapse photograph but, from a distance, the three beautiful women could almost be sisters. Michelle seems energised by her mother's presence and cooks them all a delicious lunch. In the afternoon Nelson takes George out in his buggy with Bruno cantering along beside them. Coming home, the lights are on in the house and he can see his wife, mother-in-law and daughter drinking Prosecco in front of the television. Is this the last peaceful family day they will have?

Rebecca arrives on Sunday. She's the brunette, the rebel, the one who is most like Nelson. If there's trouble, it'll be from Rebecca. His chance comes in the afternoon. After another epic lunch, Louise offers to take George out for some fresh air. She says politely that she doesn't think she can manage Bruno as well so the dog stays panting in the sitting room, looking hopefully at the door. Michelle, looking rather nervous, sits in her favourite chair. Rebecca and Laura are on the sofa, Rebecca's legs on Laura's lap. Both are on their phones.

'Girls,' says Nelson. 'I've got something to tell you.'

When Judy and Clough call round to Karen's house on Sunday morning, Annie greets them at the door.

'Mum and Pete have gone to mass,' she says. 'Do you want tea or coffee?'

Both ask for coffee and Judy makes an attempt to chat to Annie in the kitchen.

'I didn't think your mum went to church on Sundays,' she says.

'She doesn't,' says Annie, crashing cups and saucers. 'This kitchen is a mess. I'm always on at Mum to let me redesign it.'

Karen's kitchen looks tidy enough to Judy but it's definitely outdated, with blue Formica cupboards and tiles with embossed vegetables on them. It's friendly though. It reminds her of her grandmother's house.

'They've gone to mass today because they like the priest,' says Annie. 'The one doing Margaret's funeral.'

Karen, when she arrives, confirms this.

'Father Declan has been so nice about the funeral arrangements,' she says. 'We thought we ought to go to church today. It seemed only polite.' Karen is smartly dressed in a black trouser suit with a leopard-print shirt. Maybe she's from the generation that dresses up for church but Judy thinks that Karen is the sort of woman who always takes trouble with her appearance. She remembers Kim Jennings saying that Karen used to look like one of Pan's People. Judy hadn't got the reference at the time but she looked them up and it turns out that Pan's People was the name of a deeply sexist dance group that used to appear on *Top of the Pops*. From old YouTube clips it appears that the dancers specialised in routines that took song lyrics extremely literally, acting out lines like 'clouds in my coffee' whilst wearing very little clothing. Still, Judy assumes that it was meant as a compliment.

'We'll both be at the funeral tomorrow,' says Clough, as they move into the sitting room with their coffees. 'We want to pay our respects. Our boss will be there too, DCI Nelson.'

'Oh, I've heard about DCI Nelson.' Karen sounds impressed. 'It's good of him to come.'

'He wants to be there,' says Judy. 'Margaret is very important to us.'

Karen and Pete exchange a glance. 'Father Declan was asking about readings,' says Karen. 'Annie is going to do one and we were wondering if you'd do the other, DS Clough.'

'What about Luke?' says Annie. 'He might want to do a reading.'

'I've asked him,' says Karen, 'and he doesn't.'

Clough doesn't look at Judy but she knows what he's thinking. He's pleased to be the one who was asked but, at the same time, he wishes that it wasn't him.

'I'd be honoured,' he says.

They talk for a little while about readings and hymns. Clough says that his favourite is 'Amazing Grace', which surprises Judy. Hers is 'How Great Thou Art', a soaring anthem that seems as much about the glories of Nature as it is about God. Karen says that they wanted 'All Things Bright and Beautiful', which Margaret used to sing at school, but that Annie had said that it was 'feudal'.

'All that guff about the rich man in his castle and the poor man at his gate,' says Annie. 'It's obscene.'

Judy agrees in principle but she can't help noticing that Annie seems to wield a lot of power in the family. She asks who else will be attending.

'Luke will be there, of course,' says Karen. 'With Rina, his wife, and their children. They're not staying here though. It's not smart enough for them. They'll book a hotel.'

Interesting, thinks Judy.

Karen and Pete have two sons: Bradley, who is thirty, and Richard, twenty-eight. Bradley is divorced with two small children. Richard, Karen tells them rather proudly, is gay and married to a man called Brian. The brothers will be carrying the offertory gifts at the funeral.

'Of course, they never knew Margaret,' says Karen. 'But they feel as if they do. I mean, she's everywhere.' She looks up at the photograph on the wall.

She's everywhere and nowhere, thinks Judy, like one of the song lyrics so beloved of Pan's People. She wonders what it was like for Bradley and Richard, growing up with this presence in the house, this much-loved ghost.

'Annie's children will all be there tomorrow,' says Karen.

'Matt's working for a building society in Norwich, Sienna's training to be a nurse. Like her mum. And there's Star.' She smiles. Judy remembers that Carol Dunne had also smiled when she mentioned the mysterious Stella who became Star.

'Star's just had a baby,' says Pete. 'A lovely little thing. She wants to bring her to the funeral.'

'It's ridiculous,' says Annie. 'I told Star Ava's far too young. She'll only cry and upset everyone.'

'I think Margaret would have liked it,' says Karen. 'She loved babies.'

Judy wonders who will emerge triumphant from the battle of wills between Annie and Star.

'We've just got a quick question for you,' she says. 'Do any of you have any links with Scarning Fen? It's a nature reserve in Dereham.'

'Scarning Fen?' Pete looks at his wife. 'I don't think so.'

'What's this about?' says Annie. 'Has it got something to do with Margaret?'

Clough and Judy exchange glances. 'It's just a line of enquiry,' says Clough, in the soothing tone that he has now adopted for the Bensons. 'Might well be nothing but we've had some forensic reports back. Remember we thought that Margaret might have been buried somewhere else before the Saltmarsh? Well, the forensics show that she might have been buried near Scarning Fen.'

'Forensics?' says Annie. 'What forensics?' She seems outraged at the thought of such a thing in relation to her dead sister.

Judy doesn't want to go into the wildlife eating the body or the pollen in the nasal cavity. 'Moss,' she says at last. 'Moss that's unique to the area.'

'Any family links?' says Clough. 'Anyone live in Dereham?'

'No,' says Karen, sounding quite shocked even though the town is only about twenty-five miles from King's Lynn. Judy thinks of Tom Henty, 'It's an east Norfolk thing.' And of John Mostyn talking about the Roman port at Caister-on-Sea.

Before they go, Pete asks if they've made any headway with catching Mostyn's killer.

'We're following several leads,' says Clough.

But the truth is that Mostyn's killer seems to have vanished without trace. There's DNA at the scene but that's no use unless it matches some currently held on record.

'If anyone can catch him, you can,' says Karen.

Clough says modestly that the team has a pretty good clearance rate. Karen and Pete look at him admiringly. Annie is frowning in the background.

Ruth and Kate have a good day with Frank in Cambridge. They have lunch in a pub and go on a tour of the more picturesque colleges. Kate is entranced by the chapel at King's College and Ruth allows herself a brief daydream involving gowns and punting and a first in natural sciences. Of course, these places are incredibly elitist but Kate is such a clever girl and she'll be state educated . . .

'Ruth,' says Frank. Ruth comes back to earth. Frank is staring at a stone gargoyle that reminds Ruth of the Lincoln imp but it doesn't look as if he's seeing it. 'What are we doing?'

'Sussing out the right college for Kate?'

'You know what I mean.'

Ruth does know what he means and she very much wants to avoid having this conversation. She looks round for Kate but her daughter is looking up at the vaulted ceiling, apparently deep in thought.

'Do we have to be doing anything?' she says.

'I don't know,' says Frank. He runs a hand through his thick grey hair. He's wearing a heavy jacket and looks bulkier and more dependable than ever. A silver fox, he's often called by viewers of his TV programme. Ruth can't think of an equivalent compliment for a greying woman but there's no denying that Frank is still very attractive.

'I'm nearly sixty,' Frank is saying. 'I suppose I want to know if there's any future in our relationship. There's a job going at Cambridge. A permanent post. I'd like to apply. I could easily settle here. My kids are all grown and transatlantic flights aren't that expensive. It's just . . . Can you ever see us living together? I don't know about you, but I thought the other night was pretty special.'

Ruth cringes slightly at the word and at the memory of hustling Kate out of the house so that she didn't meet a semi-naked Frank on the landing. She glances over to check that her daughter is still out of earshot.

'It was great,' she says, thinking that her own word is also rather unsatisfactory. 'It's just . . . I like being with you but

I don't know if I could live with a man again. I've got used to it just being me and Kate.'

'And Flint.'

'Well, Flint would move in with you like a shot.'

'Thanks,' says Frank, rather wryly. 'What about you?'

'Can't we take it more slowly? After all, we've only just started seeing each other again. And I do like you.' She laughs, embarrassed at how lukewarm that sounds, but Frank takes her hand.

'I like you too, Ruth.'

In Frank's warm west-coast accent it sounds a lot more positive.

He tells it very badly. He'd meant to start with Katie, how sweet she is, how fond they all are of her, but instead he finds himself blurting out that he had an affair with Ruth.

'Ruth Galloway?' says Rebecca, sitting up and putting her phone down. 'The archaeologist woman?'

'It was a long time ago,' says Nelson, not entirely truthfully. 'And it wasn't even a proper affair, well, anyway . . .'

'Katie's your daughter?' Laura is staring at him with a blank, traumatised look that is worse than anything he could have imagined.

'I know it's a shock,' says Nelson. 'But I want you to know that I love you girls – and George too – more than anything.'

'Does Mum know about this?' This is Rebecca, sounding angry which is actually almost a relief.

'Yes,' says Michelle, her voice admirably steady. 'I knew about it from the beginning.'

'And you let Dad see Katie?'

'Well, it's not her fault, is it?'

'Jesus, Dad.' Laura stands up. 'I can't believe this. I thought you were one of the good guys. I thought you two had the perfect marriage. And, all this time it's been a complete sham. You've had an illegitimate daughter. You had an affair. And what about Tim?'

'What about him?' Now Michelle does sound nervous.

'He must have been in love with you. You rang him that evening, didn't you? That's why he came to save us. That's why he died.'

'This isn't about Tim,' says Nelson.

'Yes, Tim was in love with me,' says Michelle quietly, 'but I always loved your father.'

'I know it's hard,' says Nelson. 'But we do still love each other. We're still a family.'

'Bullshit.' Laura, who never loses her temper, yells so loudly that Bruno shoots out of the room. 'We're not a family. I never want to see either of you ever again.'

She storms out of the room and, with an apologetic look at her mother, Rebecca follows her. Seconds later, the door slams and they hear a car starting up. Bruno barks and then the front door opens. Nelson goes to the hall and sees Louise manoeuvring the buggy over the step.

'We've had a lovely walk,' she says. 'Georgie's been as good as gold. Where are the girls off to? Laura looked upset.'

It seems to Nelson that even Bruno is looking at him accusingly.

CHAPTER 23

'Slow down, for Christ's sake. Where are we going anyway?'

'I don't know,' says Laura. 'Away.'

'Well slow down or we'll be away to the next world.'

Laura was always the sensible one, thinks Rebecca, it's very odd to see her like this; face set, hair flying, eyes glittering with tears. But she does slow down slightly.

'That was a shocker,' says Rebecca. 'Did you have any idea?'

'It had crossed my mind,' says Laura. 'I mean, why was Dad always taking Katie to places? He brought her to the house once when Mum was out. I made her a fish finger sandwich. She was very sweet, I have to say.'

'She's our sister,' says Rebecca. 'How weird is that? I can't believe you suspected.'

'Well, I've been living at home for the past year. It's been obvious that something's up. Even you must have noticed.'

Rebecca is stung by the 'even you'. 'You're always imagining things,' she says. 'Remember when you were sure you were adopted because the date on your baptism certificate was wrong?'

'I wish I was adopted,' says Laura, taking a mini-roundabout at speed. 'I wish they weren't my parents.'

'You don't mean that,' says Rebecca, clamping a foot on the imaginary brake. 'Where are we going anyway?' They are on the Fakenham road now, full of Sunday drivers taking their time to look at the view.

'To see a friend in Wells.'

'You haven't got any friends in Wells.'

'He's my meditation teacher,' says Laura. 'I want to talk to him. He's the only person who understands anything.'

'Meditation teacher?' says Rebecca. 'Have you gone a bit nutty since the Tim thing?'

'The Tim thing? Since a man was killed in our house, you mean?'

'Yes,' says Rebecca. 'That. I mean, you finished with Chad and you never go out with any of the old gang.'

Laura is driving more carefully now but her face (so like their mother, whatever she says about being adopted) is set and serious, jaw clenched. 'I have changed,' she says. 'It feels like I've grown up at last. Cathbad says—'

'Cathbad? *He's* your meditation teacher?'

'Yes.' Laura colours slightly. 'He knows a lot about meditation techniques.'

'But he's Dad's friend. And Ruth's.'

'Mum and Dad don't know. They're so tired at the moment that they only think about George. Or this old murder case Dad's working on.'

Rebecca thinks it's a good sign that Laura is now mentioning their parents in an almost normal voice. They are taking the country route, hedges on either side, the occasional glimpse of grey winter fields. As they approach Wells, they see the sea, still exciting even if you've lived within sight of it all your life. Fishing boats are beached on the sand but the tide is coming in, streams becoming rivulets, lapis-lazuli blue in the twilight. It seems like a different world.

'Remember getting the train here when we were little?' says Rebecca, as Laura negotiates the tiny streets. Some of the shops are still open and their family name is everywhere because that other Nelson, Admiral Horatio Nelson, hero of Trafalgar, was born in Burnham Thorpe, near Wells. Nelson's café. Nelson's sweetshop. Nelson's Seaside Souvenirs. Outside a shop called Little Rocks, tiny stones glitter.

'It's a very special place,' says Laura. She even sounds like someone who takes meditation classes.

But, when they park in front of a row of fishermen's cottages, Laura seems reluctant to knock on the door that is painted an unusual turquoise colour.

'Go on,' says Rebecca. 'After all, we've come all this way.' She's curious to see Laura with Cathbad. She remembers him as a slightly oddball friend of her parents. He once gave her a dreamcatcher; she still has it above her bed in Brighton.

Laura gives her a nasty look but she gets out of the car. Rebecca watches as her sister knocks on the door and waits. After a few minutes she knocks again. There's obviously no answer. Laura starts to walk back to the car but then she stops. A man is approaching. He's got long hair. Is it Cathbad? No, this man is younger and, even from Rebecca's viewpoint, seriously good-looking. He stops and talks to Laura. Rebecca can't hear what they're saying but it seems very intense. The man has his hand on Laura's arm, bending his head down to her level. Laura flicks her hair back and laughs, all traces of the heartbroken daughter vanished. Then she comes back to the car. Rebecca winds down the window and Laura hands her the keys.

'Can you drive home? I'm going for a walk with Leif.'

'With who?'

Laura gestures at the long-haired man who raises his hand in a friendly wave.

'You're going off with a complete stranger?'

'He's not a stranger. I met him the other day. He's a friend of Cathbad's. He just came to call but they're out. It's synchronicity.'

'Is that what you call it? What shall I tell Mum and Dad?'

'Tell them I'm dead.' Laura gives her a dazzling smile and turns back to Leif.

It's dark by the time that Ruth gets home from Cambridge. Kate, who has kept up a steady flow of conversation, falls silent just as they take the road across the Saltmarsh. It's as eerie as ever, the raised tarmac with the ground dropping away on either side. One false move and they would find themselves in a ditch, prey to whatever night terrors are roaming the marshes at night. There are no lights, only that faint glimmer out to sea which might be late-night fishing boats, or phosphorescence or something altogether more sinister. Ruth hears Erik's voice, floating back through the years. Fireside tales, from that first dig, when they found the henge.

The Nix were shape-shifters. Sometimes they appear as beautiful women, sitting combing their long blue hair, their voices luring sailors to death on the jagged rocks. Sometimes the Nix is a man playing a violin, a wild tune that the traveller must follow at his peril. The Nix can even appear as a horse, a brook horse it's called in Scandinavian legend, a beautiful animal, snow white or coal black, that appears in the water by a ravine or a waterfall. If you climb on its back you can never dismount and the horse will gallop away to the ends of the earth. On dark nights you can hear the horse's hoofbeats, steady and relentless, carrying its rider to hell.

Ruth turns on the radio, wanting to silence the hoofbeats. The *Archers* theme tune fills the car.

'Can we turn it off?' says Kate from the back.

Back home, Kate panics because Flint is nowhere to be seen but Ruth senses that he's around somewhere. And, sure enough, when Kate goes up to bed, Flint is stretched out on her Hogwarts duvet.

Kate asks for a story and Ruth reads her the beginning of *Northern Lights*, the first book in Philip Pullman's His Dark Materials trilogy. The series appeals to Ruth, as an atheist, but up until now she has thought it too dark for Kate. She needn't have worried. Kate adores it. She lies propped up on one arm, listening intently, stroking Flint with her other hand. And, although it's set in Oxford not Cambridge, Lyra's world with its dining halls, gargoyles, panels and secret doors, recalls their day wandering through King's, Trinity and St John's.

'Can you read some more tomorrow?' asks Kate as Ruth bends to kiss her goodnight.

'If you like.' Ruth foresees that she will be reading His Dark Materials for the next year at least.

Downstairs, Ruth pours herself a glass of wine and tries to settle down to some marking. It's Margaret Lacey's funeral tomorrow and Ruth feels that, as the person to discover her remains, she should go and pay her respects. But it means taking a morning off work and Phil is sure to comment. It also means seeing Nelson, even if only from afar. She wonders whether Nelson has carried through with his plan of telling his daughters about Kate. She wishes that she could ring him to find out. The urge is so strong that, instead, Ruth rings Cathbad. He rarely has his phone switched on but this time he answers immediately. He and Judy and the children have been out today, visiting Judy's parents, and Ruth can hear children's voices and Thing, Cathbad's dog, barking in the background. She feels grateful for her evening peace with Kate, Flint and Philip Pullman.

'I'd like to go to the funeral,' he says. 'I visited the site with Leif a couple of days ago and there's incredible energy there. I'm sure that Margaret's remains were placed there for a purpose.'

'That's what Nelson thinks.'

'I'm not talking about the police case, I'm talking about the deeper significance. Leif says that you found another girl's bones there.'

It's a few seconds before Ruth realises that he's talking about the bones in the cist.

'Yes. I think they're early Bronze Age. An adolescent female.'

'There you are then. Perhaps Margaret was put there for the same reason as the first girl.'

'Perhaps.'

'I'd better go now. Judy's calling. I'll meet you at the church tomorrow.'

Ruth clicks off the phone, feeling more disquieted than ever. She had a breakthrough with the forensics. The unique pollen from Scarning Fen will help the police discover where Margaret was first buried and, with luck, may point them to the killer. But they will be no closer to knowing why they were put in the henge circle in the first place. Perhaps, as Cathbad says, the location itself is the clue. If the circle was a memorial to the Bronze Age girl then maybe Margaret has been placed there for the same reason and by someone who understands the significance. She thinks of the anonymous note that she received. Nelson forgot to take it with him and so it's still in her desk drawer. She gets it out and reads the words again.

You found Margaret. She called from the depths and you answered. Her soul is now at peace. May the Gods of earth, sky and sea bless you, Ruth.

There's no doubt in her mind that Margaret's remains were buried in the stone circle because someone wanted them to be discovered. Did that same person want her, Ruth, to discover them? The words are so like Erik's. So much so that, even though she knows he couldn't have written them, Ruth feels that, in some way, they are a message from him. And Leif had an actual message from him. Erik wants Ruth to travel across the country to a stone circle and pour a libation on the earth for him. For the first time Ruth thinks of the similarity between the Satanic fiddler who played until the wedding guests were turned to stone and the Nix with his violin, luring sailors into the sea. All these stories have the same moral: don't be lured by beautiful music or beautiful women or even a beautiful horse; keep your feet securely on the path; don't be lured by words from beyond the grave.

This isn't getting her anywhere. Ruth puts the note, still in its plastic bag, back in her drawer and clicks on the file marked 'Exam scripts'. But before she has read two paragraphs about 'The role of animal bone in excavations' her mind starts wandering, crossing the halls and cloisters of Cambridge, accompanied not just by Frank but now by Lyra and her dæmon too. The night when Nelson came round to look at the note was the night that she slept with Frank. And now Frank seems to be contemplating a future together. Is this so unthinkable? She likes Frank a lot, he gets on with Kate and Flint, and they all seem to coexist fairly easily. She told Frank that she doesn't want to live with a man again and this is true. But maybe they can go on as they are, with Frank at Cambridge and Ruth at UNN, but on a more formal basis. Marriage? Ruth's mind skitters away from the word as fast as it can. Ruth's mother, Jean, used to bemoan that fact that she'd never be 'mother of the bride' but now Jean is dead and her emotional blackmail can't influence Ruth any more. Though, come to think it, hasn't Erik proved that emotional blackmail can work from beyond the grave? She won't marry Frank but maybe he can be a more official partner, they can spend weekends together, meet each other's families, especially if Frank gets that job at Cambridge.

Ruth closes her file and goes onto the University of Cambridge website. She scrolls through 'Job Opportunities' before she finds it. Lecturer in Early Modern History. It's not her era, she prefers prehistory, the days before the written word made interpretation a matter of scholarship rather than detection. But, two lines below, she sees: Lecturer in Forensic Archaeology. She clicks on the link marked, 'Person Specification'.

CHAPTER 24

The church is full for Margaret's funeral. Nelson, arriving with only minutes to spare, is rather embarrassed to see that a pew has been set aside for King's Lynn CID. He wanted them to have a high-profile presence but there's something shameful about taking a seat in the middle of all the grieving relatives. He hasn't even met Karen Benson, née Lacey, yet. That must be her in the front row, a slight woman in deepest black. The larger woman with her must be her daughter, Annie. He's not sure about the other occupants of the family pews. There's a blonde girl who looks like Michelle's description of her friend Star. She has a baby in her arms which seems rather inappropriate to Nelson. But then he's hardly Father of the Year. Laura didn't even come home last night. She texted Rebecca so he knows she's safe but will his adored first-born ever talk to him again?

Judy and Clough look up as he takes his seat next to them. Clough is clutching a sheet of paper. He has been asked to read and seems extremely nervous about it. Nelson remembers reading the lesson at Scarlet Henderson's funeral, all those years ago. He'd done it very badly, stumbling over the words, unable to look at the little white coffin in front of him. He sympathises with Clough. According to Tanya, who has been left behind to hold the fort, Clough has been having coaching from his actress wife, Cassandra. It doesn't seem to have helped with the nerves. Clough's left leg is jiggling frantically. Judy gives him a slight kick and he stops.

Nelson looks round the church and is surprised, and rather pleased, to see Freddie Burnett and Marj Maccallum sitting near the back. Freddie is dressed in a black suit, his face dark brown from the Canary Islands sun. Marj is wearing a waxed jacket that looks like she uses it for dog-walking. She gives Nelson the ghost of a smile.

And there, even further back, is a face that, even in these circumstances, still gives Nelson a jolt of . . . what? Pleasure? Recognition? Love? Ruth, wearing a dark coat, sitting next to Cathbad, conservatively dressed for once in a black suit. Ted, from the field archaeology team, is with them. Ruth doesn't smile at Nelson but he knows that she's seen him. Two fair heads shine out in the gloom of the church. Maddie, some-where in the middle, and Leif Anderssen, standing at the back, arms crossed. Nelson can't see his expression but he is sure that it is irritatingly enigmatic.

The music starts and the undertakers begin their slow march up the aisle. Another white coffin, another heartbreaking floral arrangement. 'Daughter', it says in chrysanthemums and lilies. Nelson feels his eyes start to prickle. He would give his life for his daughters, all three of them, but will they ever forgive him? In the front row,

Karen lets out a low moan. Her husband puts his arm round her. A man in the row behind sobs into his handkerchief. Is that Luke, the brother?

Nelson remembers the priest, Father Declan, from a previous case. He's white-haired with a soft Irish accent and a deceptively sharp mind. Now Father Declan talks about Margaret. He didn't know her in person, he says, but he knows her from her family's memories, which are golden. Nelson thinks of the girl whom he has only known in death, her smile, her halo of hair. Everyone describes Margaret as a golden girl but gold can be dangerous, as any miner will tell you.

Clough goes up to do the reading, passing so close to the coffin that the lilies leave pollen on his dark suit.

'The souls of the virtuous are in the hands of God, no torment shall ever touch them. In the eyes of the unwise, they did appear to die, their going looked like a disaster, their leaving us like annihilation; but they are in peace . . .'

It's a curiously apocalyptic text for a child's funeral but Nelson is sure that Margaret's going was 'like annihilation' for her family. Clough reads clearly and well, not too fast and not too agonisingly slowly. Cassandra is obviously a good teacher.

'Well done,' he says, when his sergeant sits back down. Clough acknowledges this with a quick smile. The leg jiggling has stopped.

The large woman (it's Annie, he checks the order of service, gold type on white) takes the pulpit for the second reading, that bit from St Paul about love being patient and kind. It always reminds Nelson of Princess Diana's funeral and Tony Blair reading with those curious mid-sentence pauses that made the whole thing sounds like some sort of experimental poetry. He supposes it's fitting. This case started with Diana's marriage and now it ends with echoes of her death. Annie reads well but with a slight irritation in her voice as if it's not *her* fault that people don't understand about love. She steps down from the lectern, not looking at the coffin, and Father Declan moves across to read the gospel. Nelson stands up with the rest of the congregation, the choir singing 'Alleluia'. He watches the altar servers swinging incense and remembers when he used to do that job, the only enjoyable bit about serving on the altar; the rest of the time it was just a question of standing stock-still in a starched surplice. No wonder he stopped after a few years. But, now, the memory comes back to him and he finds himself mouthing the responses and touching his forehead, mouth and chest to indicate that he will live the gospel with mind, voice and heart. Clough looks at him curiously and Johnson, another lapsed Catholic, smiles to herself.

He had forgotten how similar a requiem mass is to the everyday kind. The same prayers and hymns, the same rituals and choreography. Two men with shaven heads who look like they have just been released from prison bring the bread and wine up to the altar. The offertory, it's called. Nelson wonders who the men are. They must be trusted family members if they're allowed a role. When the congregation begins its slow, swaying procession to the altar for holy communion, Nelson, Judy and Clough stay in their seats. Almost all of Margaret's family go up though. Are they still practising Catholics or is this just a nod to the solemnity of the occasion? Nelson thinks of his mother Maureen who, in his mind (and perhaps her own) is the earthly embodiment of the Holy Catholic Church. What would Maureen say if she knew about the rift with her adored eldest granddaughter? Worse still, what would Maureen say if she knew about Ruth and Katie? Maureen has met Ruth once but, for reasons of her own, remains convinced that Ruth is in a relationship with Cathbad, to whom she took one of her rare but unshakable likings. But, if everyone else knows, if there really aren't any more lies in the family, then Maureen will have to be told. She is threatening to come down in the autumn, to see Baby George, whom she persists in believing is an answer to prayer. 'A little boy after all these years. It was the same with you, Harry. How I prayed for a boy after two girls.' Nelson can see his sisters, Maeve and Grainne, rolling their eyes at that one.

More hymns, more prayers. Karen leans forward so that her head is almost on her knees. Annie pats her back. The baby starts to cry and the mother shifts it onto her shoulder. One of the convict men tries to distract it with his car keys. Then, at last, Father Declan is sprinkling the coffin with holy water and the undertakers are bearing it out of the church, followed by Karen, doubled up with grief, and the rest of the family. The daughter, Annie, is scowling, probably trying not to break down. The brother looks in a daze. The blonde girl with the baby smiles at Nelson as she passes.

'Who's that?' says Clough.

'I think she's Karen's granddaughter. She's a friend of Michelle's. From one of those mother and baby groups.'

Clough doesn't comment on the girl's youth and beauty but Nelson knows what he's thinking. In the church porch Nelson exchanges a few words with Freddie and Marj and then walks over to where Ruth and Cathbad are standing, watching the cortège drive away through the rain. He is sure that they are all thinking of the last funeral they attended; Tim borne away by a gospel choir, the Union flag on his coffin.

'Good of you to come,' he says.

'Well, I was there when she was found,' says Ruth. 'It seemed the right thing to do. God, it was so sad though.'

'Sadness is good,' says Cathbad. 'It's our way of saying goodbye.'

Nelson gives him a look but refrains from comment.

'Poor little angel,' says Ted, who is standing with them. 'May she rest in peace.' He makes a sketchy sign of the cross. Is Ted another lapsed Catholic? They're everywhere.

'Are you going to the burial?' Ruth asks Nelson.

'No, that's family only. There's a wake in the church hall but I think I'll give it a miss. I need to get back to the station. Cloughie can go. The family seem to have taken to him.'

'He read well,' says Ruth.

'He's been going to acting classes,' says Nelson.

Ruth smiles, probably thinking of Katie's ambition to be an actress. Rebecca loves acting too. Maybe now the three sisters can meet. If Laura ever comes home again.

Nelson realises that Leif has joined their group. 'Her soul is at peace,' he is saying. 'As the scripture reading said.'

Nelson is irritated. How can Leif know anything about Margaret's soul?

'Good to see you, DCI Nelson,' says Leif. 'How is the investigation going?'

'Very well,' says Nelson. 'We've made some significant forensic discoveries.'

'Science can be fallible,' says Leif.

'Yes,' says Nelson. 'But in my experience it hardly ever is. Excuse me. I'd better get back to work now.'

Ruth watches Nelson run down the church steps, his black coat flapping behind him. She thinks of all the times that she has seen Nelson hurrying, rushing from place to place, pacing the floor of his office like a caged animal, striding off into the distance. She doesn't think that she has ever, once, seen him ambling or strolling or taking an aimless walk just for the pleasure of the view. Even with Kate it's 'I'll race you to the gate' or 'Come on, love, Bruno wants a run.' Even when he's giving her a piggyback he doesn't walk, he canters or gallops. It must be very exhausting, being Nelson.

He was gone so quickly that she didn't have time to ask him whether he had told his daughters about Kate. It's hardly the place for that conversation anyway. People are drifting away now, some following the cortège, some making their way towards the church hall.

'Are you going to the wake?' asks Cathbad.

'No,' says Ruth. 'I have to get back to work.'

Judy comes over, looking very sombre in a dark suit. 'I'm dreading this,' she says to Cathbad. He puts his arm round her. 'Stay strong.' Ruth would punch anyone who told her to stay strong in these circumstances but Judy doesn't seem to mind. In the background, Clough raises his eyebrows at Ruth.

'Hi, Cathbad,' says a voice behind them. 'Hi, Judy.' It's Maddie, in a black coat with a red scarf wrapped round her neck. Her hair is in one of those complicated plaits that Ruth can never master and she looks glamorous and much older than usual.

'Hallo, sweetheart,' says Cathbad, giving her a kiss. 'I didn't know you were here.'

'I'm covering it for the paper,' says Maddie, brandishing a notebook as if in alibi. 'But I wanted to be here anyway. I met the family when I did an earlier piece on them. They're nice people.'

'Did they like your piece?' says Judy, her voice even. Ruth gets the impression that Judy was not a fan of the article.

'Yes,' says Maddie with a tilt of the head. 'I think it's so important for the family's voice to be heard.'

'This must be so hard on them,' says Cathbad. 'The mother looked devastated.'

'Yes,' says Maddie, her voice hardening. 'It's the hardest thing in the world.' Ruth knows that she is thinking of Scarlet, her half-sister. That's not surprising; Ruth has been thinking about her all day too.

'Hallo, Ruth,' says Maddie, suddenly registering her

presence. 'I hear that you found Margaret's remains. Can I have an interview sometime?'

'I don't have anything to say,' says Ruth.

'I'm sure you do,' says Maddie, giving her a look that doesn't seem entirely friendly. 'Are you coming to the wake?' She turns to Cathbad.

'Well, maybe just for a few minutes. Just to keep Judy company.'

But as Cathbad follows his daughter down the steps, Ruth wonders whether it's Judy or Maddie who needs his company more.

Back at the station, Nelson reads the post-mortem report on John Mostyn. Mostyn was killed by a single bullet to the heart. As Clough had said earlier, someone knew exactly where to shoot. Nelson wonders what will happen to Mostyn's body. No requiem mass for him, no police attendance. The only relative they have been able to trace is a cousin in Scotland. Mostyn's body will probably be cremated with only the undertakers present. Perhaps Nelson should go. It seems wrong to have a funeral with no mourners. Especially if Mostyn does turn out to be innocent of Margaret's murder.

Finding Mostyn's murderer looks as if it will be almost as difficult as tracking down the person who killed Margaret all those years ago. No one was seen entering or leaving Mostyn's house but the CCTV from the Canada Estate did capture a figure carrying what looked like a body towards the central fountain. At first Nelson had been excited by this but, in the event, the film was almost useless. The man, dressed in a dark coat with a woollen hat pulled down over his eyes, didn't look up at the cameras once. It was as if he knew where they were. The whole operation – and it did seem like an operation – was almost like a two-finger salute to the police. They couldn't even be sure that the figure on the CCTV cameras was a man, although he certainly seemed large and strong. The small bit of skin that could be seen looked darkish but they couldn't even be certain about that. The clothing gave nothing away; enlarging the image showed that masking tape had been put over the logo on the coat. The assassin had thought of everything. He even took the time to remove the bullet from the back of the sofa to prevent the gun from being identified. Clough's name for Mostyn's killer is Spectre.

The fact remains, though, that John Mostyn was murdered. Was it revenge for his supposed murder of Margaret Lacey, old emotions rekindled by the discovery of her body? But forensic reports on Margaret's remains definitely show the presence of a second person's DNA. Unfortunately, the report says that this second DNA sample has 'degraded', which means that it will be harder to get a match. However, this seems to point to the second DNA being older and therefore potentially that of the murderer. Mostyn's DNA is on the bones, which means that he handled them, presumably to move them to the stone circle, but the second DNA isn't on the bones – only on the rope and the gag – because, of course, the killer never saw Margaret's bones, these emerged many years after death and burial. Unless he was the person who moved them, of course. The killer laid his hands on Margaret's actual living, breathing body. And then she was living and breathing no more. Nelson thinks of the white coffin, the flowers spelling out the word 'Daughter'. He makes a silent vow to the dead girl, the golden girl, the angel.

I will avenge you.

It seems certain that it was John Mostyn who wrote the letters telling Nelson to search in the stone circle. Several drafts were on his computer and, searching his house, police have found scrapbooks full of old newspaper cuttings about both Margaret's disappearance and the death of Scarlet Henderson. 'Scarlet: police find body.' 'Scarlet: a family mourns.' Just reading the headlines brings it all back: the morning when they walked across the marshes at daybreak and Ruth led him unerringly to Scarlet.

In the scrapbooks there are pages from the *Chronicle* showing photographs taken by John Mostyn. There's one of the Saltmarsh: 'Lonely spot where the little girl's body was found'. Was it from the newspaper that Mostyn found out about the first letters? Nelson flicks through the file until he finds the letter sent on 12 February 2016.

Well, here we are again. Truly our end is our beginning . . . You have grown older, Harry. There is grey in your hair and you have known sadness.

It's not just the content that's the same, it's the tone,

the implication that the writer knows Nelson well and is somehow disappointed in him. *You could not save Scarlet but you could save the innocent who lies within the stone circle. Believe me, Harry, I want to help.* He thinks back to the one time he met Mostyn, when PC Campion was guiding him through giving a DNA sample. There had been something odd about the way Mostyn had looked at him, come to think of it. *I know who you are*, is what Mostyn had said. Did Mostyn really know him, in some profound and rather sinister way?

He looks at the last, unfinished, message from John Mostyn.

You have found Margaret but this is only the beginning. It is the best of times and the worst of times. You must finish what you have started. Courage, my friend. Remember we know not the day nor the hour . . .

Is this a threat or a warning? Mostyn was right, finding Margaret's body was only the beginning. They have buried her today so that, at least, is the end of one part of the story. But the second part is more difficult. They must bring Margaret's killer to justice. Did John Mostyn know who that person was? Was that why he was killed?

He hears voices in the incident room and goes in to find Judy and Clough back from the wake.

'It was so sad,' says Judy. 'I think Karen hoped that the funeral would give them some sort of closure but it just seems to have opened up all the old grief. Karen and Annie were both crying when we left.'

'Was the brother there too?' asks Nelson. 'What's his name? Luke?'

'Yes,' says Judy. 'Luke was there with his family who all seem to think they're too good for the Norfolk branch. Annie's grown-up children were there as well.'

'Yes, I think Michelle knows the girl with the baby.'

'Star? I spoke to her. She seems very nice, very together. The headmistress, Carol Dunne, mentioned her the other day. Carol was at the funeral too. And Kim Jennings and her family.'

'The place was packed,' says Clough. 'Lots of press too. I saw Maddie.'

Judy rolls her eyes. 'Maddie seems very in with the family. I left her chatting with Star, holding the baby and all that. Of course, she's not quite as big a favourite as Cloughie.'

Clough is eating some crisps left over from someone's leaving do. 'I'm starving,' he says.

'Wasn't there food at the wake?' says Nelson. He realises that he hasn't had any lunch. Does he dare send Leah, his PA, out for sandwiches?

'There was lots of food,' says Clough, 'but it didn't seem right to eat it somehow.'

'Been to a funeral, Ruth?' says Phil, when he sees Ruth's black trousers and jacket.

'Yes,' says Ruth, letting herself into her office. She has the satisfaction of thinking that she has, for once, completely silenced her head of department.

She shuts the door, hoping that everyone will assume that

she's deep in marking, and gets a rather squashed sandwich out of her bag. She hasn't had time for lunch but she needs sustenance before her three o'clock tutorial. She has just taken a mouthful of ham and cheese when there's a knock at the door. Is it Phil, come to apologise for his gaffe/find out about the funeral?

'Come in,' she says, rather indistinctly.

The door opens and a blonde woman stands framed in a sudden shaft of sunlight. For a second, Ruth thinks of Michelle, that time that she came to the cottage, to beg Ruth to see Nelson on what she thought was his deathbed. It's a memory that never ceases to fill Ruth with mingled guilt and admiration. But then she sees that this woman is much younger than Michelle and is wearing ripped jeans and a hoodie. She can't imagine Michelle in a hoodie.

'You don't know who I am, do you?' says the woman.

'Er . . .' Ruth hesitates, though she is pretty sure that she does recognise this person from some area of her life and it's not an area that makes her feel very comfortable.

'I'm Laura,' says the woman. 'Laura Nelson.'

Ah. That's it. Nelson's daughter. Kate's half-sister. Come to demand Ruth's head on a plate, by the looks of it. Salome in ripped jeans.

'Have a seat,' says Ruth, although Laura has already taken the visitor's chair.

'So,' says Laura, 'you had an affair with my dad.'

Although Ruth is, by now, expecting something of the sort, she is still thrown off guard.

'It was a long time ago,' she says at last.

'I realise that,' says Laura. 'His daughter must be about eight.'

'Eight in November,' says Ruth.

'A Scorpio like Dad. How cute.'

'I'm sorry—' Ruth begins.

'Sorry for what?' says Laura. 'For screwing my dad or getting found out?'

'Both,' says Ruth.

'He's not going to leave Mum, you know.'

'I know.'

This seems to take away some of Laura's aggression. She pushes her hair back and Ruth sees that her eyes are wet with tears. How old is Laura? In her mid-twenties, she thinks. Ruth tries to imagine how she would have reacted, at that age, if she'd found out that her father had a love child. Astounded, mainly, given that her father and late mother were ostentatiously upright Christians. But history is full of virtuous people behaving badly. She doesn't think that, whatever the circumstances, she would have confronted her father's mistress at work. Does this make her braver than Laura, or more cowardly?

'You know,' says Laura. 'I always rather admired you.'

'Really?'

'Yes. You were a professional, obviously really good at your job. Even Dad admired you. And then you were a single mother as well. Of course, I didn't realise that you weren't really single.'

'Oh I am,' says Ruth. 'Believe me.'

'Why should I believe anything you say?'

'That's up to you,' says Ruth. 'I'm sorry you're upset but there's really nothing I can do about it. I've got Kate and she deserves to see her father sometimes. Your dad's not going to leave your mum. She's been terrific about all this.'

'It's just that he lied to us,' says Laura, tears now rolling down her cheeks.

'Talk to him,' says Ruth. 'I do know one thing – he loves you very much.'

'I don't want to see him,' says Laura. 'I would like to see Katie again though. Can I come over one day?'

'Of course,' says Ruth. 'Bring Rebecca too. I'd love her to get to know you both. She'll adore you.'

She doesn't think it's worth reminding Laura that her half-sister's name is Kate.

Nelson stays late at work for a variety of reasons, some only half-acknowledged. There's a lot of work to be done on both murder cases. Michelle's mother is staying so he's not needed for moral support. And he has a superstitious feeling that the longer he stays away, the more likely it will be that Laura will be there when he gets home. She's not answering her phone and, though he's left a stream of texts saying he's sorry and that he loves her, there's been no reply, not even a sad face. Rebecca is back in Brighton and she's not answering his calls either.

Now it's nine o'clock and even Nelson can't see any reason for staying at his desk. He has organised the strategy for tomorrow: more door-to-door near Allenby Avenue, more forensic analysis, more research on the Scarning Fell area, interviews with anyone who saw John Mostyn on the day that he died. He really should be getting home, Michelle will be worrying about him. When his phone rings, he's not surprised to see his wife's name flashing up on screen.

'Hallo, love. I'm just leaving.'

'Harry!' says Michelle. 'The baby's gone!'

CHAPTER 25

'What do you mean?' he says, the room growing cold around him. 'George?'

'No.' Michelle's voice is stifled with sobs. 'Ava. Star's baby.'

Relief makes Nelson feel temporarily light-headed. He sits down at his desk.

'What do you mean, gone?'

'Star's just called me. She put Ava down in her cot and now she's vanished. She's called the police but I thought you should know as soon as possible. I told her you'd help.'

Nelson thinks fast. Control will have put the call through to the duty sergeant. Missing Persons, or Mispers, are assessed according to risk and a missing child is the highest priority of all. Uniform will probably be on the scene already. Sooner or later, Nelson and the Serious Crimes Unit will be involved. It might as well be sooner. Nelson gets the address from Michelle and promises to call round. He's about to ring Judy and ask her to meet him there when he remembers Michael. A missing child case might still be too traumatic for Judy. So he rings Tanya, who is only too pleased to leave whatever she is doing on a Monday night and join him at Star's house on Ferry Road.

Tanya is there when he arrives.

'A missing baby,' she says cheerily. 'Just like old times.'

Nelson does not dignify this with an answer.

The door is opened by Annie, last seen at the funeral. She's still in her smart black dress but her hair is loose and there's a wild look in her eyes.

'The police?' she says. 'The police are already here.'

'We're from the Serious Crimes Unit.' Nelson shows his warrant card.

Annie looks at him properly for the first time. 'So you're DCI Nelson.'

'Yes, and this is DS Tanya Fuller.'

'We're here to help,' says Tanya. 'I'm sure we'll find your baby soon.'

'It's my daughter's baby,' says Annie, but she stands aside to let them in.

The sitting room is large but it still seems very crowded. The blonde-haired girl sits sobbing on a sofa comforted by an older man. There are also two uniformed PCs, looking awkward, and another older man in a black suit.

If Judy were with him Nelson would let her take the lead, comforting Star whilst, at the same time, trying to get all the facts straight in those vital first hours. But he doesn't altogether trust Tanya so he crouches down next to Star and says, trying for his gentlest voice, 'Star. I'm DCI Nelson.

Harry Nelson. Michelle's husband. Do you think you could tell me what happened?'

Star looks at him, her face swollen with tears. 'Is Michelle here?'

'No. But she sent me. I can help you. Can you tell me what happened? Take a deep breath.' He says this because Star looks on the verge of hyperventilating. The man (her father?) pats her back and offers a glass of water. It strikes Nelson as slightly odd that it's not the mother, Annie, who's doing the comforting.

'I came back early from the wake,' says Star, 'because Ava needed a feed. Usually I don't mind breastfeeding in public but I thought it might scandalise Uncle Luke.'

The man in the dark suit, whom Nelson takes to be Uncle Luke, makes a noise of protest but Star carries on. 'I fed her and put her down in her car seat.' Her voice starts to tremble.

'In her car seat?' says Nelson.

'Yes, it doubles as a carry cot.'

'Has that gone too?'

'Yes,' says Star. She looks at Nelson, eyes wide with horror. 'Oh God. Do you think that means someone's taken her somewhere in the car? Somewhere miles away?'

'Easy, love,' says Nelson. 'Let's take things slowly. Make sure we've got all the information. So you put Ava to sleep in her car seat. Where was that? In here?'

'Yes,' says Star. 'I put her down over there, by the French windows.' As if impelled, they all look to the spot where the swagged velvet curtains cover the window. Star continues, 'Then I lay down on the sofa and I went to sleep.' She sobs, doubling up as if in pain. 'I shouldn't have gone to sleep but I was tired. I'd got up three times last night. And the funeral . . . it was so sad . . . I just closed my eyes.' She is sobbing uncontrollably now.

'You're doing well, love,' says Nelson. 'When was this? And was there anyone else in the house?'

His voice seems to calm Star a little. She looks up, wiping her eyes on her sleeve, which is black and slightly see-through, presumably worn for the funeral. 'No. I was on my own. Uncle Luke dropped me off but he went back to Grandma's house.'

Presumably to avoid witnessing any breastfeeding. 'What time was this?' says Nelson again.

'About seven. I fed Ava and put her down. Then, like I said, I went to sleep. When I woke up it was eight. I thought at first that Mum had come back and taken Ava upstairs but she wasn't back and nor was Dad. I rang her and texted her. I was running round the house in hysterics.'

'We came straight back,' says the father. 'And I rang the police.'

'I called Michelle,' says Star, 'because I know you're in charge of the police.'

Nelson half wishes Jo were here to hear this. 'Not quite,' he says. 'But you did well to let me know. We'll find Ava, I promise you. Have you done a proper search of the house? You'd be surprised how many times missing children turn out to be in the house all along.'

'We've searched the house thoroughly, sir,' says one of the PCs, sounding both awed and slightly resentful.

'I looked too,' says Luke. 'I came back with Annie and Dave.'

Why? Nelson wonders. He doesn't seem to be adding much in terms of help or moral support.

'And there's no other member of the family that could have popped in and taken Ava somewhere? For a walk or something like that?'

He looks back towards the window. It's pitch black outside and the wind is getting up but stranger things have happened. He remembers driving Laura round and round the block when she wouldn't sleep. Please God, make her come home tonight.

'We've asked everyone,' says Annie. 'Matt and Sienna have gone home. There's only Mum and Pete and the boys.'

'The boys' must be Karen's children with her second husband. By Nelson's reckoning they must be in their late twenties or early thirties.

'We need to do a fingertip search of the area,' says Nelson. 'Tanya, phone through to control and say that we're treating this as HR and need reinforcements here as soon as possible.' He doesn't want to say the words High Risk aloud, though, with a newborn baby and a cold March night, it's pretty obvious.

He asks the constables if they've spoken to the neighbours and they haven't. 'We'd only just got here when you arrived and we searched the house first.'

'Well, do it now,' says Nelson. 'I want a list of everyone who has been in and out since seven p.m.' He looks back at Star, sobbing on the sofa, now with a parent at either side.

He turns back to Luke. 'Could you show me the layout of the house?' he says.

They search all night. The house and garden on Ferry Street are taken apart and put together again. Police in protective clothing trawl through the nearby gardens, torches illuminating lawns and shrubbery, watched from above by curious and resentful householders. Nelson's friend Jan Adams, the famous police dog handler, arrives with Barney, a distant relative of Bruno. Barney sets off efficiently, nose down, tail waving. Jan is uncharacteristically subdued, calling her dog with strange staccato commands. They all know that a search for a missing baby rarely ends well.

From the start Nelson was worried about the proximity of the river. Is it possible that someone has taken Ava and put her in the dark water, like a horrible version of the Moses story, without the kindly princess pulling the wicker basket to shore? At midnight he calls for the frogmen and they add to the strange procession through the Lynn streets, amphibious creatures who disappear into the depths with barely a sound. But the frogmen find nothing.

At three Nelson goes home for a few hours' sleep. Michelle is up, feeding George, and they confer in whispers because of Louise sleeping next door. Michelle hasn't heard from Laura but she thinks she has been home to collect some of her belongings. Laura is in touch with Rebecca but Rebecca won't say where she is. For her part, Rebecca is angry with her father but this is almost trumped by her curiosity about Katie. Rebecca will come round. Neither of them are sure about Laura who, although generally sweet-tempered, possesses a strength of will that her parents often call stubbornness. Michelle weeps about Ava and holds George so tightly that he squeaks. 'What do you know about the family?' asks Nelson, getting into bed.

Michelle looks at him. 'You can't suspect . . .'

'The family are always the first suspects,' says Nelson, 'you know that.'

'I'm sure there's nothing like that with Star's family,' says Michelle, switching George to her other breast. 'I mean, she's living with her parents. They seem to get on well.' Nelson tries to frame another question, something about Uncle Luke and Star's obvious preference for her father over her mother, but he's asleep before he finds the right words.

The briefing is at seven. The team are all there: Tanya full of satisfaction at being the first DS on the scene, Clough chewing thoughtfully, Judy . . . Nelson finds it hard to read Judy's face. She looks pale but composed enough, making notes in her leather-bound book as she always does. Is she thinking about Michael? Is she resentful that Nelson took Tanya with him last night? Judy gives little away, a quality Nelson admires in principle but, at the moment, he feels that he's had enough of enigmatic women.

'The timeline is quite tight,' says Nelson. 'Star left the wake at six thirty and was driven back to her house by Luke Lacey. He left her at about six forty-five and drove to Karen's house, where the remaining family members were gathering. Star says she fed Ava at seven, then woke at eight

to find that the baby had disappeared. She called her parents at once and they contacted the police. First responders
were there at eight thirty. Fuller and I got to the house at
nine eighteen.'

'What time did Luke get back to Karen's house?' asks
Clough.

'That's something we've got to ascertain today,' says
Nelson. 'We've got to interview all the family members.
We need a clear strategy for this.'

'Luke's the one with the opportunity,' says Clough.
'What's he like?'

'Serious, smartly dressed, possibly a bit strait-laced,' says
Nelson. 'Star said that she didn't want to breastfeed in front
of him. Fuller, you interviewed him. What did you think?'

'He still seemed very cut up about Margaret,' says Tanya.
'As if nothing was ever the same again after she disappeared.
Luke went out searching for Margaret that night. He was
with his dad and it sounds as if the dad completely went
to pieces. That must have had an effect on Luke. And he
seemed a bit negative about Annie, Star's mother. He said
she had anger management problems.'

'Were those his exact words?' says Judy.

'No,' says Tanya, with dignity, 'but he said that she had
a temper when she was a child. They were close then but I
got the impression that they aren't now. I mean, he didn't
come rushing down as soon as the bones were found, did
he? He did mention Star's baby to me, said that Annie had
recently become a grandmother. He said that Star's name
was really Stella.'

'Carol Dunne, the headteacher, told me that too,' says Judy. 'She taught Annie and Luke. Might be worth talking to her again.'

'Do we think this is linked to Margaret in some way?' asks Clough. 'I mean, it's the same family, the day of Margaret's funeral. Seems too much of a coincidence to me.'

Nelson is glad to see that the team have absorbed his suspicion of coincidence.

'Do you mean that the person who killed Margaret also abducted Ava?' says Tanya, ever literal.

'Not necessarily,' says Clough. 'For one thing, they would be getting on a bit now. But maybe this is an attack on Star. When I saw her I did think that she looked a bit like pictures of Margaret.'

Once again, Nelson is impressed. And, now that Clough mentions it, he can see the resemblance. Could there be a link between the two cases?

'We won't rule anything out,' he says, turning to the whiteboard. 'We need to talk to Karen and Pete and to their grown-up sons Bradley and Richard. We need to interview Star's parents, Annie and David, and Uncle Luke. We also need to talk to Star again. Johnson, are you up to doing that?'

'Of course,' says Judy.

'Fuller, you take Luke and his wife. Clough, you talk to Karen's family as you have the rapport there. It goes without saying that time is of the essence. Ava has been missing for twelve hours and she's only twenty-three days old.'

He has no trouble calculating Ava's age because she's only a day older than George.

'The best we can hope is that someone has taken her, for whatever reason, and is keeping her safe,' he says. 'But we need to move fast. I'll brief Superintendent Archer when she comes in and I expect she'll want to talk to the press. Until then, no comment.'

'There are already reporters outside,' says Clough. 'No sign of Maddie yet.'

'She'll turn up,' says Judy.

'No word from Cathbad?' says Nelson. 'No psychic insights for us?' He's only half-joking.

'He was asleep when I left,' says Judy.

Nelson always finds it hard to imagine Cathbad sleeping. Somehow he pictures him hanging from the ceiling like a bat.

CHAPTER 26

Ruth doesn't hear the news until midway through the morning. And her informant is Cathbad himself. She comes back from a lecture to find him waiting outside her office, in everyday clothing of jeans and a heavy jacket. It reminds her of the time – more than eight years ago now – that she arrived one morning to find Nelson waiting there for her with Phil. 'This is Detective Chief Inspector Harry Nelson. He wants to talk to you about a murder.'

'Hi, Cathbad,' she said, unlocking the door with her card. 'What brings you here?'

'Have you heard?' he says. 'A child has gone missing.'

'A child?' For a moment, Ruth thinks of George, that swaddled baby in Kate's arms, her half-brother.

'A relation of Margaret's, the girl whose remains were found in the stone circle. Judy's involved in the search. The child, just a baby, a few weeks old, went missing last night. They're searching the river. Everything.'

'My God,' says Ruth. 'How awful. Can it be related to Margaret in any way?'

'I don't know,' says Cathbad, sitting in her visitor's chair. 'I only had a quick call from Judy. She's interviewing the baby's mother now. Poor thing. She's only twenty-one. Almost a child herself. I know her quite well. She goes to my meditation class.'

Somehow, thinks Ruth, Cathbad manages to know everyone. But then she thinks of the mother, that primal cord that ties you to your baby, long after the physical umbilicus is cut. What must it be like to have your child wrenched from your arms?

'They'll find her,' she says. 'Nelson will find her.' She remembers how her thoughts first went to George and, even now, she can't help feeling that he's in danger in some way. She is surprised how protective she feels towards Nelson's baby, the child who, however innocently, came in the way of their happiness. She wonders what Nelson is feeling as he leads the search for this unnamed infant. Then she sees Cathbad's face and she remembers Michael.

'I'm sorry,' she says. 'This must bring it all back. How's Judy coping?'

'She'll have her professional face on,' says Cathbad. 'She won't show what she's feeling. But yes, the searching, the waiting, it brings it all back.'

'But Michael was found safe and well,' says Ruth. 'Let's hope this baby is too.'

'I pray to the goddess that she is,' says Cathbad. 'But that's not what I came for. I've had a message from Leif. A message from beyond the grave, in a way.'

'You too?' says Ruth, before she can stop herself.

Cathbad looks quite put out. 'What do you mean?'

'Leif met me here the other day. He read me part of a letter that Erik had left for him. It mentioned me and something about dancing with the stone wedding guests.'

'The letter mentioned me too,' says Cathbad. 'Erik said that he was sorry for involving me in his affairs. He wished me well and told me to dance in the stone circle.'

'I think it means Stanton Drew in Somerset,' says Ruth. 'It's a Neolithic stone circle and there's a local legend that the stones represent a wedding party who danced on the Sabbath. I rang you up to tell you about it but you were out. Teaching your meditation class, actually.'

'I know,' says Cathbad. 'Leif's been researching it too. And he wants you and me to go to Stanton Drew with him tomorrow.'

'Tomorrow?' says Ruth. 'Why?'

'I said that it might be difficult for you,' says Cathbad. 'For me too, come to that. Judy will probably be working late. I might have to take Miranda with me.'

'It's a four-hour drive,' says Ruth. 'Why can't we leave it until the weekend?'

'He was very insistent that it has to be tomorrow,' says Cathbad.

Ruth thinks. She has no lectures on a Wednesday and, as a matter of fact, Kate has been invited to a sleepover with her best friend Tasha, a midweek treat for Tasha's birthday. But Leif can't have known this and she resents the high-handed way that he's dictating the terms.

'What's so special about tomorrow?' she says.

'I don't know,' says Cathbad. 'I just have this feeling . . .
I know it's stupid but I feel that Erik wants us to go. I feel
like I've been getting messages from him all day. A black cat
walking across my path, three magpies in the apple tree, a
white feather that just fell into my hand as I walked across
the campus just now.' He opens his palm to show the tiny
feather, downy and pale.

'The baby birds are starting to be born,' says Ruth, 'that's
all.'

'I know what it *is*,' says Cathbad patiently, 'just not what
it *means*.'

'I'll think about it,' says Ruth.

'You do that, Ruthie,' says Cathbad. 'Let me know. I'd
better be going back now. I'm helping in the school library
this afternoon.'

Ruth feels guilty. She never helps in the school, never
goes to PTA meetings, only attends the Christmas fair for
long enough to buy a raffle ticket and to let Kate meet
Father Christmas (Mr Evans, the Year 6 teacher, in a fat suit).
Cathbad, despite his eccentricities, is a valued member of
the school community. She really must try harder.

It's only when Cathbad has gone that she thinks of the
three magpies. Three for a girl.

Judy sees immediately that Star is still in shock. The girl
– she still seems like a girl to Judy – is sitting on the sofa
hugging her knees to her body. She is shaking and her eyes
have a glazed, unfocused look. Her parents hover around
her, clearly not sure what to do.

Judy sits next to Star. She has already worked out what she will say. It is stepping over the line to offer personal information but, in this case, she thinks it is justified.

'Star,' she says. 'I'm Judy. I'm a police officer. We met the other day when I came to talk to your mum.'

Star looks at her. She has large blue eyes that remind Judy, rather disconcertingly, of Maddie. 'Ava's gone,' she says. 'My baby's gone.'

'Star,' says Judy. 'Listen to me. I know what you're going through. My little boy was taken five years ago. It was terrible. I wanted to die. But the police found him. He was fine. He's seven now.'

Star says nothing, picking at a thread on her loose trousers – or are they pyjamas? Judy thinks she hasn't taken her words in but then she says, 'Who took him? Your little boy?'

Judy hesitates, not wanting to give a name, although the case was in the papers at the time. 'Someone who didn't mean him any harm,' she says. 'Someone . . . not quite in their right mind.'

'How did the police find him?'

'By following the clues,' says Judy. Plus guesswork and a handy medium, she adds silently. 'That's why it's important that you tell me everything that you remember about yesterday. Can you do that?'

'Yes,' says Star. Judy can hear Star's parents exhaling with relief behind her. To get them out of the room, she asks for some tea.

'I drink blessed thistle,' says Star. 'It's very good when you're breastfeeding.' Her eyes well up again.

'My partner gave me all sorts of herbal infusions when I was breastfeeding,' says Judy. 'Most of them were disgusting.'

Star manages a watery smile.

'So, can you tell me what happened yesterday, from the time you left the wake?'

'I wanted to come back to feed Ava,' says Star. 'Normally I just feed her where I am but . . . I don't know . . . I felt tired and sad after the funeral. I just wanted to be at home with my feet up. Also stuffy Uncle Luke was there and I'm sure he wouldn't approve of me breastfeeding in public. So I said I wanted to go home and Uncle Luke offered me a lift. He dropped me at the door, wouldn't even come in, so I just came into the sitting room and fed Ava and left her in her car seat, there by the window. Then . . . Oh God . . . I fell asleep.'

She starts to rock back and forth. 'I shouldn't have gone to sleep. It's all my fault.'

'It's not your fault,' says Judy, 'but you've got to hold it together, OK? For Ava's sake. Now, who knew you were at home yesterday evening?'

'Mum and Dad, of course. And the rest of the family. Granny and Granddad, Bradley and Richard.'

'Did you text any of your friends? Send a snapchat?'

'No,' says Star. 'I don't even have a smartphone. I don't approve of them really.'

Once again, Judy is reminded of Maddie, that high-minded earnestness, charming in the young, less charming when it crystallises into prejudice later.

'Do you have a boyfriend?' she asks. 'What about Ava's dad?'

'Ryan? We're not together any more.'

'Does he know about Ava going missing?' Judy thinks of the time when Michael was abducted, the added strain of having his two fathers at her side, all of them suffering in their different ways.

'I think he's abroad,' says Star vaguely. 'He hasn't even seen Ava yet.'

'What about a boyfriend?'

For the first time, some colour seeps into Ava's cheeks. 'There is someone. I met him at my meditation class.'

'You go to meditation classes?'

'Yes, at the community centre. I met Leif there.'

'Leif?' Judy's knows that her tone is too sharp.

'Yes, Leif Anderssen. He's an archaeologist. Do you know him?'

'Slightly. How long have you been going out with him?'

'Oh, we're not going out,' says Star and Judy remembers that this means something different to the new generation. She's vague about the stages: hooking up, hanging out, being exclusive. Judy's thirty-six and she's only had two serious relationships in her life.

'When did you last see Leif?'

'Last week. He met me after my class. We went for a drink but I had to come back because of Ava.'

'We'll need to speak to Leif and any other close friends,' says Judy. 'Can you make me a list?'

'OK,' says Star. She is sitting up and the shivering has stopped. Annie, coming into the room with the tea, says, 'Oh you do look better, sweetheart.' Judy thinks that Annie looks almost as harrowed as her daughter; there are dark circles under her eyes and the tray is jangling in her hands.

Star sips her blessed thistle tea. 'My boobs are agony,' she says. 'I'll have to express.'

'Do you often express?' says Judy. 'Where do you keep it?'

'In the fridge,' says Star. 'Why?'

'Can I see?'

Star's father, Dave, is in the kitchen. When he hears Judy's request he goes to look in the 'small fridge', which is hidden behind one of the shiny units. The other fridge is a massive chrome American affair with a mechanism for making ice. A two-fridge family, thinks Judy.

Dave opens the door and gives an exclamation.

'What's wrong?' says Annie.

'Star's expressed milk. It's gone.'

CHAPTER 27

'So whoever took Ava took the milk too,' says Nelson. 'That means they knew where to look. In this second fridge.'

'It also means they want to keep Ava alive,' says Judy. She's in her car, a few streets away from Star's house. It's a grim, grey day and starting to rain.

'True,' says Nelson and Judy can almost hear him pacing. 'It may be someone who thinks they have a claim on Ava. What about her father?'

'Star says he's abroad. I don't think they're in touch.'

'All the same, check him out. And his family. They might resent the fact that they're not involved in Ava's life.'

'There's another thing, boss.'

'What?'

'Star's been seeing Leif Anderssen.'

'Bloody hell. Seeing as in having a relationship?'

'I don't think it's that serious. But they've been out a few times.' Judy guesses that Nelson will be even less au fait with dating terminology than she is.

'Where did she meet him?'

'At Cathbad's meditation class.'

'Jesus. I don't like this. Leif's a coincidence too far. He was the one who discovered Margaret's body, for God's sake. One of his team, anyway.'

'I know.'

Nelson is silent for a few minutes, then he says, 'Leave Leif to me. You check out Ava's father and his family. Briefing at five.'

'OK, boss.'

He rings off, leaving Judy sitting in her car staring at the rain.

Clough doesn't like to admit it but he misses having Judy alongside him. Karen and Pete seem utterly shell-shocked by Ava's disappearance and he needs Judy's calm empathy to get the interview back on course.

'Who would take a baby?' Karen keeps asking, as if he could possibly know the answer.

'She's only tiny,' adds Pete, unhelpfully. 'A newborn.'

'We'll find her,' says Clough. 'We've got officers from four forces searching. We'll find her. But it would help if you could tell me what happened yesterday. After the . . . after Margaret's funeral.'

'The burial was terrible,' says Karen, 'seeing her coffin go into the ground. It was as if I'd lost her all over again. But, when we got back to the wake, I don't know . . . it seemed almost joyful. All the family together. It's a long time since I've had Annie and Luke in the same room.'

'Why?' asks Clough. 'Don't they get on?'

'They've always rubbed each other up the wrong way,' says Karen. 'Annie's always been a bit prickly and, after Margaret went, it got worse. She's always been a bit . . . well, forceful, and she used to niggle away at Luke all the time, saying that he was lazy, didn't pull his weight at home, that sort of thing. Luke went away to university, got a job in London and hardly ever came home. But, this weekend, they seemed really close, talking together for ages. Don't you think, Pete? You went to the allotment with them on Saturday, didn't you?'

'Yes, they seemed to be like a proper brother and sister for a change,' says Pete. His own sons, Bradley and Richard, quiet men with tattoos and closely shaven heads, sit silently in the background.

'Can you remember what time Star left the wake?' asks Clough.

'I think it was after six,' says Karen, 'because it was getting dark outside. She came to say goodbye. She wanted to get home to feed Ava. She's such a lovely mum.' She dabs at her eyes, Pete pats her on the back, ever the comforter.

'Luke drove Star and Ava home, didn't he?'

'Yes,' says Karen. 'He's got a company car. It's very comfortable.'

'Did you notice what time Luke got back?'

'After Star left, we all decided to go home,' says Karen. 'Annie stayed behind to help clear up. She's good like that. But the rest of us – me, Pete and the boys – came back here.'

'And did Luke join you here? What time was that?'

'I couldn't say,' says Karen. 'We were all sitting in here, looking at photos of Margaret.'

'Had you been home for some time?' Clough knows that he has to persist on this. It's vital to know whether Luke had time to abduct his great-niece before returning to the family party.

'I don't think so,' says Pete. 'I remember Bradley asking Luke if he'd go out and get some more beer. He wasn't drinking, you see.'

'So Luke went out again?'

'No,' Bradley cuts in. 'He was just about to but then Dave got the call from Star.'

'Dave's Star's dad?'

'Yes,' says Karen. 'They've always been close. Dave got the call and he and Annie left immediately. Luke went too, to see if he could help.'

Why? wonders Clough. Why was Luke, the man who hadn't bothered with his family for years, being so helpful all of a sudden? He hopes that Tanya is making some progress with Luke and his wife. They're staying at a smart hotel near the quay. None of this mucking-in sleeping-on-sofas stuff for them.

'Do you have any idea who could have taken Ava?' he asks. 'Any idea at all?'

'I thought Star was making it up at first,' says Bradley. 'She always used to make things up when she was little.'

'How can you say that?' says Karen. 'Annie says that she's devastated.'

'She's a good actress,' says Bradley.

'No one's that good an actress, son,' says Pete.

But Clough is married to an actress and he knows that the audience believe what they want to believe.

Nelson knows that he should stay at headquarters, masterminding the search for Ava. It's not the role of a DCI to go out interviewing suspects. And Leif's not a suspect or even a person of interest. But by early afternoon he's going stir-crazy. The rain has set in and he's pretty sure that Leif won't be doing any digging today. He tells Leah that he's popping out and takes the back stairs to avoid bumping into Super Jo.

Leif is staying in a flat overlooking the river. In fact it's very near the place where Margaret was last seen by Kim Jennings, crossing the narrow bridge in front of the Custom House. There's an entry phone but someone is coming out of the double doors so Nelson just pushes past and barges up the stairs. He always likes to take people by surprise if he can. He hammers on Leif's door, one of four identical doors on the second-floor landing. He has to restrain himself from shouting 'Police!' After a few minutes the door is opened but Nelson does not shoulder his way into the apartment. Instead he stands there, mouth slightly open.

'Dad!' says Laura. 'What are you doing here?'

CHAPTER 28

'Laura,' says Nelson. 'I was looking for Leif Anderssen.' For a moment he really believes that he's come to the wrong address.

'Leif's out,' says Laura. 'He went to the university.'

Nelson stands there staring at his daughter. He tries to frame a question but the words won't come.

'Well, if that's all . . .' Laura goes to shut the door.

'No!' With instinct born of years of policing Nelson gets his foot in the gap. 'We need to talk.'

Laura looks as if she wants to refuse but then shrugs and stands aside to let him in.

The small flat shows signs of dual occupancy. Laura's laptop on the coffee table, her trainers on the carpet. She's wearing leggings and a T-shirt as if she's just been to the gym.

'No uni today?'

'No,' says Laura. 'I start my first placement in a school next week.'

His daughter is nearly a teacher, a role Nelson regards

with utmost respect. He feels the familiar surge of pride in his first-born followed immediately by an equally familiar urge to protect her.

'Why are you living with Leif?'

'Don't tell me you're going to give me a moral lecture,' says Laura. 'You of all people.'

'Laura . . .' He takes a step towards her.

'Don't,' says Laura, backing away. 'I don't want to talk to you.'

'I'm sorry, love. Please come home.'

'No,' says Laura. 'I'm happy with Leif.'

'You don't know anything about him,' says Nelson. 'Do you know why I'm here? Because a baby has been abducted and we've been told that the baby's mother is Leif's girl-friend.' He wants to shock Laura and he succeeds. She stares at him, eyes wide. 'What?'

'She's called Star. Apparently she met Leif at Cathbad's meditation class.'

'Star?' Laura sits on the sofa. 'Oh my God.'

'Do you know her?' Nelson sits next to his daughter.

'Of course I do. I go to the same class, remember?'

But Nelson has never sorted out all of Laura's extra-curricular activities: gym, spinning, weight-training, hot yoga. She always seems to be dashing off somewhere with a mat under her arm. And it turns out that she was dashing off to one of Cathbad's lunatic fringe activities. Now he dimly remembers Laura saying that Cathbad was kind to her after the shooting last year, that he had listened and understood, something to do with them both being scientists. Nelson has never thought of Cathbad as a scientist although, when they first met, he was working at the university as a lab technician.

'Leif's not going out with Star.' Laura sounds quite contemptuous. 'They're just friends.'

'He's got a friend at UNN too,' says Nelson. 'She's called Chloe Jackson and she teaches history.' He thinks that this is news to Laura. Her eyes narrow but she says nothing.

'How do you know Leif anyway?' he asks.

'I met him outside the class one evening,' says Laura. 'Then, that day . . . when you told us . . . I went to talk to Cathbad but he was out. Leif was there, he was calling on Cathbad too. We went for a walk and we talked. He was kind, he listened.'

Then he lured Laura back to his flat, thinks Nelson. That good listener act is the oldest trick in the book.

'I need to interview Leif,' says Nelson. 'When's he back?'

'In an hour or so,' says Laura. 'He's organising some sort of trip for tomorrow.'

'Tell him to call in at the station later today,' says Nelson. 'It's important.'

'OK.' Laura isn't looking at him.

'Look, love,' says Nelson, trying for the tone that often works with Laura, though rarely with Rebecca. 'I'm just thinking about you. I'm worried about you. Mum is too.'

Laura turns towards him, her eyes full of tears. 'How is Mum?'

'She's OK. But she misses you. George does too.'

'Rubbish.' But this draws an unwilling smile. 'He only worries about his next feed.'

Nelson thinks about Ava. Is she missing her mother? Is she thinking about her next feed, delivered by the person who stole expressed milk for her?

'Bruno really misses you,' he says. 'He's pining.'

'Stop trying to stop me being cross with you.'

Nelson reaches for Laura's hand. 'I'm sorry. I really am. If I could change the past, I would.' But, even as he says this, he wonders if it's really true.

Laura pulls her hand away. 'I went to see Ruth yesterday,' she says, in a tight, hard voice that he hasn't heard before. 'At the university.'

'You did?'

'Yes. I was angry with her. I wanted to tell her that she'd broken up our family. But, when it came to it, I couldn't. She's just an ordinary woman. She said that she always knew that you weren't going to leave Mum. I actually felt a bit sorry for her.'

Nelson says nothing. Laura is having spiritual guidance from Cathbad, she's visiting Ruth at the university. It's as if all the separate areas of his life are suddenly colliding, making him feel jolted and uneasy.

'I'd like to see Katie again,' says Laura. 'I remember the time you brought her to the house. I didn't realise why you were babysitting Ruth's child. I must be so stupid.'

'Of course you're not stupid. You're a hundred times cleverer than me.'

'That's not difficult,' says Laura. Then, softening slightly, 'Katie was sweet though.'

'I think you'd like her,' says Nelson carefully.

'Ruth told me to talk to you,' says Laura. 'She was quite nice really.'

'Come home, love,' says Nelson. 'Then we can talk. All three of us. You can't stay here. I don't trust this Leif. I knew his father and he was a very strange character.'

This is a mistake. Laura stands up. 'You don't know anything about Leif.'

'He's too old for you.' He falls back on an old favourite.

'He's only thirty-five. Anyway, age is just a number.'

'Is that one of Cathbad's pearls of wisdom?'

'Get out,' says Laura, flaring up. 'Go away and leave me alone.'

'Please, love—'

'Just go,' says Laura. 'I never want to see you again.'

Tanya is finding Luke and his wife, Rina, rather hard going. She interviews them in their room at the charming Bank House Hotel which makes the occasion seem oddly intimate. Tanya sits in a chintzy armchair while the Laceys perch on the bed. She is distracted by an open suitcase on the floor. Why can't they hang their clothes up like civilised people? She and Petra have a wardrobe each.

Luke seems very nervous and keeps getting up to pace the room, once knocking his head quite hard on the sloping ceiling. Rina seems calm, almost too calm. She's a poised, elegant woman who, in Tanya's estimate, is about five kilos underweight.

'Can you tell me what happened after you left Star at her parents' house last night?' Tanya asks Luke. 'Any detail, however seemingly insignificant, might be important.'

'I saw her inside the house,' says Luke, fiddling with the tassels on one of the numerous cushions on the bed. 'Then I went back to Mum's house. I knew everyone was meeting up there.'

'Why didn't you go in with Star?' asks Tanya.

'I got the impression she wanted to be alone,' says Luke. 'She's very self-contained although she's so young.'

'Did you see anything unusual near the house? Any cars parked outside it?'

'No.' Fiddle, fiddle, fiddle. 'I don't think so.'

'What did you do next?'

'Drove straight to my mum's house.'

'What time did you get there?'

'About seven, I think.'

'Who was there?'

'Mum, Pete, Bradley and Richard. Annie and Dave arrived at about the same time as me. They'd been clearing up in the church hall.'

'What happened next?'

'Bradley wanted me to go out for some beer. I thought he'd had enough but I said I would.'

'Nothing's ever enough for Bradley,' says Rina. 'He's a borderline alcoholic.' Tanya thinks this is interesting. She gets the impression that Rina is not close to her in-laws.

'But, then, just as I was leaving, Dave said he'd had a call from Star saying Ava was missing. He and Annie left immediately. I followed them in my car.'

'Why?' says Tanya.

'Why?' Luke looks bemused.

'Yes, why? What could you do?' Tanya realises that sounds rather rude and amends it to, 'Weren't her mum and dad enough?'

'I thought they might need to someone to drive somewhere,' says Luke. 'Talk to the police, that sort of thing.'

'Luke's a professional, you see,' says Rina. 'He's used to talking to people in authority.'

But Dave is a teacher and Annie is a nurse, thinks Tanya. Both highly responsible, professional jobs. Why would they need Luke to liaise with the authorities?

'At what point did you call the police?' Tanya asks.

'Almost immediately,' says Luke. 'Star was hysterical. Annie and I had a quick search of the house. It was obvious the baby wasn't there. Dave called the police. They came very quickly,' he adds, in a conciliatory tone.

'Do you have any idea who could have taken Ava?' Tanya addresses both of them.

'No,' says Luke. 'Who would do a thing like that?'

'That's what we're trying to find out,' says Tanya, hoping that she doesn't sound too pompous. It's hard work, being nice to irritating people.

Ruth, popping into the cafeteria at lunchtime, is surprised to see a long blond ponytail in the queue in front of her.

'Leif! What are you doing here?'

'Ruth!' Leif turns in apparent delight. 'How are you?'

'Fine,' says Ruth, conscious of looking sweaty and untidy in her crumpled shirt and dark trousers. It's cold and rainy outside but, for some reason, the temperature in the Natural Sciences block is tropical.

'Did Cathbad mention tomorrow to you?' says Leif. 'Visiting Stanton Drew.'

'Yes,' says Ruth. 'It seems a long way to go.'

There's a hiatus while Leif pays for his lentil salad and carrot juice and Ruth tries to hide the fact that she's having a ham and cheese toastie. While Ruth's waiting for her food Leif turns to her with the full force of his blue-eyed charm; so like Erik, so horridly, wonderfully like Erik. 'Please, Ruth. I can't explain but I really think it's important that we do this tomorrow. Bring your daughter if you like. Surely the school will understand if it's educational?'

Shows how much you know about the British education system, thinks Ruth, collecting her toastie, steaming gently in its greaseproof paper. 'Kate's been invited on a sleepover,' she says.

'Well, then,' says Leif, spreading his arms wide. 'What's stopping you?'

And Ruth finds herself agreeing to go to the stone circle.

The briefing is a rather tense affair. They all know that time is running out. The search parties have found nothing and the press are camping outside the police station. Jo Archer keeps reminding Nelson that the eyes of the world are on them which, even if not strictly true, doesn't help with the stress levels.

'It's such a narrow window of opportunity,' says Nelson. 'Star went into the house at six forty-five, Ava was gone by eight. Someone entered the house, probably with a key – there's no sign of forced entry – took Ava and the milk and left. It must have been someone who knew the place well. Is there anything from the neighbours? Any CCTV?'

'No.' Judy is flipping through the reports. 'Nobody saw anything unusual and none of the houses have CCTV. It was a dark evening. Probably everyone was inside watching TV.'

'What about Luke?' says Nelson. 'He's still our best bet. He could have waited in the car and come back when Star was asleep.'

'But where would he put her?' says Tanya, managing to make it sound as if Ava were an inconveniently shaped parcel. 'He's staying in a hotel.'

'Bradley – Karen and Pete's son – thought that Star might be making it up,' says Clough. 'Is it worth following up that line of enquiry? Could Star just want to be the centre of attention? A bit like what's-it-called . . . Munchausen's.'

Nelson is impressed that Clough has remembered the name of the syndrome where a person invents medical symptoms in order to gain sympathy and attention. He turns to Judy. 'What did you think of Star? Is this possible?'

'It's called Facititious Disorder now,' says Judy. 'I suppose it's possible. After all, yesterday was all about Margaret, not Star. She might want to be back in the limelight. But I could swear that she's genuine. And Star's been a devoted mother up until now. I spoke to her health visitor.'

'Michelle said the same,' says Nelson. 'She said that Star seemed to really enjoy being a mum. What about the dad? Ryan? Any luck there?'

'He's in the States,' says Judy, 'working at Camp America. I saw his parents. They seemed very shocked. They knew about Ava but I don't think they've seen her yet. I got the impression that they don't want to be involved. What about possible boyfriends? Did you contact Leif Anderssen?'

'I called round but he wasn't in,' says Nelson. 'I left a message for him to come into the station later.'

'The archaeologist bloke?' says Clough. 'Could there be a link there?'

'It's a coincidence,' says Nelson, 'and I don't like coincidences. But it's hard to see why Leif would snatch Ava. And, like Fuller said earlier, where would he be keeping her?'

'What about Star's mother, Annie?' says Judy. 'She seemed really distressed today. Could she know something?'

'Karen said that Annie was a difficult character,' says Clough. 'And Pete, her stepfather, said the same. He spent a lot of time with Annie and Luke at the weekend apparently. On his allotment.'

'Pete has an allotment?' says Judy.

'Yes,' says Clough. 'Why? Lots of people do.'

Judy is flipping through her notebook. 'When we went to see Karen and Pete to ask about Scarning Fen, did either of them say that they had links to the area?'

'No,' says Clough. 'What are you getting at?'

'When I interviewed Steve and Alison Jennings, Kim's parents, they said that Pete used to live "out Swaffham way". I made a note. Look.' She pushes the page, filled with her small, neat handwriting, towards Clough. 'Swaffham's near Scarning Fen. Why didn't Pete say that when we asked him? And he's got an allotment. What if he had an allotment when he lived in Swaffham?'

'And you think he killed Margaret and buried her in his allotment?' Clough's voice is rising.

'Well, it's possible,' says Judy, rather defensively. 'Pete knew Karen when Margaret went missing, the two families were friends.'

'He killed her daughter and then married the mother?'

'It is possible,' Nelson cuts in. 'And the Swaffham link is interesting, especially the fact that Pete Benson didn't mention it when interviewed. But now our focus has to be on Ava. She's been missing for almost twenty-four hours now.'

He doesn't turn to look at the clock but everyone is conscious of the second hand moving towards six.

CHAPTER 29

Nelson almost doesn't expect Leif to obey his summons but, when he comes out of the briefing, he is told that he has a visitor in the interview suite. He's grateful to Tom Henty for putting Leif into this room because it has a two-way mirror. He spends a few minutes observing Leif who is sitting, seemingly completely at ease, in one of the armchairs (this is a so-called 'soft interviewing space' which means that it has IKEA furniture and a plastic fern). Leif is leaning back, legs crossed at the ankle, staring at the ceiling. He isn't checking his phone, as most people do now whenever they have an off-duty moment. He doesn't look nervous or ill-at-ease even though he's in a police station. He is smiling gently, hands relaxed on the chair's chintz arms. Leif is taller than his father and more heavily built. Nelson supposes that he's good-looking, although that long hair is ridiculous and his eyes are too pale and he doesn't blink enough. Still, he is pretty sure that his daughters would say that Leif is 'fit'. Well, one of his daughters clearly does think so. He pushes open the door.

'DCI Nelson.' Leif smiles in apparent delight but doesn't get up.

'Good of you to come in,' says Nelson, not smiling back.

'Laura passed on your message,' says Leif. 'It sounded urgent.'

Nelson grinds his teeth at the mention of his daughter.

'It is urgent,' he says, taking the armchair beside Leif's and moving it back slightly. 'We're conducting an inquiry into a missing child. I'm sure you've seen it on the news.'

'I don't follow the news,' says Leif. 'I try to keep myself free from negative influences.'

'Bully for you,' says Nelson. 'I'm a policeman and negative stuff is my job. I believe that Star Simmonds is a friend of yours.'

'I know her a little,' says Leif. Is it Nelson's imagination or does the Vedic calm seem to falter slightly?

'Well, it's her child that has gone missing. Ava was snatched from Star's parents' house yesterday evening.'

'Laura told me,' says Leif. 'Poor Star. How terrible. Do you have any idea who could have done it?'

Nelson ignores this. 'Your name has come up as a possible boyfriend of Star's,' he says. 'And we need to check out all her close associates. Can you tell me how you met her?'

'I went to see Cathbad after his meditation class,' says Leif. 'I wanted to talk to him about my dad. I'm working through my relationship with Erik and I knew that he and Cathbad were close. Star was there, asking Cathbad some questions about meditation. I was impressed with her open mind.'

I bet you were, thinks Nelson. 'This must have been just

after Ava was born,' he says. 'After all, she's only twenty-three days old.' Once again, the number comes automatically.

'Yes, I was impressed with that too. The fact that she was going to classes so soon after having a child.'

'So you found Star impressive,' says Nelson. 'Did you go out with her?'

'Once or twice. Just for coffee and a chat.'

'Did you ever meet Ava?'

'She had the baby with her, of course. She had her in one of those . . . what's the word? . . . baby slings.'

'Did Star ever say that she was worried about anything? Anyone threatening Ava?'

'No. She seemed delighted with the whole experience of motherhood.' This is pretty much what Michelle said, but without Leif's smug expression. Nelson wonders whether Leif's amorous intentions were thwarted by the presence of the baby in the sling. Maybe that's why Leif moved on to Laura. Be careful, he tells himself. Hitting a member of the public is never a good idea.

'When are you going back to Norway?' he asks.

'At the end of the month,' says Leif. 'The dig should be finished by then. We've had some very interesting results from the bones in the cist. They're the remains of a young girl. I'm hoping to commission a facial reconstruction.'

Nelson is rather shaken by the fact that another young girl was buried in the circle on the beach. But Leif just looks, if anything, even more pleased with himself.

'Don't leave the country without letting me know,' says Nelson, standing up to show that the interview is over.

'I won't,' says Leif. 'Good luck with the search. I will pray to the goddess for Ava.'

'Very kind of you,' says Nelson. Then he leans in. 'If you hurt my daughter,' he says, 'I'll kill you. Understand?'

Nelson tells the team to get a good night's sleep. 'There's nothing more we can do today. The search teams will keep going all night. I need you all back here tomorrow in top form.' Judy considers staying at work until the kids are in bed. All that bath, story, bedtime romping is so exhausting. But she also longs to see her children, to hold them tight and feel their solid little bodies against hers. The memories, the ones that have been hovering ever since she heard that Ava was missing, are threatening to engulf her. That terrible moment when her childminder turned to her and said, 'He's gone . . . Your friend came to pick him up . . .' The dark days afterwards, the waiting, the dreadful draining away of hope. Cathbad had saved her then. The least she can do is be at home for bath time.

She gets back to find a cosy domestic scene. Cathbad cooking vegetarian spaghetti carbonara and three of his children sitting at the kitchen table: Michael, Miranda and Maddie. Thing is watching hungrily from under the table.

'Hi, Judy,' says Maddie. 'Just in time. Dad's such a good cook.'

'Maddie's here,' says Miranda, gazing adoringly at her half-sister.

'So I see,' says Judy, searching in the fridge for wine. She suspects Maddie's motives for this visit and doesn't want to spend the entire evening avoiding the subjects of Ava or Margaret. Also, it's very rare for Maddie to call Cathbad 'Dad'.

Judy splashes wine in two glasses and passes one to Cathbad.

'Tough day?' he says, beating eggs.

'Yes,' says Judy. 'I'll tell you about it later.'

'We're going to Granny and Granddad's tomorrow,' says Michael who, as ever, is watching Judy intently.

'Are you?' says Judy, taking a gulp of native Norfolk Winbirri white. 'Why?'

'I'm going to Somerset with Ruth and Leif Anderssen,' says Cathbad. 'Apparently Erik wrote a letter to Leif before he died. In it he said that he wanted us all to meet at a stone circle called Stanton Drew. Leif wants us to go tomorrow. I asked your mum and dad if they would pick up the kids. They were delighted. They'll take Thing too.'

Judy bets they were thrilled to be asked. Her parents live locally and are devoted grandparents. Even so, she feels slightly aggrieved that Cathbad hadn't mentioned his plans to her.

'I only decided today,' says Cathbad, reading her mind. 'I thought you'd be busy at work.'

'It's pretty frantic,' says Judy. 'Ava's still missing.'

'Have you got any leads?' asks Maddie, turning in her chair. 'Can I have some wine?'

'Sorry,' says Judy. 'I forgot you were grown-up.'

Miranda laughs delightedly.

Cathbad serves the pasta, getting all that last-minute egg

and cheese stuff just right. There's an appreciative silence at the table as people eat, some more successfully than others. Cathbad, who has lived in Italy, twirls like a native, Michael cuts his up and Miranda makes slurping sounds that are only just permissible in one under five. Thing takes up his position beside Miranda, licking his lips.

'How are you getting on with the Margaret Lacey case?' asks Maddie, putting a tiny piece of pasta into her mouth. Judy never thinks that she eats enough.

'The missing child is taking precedence,' says Judy.

'Aren't they linked?' says Maddie, eyes wide. 'After all, Ava is Margaret's great-niece.'

Judy has never thought about the relationship in this way before.

CHAPTER 30

It's only when Ruth sees the jeep-like Honda that she realises that Cathbad is driving. She had assumed somehow that Leif would be at the wheel but, come to think of it, she has only ever seen him on a bike. She always feels that Cathbad, too, is more comfortable on two wheels, better still on two feet. He's a dreamy and erratic driver. Judy, on the other hand, loves cars and always drives when the family are together. The Honda is the family car. Judy must have taken the sportier Fiat to work.

Ruth has already dropped Kate at her childminder's house. Sandra will take her to school. Cathbad must have picked up Leif on his way home from the school run. Ruth is waiting for them and comes straight out of the house. Leif gets out of the car, all the same.

'So this is the famous cottage,' he says. 'What a stunning situation.'

Actually, it's a grey and misty day, the marshes and the sea lost in a hazy, mutable light. There's something about Leif's tone that Ruth doesn't quite like. Why is her home 'famous' to him? She remembers the last time that Erik visited her, the mad chase across the dangerous no-man's-land, a chase that ended in death.

'It's better when you can see the view,' she says, opening the back door.

'Would you prefer to sit in the front?' asks Leif.

'No, this is fine.'

At least, in the back, she won't have her foot clamped on a phantom brake.

There's actually something quite pleasant about sitting in the back. It's like being a child again, the fields and houses sliding past, the sense of being taken rather than being in charge of the journey. She has to resist the temptation to ask if they are there yet. Cathbad and Leif are talking about stone circles, ritual and sacrifice, the cycle of the seasons, the need for state funding of archaeological digs. Ruth closes her eyes.

It's a long journey though. Right across England, from coast to coast. 'Just think of the journey from Wales to Stonehenge,' says Cathbad helpfully, 'and we're not dragging massive megaliths behind us.' Ruth knows that the so-called Stonehenge bluestones were transported from Wales to Wiltshire and, whilst this was undoubtedly an impressive and mysterious achievement, she doesn't feel like discussing Neolithic building methods now. She feels tired and slightly sick, possibly the effects of Cathbad's motorway driving.

They stop for coffee and sandwiches on the M42 near Birmingham. Ruth feels slightly revived and texts Shona:

'On an adventure with Cathbad. Scary!' Leif, unable to find food pure enough for him in a motorway service station, is drinking what he says is pea protein from a flask. Cathbad eats an M&S sandwich with apparent relish. Ruth remembers a trip to Blackpool with Cathbad and Kate, six years ago. They stopped at Preston Services and Kate had wanted to ride on the Thomas the Tank Engine machine over and over again. The maddening theme tune comes back to her now and the memory makes her smile even though the holiday itself had been at best stressful and, at worst, terrifying.

Cathbad is telling Ruth an alternative Stanton Drew story. 'It's said to be impossible to count the stones,' he says, 'because they're of the devil's number. Or else no number at all. If you succeed, you drop down dead. Stone dead.' He grins and takes a swig of mineral water.

'Well it is a big site,' says Ruth. 'Bigger than Stonehenge and only slightly smaller than Avebury. Between twenty-five and thirty stones, I read.'

'You see,' says Cathbad. 'No one knows the exact number.'

It is quite exciting as they get nearer the site, the first glimpse of the sea, the picture-perfect villages, the sudden sighting of a lichened stone looming over a thatched roof. They park by the church and follow the signs 'to the stones'.

The day is still grey and overcast. The stones, when they appear, seem sullen and menacing. They are oddly shaped, bulging as if with some secret stone pregnancy, some upright, some recumbent. It's hard to get a sense of a circle, or even of a pattern. 'It used to be thought that the number and positioning of the stones corresponded to the

Pythagorean planetary system,' says Cathbad. 'The three circles correspond to the solar, lunar and earth cycles.'

'I thought you said it was impossible to count them,' says Ruth. 'And there's no sun today.' She is finding Cathbad rather irritating; he has donned his purple cloak and frequently pauses – head up, eyes closed – to 'absorb the energy of the place'. Leif is walking on ahead. He seems preoccupied, constantly checking his phone, more like a bored teenager than a spiritual seeker after truth.

The English Heritage site described the largest collection of stones as The Great Circle but, even when you are standing in the centre, it's still hard to see the shape. You probably need to see it from above, thinks Ruth, which gives rise to one of the many unanswered questions about stone circles: how did prehistoric builders manage to create a design that was best appreciated from the air? If you discount the alien theory – which Ruth does – then you are left with Cathbad's planetary system, which is unsatisfactory in its own way. Henges are also sometimes called stone gallows. The theory is that the stones form some sort of portal, either for use in some ancient ritual or, for the more fancifully inclined, a gateway between life and death. It's said that if you pass through the gateway, on the right hour of the right day, then you will see death itself.

Cathbad now has his hand on one of the stones and his face to the sky. Ruth reaches out to touch one of the megaliths. It's scratchy with lichen but oddly warm, a disconcerting sensation given the coldness of the day. Ruth snatches her hand away and, when she turns around, she has the oddest feeling that the stones have moved closer. A mist has blown in from the sea and she can't see Cathbad or Leif. For a moment it feels as if she's completely alone, at the centre of the circle, watched by its silent guardians.

'Cathbad?' she says, hearing her voice sounding high and rather panicky.

'I'm here.' He is much closer than she had thought, materialising between two boulders, his cloak bright against the grey. Irritation forgotten, she has to resist an urge to grasp hold of Cathbad's arm.

'Where's Leif?' she says.

'Probably gone to look at the other circle,' says Cathbad. 'There's a kind of avenue to the left.' He raises his voice. 'Leif!' His voice echoes against the silent stones.

'Where is he?' Even Cathbad sounds quite rattled. He calls again. 'Leif!'

'I'm over here.' Ruth can't tell where the voice is coming from. She squints at the stones forming the Great Circle. Have they moved again? Will they be trapped, unable to escape until the devil plays his wild tarantella? She can hear seagulls calling, high above the clouds, but otherwise everything is silent. Beside her Cathbad says, 'Leif! Where are you?' Then, suddenly, the mist clears and a figure is walking towards them. No, two figures. Three. Leif is in front, followed by a woman with long hair that flows back behind her.

The woman is carrying a baby.

Carol Dunne is teaching but the receptionist says that she will fetch her. Judy waits in the area with the coloured mural which, on closer inspection, depicts St Paul's and the surrounding countryside, the school a blob of red against yellow houses and green fields, the sea – or the sky – a line of blue on the horizon. On the opposite wall there's a display of photographs of 'our school family'. The road-crossing attendant with her lollipop is at the centre. There are also certificates declaring that the school is green, accessible and anti-bullying. The list of safeguarding officers adds a more sober note but Judy is pleased to see that it's up to date.

Carol arrives, as sunny and youthful as ever in a green dress and flat brown boots.

'Sorry,' she says. 'The Year 4 teacher is off sick and I'm taking her class today. I can only spare you five minutes, I'm afraid. The teaching assistant's in there but they're quite challenging today. It's the rain. Wet play and all that.' It has been drizzling all morning but now the rain is hammering against the skylight above their heads. As Judy follows Carol to her office, she sees several buckets placed at strategic intervals.

'Maintenance never ends,' says Carol. 'Sometimes I feel more like an odd-job man than a teacher. It's not what I came into the profession for.'

'I just wanted a quick word,' says Judy, taking the visitors' chair opposite Carol. The office has a view over the wet playground. A soggy banner exhorts pupils to 'Learn Well and Play Well'.

'You've heard about Ava Simmonds going missing?' says Judy.

'Yes,' says Carol. 'I heard it on the news this morning.

What a terrible thing. As if that family hasn't suffered enough.'

'I know you used to teach Star,' says Judy. 'Or Stella as she was then. We're following up every avenue in the search for Ava and one of the family made a remark about Star which I'd like to follow up.'

Carol says nothing but she is looking at Judy intently.

'One of Star's uncles suggested that she might have made the whole thing up,' says Judy. 'To gain attention, perhaps because the previous day – the funeral – had been all about Margaret. I just wanted your opinion on this theory.'

Carol holds up her hand, like the road-crossing attendant in the photograph.

'Absolutely not,' she says. 'Stella, Star, wasn't like that at all. She wasn't the most conventional child but she was actually very firmly rooted in the real world. You often do get children who lie, who embellish the truth, who crave attention, but Star wasn't one of them. She was confident, happy in herself.'

Judy has only known Star in time of crisis, but, even so, she recognises this image. Star has obviously embraced being a single parent with clear-sightedness and practicality. She attended mother and baby groups, she expressed her milk, she drank blessed thistle tea. She is living at home with both her parents in attendance. It seems very unlikely that she would harm her precious baby just to gain attention.

'In cases where children do make up stories,' says Carol, 'it's often to make themselves feel safe. If you are telling a story then you're in control of the narrative, you're empowered.'

'My son likes making up stories,' says Judy. 'Not about himself but about made-up characters. My partner says that storytelling is an essential human activity.'

Carol smiles. 'Your partner is right. Perhaps they . . .' Judy can see Carol hesitating over the pronoun, 'could come in to one of our storytelling sessions in Book Week.'

'I'm sure he'd love to,' says Judy.

'Funnily enough,' says Carol, 'I was thinking of Margaret just then. Margaret sometimes used to tell stories, part truth, part embellishment. When she went missing some of her friends said that Margaret had told them that she had a boyfriend in London. The police investigated and there was no truth behind it at all. But the fact that she told that story made me wonder . . .'

She is silent so long that Judy prompts, 'Made you wonder what?'

'As I said, telling stories makes us feel safe. Usually, as your partner says, it's a benign activity that helps us make sense of the world but sometimes . . . sometimes you have to wonder why a child feels unsafe. Inventing a boyfriend, for example, could be a way of saying that "I'm OK, someone loves me, someone will protect me."'

'You said that everyone loved Margaret.'

'Yes, she was very popular. But, after she disappeared, I did wonder if she was completely happy at home.'

'You never met her father, Bob, did you?'

'No,' says Carol, 'and I'd be very wary about throwing out

allegations of abuse, especially as the poor man is dead. But there's no doubt that shame is often at the bottom of persistent lies.'

'Shame?'

'Victims often feel shame,' says Carol. 'Shame, guilt, anger and fear. You asked me if Star fitted the profile of a compulsive liar. I would say absolutely not. But I can't say the same about Margaret. Or even Annie. I taught her too, remember? Just briefly, before I left the school.'

'Annie? Star's mother?'

'Annie was a bright girl,' says Carol, 'and, of course, she suffered a lot. Her sister disappearing, her parents breaking up. She reacted by being permanently angry. It sometimes takes children like that but I've often wondered if there could have been more going on beneath the surface. Annie and Luke both did well at school and I've heard they're happily married now but maybe there was damage that we didn't see, or weren't trained to see.'

Judy thinks about the conversation as she drives to Star's house through the rain. Is it possible that Margaret was abused and, if so, does the focus need to come back to the immediate family? She still has her suspicions about Pete. He seems nice enough, supporting Karen, always at her shoulder with a comforting pat and a kind word. But she can't forget that he denied all knowledge of Scarning Fen when he had actually lived fairly near there. And he had an allotment. Could Pete who, according to his brother-in-law, had always liked Karen, have been hanging around to abuse her children? It's a dark thought but darker things have happened.

And what about Annie? 'Damage' was the word used by Carol Dunne. If Annie too had been abused by Pete, that might account for her anger, which a few people have mentioned. Judy hasn't really seen this side of Annie. She seems a rather distant parent, hovering around Star but often appearing not to know what to do to comfort her. It's Dave who puts his arms round Star, who tells her that it's going to be all right. But, then again, in their family it's Cathbad who's the more nurturing parent. He's the one the children call if they get scared in the night. Judy provides stability and (she hopes) unconditional love. But would an outsider judge her for checking her phone messages while on the sofa watching *Peppa Pig*?

She wonders how Cathbad is getting on in Somerset. She hopes it's not raining there, Cathbad's not the best at driving in challenging conditions. She feels slightly envious of Ruth, wandering through the countryside looking at stones, while she is stuck in the grim reality of missing children. But being with Cathbad would mean spending the day with Leif, whom Judy found a rather disturbing presence. She hopes that Cathbad remembers to tell her that he's arrived safely. He has an annoying habit of leaving his phone switched off.

The house on Ferry Road already feels claustrophobic, both too big and too small. When Judy arrives, Star is huddled on the sofa, still in her pyjama-type trousers. Dave is sitting beside her and Annie is in the background, offering food, herbal tea and backrubs, all of which are rejected.

Today there is also Star's elder sister, Sienna, who has come over from Loughborough. Sienna is a tall, athletic-looking woman who seems to get on Star's nerves. 'A walk would do you good,' she keeps saying, 'get some fresh air.'

Star shivers, wrapping her arms round herself protectively. 'I'm cold,' she says, 'I never want to go outside again.'

Judy manages to get the family out of the room on various pretexts. Then she turns to Star. 'Today's the worst day,' she says. 'A whole night has gone past and you're thinking that Ava will never be found. But she will be.'

Star looks at her, eyes shadowed and huge. 'How long was your baby missing for?'

'Four days,' says Judy. 'Three nights.'

'I don't know how you survived.'

'I almost didn't,' says Judy. 'But the police found him. My colleagues found him. We're really good at this sort of stuff. We'll find Ava.'

'What's your little boy's name?'

'Michael,' says Judy, rather reluctantly. She always feels that giving away her children's names makes them vulnerable in some way.

'Does Michael remember anything about it?'

'I don't think so,' says Judy. 'Once he said the name . . . the name of the person who took him. It gave me a terrible shock but I don't think he remembers. He was only a year old.' But Michael claims to remember being born ('It was like a door being opened in space . . .') and Cathbad believes him.

'Ava's not even a month old,' says Star. 'I was looking forward to saying her age in months and not days.'

'You will,' says Judy.

'Mum and Dad are being really kind,' says Star, 'but they don't understand. Nor does Sienna. I suppose if I had a partner it might be different because he'd love Ava as much as I do. Have you got a partner?'

'Yes,' says Judy. She doesn't feel like going into the complications of Michael's paternity. 'He was really traumatised by the whole thing. But it's fine now. We've got another child. A girl.'

'That's lovely,' says Star, giving Judy a smile of such sweetness that she blinks.

'I saw Ryan's parents,' she says. 'They were very shocked. They send their . . . their best.' It's not much, coming from Ava's grandparents, but Star seems genuinely touched.

'That's nice. They're nice people. They just didn't want Ryan to be tied down with a baby. That's why they sent him away to Camp America. But I never expected anything of Ryan. I always knew that I'd be bringing Ava up on my own.'

'That's very brave.'

'I'm luckier than most single mothers,' says Star. 'I've got my parents, a nice house, lots of friends.'

Judy is working her way down the list of friends given to her by Star but it seems that most of them haven't seen Star since she gave birth. She wonders if Star is a bit lonely, despite the parents and the nice house. After all, she seemed very keen to be friends with Michelle, who is more than twenty years older than her. The boss says that Michelle is planning to visit Star this afternoon.

'Is Leif Anderssen a good friend?' she asks.

'I like Leif,' says Star. 'He's a very beautiful person. Physically, I mean. But he'll be going back to Norway soon. My next relationship has to be with someone special. Like Cathbad.'

'What?'

'Cathbad. The man who runs my meditation class. I'd like to meet someone like him. He's so spiritual and wise. He knows all the answers.'

Only if you ask the right questions, thinks Judy. She knows that she should tell Star that Cathbad is her partner but she can't find the words.

'How about some camomile tea?' she says.

The woman comes closer, wearing a homespun cloak, her hair gleaming. For a moment Ruth genuinely wonders if she has slipped through a portal and gone back in time. This could be some Neolithic woman, come to lay her baby in the centre of the stone circle and ask for blessings from the nature spirits. She could be a Bronze Age hunter-gatherer, tending the fields with her child strapped to her back.

'Ruth,' says the woman. 'Ruthie.'

It's Magda. Erik's wife. Leif's mother.

Magda passes the baby to Leif and holds out her arms. Ruth moves forward and is enfolded in a hug that smells of lavender and wood smoke. Once she had loved Magda, seen her as the mother she wanted and needed, rather than the one she had. But, since Ruth's mother has died, Ruth has started to see her in a more favourable light. She actually misses her a great deal. And Magda, like Erik, turned out to be not quite what she seemed.

'I wanted to see you.' Magda holds Ruth's face in her hands. 'I got Leif to arrange this meeting with you. With both of you.' She turns to Cathbad.

'Hallo, Magda.' Ruth can hear her own wariness in Cathbad's voice.

'The baby?' says Ruth. She turns to look at the child in Leif's arms. It is blonde and cherubic but it's not a newborn. It's not Ava.

'This is Erik's child,' says Magda, smiling at them both. 'Freya. Our miracle baby.'

Nelson is about to leave the station to visit the search teams when Leah tells him there's a call on the line.

'This is Inspector Per Amundsen from the Norwegian police. I believe you were asking about Professor Leif Anderssen.'

'Yes, I was.' Nelson always believes in double-checking. Especially when the person is question is living with his daughter.

'There are no convictions on his file. He's a well-respected academic.'

'Oh well,' says Nelson. 'Thanks for calling anyway.'

'There is just one thing,' says Inspector Amundsen, in carefully perfect English. 'There was once a complaint made against Professor Anderssen. The case was never taken any further though.'

'A complaint? What sort of complaint?'

'Assault,' says Amundsen. 'On his then girlfriend. But, as I say, she withdrew the allegations and the case never came to court. I just thought that you should know.'

'Thank you,' says Nelson. 'Thank you very much.'

CHAPTER 31

'She was a miracle,' says Magda. 'A gift from the universe.'

'Pa had his sperm frozen,' says Leif.

Ruth thinks that Leif seems different in his mother's presence. He's diminished, hard as that is to achieve when you're about six foot five and look like a Viking. He appears, in fact, to be torn between embarrassment and affection, an expression that Ruth already recognises from Kate.

They have repaired to a café because the fog is now even thicker, bringing with it a bitter cold that seems almost malevolent, cutting into their faces as they walk through the shrouded stones. Freya is cocooned in a fur-lined snow-suit but, in the café, Magda unwraps her and Ruth sees that she's an enchanting child of about eight months. She has Erik's eyes.

'We felt that Erik's DNA should be preserved,' Magda is saying, 'so he had his sperm frozen. Last year I found a wonderful host mother, a PhD student called Agnetha. I was present at the birth and Agnetha put Freya straight into my arms. It was love at first sight.'

This must mean that Freya is not genetically Magda's child, thinks Ruth. Still, genetics are not everything and Magda obviously dotes on the baby.

'I wanted us all to be together in this sacred place,' says Magda. 'So I asked Leif to arrange it.'

'That letter,' says Ruth. 'Was it really from Erik?'

'I'm sure it's what he would have wanted to write,' says Leif. 'He was so fond of you both.' He glances at Cathbad. 'But, no. It was a little tease from me. I know how much you like a puzzle, Ruth.'

A tease. Leif has dragged them all the way across the country for a tease. Rather than Erik speaking to her from beyond the grave, in fact it was just his son trying to be clever. She remembers the way she had obediently rushed home and looked up 'stone wedding guests' as if she were a student again, completing one of Erik's assignments. Will she ever stop seeking Erik's approval? She looks at Cathbad who raises his eyebrows and shrugs. She wonders if he's thinking the same thing.

'Can I hold the baby?' Cathbad asks.

'Of course.' Magda gives him a glittering smile and passes Freya across the table. The child, who was grizzling slightly, looks up at Cathbad, almost in awe, and starts to smile. Judy calls him the baby whisperer.

'It's wonderful to see you, Ruthie,' says Magda and, despite herself, Ruth feels the familiar glow that comes from basking in the all-encompassing warmth of Magda's affection.

'Great to see you,' she says.

'But I really want to see your gorgeous little girl. How old is she?'

'Seven.'

'A magical age. What is she like?'

Ruth wonders how to sum up the glory that is Kate. 'She's very bright,' she says at last. 'Interested in everything. She loves books and acting and animals. She's great.'

'She's a star,' says Cathbad.

'And you have children too, Cathbad? I know you have a daughter. She must be grown-up now.'

'Yes, Maddie – my daughter with Delilah – is twenty-four. I've got two younger children with my partner, Judy. Michael is six and Miranda is three.'

'You are blessed.'

'Yes, I am,' says Cathbad, making Freya laugh by hiding his face behind his cloak.

The waiter brings their drinks. Cathbad and Ruth have ordered sandwiches too. Leif gets out a Tupperware box of mixed seeds.

'Still eating healthily?' says Magda.

'Yes,' says Leif, sounding slightly like a sulky teenager. 'Chia seeds are high in iron and magnesium.'

Magda has asked the waiter to bring a mug of hot water. Now she puts a bottle of milk in it to warm up. Ruth thinks of the missing baby in King's Lynn, the mother longing to hold her baby and care for it, as Magda is doing now. She knows that Nelson, Judy and Clough will be working flat out but she hopes that Judy will tell Cathbad if the baby is found.

'Your baby's father,' says Magda to Ruth with a smile, taking Freya from Cathbad and settling her in the crook of her arm before giving her the bottle. 'It's the policeman, isn't it?'

Ruth is not expecting this Erik-like sixth sense. 'Yes,' she says, rather stiffly. 'His name's Harry Nelson. He's a detective chief inspector.'

'DCI Nelson?' says Leif. 'I met him yesterday.'

'Did you?' says Ruth.

'Yes,' says Leif. 'I know the girl, you see. The one whose baby went missing.'

'Her name's Star,' says Cathbad.

'I don't think Nelson cares much for me,' says Leif. 'But then, I am living with his daughter.'

'You're living with Laura?' says Ruth. She thinks of the furious girl in ripped jeans. She supposes that Laura left home after Nelson's revelation but somehow she doesn't like to think of Laura living with Leif.

Perhaps Cathbad feels the same because he says, 'I think Laura's in a vulnerable state just now.'

'Sure she is,' says Leif. 'I'm counselling her.'

He smiles at Ruth and Ruth suddenly sees the other side of the Viking; not the adventurer but the destroyer, the raider who invades Anglo-Saxon settlements and carries off their womenfolk.

She supposes that Leif himself is a message from Erik.

Michelle feels slightly nervous as Star's mother ushers her into the sitting room. She thought long and hard about bringing George. Would the sight of him cheer and distract Star? Or would he be a reminder of the missing Ava, his almost-twin? On balance she decided to leave him behind with her mum but now she feels his absence acutely. Is it possible that she's only known this baby for twenty-odd days? Now she feels lost without him. Besides, George would have given them something to talk about.

Star is on the sofa. When she sees Michelle she bursts into tears. Michelle puts her arms round her. 'There, there. It'll be all right.' This, at least, she can do. Memories of comforting the girls when they were young. Broken toys, grazed knees and – later on – arguments with friends and the unfathomable strangeness of boys. She knows what to say for all of it. Which is to say, she says nothing. 'There, there,' she says, patting Star's back. 'There, there.'

Eventually Star hiccups and pulls away, wiping her eyes on what looks like one of Ava's muslin cloths. Star's mother, Annie, offers tea which Michelle accepts because she thinks drinking something might be good for Star. She thinks that Annie looks almost as traumatised as her daughter. She can only imagine how she'd feel if this happened to one of her girls and their mythical offspring.

'I met your husband yesterday,' says Star, still hiccupping slightly. 'He's very nice.'

'Yes, he is,' says Michelle. 'And he's very good at his job. He'll find Ava. He's done it before.'

'With Judy's baby? She told me. She's nice too.'

'Yes, she is.'

'Oh, Michelle.' The tears start again, welling in Star's blue eyes and falling unchecked down her face. 'I just miss her so much. She's my baby. She needs me.'

'That's why you have to stay calm,' says Michelle. 'For Ava's sake. She'll need you when she comes home. She'll need her mum.'

Looking towards the door, Michelle sees that Annie hasn't left the room. She's standing in the doorway and she, too, has tears running down her cheeks. Go to your daughter, Michelle wants to say. Comfort her. We all need our mothers to comfort us sometimes. But they stay frozen in their positions, Star on the sofa with Michelle beside her, Annie in the doorway. They all jump when there's a knock on the door. Annie goes to answer it and comes back with Judy.

'No news,' she says immediately. 'I'm sorry.' She sits on the other side of Star.

'Hi, Michelle.'

'Hallo, Judy.'

They sit on the sofa in silence whilst, in the background, a clock chimes the hour. Three o'clock.

Nelson is feeling the frustration of being left at the station while the action goes on elsewhere. He leaves a message for Laura and asks her to ring him back but he's not really surprised when she doesn't. At half past three he gets a message from Mike Halloran, who is in charge of Forensics.

'We've got something from the search team,' he says. 'It may or may not be significant.'

This is a typical Mike phrase.

'What is it?' says Nelson.

'A piece of brown paper caught on the hedge outside the house on Ferry Road. Looks like it might be from a bag. You know, the sort you find in greengrocers sometimes.'

'A brown paper bag?'

'Yes.'

Nelson thinks of the bag containing the witch stone that was left on his doorstep. *Greetings from Jack Valentine.* But they had been sure that John Mostyn had been Nelson's mysterious Valentine. After all, he was from east Norfolk and he collected stones. The handwriting, of course, had been impossible to match. Could this possibly be linked? He can hear Tom Henty's slow voice now: *Then there's Snatch Valentine . . . Present on the doorstep with a string attached. Child goes to grab the parcel but the string moves it just out of reach. Child chases the present until it's out of sight. Child is never seen again.*

But, then again, it could just be part of a paper bag, one that had once held oranges or apples, blown by the wind onto the Simmondses' hedge.

'The hedge is quite overgrown,' Mike is saying, 'and it's the side near the road. It's possible that this bag got caught there while someone was trying to manoeuvre themselves into their car.'

'Themselves or something else. A baby in a baby seat perhaps?'

'Perhaps. We'll check it for prints, of course. Pity it's not bigger.'

It's a pity we haven't got any more evidence, thinks Nelson. It's a pity we haven't got CCTV of someone abducting Ava.

It's a pity we haven't found her. He thanks Mike and tells him to keep him informed.

Putting down the phone, Nelson paces round the office. He wants to drive to Leif's apartment and confront him but he's worried that the confrontation will end with Nelson, not Leif, being charged with assault. Better to speak to Laura first. Or should he ask Michelle to ring her? He texts Michelle but she doesn't reply. Then he remembers that Michelle is going to visit Star this afternoon. Well, he hopes that she can be some comfort to the poor girl.

Maybe he should call in on Star too? Check in with Judy, reassure the family that they're doing all they can. He picks up his jacket and phone but, as he does so, the internal line rings. 'Someone to see you, DCI Nelson. Her name's Rita Smith. She says it's about the Ava Simmonds case.'

The name means nothing to Nelson but he's willing to meet the devil himself if he'll help him find Ava. A few minutes later a middle-aged woman comes into the room, clutching a large handbag and smiling serenely.

'I'm Madame Rita,' she says. 'You consulted me when Michael Foster went missing. I spoke to a nice policeman called Clough.'

Oh Christ, it's the medium. They had only consulted her last time because Cathbad had insisted. Nelson remembers that Clough had been sure that she'd given him vital information although he remains unconvinced.

'I haven't got much time,' he says.

'No, none of us have got much time,' says Madame Rita.

'Not on this earth anyhow. But I was able to help last time so I've asked my spirit guide if he can see Ava.'

'And can he?'

'Yes. She's with lots of other motherless children.'

Despite himself, Nelson's skin prickles. 'What do you mean? Is she dead?'

'Bless you, no.' Madame Rita gives a chuckle. 'She's alive and she's not far away.'

'Any ideas as to where she might actually be?'

'As I said to Sergeant Clough five years ago, the spirits don't deal in addresses. If you can bring me something that belongs to Ava, I might be able to feel her spirit more powerfully.'

And Nelson finds himself promising to get one of Ava's possessions to give to the medium.

Outside the café it's almost dark and the fog is thicker, adding its own visual effects of smoky vapour and lowering grey cloud. Ruth and Cathbad walk ahead across the fields while Leif follows with his mother and her baby. They are looking for the Cove, the name given to the three megaliths said to depict the bride, groom and pastor. The waiter at the café told them that the stones were in the grounds of the pub, appropriately named the Druid's Arms. In fact they are lying between the church and the pub, glowing slightly in the dusk, reminding Ruth of the phosphorescence that she sometimes sees on the marshes late at night.

One of the stones looks like a petrified golf flag, a vertical

post with a protrusion at the top. The other is vaguely trian-
gular and the third is lying horizontal on the grass.

'That's the preacher,' says Cathbad.

'Why's he lying down?' says Ruth. Her breath billows
around her like the fog.

'Maybe he's drunk,' says Cathbad, waving a hand towards
the pub. The bench seats, complete with holes for umbrellas,
are only a few metres away.

'These stones are older than the circle,' says Leif, appearing
out of the gloom. 'It's thought they might have formed the
portal to a tomb.'

'They found a burial chamber under here, didn't they?'
says Ruth, keen to show that she too has done some research.
'There was a study in 2009.'

'And, in the seventeenth century, when some of the
stones fell,' says Leif, 'human remains were found buried
underneath.'

'Were there any grave goods?' asks Magda. She is clutching
Freya to her chest but her tone is very much that of the
archaeologist.

'A strange round object,' says Leif, 'described as being like
a large horse bell.'

'Maybe it was like Victorians having bells in their coffins,'
says Cathbad, 'in case they got buried alive.'

Ruth shivers. This conversation, carried out in the ghostly
fog, seems unsuitable for the day's purpose. But, then again,
Erik enjoyed a chat about the undead as much as the next
archaeologist. She can't help thinking of the burial chamber
which is, presumably, directly beneath their feet.

Magda too seems to be remembering why they're there. From her capacious nappy bag she produces a bottle of red wine. Bull's Blood.

'For the libation,' she says.

Instinctively, they all look towards Cathbad and he rises to the occasion.

'Spirits of the other world,' he says, raising his arms. 'We ask you to receive our offering. Just as water, when poured on barren earth, causes seeds to germinate and flower, may this wine restore the spirit of our dead husband, father and friend, Erik Anderssen. Though you are gone from our sight, Erik, you are never forgotten. May your ship carry you safely to Valhalla. Rest in peace and rise in glory.'

Like most of Cathbad's incantations, this is a mixture of pagan and Christian, with a bit of Norse mythology thrown in for good measure, but it's curiously effective. Cathbad takes the bottle and, from a height, pours wine onto the grass.

'Rest in peace,' echoes Leif, 'and rise in glory.'

'Farewell, dear Erik,' says Magda, holding Freya high above her head. 'May the rainbow bridge carry you to Asgard.' The baby starts to cry and Ruth doesn't blame her. They are all looking at her expectantly.

'Goodbye, Erik,' she says. It's the best she can do.

'We should all drink of the wine,' says Leif, taking an enthusiastic swig of Bull's Blood.

'I can't,' says Cathbad. 'I'm driving.'

Ruth is grateful for this piece of non-druidical common sense.

*

Nelson drives over to Star's house, knowing that he has seized on a pretext to visit the crime scene, for that is what the house in Ferry Road has become. He's clutching at straws and he knows it but there was something about Madame Rita's demeanour that means that he cannot entirely dismiss her as a crank. *She* believed what she was saying, that much was obvious, and in the face of such certainty Nelson felt his scepticism start to waver. He feels the same when he's in Cathbad's company sometimes. Doubting Thomas, he remembers, was only convinced that Jesus had come back from the dead when he put his hands into his open wounds. He is not going to wait until he sees blood. Oh ye of little faith.

It's almost dark and raining hard by the time that he gets to Ferry Road. He can just see the search team at the end of the street, their blue overalls almost invisible in the hazy light. They are concentrating on the path down to the river. Please don't let Ava be in the water. What did Madame Rita say? *She's with lots of other motherless children.* That must, at least, rule out the river.

When he approaches the house he sees Judy in the porch looking at her phone.

'Hallo, Johnson. What's the news?'

'Nothing. Star's in a pretty bad way. Michelle came round earlier. She was really good with her. Got her to eat something and have a shower. That's more than her mother or I could do.'

Michelle, Nelson thinks, was always good when the girls were upset. She usually suggested something practical: have a shower, go for a walk, drink some water. It might not have solved the problem but it gave them something to do. He must get Michelle to talk to Laura again.

'Any news from the search teams?' asks Judy.

'You heard about the brown paper bag?'

'No.'

'Halloran's team found a piece of paper on the hedge here, outside the house. They think it was from a brown paper bag.'

'Like the Jack Valentine bag?'

'That was my first thought but we mustn't jump to conclusions. Besides, we were sure that John Mostyn was Jack Valentine.'

'I know,' says Judy. 'It's just that I'm so desperate for a lead. I'm clutching at straws. Though a drinking straw would be good. It would have DNA on it.'

'I'm the same,' says Nelson. 'That medium woman came in again. Madame Rita. And I found myself agreeing to see her.'

'Really?' says Judy. 'Madame Rita gave us a clue about Michael, didn't she?'

'Cloughie always thought so but it was all so vague. It was the same this time.'

'What did she say?'

'She said that Ava was alive and that she was with other motherless children.'

'Other motherless children? Ava isn't motherless.'

'These people always talk in riddles. Madame Rita wants a possession of Ava's so that she can feel her spirit more powerfully.' He puts ironical quotation marks round these words but Judy seems to take them seriously.

'I'll pop in and get something.'

'Why are you out here anyway?' says Nelson. 'Poor signal?'

'No, I wanted to ring Cathbad. He's gone gallivanting off somewhere with Leif and Ruth and now his phone is switched off.'

'Cathbad's gone somewhere with Ruth? And Leif Anderssen?' Nelson's antenna are on full alert. 'Where have they gone?'

'To see some stone circle in Somerset.'

'Is Katie with them?'

'No, she's at school. I think she's going on a sleepover tonight. My parents are looking after Michael and Miranda.'

But Nelson has already got out his phone. 'Call me,' he texts Ruth.

It's completely dark by the time they start the drive home. The fog is thicker too. As they drive through the country roads it's as if the outside world has vanished, reminding Ruth of the road across the Saltmarsh. This time Ruth is in the front seat while Leif lounges in the back, scrolling through his phone, still slightly in his teenager persona.

Ruth is unaccountably tired (after all, she's been in the car most of the day). She closes her eyes but forces herself to reopen them. Cathbad might need a co-driver. Looking in the passenger-side mirror she sees Leif has fallen asleep, his handsome head thrown back, like a lion at rest. The motorway is a relief; lights and signposts and the reassuring presence of other cars. All of them, Ruth imagines, on their way home. Ruth and Cathbad chat about Stanton Drew and the symbolism of circles. 'A circle is totality, wholeness, perfection,' says Cathbad. 'Think of a zero. It symbolises eternity.' 'Or nothingness,' says Ruth. Kate once asked her if nought was a number. Maybe she was thinking of something altogether more profound than number bonds.

Just outside Bristol the rain starts. The windscreen wipers slick back and forth, barely coping with the torrent. Cathbad starts to hum under his breath so Ruth knows he is nervous. It's dark now but the mist is still there, billowing around them like dry ice. They join the M4, hardly able to see a few metres in front of them, lorries passing them in a sheet of spray.

'Are we there yet?' says Leif, waking up. 'Some weather, eh?'

No one answers and he goes back to sleep. Cathbad leans forward, concentrating on the road ahead. Ruth tries to keep up a flow of calming chat but, eventually, she too falls silent. Then, just before Peterborough, they see a red sign flashing in front of them. 'Road closed.'

'What shall we do?' says Ruth.

'We'll have to go across country,' says Cathbad. His knuckles are white on the wheel and he starts to hum again.

They head towards Downham Market. At first there seem to be many cars going in their direction and their presence is comforting. But, one by one, the other vehicles veer off and they are alone on the featureless road. The rain thunders against the roof and their headlights seem only to reflect the darkness back to them. It's only eight o'clock but it feels like midnight and it seems as if this road will never end. Only about an hour more, thinks Ruth. Then she'll be home, sitting on the sofa with Flint and drinking a glass of wine. She has already had a text from Tasha's mum saying the two girls are happily watching a Disney film. Before bed she'll text again just to say goodnight to Kate. Nearly home, nearly home.

Their headlights illuminate a sign for Cambridge.

'We can call in on Frank,' says Cathbad.

'I'm thinking of applying for a job there,' says Ruth.

Cathbad flicks her a quick glance. Keep your eyes on the road, thinks Ruth.

'Are you serious?'

'Well, I'm just thinking about it but I can't stay at UNN all my life. I'll never get promotion unless Phil leaves.'

'Maybe he will leave.'

'Not him. He likes being a big fish in a small pool.'

'What about you?' says Cathbad, leaning forward to see through the deluge. 'Do you want a new pool?'

'I don't know,' says Ruth, 'but recently I've been thinking that I want *something* new. I'm just not sure what it is.'

Cathbad is about to answer when, with terrifying suddenness, a figure rises up in front of them. A massive creature, a mythical beast crowned with horns.

She distinctly hears Leif saying 'Herne the Hunter' before the car leaves the road and crashes headlong into a ditch.

Darkness.

CHAPTER 32

By the end of the day the searchers have found nothing. Judy finds it increasingly difficult to keep Star calm. Eventually Annie calls a doctor and Star is given a sedative. She lies on the sofa, eyes open, apparently in a daze. Annie and Dave sit in the kitchen talking in hushed tones. Luke is there too and Karen, who busies herself cooking a meal which Judy is sure no one will eat. At eight o'clock Judy leaves them to go back to the station for a briefing. Outside it's pouring with rain and, although she hopes and prays that Ava is safely inside somewhere, her heart sinks. She's increasingly worried about Cathbad, who hasn't rung all day. In the car she checks her phone, hoping to hear that the travellers have safely returned. But, instead, there's a missed call from Shona Maclean.

'Shona? What's up?'

'Hi, Judy. Have you heard from Ruth?'

'No. I think she's out somewhere with Cathbad.'

'I know. She sent me a message. "On an adventure with Cathbad. Scary."'

'Scary? She must mean his driving.'

'I didn't think anything of it but I've been trying to ring her and her phone seems to be switched off.'

Judy's skin prickles. If there's one thing she knows it's that working mothers never, ever switch off their phones.

'They've gone to Stanton Drew, haven't they?' says Shona.

'Yes,' says Judy. 'How do you know?'

'Leif asked me too. He said that Erik, his father, had left a message for me, something about dancing in a stone circle. He wanted me to go to Stanton Drew today with Ruth and Cathbad but I couldn't go because I had lectures.'

'Erik seemed to leave messages for a lot of people.'

'That's what I thought. There's something fishy about it all.'

'Cathbad's phone is switched off too.'

There's a second's pause and then Shona says, 'I know it sounds silly but I looked at Ruth's Fitbit. I can see her stats because we're friends. And she's hardly done any steps today and nothing since four o'clock.'

Judy looks at the time on her dashboard. It says 20.05.

'They're probably in the car,' she says.

'I know,' says Shona. 'I was just worried. The weather's so awful too.'

Judy has never been able to shake a slight suspicion of Shona, dating back to the time when she first interviewed her about the letters, but now she feels an unprecedented rush of goodwill towards her. Whatever else she may be, Shona is clearly genuinely fond of Ruth.

'I'll let you know if I hear from them,' she says. 'I've got to get back to the station now.'

Nelson's first question is, 'Have you heard from Cathbad?'

'No. Have you heard from Ruth?'

'No. I left a message telling her to call me.' Telling not asking, notes Judy. No wonder Ruth hasn't replied.

'The A47 is closed,' says Clough, who always knows that sort of thing.

Judy relaxes slightly. Cathbad must be held up in traffic somewhere. Even so she wishes that Cathbad or Ruth would call. It's still raining heavily and Clough says that there's freezing fog on the Downham Market road.

'Let's get going,' says Nelson. They sit around the table in the briefing room. Leah has been out for sandwiches but Judy doesn't feel like eating. Clough has her share.

'Ava has been missing for forty-eight hours now,' says Nelson. 'Things are getting very serious. We think the abductor took some of Star's expressed milk but that must be running out now. Ava is only twenty-four days old. Our only real clue is a piece of brown paper caught on the hedge outside Star's parents' house. There's no CCTV in the street and none of the neighbours saw anyone entering or leaving the house on Monday evening. The family don't seem to have anything to offer although one of her uncles suggested that Star might be making it up.'

'I'm sure she isn't,' says Judy. 'And Carol Dunne, her ex-teacher, agrees. She said that Star isn't the type to make up stories. Although, interestingly, she thought that Margaret may have been the type. And Annie too. Carol taught Annie and she described her as being damaged in some way. She suggested that telling stories was a way of making children feel safe, in situations of abuse, for example.'

'Who might have been abusing Margaret?' says Clough. 'Her dad?'

'Maybe. Or her stepdad,' says Judy.

'You're not still going on about that, are you? Pete Benson wouldn't hurt a fly.'

'Appearances can be deceptive,' says Nelson. 'But it's Star and Ava we have to focus on here. Star hasn't shown any sign of compulsive lying up until now. I think we can discount that theory. How was she when you left her?'

'In a pretty bad way,' says Judy. 'The doctor had to give her a sedative.' She looks at the mobile in her lap. No messages.

'What about Uncle Luke?' says Nelson. 'He's the only one with opportunity.'

'He's with Star now,' says Judy. 'He's a bit of an oddball but seems genuinely concerned. And, even if Luke did take Ava, it comes back to the same question. Where is she now?'

'We searched the grandparents' house,' says Clough. 'They were very cooperative.'

'What about Pete's allotment?' says Judy.

'Yes,' says Clough with elaborate patience. 'The allotment has been searched as have the homes of Bradley and Richard Benson.'

'I checked all the door-to-door interviews,' says Tanya. 'Everyone says they're a lovely family, respectable jobs and all that. No scandal, except Star getting pregnant and not being married but everyone does that now. And Star was a devoted mother, by all accounts.'

'*Is* a devoted mother,' says Judy.

Nelson gives her a rather anxious look. He must be worried that she's about to crack up.

'The next thing—' he says. But they never hear what the next thing is. Judy's phone rings and she pounces on it.

'Judy,' says Cathbad. 'There's been an accident. Ruth is hurt.'

Judy insists on driving.

'You're in no fit state,' she says to Nelson. The fact that he gives way without any further argument tells her how worried he is. Cathbad and Ruth are in the King's Lynn Hospital which is only ten minutes away from the station. The roads are clear but it's still raining hard. Judy drives as fast as she dares. She's a good driver, the best on the team. This doesn't stop Nelson telling her, several times, to get a move on.

'Bloody Cathbad,' he says, pounding his knee with a fist. 'He's a danger on the roads. I'll revoke his licence.'

'It wasn't his fault,' says Judy, firing up immediately. 'He said they hit a deer.'

'What did he say about Ruth?'

Judy has told him this three times but she repeats, patiently, 'She's unconscious, he said, and the doctors are with her now. They don't know how badly hurt she is.'

'And Cathbad hasn't got a scratch on him. He's got the luck of the devil, that man.'

Both of them have completely forgotten about Leif Anderssen.

'You love Ruth, don't you?' says Judy. She would never have dared to say this normally but, just for the moment, she feels that they are equal, driving in the dark through the rain, both worried about their loved ones.

'Concentrate on the road,' growls Nelson. Then, in a different voice, 'Yes, I love her. Sometimes I think it's killing me.'

'I thought the same when I was married to Darren and in love with Cathbad,' says Judy. 'When I left Darren it was awful but the awfulness doesn't last. Sometimes you just have to be with the person you love.'

Nelson says nothing and the rain continues to fall.

CHAPTER 33

Nelson is out of the car before Judy has parked. She watches him run towards the entrance to A&E, pushing porters out of the way. Then she drives round to the car park and goes through the labyrinthine system of getting a ticket and finding a space, surely designed to give a heart attack to any worried relative. When she finally makes her way back to reception, Cathbad is there. He has a bruise on his cheek but otherwise looks exactly like his dear, infuriating self.

He comes over and wraps his arms around her. 'I'm sorry,' he says.

'At least you're safe,' says Judy, muffled in his shirt. 'Nelson says you've got the luck of the devil.'

'No, it's the angels who're on my side,' says Cathbad. 'They're looking after Ruth now.'

'Have you heard how she is?'

'No. The doctors are with her. Nelson went steaming in, of course. He said he was her next of kin.'

'Well, I think he is, in a way.'

Cathbad looks at her quizzically but obviously decides to let this go.

'They think Leif has a broken leg,' he says.

'Leif?'

'Leif Anderssen. He was in the back seat.'

'This is all his fault,' says Judy, breaking away. 'Why did he have to drag you all the way to Somerset? Shona rang up. She said he asked her too.'

'He wanted us to meet his mother and her miracle baby,' says Cathbad.

'What?'

'It's a long story. I've rung your mum and dad, by the way. They're staying the night at the house.'

'That's good,' says Judy, rather ashamed that she didn't do this herself.

'Maddie's there too,' says Cathbad, 'but I thought you'd still want your parents to stay.'

He's right but Judy doesn't quite want to articulate why she doesn't think that Maddie is an adequate babysitter.

'I feel terrible about the deer,' says Cathbad. 'Such a beautiful, noble creature. I'd like to make some reparation.'

'I'm sure there's a charity you can donate to,' says Judy.

'Do you want to go home?' Cathbad asks. 'The car's a wreck, I'm afraid. But we could go in yours.'

'I'd like to find out about Ruth first,' says Judy.

'So would I,' says Cathbad. 'I'll get us some coffee. There's a machine here somewhere.'

Judy sits on one of the nailed-down chairs in the reception area surrounded by the halt and the lame; the boy in rugby kit with his arm in a sling, the two young women chatting on their phones about a third woman who is apparently 'having her stomach pumped', the bearded man who seems to be dying of sadness, tears rolling down his cheeks. After a while Cathbad appears with two polystyrene cups. 'I put sugar in,' he says, 'for the shock.' Judy leans against Cathbad and sips the disgustingly sweet liquid. She feels ashamed of the wave of contentment that flows through her.

Ruth is floating. She's in a black sea and the devil is playing the fiddle. She's in the stone circle and the bride is dancing. She is digging through the mud and a hand is rising up to grasp hers. She sees Kate walking between two women. They seem familiar but she can't see their faces. She tries to call out but it's too difficult . . .

'Ruth.'

She sees Nelson. His face is close to hers, his brown eyes both intent and tender, an expression that she's only seen on a few, never-to-be-forgotten, occasions. She can see the small scar on his cheekbone, his dark eyelashes, the stubble on his chin.

'Ruth.'

She opens her eyes. 'Nelson. Where's Kate?'

'She's fine. She's safe. She's having a sleepover with her friend.'

'She was with two women. I didn't recognise them.'

'You were dreaming.'

Was she dreaming? But she's not asleep. She can see

Nelson but there's a blue curtain behind him and she doesn't recognise the room.

'Where am I?'

'You're in hospital. Bloody Cathbad crashed the car.'

'Herne the Hunter. We saw Herne with his antlers.'

'You hit a deer apparently. The car went off the road. It's a write-off.'

The room comes into sharper focus. It's a cubicle really and Nelson is sitting by her bed. She tries to sit up but Nelson pushes her gently back down on her pillows.

'You've got to stay quiet. That's what the doctor said. You've got concussion but they don't think there's anything else wrong with you.'

'I want to go home. I need to feed Flint.'

'That cat's as fat as a house. He won't starve because he misses a meal.'

'He's not fat. He's big-boned.'

'He'll be fine. As soon as you're discharged, I'll drive you home.'

'My head hurts,' says Ruth.

'Just lie still,' says Nelson.

Ruth closes her eyes.

For a while Nelson just watches Ruth sleep. He knows he should go and update Judy. He should go back to the station and continue the search for Ava. He should go home to his wife. But for the moment he watches Ruth. She has a bandage wound diagonally across her head which gives her an oddly rakish appearance. Her hair is in disarray and, for the first time, he sees threads of grey in the brown. She is frowning slightly as she sleeps. Probably working out the exact date for some obscure piece of prehistorical pottery. Nelson reaches out a hand to touch her hair. It's so soft – that's something he always remembers – unlike Michelle's which is sometimes stiff with the spray she uses to keep it in perfect waves. Nelson wants to kiss Ruth but what would the nurses think? He can see a gang of them through the cubicle curtains, standing at the end of the ward, talking earnestly. As he watches, a figure passes the double doors, another nurse, large and purposeful in navy blue. Why does she look so familiar? But then it clicks. It's Annie Simmonds, Star's mother, who should be at home looking after her daughter.

Nelson gets up and goes to the ward entrance. Annie is just disappearing around a corner. Nelson follows, keeping a discreet distance between them, up two flights of stairs, along several identical corridors, characterless and institutional, punctuated by hand-washing stations and fire extinguishers. Annie is walking quickly, not looking to left or right. Finally she reaches a locked door with 'Neonatal Unit' written on it. Annie punches in a password and is admitted. The door doesn't quite shut behind her and Nelson catches it before the latch hits the lock.

Annie is moving in a kind of trance, unaware of the footsteps behind her. She is walking through a room full of Perspex cots, all of which are surrounded by monitors, wires and drips. All except one, furthest from the door. As Nelson watches, Annie approaches this cot and lifts up the baby.

'I see you've found Ava,' says Nelson.

CHAPTER 34

'This isn't Ava,' says Annie.

'Of course it is,' says Nelson. 'The perfect place to keep her, you being in charge of the neonatal unit and all. But I think her mum wants her back now, don't you?'

'This isn't Ava,' says Annie, but her face is suddenly completely blank. Nelson has seen that look many times before and it always means guilt.

'Let me see,' he says, keeping his voice quiet and reasonable. He walks between the Perspex cots. He thinks of Madame Rita. *She's with lots of other motherless children.* These babies are not so much motherless as temporarily separated from their parents but he's got to give the medium some credit all the same. Shelves at the end of the room contain baby supplies: sterilisers, blankets, changing mats. Brown paper bags full of nappies.

Annie is holding the baby tightly to her chest, wrapped in one of those blankets that seem to be mostly holes. As Nelson approaches she loosens her hold slightly and he can see a tiny face and a single curl. He has never met Ava but he's seen photographs and that silver-blonde hair is unmistakable. He feels a rush of pure relief, so strong that his head spins. He had almost given up hope of finding Ava alive.

'Annie,' he says, still trying for the calm tone, channelling Judy at her most persuasive. 'Annie. Give Ava to me. We need to get her back to Star. She's in a terrible state and this baby needs her mother.'

'I did it for Star,' says Annie. She doesn't hand over the baby but the fight seems to leave her. Her shoulders, so square and determined in their uniform, slump. 'I did it to protect Ava from him.'

'From who?'

'Pete,' says Annie, as if this is obvious. 'Pete killed Margaret and now Ava's in danger from him. Star was even talking about letting Mum and Pete look after Ava when she goes back to work. If you can call it work, pretending to cure people with massage and a bit of oil.'

'Why do you think Pete killed Margaret?' Nelson edges closer. He should have called for back-up as soon as he saw Annie. Judy is probably still in the hospital somewhere. He could arrest Annie now, seize the baby and drive off to Star with all the sirens blazing. But, right now, it seems better to stick to the softly-softly approach.

'We never liked him, me and Luke,' says Annie. 'Everyone else said that he was so nice, so dependable, such a good stepfather, nothing like our dad, the no-good alcoholic. But I loved my dad, even if he did drink and shout a bit. I thought Pete was a creep. He was always hanging round

Mum, even when Dad was still alive. I didn't see him at the street party but he must have been there, lurking somewhere. Then, that day, a week ago, DS Johnson was asking about Scarning Fen. She said that Margaret had been buried near there. Luke and I remembered that Pete was living in Swaffham when Margaret went missing. He had an allotment near Scarning Fen. We realised that he must have killed Margaret and buried her there. So I knew we had to protect Ava.'

'Why didn't you go to the police?'

'The police!' Annie snorts with contempt. 'They wouldn't believe us. I saw DS Clough with Pete. All chummy, thinking he's such a nice man, such a good husband and father. No, Luke and I knew that we were on our own.'

'Did Luke help you?'

'Yes, he took Ava when Star was asleep. I drove her straight to the hospital. I knew she'd be safe here.'

And you let your own daughter almost die from worry, thinks Nelson. It doesn't seem the moment to say this now.

'Annie,' he says, 'if Pete is guilty we'll arrest him but, right now, we need to get this baby back to her mother.'

'Mum doesn't want to see,' says Annie, sounding for all the world like an aggrieved teenager, the age she was when her sister vanished for ever. 'She thinks that Pete is such a good guy. She'll never believe the truth.'

'What about Star?' says Nelson. 'Your daughter. She wants her baby back.'

'Star never listens to me,' says Annie, as if she's talking about undone homework rather than child abduction. 'She thinks she knows it all.' But she seems to relax her hold on the bundle in the pink blanket.

Nelson seizes his moment. He texts Judy. 'Got Ava. Meet me at hospital entrance.' Then, gently, he takes the baby from her grandmother.

Judy doesn't ask any stupid questions. She is waiting by the main door and has called for back-up. When the squad cars arrive, Nelson, still holding Ava, gets in the back of one of them. Judy gets into the other car with Annie, who has been charged with child abduction. They drive fast through the empty streets. The rain has stopped but there is still a lot of water on the ground. Several times they almost aquaplane, spray flying up as if they're on a theme park ride. Holding the tiny baby, who is now making little mewing sounds, Nelson is reminded of his own daughters. They both used to love theme parks and there's a big picture in the sitting room of the four of them – Nelson, Michelle, Laura and Rebecca – on something called The Deadly Rapids. The girls are about eight and ten, gap-toothed grins above their life jackets. Please God, let Laura forgive him.

Judy has radioed ahead and Tanya and Clough are both at the house. As soon as the car comes to a halt, Star comes flying out of the house. Nelson gets out and Star snatches Ava from his arms.

'Oh my baby, my baby.'

'Come on, love,' says Nelson. 'Let's get inside. It's too cold out here for Ava.'

He can see Dave, Star's father, in the doorway, Tanya at his side. Clough comes out to meet them, a thousand questions on his face.

'How did you find her, boss?'

'Let's just get inside first.'

Nelson watches as Dave hugs Star, who is still clutching Ava to her chest. Together, father and daughter move into the house. Tanya and Clough follow. Nelson waits in the porch. He wants Star to have a few minutes with Ava before he tells her that her mother was the person who abducted her baby.

When Ruth wakes up she thinks that she only dreamed that Nelson was there. Sitting beside her bed, her hair a fiery splash of colour against the blue curtains, is Shona.

'Hi,' says Shona. 'How's the head?'

Ruth touches her forehead gingerly. 'OK, I think. A bit sore.'

'Judy rang me,' says Shona. 'They say that you can be discharged if there's someone with you tonight so I'm taking you home with me.'

Shona's home is also Phil's home so Ruth says, 'I'll be all right on my own. We don't need to tell the hospital.'

'No. I'd never forgive myself if you slipped into a coma or something,' says Shona. 'I'm all set to be Florence Nightingale and you can't dissuade me. I knew something would happen if you went off with Leif. That man's trouble. Just like his father.'

'How is Leif?' asks Ruth. 'Is he OK?'

'Judy says they think he's broken his leg,' said Shona. 'He's waiting for an X-ray.'

'I met Magda,' says Ruth. 'She had a baby. It was Erik's. Artificial insemination using his frozen sperm.'

'Too much information,' says Shona lightly but, too late, Ruth remembers that Shona was once pregnant with Erik's child and, at his insistence, had an abortion. She's not thinking clearly. It must be the bang on the head.

'We're just waiting for a doctor to discharge you,' says Shona. 'Phil's making up the spare room bed.'

'It's very kind of you,' says Ruth. 'Of you both.' On reflection she thinks that it might be rather nice to spend the night in Shona's spare room, rather than on her own in her cottage. Her head feels as if it's full of cement.

'Was Nelson here?' she asks.

'Nelson?' says Shona. 'I don't know. Judy just rang and asked if I could pick you up. Apparently they've found the baby. The one that was missing.'

'Ava?' says Ruth. 'Oh, that's great news.' Perhaps she did imagine Nelson. She remembers a dream about the devil and Nelson saying that Flint was too fat. Flint!

'I've got to go back,' she says, struggling to sit up. 'No one's fed Flint.'

'Relax,' says Shona. 'I sent a message to your neighbour, Sam. She and Ed are down for a few days. She'll feed Flint.'

'How do you know Sam?'

'Turns out we're friends on Facebook. You see, Ruth, social media does have its advantages.'

Ruth doesn't answer this, her brain is still too muzzy.

Shona sits by her bed talking about Louis and Phil and a lot of people whom Ruth doesn't know. Eventually a doctor and nurse arrive to discharge her. After the doctor has looked into Ruth's eyes with her torch and pronounced herself satisfied, the nurse says, 'Has your husband left?'

'My . . . I don't have a husband.' Has she woken up in some parallel universe where she's married with two point four children?

'Oh, sorry. I should have said your partner. The tall, dark-haired man who was with you earlier. He said he was your next of kin.'

So Nelson must have been here after all. Ruth supposes he left because Ava was found. 'He's just a friend,' she says.

'Well, he looked a very close friend,' says the nurse. 'Sitting beside you and stroking your hair.'

'Stroking my . . .'

'And he yelled at the A&E consultant earlier. Demanding to know if you were all right.'

That sounds more like Nelson.

'He can be rather domineering.'

'Tell me about it,' says the nurse. Though he doesn't say whether he's speaking from the position of a yeller or a yellee.

'Come on, Ruth,' says Shona. 'You're free. Time to go.'

There seem to be lots of police cars outside the hospital but Ruth assumes that this is just part of the routine emergency of hospital life. By the time they reach Shona's car, on the top floor of the multi-storey, she is feeling tired and rather sick. Shona must realise this because she doesn't try to talk. Instead she switches on Radio 4 and lets *Midnight News* accompany them home.

Nelson also arrives home at midnight. He presses the button to open the garage, so tired that he's almost in a dream, a weightless feeling that's not unpleasant. He feels as if he has run through a lifetime's emotions in a day but the predominant feeling now is one of satisfaction. Ava has been found, alive and well. The complications around her abduction will have to wait until another day. Tonight Star can sleep with her baby beside her.

The house is quiet when he lets himself in. No sound from George upstairs and, more worryingly, no sound from Bruno downstairs. When he doesn't hear Bruno running to meet him, nails clattering on the wooden floor, tail hitting the wall, Nelson feels a sudden lurch of fear. What has happened to his guard dog? Has he been lured away by a piece of poisoned meat? Such things have happened before. But when Nelson lets himself into the sitting room, Bruno is lying on the sofa next to Laura, both of them fast asleep.

Bruno sees him first. He opens his eyes and wags his tail but doesn't move. After a few seconds Laura sits up, rubbing her eyes.

'You're back,' says Nelson. He knows that he's grinning like a goon.

'Just for a bit,' says Laura. 'I'm going to look for my own place soon. I can't keep looking after you two for ever.'

'No, you can't,' says Nelson. 'But this is always your home. I'm so pleased to see you, love.'

He pushes Bruno aside to sit on the sofa and Laura puts her head on his shoulder. She doesn't say so but he knows that he's forgiven.

It's so much more than he deserves.

CHAPTER 35

'The trouble is,' says Nelson, 'we've got no evidence.'

The team are back in the briefing room and, despite each of them only having had a few hours' sleep, the atmosphere has changed completely. When Nelson got into the office at nine, all the admin staff stood up and applauded him. It's rare, in policing, to have so complete a success. One baby lost, one baby found. Super Jo herself even received a tepid ovation when she wafted in to congratulate Nelson. 'It's a complete good news story,' she said.

'Well, hardly,' said Nelson. 'The baby's grandmother's been charged with abduction.' Annie Simmonds has been released on bail. Nelson doesn't know whether she has gone back to the house that she shares with her daughter. Luke Lacey has also been charged with abduction though his solicitor is fighting hard for the lesser charge of wasting police time.

'The child is safe,' said Jo. 'That's all that matters for now. Do you want to do the press conference or shall I?'

'Be my guest,' said Nelson.

And now, they are tackling the next big question. Was Annie right and did Pete Benson kill Margaret, all those years ago?

'We've got a team at his old allotment near Scarning Fen,' says Nelson. 'It's owned by someone else now. SOC think there's evidence of recent digging but, then again, it *is* an allotment. We really need Ruth there to do her stuff.'

'How is Ruth?' asks Judy. She feels a bit guilty about leaving Ruth at the hospital last night. She hopes that Shona is looking after her.

'I rang her earlier,' says Nelson, not meeting Judy's eyes. 'She's OK. Just got a bit of a sore head. She wanted to go to Scarning Fen today but I told her to wait until she was feeling stronger.'

Would Ruth listen? Judy wonders.

'So, if John Mostyn's DNA was on the bones,' says Clough, who is meditatively eating a breakfast Mars bar, 'does that mean that he knew Margaret was there and that he dug up her remains and buried them on the Saltmarsh? Why?'

Unconsciously they all look towards the cage where Sonny and Fredo are curled up in the straw. As if he recognises his former owner's name, Fredo stirs and chirrups in his sleep.

'He wanted us to find them, I suppose,' says Nelson. 'That's why Mostyn wrote those letters, basing them on the ones I received about Scarlet. He must have known about the originals because he worked for the *Chronicle*. Mostyn wanted us to find Margaret. Maybe he waited all these years until the archaeological dig gave him the opportunity.'

'And then someone killed Mostyn,' says Clough. 'Was that Pete Benson too?'

'He has an alibi.' Judy is leafing through her notebook. 'Pete and Karen were both in all evening when John Mostyn was killed, watching television.'

'Married alibis don't stand up in court,' says Nelson. 'But the way that murder was committed, so cold and clinical, I can't quite see Pete Benson pulling off a crime like that.'

Clough is frowning at the hamsters. 'Why would Karen cover up for Pete if she thought that he'd murdered Margaret? Come to that, why would she stay married to him all these years? They've got grown-up children, for God's sake.'

'Annie said that Karen didn't know,' says Nelson. 'That's what she said to me. "Mum refused to see." She said that she and Luke had never liked Pete. Maybe they had their suspicions for years. It was us asking about Scarning Fen that finally decided them.'

'It's a bit extreme though, isn't it?' says Tanya. 'I mean, I always thought Luke Lacey was a bit odd but to kidnap your own niece – great-niece – like that just because of something you suspected.'

'I think it must have festered for years,' says Nelson. 'Annie and Luke might both have felt guilty about Margaret and neither of them liked their stepfather. Last weekend, seeing each other again, Margaret's funeral, it must have brought it all back. They probably worked each other up so that kidnapping Ava seemed the only thing to do.'

'Folie à deux,' says Judy. 'Alone, they might never have

acted, but together they convinced themselves that they were doing the right thing.'

'"It was just Annie and me again",' says Tanya. 'That's what Luke said to me when he was talking about Margaret going missing. And he said that Annie used to "make him do things". I think she was always the dominant one.'

'Annie had a serious breakdown in her late teens,' says Nelson. 'Michelle says that Star hinted as much to her, and Dave confirmed it last night. Finding Margaret, the birth of Ava, her suspicions about Pete, it must all have pushed her over the edge.'

'And Annie knew that she could keep Ava safely in the neonatal unit,' says Judy. 'She even took Star's expressed milk for her. Although I still can't believe that Annie managed to smuggle a baby into the hospital without any of the medical team knowing about it.'

'There's a safeguarding inquiry going on as we speak,' says Nelson. 'But Annie was in charge of the neonatal unit. I don't think anyone else would have challenged her. When I saw Annie last night, it was obvious that she wasn't in her right mind. The thought of putting her own daughter through something like that.'

'I never thought that Star seemed close to her mother,' says Judy. 'She obviously had a better relationship with her father.'

'Even so,' says Nelson. 'Annie put Star through hell. "Star never listens to me," she said, "she thinks she knows it all." As if it was Star's fault.'

'Star seemed remarkably calm when I saw her this

morning,' said Judy. 'She's so pleased to have Ava back that I don't think the rest has sunk in.'

Nelson is looking at the incident board. The word 'Found' is scrawled across Ava's picture but Margaret is still there, golden-haired and innocent in her bridesmaid's dress.

'We haven't got enough to arrest Pete Benson,' he says. 'But we should interview him under caution. Scare him a bit. Can you bring him in, Cloughie?'

'Sure thing,' says Clough, standing up. 'Coming, Judy?'

'I want to call in on Star again,' says Judy. 'Tanya will go with you.'

Tanya already has her coat on.

Judy finds Star sitting on the sofa with Ava in her arms.

'I can't seem to let her out of my sight,' she says. 'I think that's quite normal, considering.'

'I think so too,' says Judy. Dave, who had met her at the door, told her that Annie was staying with Sienna in Loughborough. 'I can't see how Star can ever forgive her mum,' he said, his ruddy face pale with distress, 'but Star says she can. Of course, she knows what her mum went through as a girl but, even so, she's a wonder, my daughter.'

And Star does look rather wonderful this morning, sitting in the sunlight with the glass constellation glittering above her. Ava sleeps peacefully on her lap. 'Star's a strong spirit,' Cathbad had said that morning. 'She's got a powerful sense of self-preservation. I think she'll be just fine.' As usual, it seems that Cathbad is right. Judy asks after the baby.

'The doctor checked her over last night,' says Star. 'She

said she was fine. And she'll take a bottle now, which I suppose is a good thing.'

'And how are you?' asks Judy.

'I'm just so happy to have Ava back,' says Star. 'I can't really think of anything else. But when I do think about it . . . Dad says that Mum took Ava because she thought that Granddad had killed Margaret. That's horrible. I love Granddad. He'd never do anything like that. You don't think it's true, do you? It was just Mum . . . Mum getting ill again, wasn't it?'

'We have to investigate,' says Judy. 'But the best thing you can do is put it out of your mind for now. I know it's difficult.'

'I've been meditating,' says Star. 'That helps.' She looks rather coyly up at Judy. 'The other policewoman, Tanya, she told me that Cathbad's your partner. Why didn't you tell me?'

'I don't like to talk about my private life,' says Judy. 'I'm not the important one here.'

'But you told me about your baby being abducted.'

'Because I thought it might help.'

'It did,' says Star. 'It was the only thing I clung on to during that first awful night. I'll always feel a special kinship with Michael.'

Judy wishes that she hadn't remembered the name. 'Concentrate on Ava,' she says. 'Babies are good at making you live in the present.'

'The secret of health is not to mourn for the past or worry about the future but to live in the present wisely,' says Star. 'That's what Cathbad says.'

'I think Buddha or someone said it first,' says Judy. 'But it sounds like a good idea.'

When Judy leaves the house she is irritated, if not entirely surprised, to see Maddie sitting on the low wall of the front garden. She is scrolling through her phone but looks up when Judy emerges. 'Hi.'

'Are you following me again?' says Judy.

'Is it true that Star's mum abducted Ava?'

'There's a press conference on now,' says Judy, looking at her watch. 'Why aren't you there?'

'I thought this was where the story was.' Maddie gives her a wide smile, eyes big and innocent. Even though she knows it's an act, Judy can't help smiling back.

'Let's leave the family in peace,' she says. 'Ava's back with her mother. That's all you need to know. Can I give you a lift somewhere?'

She expects Maddie to refuse – like her father, she's an indefatigable walker – but she says, 'Could you drop me in Wells? I'm meeting someone for lunch.'

'OK,' says Judy. It's not far and she enjoys the drive along the coast. After last night's rain, it's suddenly a beautiful day with the promise of spring in the air. Maddie doesn't ask any more about the case but chatters on about her flatmates and the prospect of a trip to Greece in the summer. When they get to Wells, the sea sparkling like a Sunday night TV show, boats clinking in the harbour, Maddie says, 'You can drop me here.'

Judy stops the car. They are outside a small shop, trays of

jewels catching the light, red, green and gold. Little Rocks, reads the sign.

'Who are you meeting for lunch?'

'Roxy. She's an old schoolfriend. She works here.'

Judy looks at her almost stepdaughter. Does she know about the link between this shop, and its owner Kim Jennings, and the death of Margaret Lacey? It's possible that she doesn't. Maddie was, after all, brought up in the area. She could well have a schoolfriend who works here.

Judy watches as Maddie enters the shop, the bell ringing as the door shuts behind her. She looks at the trays displayed outside, jewellery, seashells and souvenirs of sunny Norfolk. She remembers Annie's scathing description. *Full of old tat covered in glitter.* Judy gets out of the car and moves closer. There's a whole tray of seahorses: coloured stone, silver, silk and satin embroidered in bright colours.

It came to me about five years ago that Margaret had said something about a seahorse..

That's what Kim Jennings had said when Judy asked her about the day when Margaret went missing.

Seahorses.

See horses.

Pete Benson seems confused by Clough's request.

'You want to talk to me about Margaret. Why?'

'We have received some new information,' says Clough. He is finding the whole thing rather difficult. Karen and Pete have always been nice to him. They asked him to read at Margaret's funeral. Now he is having to use phrases like 'information received' and 'interview under caution'.

'Is it about Ava?' says Pete. 'Dave rang us last night and said she'd been found. He sounded odd on the phone.'

'Ava's back home with her mother,' says Clough. 'As far as I know, she's in good health.'

'But who took her?' says Karen, who also seems bemused. She is youthfully dressed in white trousers and a sparkly top but, as she hovers around her husband in the hall, she suddenly looks like an old woman. 'I keep ringing Annie,' she says, 'but she's not answering her phone.'

'Ava is safe,' says Clough. 'That's all we can tell you at present.' Keep him in the dark, Nelson had said, then we can spring the questions about Margaret. That's all very well but the boss isn't having to shepherd a confused elderly man into a police car. Karen comes out to the car with them. 'When will you be back?'

'I don't know,' says Pete. His hands are shaking.

'We'll be as quick as we can,' says Clough. He opens the back door for Pete and then gets into the passenger seat. Tanya is driving.

They drive slowly through the estate. Haig Road, Marshall Drive, Byng Place, Allenby Avenue. John Mostyn's house still has police tape outside. The windows have been boarded up, presumably to stop the locals breaking them.

'Why are you taking me to the police station?' asks Pete, querulously, from the back seat.

'There are just some questions we need to ask you,' says Clough.

'Under caution,' adds Tanya, from behind the wheel. Clough thinks that she is enjoying herself far too much.

The skewbald is still grazing in the paddock outside the house belonging to Steve and Alison Jennings. What was its name? Patch, something like that. But Steve had said that, at one time, the family had owned a few rescue horses, including Cuddles, the pony belonging to Kim Jennings.

At first Judy thinks that there's nobody in but after a few minutes the door is opened by Steve, wearing another of his woolly jumpers.

'Hallo?' He doesn't recognise her.

'Hi. I'm DS Judy Johnson. I came to talk to you the other day, about Margaret Lacey. There's something else I wanted to ask you.'

'Come in,' says Steve but Judy thinks that he looks wary. There's little trace of the cosy granddad today.

There's no trace of the grandchildren either, or of his wife. Only the elderly dog snores by the electric fire with its fake coals. Even the cockatoo's cage is covered by a cloth.

'Ali's collecting Daisy-Mae from school,' says Steve, in answer to Judy's query. He doesn't say who Daisy-Mae is.

Judy is beginning to wish she hadn't rushed over to the Jenningses' house so recklessly. She texted Clough saying where she was going but, if he's in the middle of an interview, he won't look at his phone. She should have waited for proper back-up. But she's here now, so she might as well get on with it.

'Mr Jennings,' she said. 'Did you see Margaret alone on the day that she disappeared?'

She had thought that Steve's face had changed earlier, when he saw her at the door. But she was wrong; it changes now.

'What are you talking about?' he says.

'Kim told me that Margaret said something about a sea-horse. But I think she said that she was going to see the horses, your horses.' Judy remembers Karen being quoted, in Maddie's article, as saying that Margaret had liked 'dancing and ponies and dressing up'. She thinks it was Margaret's love for ponies that had led her to accompany Steve Jennings on the sunny July day. And, after all, the man was her best friend's father; she had trusted him. What had Annie said? *There was no one strange there. It was just our friends and family.*

'What happened, Steve?' says Judy. 'Did you take Margaret back here, to your house?'

'Of course I didn't,' says Steve. 'This is slander. I'll sue.'

'You were seen,' says Judy, suddenly sure of it. 'John Mostyn saw you.'

'That nutter,' says Steve. 'You can't believe a word he says. Anyway, he's dead now. Dead men tell no tales.'

The cliché sounds very sinister in Steve's flat Norfolk accent. Suddenly, despite the fact that it is midday and she's in a sitting room filled with pictures of smiling children, with a dog snoozing on the hearthrug, Judy is afraid.

'What happened?' she says again. 'What happened to Margaret?'

Steve turns away and seems to be looking for something

in a drawer. With his back still turned, he says, 'It was an accident. I just wanted a kiss. She was a tease, that girl, prancing about in shorts and skimpy tops. "Hallo, Uncle Steve." She knew what she was doing.'

'She was twelve,' says Judy.

'Twelve going on thirty,' says Steve. He turns to face her. He's smiling now and it's a few seconds before Judy realises that he's holding a gun.

Pete still seems confused when he's ushered into Interview Room 1.

'What's going on?' he keeps saying.

'Interview with Peter Benson under caution,' says Tanya into the microphone. 'Present, DS Tanya Fuller and DS David Clough.'

'We wanted to talk to you about Margaret,' says Clough, still feeling slightly awkward. Pete fixes him with mild blue eyes, clearly thinking that Clough is his only friend in the room. 'I believe you knew the family before you married Karen. Did you know Margaret?'

Pete blinks twice. 'I did know them,' he says slowly. 'My brother-in-law Steve was a friend of Bob's, Karen's first husband. I met the family at his house a few times.'

'How well did you know Margaret?' asks Tanya.

'Not well. I mean, she was a young girl, always playing with Steve's daughters. I don't think I spoke to her more than twice. But I feel that I've come to know her since she went missing, if you know what I mean. She's a big part of our lives still.'

Clough, remembering the wall of photographs, thinks that he does know what Pete means. Marrying Karen must have meant marrying into the shared family grief.

'Were you at the King's Lynn street party on the twenty-ninth of July 1981?' asks Clough.

'No,' says Pete. 'I lived near Swaffham then. I think I watched the wedding on television at home and then went to the pub for a quick pint. I only heard about Margaret going missing when it was on the news the next day. I rang Steve. He was quite distraught.'

'You had an allotment, didn't you?' says Clough.

'Yes,' says Pete. 'I've always enjoyed gardening. I've got an allotment now too.'

'Why didn't you tell us that you used to live near Scarning Fen?' says Clough. 'We asked if you had any connection to the area.'

'I don't think I realised it was near there,' says Pete. 'I didn't recognise the name. What's all this about? Why are you asking me these questions?'

Clough glances at Tanya. They have discussed this beforehand. It's just a matter of who says the words.

'How well do you get on with your stepchildren Annie and Luke?' asks Clough.

Pete shakes his head, seeming bewildered again by the change in direction.

'Well enough, I think. They were teenagers when I married Karen. Luke was almost an adult. So things were a bit tricky sometimes. Luke had got used to being the man of the house, I think. Annie too. It was almost like she was in charge. She used to order Luke to do things and he'd do them. It was like he didn't have any free will. Both of them tried to look after Karen, they were very protective of her, but it sometimes looked like bullying to me. Things were easier when they left home to go to university. Then Karen and I had Richard and Bradley.'

'Did the siblings get on?' asks Clough.

'Yes. Annie doted on the boys when they were young. She was always good with babies. I think that's why she became a paediatric nurse. Luke was always more distant. I think I spoke to him more when he came home for Margaret's funeral than I ever have before.'

Was that because Luke already suspected him of killing his sister? thinks Clough. And was Annie, the girl who had loved babies, already planning to abduct her own daughter's child?

But Pete's mind has been moving in the same direction.

'Is this to do with Annie and Luke? Did *they* think I killed Margaret? Oh my God.'

Clough lets silence answer him.

Steve levels the gun at Judy. It looks like an old service pistol, old-fashioned but, unfortunately, still in working order. Steve's voice is now quiet and reasonable, as it was the first time Judy met him. 'I tried to kiss her,' he says. 'I took hold of her, just to steady her, but she pulled away and she fell and hit her head. There, on the fireplace.' He points at the fire surround, which is made of rough-hewn stone, a sixties attempt at antiquity. 'When I went to pick her up, there was blood coming from her head and she was an awful colour, sort of grey. I went to get something to put over her and, when I came back, she was dead. No heartbeat, nothing. I didn't know what to do. Ali and the kids were due back from the street party any minute.'

Judy remembers Kim Jennings saying that, after she had parted from Margaret, she went back to the party to sit with her 'mum and sisters'. No mention of her dad, who was presumably, at that very moment, driving Margaret away on the pretext of seeing his horses. Yet, later, Steve had been one of the men out looking for Margaret, even though he knew that she would never be found.

'Why didn't you call an ambulance when she first fell?' says Judy. 'You might have saved her.'

'I told you,' says Steve. 'I panicked. I didn't know what to do. It was a terrible shock. Imagine Kim coming back to find her friend dead on the carpet. I had to act quickly.' He actually sounds quite sorry for himself.

'What did you do?' asks Judy.

'I wrapped her in a blanket and tied her up,' says Steve, as if this is perfectly normal behaviour. 'Then I put her in the boot of my car and went to join the search party. Later that night I buried her.'

'In your brother-in-law Pete's allotment near Scarning Fen.'

'What a clever policewoman you are,' says Steve. 'Such a shame about the way you're going to die. The gun just went off accidentally, that's what I'll say. I'll probably only get a suspended sentence, what with having such a good name in the community. Devoted family man and all that.'

And that's precisely how Judy had thought of him, until about half an hour ago. She thinks of Kim Jennings and the way her face looked sad in repose. Did she somewhere, deep down, know what her father was?

'My colleagues know where I am,' says Judy. 'They'll be here any moment.'

'Rubbish,' says Steve. 'I saw your face just now. You were terrified.'

'Police!' shouts a voice behind them. 'Drop that gun!'

Steve doesn't drop it but he half turns and that's enough for Judy. She swings her arm upwards and knocks the gun from Steve's hand. Then she punches him in the stomach. He groans and doubles up, his head near the spot where Margaret breathed her last. Somehow the dog sleeps on.

Judy is bending over Steve's hunched body and putting on handcuffs.

'Call the police,' she says to Maddie.

'I have.' Maddie's voice has gone back to normal now. Where did she find that commanding tone earlier? The shout of 'Police' had almost convinced Judy herself.

Judy kneels on the carpet beside Steve, who is still breathing heavily.

'Are you OK?' says Maddie.

'I'm fine. How did you find me?'

'I followed you.' Maddie gives her a sudden grin. 'Like you're always telling me not to do. Roxy gave me a lift up here. I knew you were on to something.'

'Well, I'm very grateful,' says Judy. 'That shout was amazing. I thought you were the real thing for a moment.'

'I tried to sound like that superintendent. The one who's always doing the press conferences.'

'Jo Archer. Yeah, that's who you reminded me of.'

'Did he confess?' Maddie nods towards the crumpled figure on the hearthrug.

'Yes. This is the man who killed Margaret Lacey.' Steve mutters something indistinct. 'He'll be confessing it again later in a taped interview.'

'Can I have an exclusive afterwards?'

'You certainly can,' says Judy, as the sirens sound in the distance.

CHAPTER 36

Despite her words to Maddie, Judy half expects Steve to deny everything when he is questioned at the police station. But, in a recorded interview with Judy and Clough, live-streamed to Nelson in the viewing room, Steve Jennings describes how Margaret Lacey died. It's murder, in Judy's book, but she knows that a lawyer might try for a plea of manslaughter. Luckily Steve has waived his right to a solicitor and Judy makes sure that she gets on tape the fact that Steve didn't call for an ambulance when Margaret first fell and hit her head. He says he went for something to put over her but did he really just wait for her to die? Maybe he even hastened her death by smothering her? Traces of material were found around Margaret's jaw bone and Judy is willing to bet that Steve's DNA is on them and on the rope that bound her body. Steve is helpfully quite expansive about his feelings for Margaret, which should damn him in the eyes of any decent-minded jury. 'She knew what she was doing, that girl. She was the type who could wind men around her little finger.'

Clough, who is less good at hiding his feelings than Judy, clenches his fists under the table.

'I only wanted a kiss,' says Steve. 'Was that so bad?'

'She was twelve years old,' says Judy. She wants this clearly on the tape.

Steve laughs. 'She was no innocent, believe me. She was just like her mother. A right little prick tease. I could see it when Margaret used to come to the house. She was always looking at me under her eyelashes. Flaunting herself. Tempting me.'

'You're talking about the times when Margaret came to play with your daughter, Kim?'

'Margaret never had much time for Kim, to be honest. I think she came to see me.'

Can he really have believed this? thinks Judy, looking at the grey-haired man across the desk, even now smiling complacently, hands folded across his paunch. And what about Kim, the little girl who was always in Margaret's shadow? Did she know that her father was lusting after her schoolfriend? Judy hopes not.

'I went to kiss her,' says Steve. 'And she pulled away. I grabbed her. I knew she wanted it really. And she fell. She hit her head on the fireplace. It was an accident.'

Judy asks again about the ambulance. 'Why didn't you call for help? It's possible that you could have saved her. Didn't you want to save her?'

'I didn't know what to do,' says Steve. 'I didn't want her lying there dead on my carpet.' Judy gets Steve to recount, in painstaking detail, how he hid Margaret's body in the boot of his car, went to join the search party and later buried Margaret in his brother-in-law's allotment. She hopes that this will sound particularly cold and calculating in court.

'Did Pete know that you had killed Margaret?' asks Clough.

'No,' says Steve. 'He's a wimp, Pete. Always has been. He would have gone to pieces.'

'Didn't he notice that the ground had been disturbed?'

'No. It was a new allotment then. Pete had just dug it over and put the compost down. I gave him the horse manure. It was easy to bury her. Pete planted his vegetables on top and never knew a thing. The plants always grew well there and I always wondered whether that was due to Margaret. And my manure, of course.'

Did he really say that? Judy glances towards the camera and wonders what the boss is making of all this.

'What did you think when Pete married Margaret's mother?' she asks, really wanting to know.

'I was pleased for Pete. I never thought he'd have the guts to ask her. And she was a good-looking woman. Though she'd gone off a bit by then.'

Karen would have been in her thirties when she married Pete but Steve's tastes obviously lay in other directions. Judy wonders again about his own daughters, not to mention Steve's grandchildren and great-grandchildren.

'Are we nearly finished?' says Steve. 'I need to get home. I'm taking Daisy-Mae to her ballet class.'

'We're nearly there,' says Judy.

She can only hope that Steve's babysitting days are over.

While Steve is being charged with murder and possession of a firearm with intent to endanger life, Judy and Clough retreat to Nelson's office.

'Good work,' says Nelson. 'We've got a full confession. We'll try hard to make the murder charge stick. After all, he assaulted an under-age girl and didn't call for help when she was hurt. Bastard. What made you realise it was him?'

Judy explains about the seahorses. Nelson makes a noise that seems halfway between admiration and exasperation.

'What were you thinking of, going there without back-up?'

'I texted Clough.'

'I was in the interview room,' says Clough. 'By the time I saw your text you were back here handcuffed to Steve Jennings.'

'I know,' says Judy. 'It's not your fault. I should have waited for back-up.'

'Instead you had Maddie storming in pretending to be Jo Archer,' says Nelson. 'That I would have liked to see.'

'Is Maddie OK?'

'Seems so. She's given a statement and she's waiting for you downstairs.'

'I've promised her an exclusive.'

'She can have one as soon we've done the paperwork. She deserves it. Seems she's like her father, always turning up at the right moment.'

'She is like him,' says Judy. 'She's been driving me mad following me around but she probably saved my life today.'

'You should never have put yourself in that position,' says Nelson, glowering again.

'I know. I'm sorry.'

'So,' says Nelson, sitting down at his desk. 'We've got Margaret's killer. And we've found Ava. Not bad going.'

'We just need to solve John Mostyn's murder and we're done,' says Clough. 'Any chance that Jennings could have done it?'

'He's got an alibi,' says Judy. 'He was at home with Alison. They had the great-grandchildren staying.'

'It's another married alibi,' says Clough. 'Could be broken. Especially when the wife finds out about this.'

'I think Mostyn suspected Steve all along,' says Judy. 'Maybe he even saw him with Margaret on the day of the street party. Somehow, he must have realised that Steve had buried Margaret in Pete's allotment. Remember when we spoke to Pete? He said that he'd talked to John Mostyn about gardening. Maybe that gave him the idea.'

'Why did he dig her up and bury her at the Saltmarsh though?' says Clough.

'So we would find her,' says Judy. 'He must have read about the dig and seen his chance. There may have been some other significance too. Remember the witch stones that were found at the site? John Mostyn loved stones and the beach. Maybe that's why he buried Margaret there.' Judy still has the witch stone that John Mostyn gave her. It's in her bag and several times a day she feels for it, the smooth surface, the satisfying void at the centre.

'I still think Jennings could have killed Mostyn,' says Clough. 'Who else could benefit?'

'Dead men tell no tales,' says Judy. 'That's what Steve said to me.'

'Steve Jennings didn't kill John Mostyn,' says Nelson.

Judy finds Maddie in reception, scrolling down her phone as usual.

'Want a lift?' she says.

'Hi, Judy,' says Maddie, for all the world as if this is a casual meeting. 'That would be great. Actually, I was wondering if I could stay at your place tonight.'

'Of course,' says Judy.

'In fact, my flatmates are getting on my nerves a bit so I was wondering . . .'

'You can move in with us,' says Judy. 'Cathbad would be delighted.'

'It's only temporary,' says Maddie, putting on her backpack. 'I think I'm destined to be a nomad.'

'Maybe for a while,' says Judy. 'But I think you'll settle down one day.'

'Like Dad?'

'Just like him.'

They go towards the exit but, at the swing doors, Judy asks Maddie to wait for her and sprints back upstairs. She comes back down carrying the hamster cage.

'What's that?' says Maddie.

'Two new pets.'

The more the merrier, she thinks. And she actually means it.

By the end of the day, Ruth is feeling exhausted. Last night hadn't been too bad. Shona had been really kind, offering hot drinks and popping in several times during the night to check that Ruth was all right. And even Phil hadn't asked too many questions. After Nelson's phone call Ruth had driven today to Scarning Fen and, ignoring his advice, had examined Pete Benson's old allotment for signs of disturbance. It was difficult because the soil had been turned over fairly recently – the current allotment owners seem keen on crop rotation – but she thought that, in one place, the earth appeared darker and richer, which could point to something organic having been buried there. She took samples and filled in a report and then she drove to the hospital to see Leif. She had been feeling rather guilty about him. After all, Cathbad had Judy and she had Shona. Who was looking after Leif?

The answer is, half the hospital. Leif, his leg in plaster up to his thigh, is in a small room off the main ward but nurse after nurse comes in to enquire after his progress and to offer fruit drinks and vitamin supplements.

'I know you're fussy about your food,' says one pretty redhead, as if she has known Leif since childhood.

'You're really kind, Kerry,' says Leif. He is on first-name terms with all of them and many have signed his plaster with accompanying hearts and kisses.

'How are you feeling?' asks Ruth during a brief lull.

'OK,' says Leif, although, close up, his eyes are rather shadowed. 'We were lucky, I guess.'

'You came off worst,' says Ruth, although her head is splitting and she still feels rather sick.

'The deer came off worst.'

'Yes. Poor thing. Cathbad feels terrible about that. And about you,' she adds hastily.

'I know. He was in earlier. But it wasn't his fault. Driving conditions were terrible and the stag just appeared in front of us out of nowhere. I still think it might have been Herne the Hunter. I'm just annoyed about this,' he gestures at his leg, 'just when I need to tie up the loose ends at the dig.'

'If there's anything I can do to help,' says Ruth, although she knows she sounds unconvincing.

'Don't worry,' says Leif. 'It's really just waiting for the lab results now. And for the facial reconstruction. When I'm discharged I'm going to stay with my mother for a few days.'

So Leif does have someone to look after him, thinks Ruth, feeling slightly envious as she often does now when people mention mothers. She wonders what has happened with Laura. If she was living with Leif, she obviously isn't now.

'I'm sorry,' says Leif suddenly. 'If I hadn't dragged you all the way to Stanton Drew, this would never have happened.'

'It's OK,' says Ruth. 'It's all part of the great web. That's what Cathbad would say.'

'He did say it earlier,' says Leif. 'But I'm sorry all the same. We're still friends, aren't we?'

Were they ever friends? thinks Ruth. Erik had been her friend. Perhaps he still is. She's not sure what she thinks about the handsome wounded lion in front of her. She still doesn't quite trust him but she takes the outstretched hand and squeezes it.

'Of course we're friends,' she says. 'I have to go and collect Kate now.'

Kate is fascinated by the plaster on Ruth's forehead, which is now looking a bit grubby at the edges. She wants to hear the story of the crash again and again: the stone circle, the rain, the deer in the road.

'Remember our crash?' she says. 'With the rabbit?'

It takes Ruth a few minutes to realise that Kate is talking about the first time that she met Frank. He had literally crashed into them, driving his hired car on the wrong side of the road. There had been a dead rabbit on the verge, completely unrelated to the accident. Ruth hadn't known that Kate had noticed it.

'Are we going to see Frank today?' asks Kate after they have reminisced about the time a man with a 'funny accent like a cowboy' drove his car into them.

'Not today,' says Ruth. 'I'm too tired today.'

'I'm tired too,' boasts Kate. 'Tasha and I didn't sleep all night. We played games on her tablet and we ate Haribos at midnight.'

Kate seems lively enough when they get back, rushing to tell Flint all about her sleepover. Flint is slightly offish with Ruth for abandoning him last night but he consents to eat a special tuna supper and to sit with them while they watch some teenage TV show that Ruth is too lethargic to turn off.

Kate must be a bit tired though because, when Ruth tells

her that it's time for bed, she only puts up a token resistance. Ruth heaves herself off the sofa, ready to run the bath, when there's a fusillade of knocks on the front door. Only one person knocks like that.

'Nelson. What are you doing here?'

'Came to see how you were,' says Nelson, thrusting a rather battered bunch of carnations at her. Ruth recognises the wrapping from her nearest petrol station but she appreciates the gesture. She remembers Valentine's Day and her vision of Nelson presenting Michelle with beautifully wrapped red roses.

'Dad!' Kate comes downstairs and barrels into Nelson's chest. 'I had a sleepover last night. I ate sweets at midnight.'

'That's nice, love.' Nelson sits on the sofa and, despite often declaring herself nearly grown-up, Kate climbs onto his lap. Flint, on the other hand, walks off in disgust.

'I had a sleepover too,' says Ruth.

'Did you?' Nelson gives her a sharp look. 'Who with?'

Ruth feels like telling him to mind his own business but it seems too much hassle so she says, 'With Shona and Phil. The hospital said that I shouldn't go home on my own.'

Nelson's face seems to relax. 'But you're OK now?'

'I'm fine,' says Ruth. 'I went to Scarning Fen today.'

'I told you not to.'

'It's lucky that I don't have to do what you tell me,' says Ruth sweetly. 'I examined the soil at the allotment and I think it's possible that a body was buried there until fairly recently.'

'Oh, we've found Margaret's killer,' says Nelson.

'You have?' says Ruth. 'Who is it?'

'A family friend called Steve Jennings. It'll be in the press tomorrow, probably in an exclusive written by Maddie Henderson.'

'Maddie? How come she's involved?'

'It's a long story. Johnson made the breakthrough but nearly got killed for her efforts. Maddie saved her.'

'Wow,' says Ruth. 'That *is* a good story.'

'Will you read me a bedtime story?' Kate asks Nelson. 'I still have stories sometimes.'

So Nelson stays to read Kate a bedtime story and, afterwards, he and Ruth drink wine in front of the fire. It's almost like the first time, when Nelson turned up at Ruth's door after Scarlet's body had been found. Except, this time, they're not going to sleep together. Ruth is quite certain about that.

But it turns out that she's wrong about this too.

CHAPTER 37

Nelson and Freddie Burnett are sitting on Cromer pier. The tide is out and the sand stretches in bands of blue and gold. They have brought coffee from the café and sit companionably in deckchairs watching the cockle-pickers pulling their nets along the beach.

'It's a beautiful spot, isn't it?' says Freddie. 'I always thought that I'd end my days here.'

'It's a nice beach,' says Nelson. Though, in his opinion, it could be improved by a roller-coaster and a few donkeys.

'How are they doing?' says Freddie. 'Margaret's family?'

'Not bad,' says Nelson. 'I think it was a relief to learn the identity of Margaret's murderer, although it was a shock too, especially for Pete, the stepfather.'

'Killer was his brother-in-law, wasn't he? Are you telling me this Pete had no idea?'

'He says not and I believe him. Pete's a gentle soul. I don't think he ever realised what his brother-in-law was.'

'Scum, that's what he is,' says Freddie. 'They should throw away the key. What about the other business, with the baby?'

They have, so far, managed to keep Annie's name out of the press. It was helpful that Steve Jennings' arrest, and Maddie's exclusive on it, led the news for many days. Annie is out on bail and receiving psychiatric treatment. Her psychiatrist says that Annie abducted Ava while suffering from delusions brought on by the stress of Margaret's body being discovered. Her family seem to have accepted this and, according to Judy, Star has seen her mother and apparently forgives her. Ava is still doing well. She's currently at Nelson's house for a 'playdate' with George.

'The baby's fine,' says Nelson. 'The family are coping well. Considering.'

'What about Mostyn?' says Freddie. 'You pinning that on Jennings too?'

'Freddie,' says Nelson, 'Steve Jennings didn't kill John Mostyn. You did.'

Freddie turns to look at him, his still-bulky frame blotting out the sun.

'What are you talking about?'

'I suspected from the beginning,' says Nelson. 'It was such a professional killing. I knew it either had to be a criminal or a copper. The way he was killed, just one shot and the bullet taken away. No prints on anything. The body moved just for a bit of misdirection. Even the CCTV at the Canada Estate. The killer knew where the cameras were, they'd even covered up the logo on their coat. I did see some dark skin though. You got very tanned in Tenerife, Freddie.'

Freddie stares at him, his eyes bright in a face which is still the colour and texture of shoe leather.

'You've got no evidence.'

'Then I remembered the phone call,' says Nelson. 'You phoned me when we had Mostyn in for a DNA test.'

'I asked you if he was going to get away with it again. And you gave me some crap about doing things by the book.'

'The thing is,' says Nelson, 'you were meant to be in Tenerife but, when I checked the call location, you were ringing from Norfolk.'

'Bloody mobile phones,' says Freddie. 'There's no privacy these days.'

In Nelson's opinion, being watched is no problem if you don't break the law. But he doesn't say anything. He wishes, more than anything, that he could leave Freddie sitting on the pier enjoying his retirement. No one's going to worry too much if John Mostyn's murder goes unsolved. They've caught Margaret's killer and they've restored Ava to her mother. The golden-haired girl and the innocent baby, those are the victims that the public cares about. Not a seventy-year-old man who collected stones and lived alone with his hamsters. Funnily enough, it's the thought of Sonny and Fredo, now happily residing with Cathbad and Judy, that strengthens Nelson's resolve. John Mostyn deserves justice and Nelson, like Agatha Christie's Poirot, does not approve of murder.

'You'll have trouble making it stand up in court,' says Freddie.

'I'm confident we'll get your DNA from the scene,' says Nelson. 'It's a different world now, Freddie. It's almost impossible to get away with these things. DNA has changed everything.'

'Changed it for the worse,' says Freddie. 'There's no real policing any more.'

That depends on your definition of policing, thinks Nelson.

In a different voice, Freddie says, 'I thought you'd let him off. You're getting soft in your old age. All that "innocent until proved guilty" crap.'

'He was innocent,' says Nelson.

Freddie gives a mirthless laugh. 'Well, I know that now, don't I?'

They are both silent, looking out towards the sea, now only a line of darker blue against the sky.

'What'll I get, do you think?' says Freddie. 'Ten years with good behaviour?'

'Maybe less,' says Nelson, 'and you could serve most of it in an open prison.'

'I'm sixty-eight,' says Freddie, 'and I've got prostate cancer. I'm not going to see the outside world again.'

It's the first time that Nelson has heard about the cancer. He watches Freddie as the older man sips his coffee, eyes narrowed against the spring sunshine.

'Give me a day to get my things in order,' says Freddie. 'I'll turn myself in tomorrow. You have my word on that.'

'All right,' says Nelson. And they sit in silence, watching the tiny figures walking across the bay.

CHAPTER 38

'When are they coming?' asks Kate, for the tenth time.

'Soon,' says Ruth. 'They said eleven o'clock.'

But Kate has been watching at the window since ten. She has changed her outfit three times. She's now wearing jeans and a black top with a sparkly Hello Kitty on it. She's even tried to persuade Flint to wear a bow tie. He is currently sitting on top of Ruth's wardrobe, tail fluffed out in outrage.

Ruth, on the other hand, is feeling extremely nervous. When Laura rang her she had been expecting more abuse, not the suggestion that Laura and Rebecca should pay a visit 'to get to know Katie'. But she had known that Kate would love a visit from her half-sisters so they have fixed on this Saturday morning, a week after Steve Jennings was charged with the murder of Margaret Lacey and a retired copper called Freddie Burnett was found dead at his bungalow in Cromer, a gun at his side.

'Is this them?' squeaks Kate as a car pulls up outside.

'I think so,' says Ruth.

The two young women, one dark and one fair, look very

similar as they walk down the garden path. But, when she meets them properly, Ruth realises how different the sisters are. Rebecca immediately bonds with Kate and, within minutes, is upstairs playing Sylvanians with her. Laura, though she gives Kate a lovely hug, holds back a little. She and Ruth are left downstairs listening to sounds of riotous play from above.

'Rebecca always gets on with children,' says Laura. 'She's the one who should have been a teacher.'

Ruth is making coffee. She thinks that Laura sounds a little wistful.

'I'm sure you'll make a great teacher,' she says.

'Cathbad says that it's my calling,' says Laura. 'And I must say I did enjoy my placement.'

'I was terrified when I taught my first undergraduates,' says Ruth. 'But I love it now.'

'It must be wonderful being a university lecturer,' says Laura. 'You can really impart knowledge.'

'The longer I do it the more I wonder if I ever teach my students anything,' says Ruth. 'But, if I can make them interested in archaeology, that's the main thing. Your job is more important. You're creating lifelong learners. God, that sounds like a government pamphlet.'

Laura laughs then looks rather constrained. Perhaps she realises that she is talking and laughing with her enemy, the scarlet woman who is threatening her parents' marriage. And, remembering the night when Nelson called round with his bunch of carnations, Ruth feels guilty all over again.

'I'm back living with my parents,' says Laura. 'But I'm

looking for a flat. I want to live on my own for a bit. I've never done that before.'

'Living on your own is great,' says Ruth. 'And, if you want company, get a cat.'

Laura brightens. 'I do like cats. And we could never have one at home because of Bruno.'

Ruth wonders again what happened with Leif. Perhaps he and Laura were never really seriously involved. She hasn't seen Leif since she visited him in hospital. She assumes that he's in the West Country with Magda and her miracle baby.

They drink their coffee and Rebecca and Kate come clattering downstairs. Rebecca is wearing Kate's pirate hat and Kate has drawn a curly line on her upper lip.

'I'm a lady pirate,' she says, grabbing biscuits with both hands, 'but I've got a moustache.'

'I've got one too,' says Rebecca, 'if I don't wax it off.'

Looking at her smooth, glowing face, Ruth doubts this. All three of Nelson's daughters are beautiful, she realises. Laura in particular takes after Michelle but she, Ruth, must surely take some credit for Kate.

It's a beautiful early spring day and Ruth suggests a walk over the marshes. Anything to work off Kate's excess energy. She has no particular route in mind but she is not surprised when they find themselves following the ancient path towards the place where the wooden henge once stood. As Cathbad would say, the Saltmarsh has its own ideas about destiny. It's a long walk though and Ruth finds herself looking at her Fitbit before remembering that it got broken in the crash. She's not going to replace it. Shona is a good friend but Ruth doesn't want her knowing all about her cardiovascular fitness, such as it is.

'It's so beautiful here,' says Laura. 'You can see for miles.'

'Not what Dad says,' says Rebecca. She adopts a comedy Northern voice. 'Ee bah gum, it's full of ghosts and ghoulies.'

'Not like Blackpool,' says Laura, in the same voice. 'Now that's a proper beach.'

Kate laughs delightedly but Ruth hears the affection in the teasing and feels rather sad. This is the family life that she can never share. She and Nelson haven't spoken since the night with the carnations. Is this what her future is going to be, hanging round on the outskirts of Nelson's life with her only reward being the occasional night of (admittedly fantastic) sex? She shouldn't settle for it. She mustn't settle for it. She thinks of the still unsent job application on her computer. Can she really do it, move from UNN to Cambridge? It would be great for her career, there's no doubt about that, but what about the rest of her life? And, when it comes down to it, could she bear to leave this place, the shifting marsh, the ever-changing sky, the sand dunes suddenly giving way to sea, wide and clear under a bright blue sky?

The dig is now over so she expects the site to be deserted but, when they get nearer, they see a man standing by the trenches. At first it looks as if he has four legs but, getting closer still, Ruth sees that he is on crutches.

'Oh no,' says Laura. 'It's Leif.'

'Laura split up with Leif,' says Rebecca, 'because Dad told her that he beat up his old girlfriend.'

'That wasn't why,' says Laura. 'And Leif was never charged. He says it didn't happen.'

'They all say that,' says Rebecca.

It doesn't surprise Ruth that Nelson has been checking up on Leif. He is insanely protective where his daughters are concerned. And nor does it totally surprise her to hear about the domestic abuse. She has always suspected that there was a darkness in Leif, something ugly beneath the handsome exterior. She felt the same about Erik, she realises now.

Laura greets Leif with some embarrassment and they speak in private for a few moments. Then Leif swings himself over to talk to Ruth. Apart from the leg, he seems fit and well, his face tanned and his hair, loose today, a burnished mane.

'I'm going home tomorrow,' he says, in answer to Ruth's question. 'I just wanted a last look at this place. The stone circle.'

Ruth remembers Stanton Drew and the stones looming up out of the mist. This is an altogether friendlier place, a hymn to the sea and the sky. But it is also a place where a young girl was buried, with a witch stone at her side. And the place where John Mostyn, the Stone Man, laid Margaret to rest. The landscape itself is important, as Erik so often used to say.

'I heard that they were able to get some DNA from the bones in the cist,' says Ruth.

'Yes,' says Leif. 'Look at this fantastic reconstruction that Oscar did.'

He produces a phone and, with some difficulty because of

the crutches, scrolls down until he finds a photograph. Ruth looks at a young girl, aged about sixteen, gazing out at the world with a mixture of curiosity and defiance.

Ruth thinks of the Bronze Age girl and of Margaret Lacey, neither of whom ever lived to see adulthood. They left their mark all the same, she thinks. Kate, Laura and Rebecca have gone down to the beach and, watching them, Ruth remembers her dream, Kate walking between two unknown women. Well, they are unknown no longer. Has she any right to take Kate away from this place, away from her family? As she watches, the three sisters start to run, their footsteps dark on the white sand, soon to be washed away by the tide.

ACKNOWLEDGEMENTS

The Stone Circle mainly features real places, although characters and events are all fictional. A second circle was found near the famous Seahenge in Norfolk although the stone cist and its contents are imaginary, as is the entire story of Margaret Lacey. King's Lynn is obviously real, with its quay, Custom House and Tuesday Marketplace, but the events described in this book are all invented by me. The stone circle at Stanton Drew, too, is real and well worth a visit. Incidentally the sculptor Oscar Nilsson is also an actual person and his work can be seen at the new archaeology gallery at Brighton Museum.

Lots of people have helped with this book but I must stress that I have followed their advice only as far as it suits the plot and any subsequent mistakes are mine alone. Thanks to Linzi Harvey for being brilliant on bones as usual and to Graham Bartlett, police consultant extraordinaire, for trying to keep the procedural side of the book within the bounds of reality. Special thanks to Matt Pope and Letty Ingrey from the UCL Institute of Archaeology for coming up with Scarning Fen, which is a real place and does contain some unique flora and fauna. Thanks also to Lee Mason at Beccles Books in Suffolk for telling me about Jack Valentine. I don't think I have nearly exhausted all the myths and legends of East Anglia, let alone its archaeological wonders.

Thanks to Carol Dunne for taking part in a charity auction to become a character in this book. All proceeds go to CLIC Sargent, the charity supporting teenage cancer sufferers, so a huge thank you to Carol and everyone else who took part. Although Carol is a headteacher, she bears no resemblance to her fictional counterpart in these pages. St Paul's School is also imaginary. Thanks to Jan Adams and Marj Maccallum, previous auction winners whose namesakes are now regular returning characters.

Heartfelt thanks to my publishers Quercus and the amazing Team Elly: Therese Keating, Hannah Robinson, Olivia Mead, Laura McKerrell, Katie Sadler, David Murphy and so many others. I'm so grateful for everything you have done for me and Ruth. Special thanks, though, must go to my editor, Jane Wood. Jane has edited all my 'Elly Griffiths' books and has, in the process, become a mentor and friend. We always agreed that there would be ten Ruth books so it's only right that this eleventh should be dedicated to her, with love and thanks.

Thanks, as always, to my wonderful agent, Rebecca Carter, and all at Janklow and Nesbit. Thanks to Kirby Kim in New York and to Naomi Gibbs and all at HMH. Thanks to all the publishers around the world who publish these books with such dedication and care. Thanks to my crime writer friends for their support and to anyone who has bought my books or borrowed them from a library. I appreciate you more than I can say.

Finally, love and thanks always to my husband, Andrew, and to our children, Alex and Juliet.

EG 2019

WHO'S WHO
IN THE DR RUTH GALLOWAY
MYSTERIES

Dr Ruth Galloway

Profession: forensic archaeologist

Likes: cats, Bruce Springsteen, bones, books

Dislikes: gyms, organized religion, shopping

Ruth Galloway was born in south London and educated at University College London and Southampton University, where she met her mentor Professor Erik Anderssen. In 1997, she participated in Professor Anderssen's dig on the north Norfolk coast which resulted in the excavation of a Bronze Age henge. Ruth subsequently moved to the area and became Head of Forensic Archaeology at the University of North Norfolk. She lives in an isolated cottage on the edge of the Saltmarsh. In 2007, she was approached by DCI Harry Nelson who wanted her help in identifying bones found buried on the marshes, and her life suddenly got a whole lot more complicated.

Surprising fact about Ruth: she is fascinated by the London Underground and once attended a fancy dress party as The Angel Islington.

Harry Nelson

Profession: Detective Chief Inspector

Likes: driving fast, solving crimes, his family

Dislikes: Norfolk, the countryside, management speak, his boss

Harry Nelson was born in Blackpool. He came to Norfolk in his thirties to lead the Serious Crimes Unit, bringing with him his wife, Michelle, and their daughters, Laura and Rebecca. Nelson has a loyal team and enjoys his work. He still hankers after the North, though, and has not come to love his adopted county. Nelson thinks of himself as an old-fashioned policeman and so often clashes with Super-intendent Archer, who is trying to drag the force into the twenty-first century. Nelson is impatient and quick-tempered but he is capable of being both imaginative and sensitive. He's also cleverer than he lets on.

Surprising fact about Nelson: he's a huge Frank Sinatra fan.

Michelle Nelson

Profession: hairdresser

Likes: her family, exercising, socializing with friends

Dislikes: dowdiness, confrontation, talking about murder

Michelle married Nelson when she was twenty-four and he was twenty-six. She was happy with her life in Blackpool – two children, part-time work, her mother nearby – but encouraged Nelson to move to Norfolk for the sake of promotion. Now that her daughters are older she works as a manager for a hair salon. Michelle is beautiful, stylish, hard-working and a dedicated wife and mother. When people see her and Nelson together, their first reaction is usually, 'What *does* she see in him?'

Surprising fact about Michelle: she once played hockey for Blackpool Girls.

Michael Malone (aka Cathbad)

Profession: laboratory assistant and druid

Likes: nature, mythology, walking, following his instincts

Dislikes: rules, injustice, conventions

Cathbad was born in Ireland and came to England to study first chemistry then archaeology. He also came under the influence of Erik Anderssen though they found themselves on opposite sides during the henge dig. Cathbad was brought up as a Catholic but he now thinks of himself as a druid and shaman.

Surprising fact about Cathbad: he can play the accordion.

Shona Maclean

Profession: lecturer in English Literature

Likes: books, wine, parties

Dislikes: being ignored

Shona is a lecturer at the University of North Norfolk and one of Ruth's closest friends. They met when they both participated in the henge dig in 1997. On the face of it, Shona seems an unlikely friend for Ruth – she's outgoing and stunningly beautiful for a start – but the two women share a sense of humour and an interest in books, films and travel. They also have a lot of history together.

Surprising fact about Shona: as a child she won several Irish dancing competitions.

David Clough

Profession: Detective Sergeant

Likes: food, football, beer, his job

Dislikes: political correctness, graduate police officers

David Clough ('Cloughie' to Nelson) was born in Norfolk and joined the force at eighteen. As a youngster he almost followed his elder brother into petty crime, but a chance meeting with a sympathetic policeman led him into a surprisingly successful police career. Clough is a tough, dedicated officer but not without imagination. He admires Nelson, his boss, but has a rather competitive relationship with Sergeant Judy Johnson.

Surprising fact about Clough: He can quote the 'you come to me on my daughter's wedding day' scene from *The Godfather* off by heart.

Judy Johnson

Profession: Detective Sergeant

Likes: horses, driving, her job

Dislikes: girls' nights out, sexism, being patronised

Judy Johnson was born in Norfolk to Irish Catholic parents. She was academic at school but opted to join the police force at eighteen rather than go to university. Judy can seem cautious and steady – she married her boyfriend from school, for example – but she is actually fiercely ambitious. She resents any hint of condescension or sexism which can lead to some fiery exchanges with Clough.

Surprising fact about Judy: she's a keen card player and once won an inter-force poker competition.

Phil Trent

Profession: professor of Archaeology

Likes: money, being on television, technology

Dislikes: new age archaeologists, anonymity, being out of the loop

Phil is Ruth's head of department at the University of North Norfolk. He's ambitious and outwardly charming, determined to put the university (and himself) on the map. He thinks of Ruth as plodding and old-fashioned so is slightly put out when she begins to make a name for herself as an advisor to the police. On one hand, it's good for the image of UNN; on the other, it should have been him.

Surprising fact about Phil: at his all boys school, he once played Juliet in *Romeo and Juliet*.